Forgetful of Strangers

ISBN-13/EAN-13: 978-0-9704974-3-7

Manufactured in the United States of America

As Always…To Helen

Forgetful
of Strangers

Chapter 1

Bad things happen in an instant. The worse a thing is, the quicker it strikes– as if the devil knows full-well it's best to not let you see it coming. Five-minutes earlier, four teenage boys had made their way into the woods thinking of nothing but getting home and getting fed. But the devil was in one of them, and in an instant he pounced.

Along a small pathway cutting through the front edge of a local South Carolina woodlands, there is a sudden rash of the color red. Spattered, blotted, and absorbed by the Spanish moss; sprayed and lightly dripping from shiny kudzu leaves; the color radiates outward from a distinctive shape pressed into the foliage. Standing alone over the still body of one of the teenage boys, the biggest of the four dangles a baseball bat from his left hand. Gripped by the handle, the bat isn't long enough to reach to the ground, and the new color drips from the end of it as well.

"Oh, please Lord," the big boy cries out in a sobbing voice. "Won't you please just wipe all this away?"

With tears flowing, he reaches down with his free hand and tries desperately to push back the color gray oozing out of a large crack in the head of the unmoving form. Blood covers his hand to the wrist, and as he wipes away tears collecting in his eyes, he is unaware of the effect it has on his appearance.

"God, please!" he shouts, raising the bat to the heavens. "I want to wake up now!"

In his delirium, the big boy doesn't notice the sound of people running up the path behind him.

"There he is!" one of the original four boys shouts. "I told you he was crazy. He kilt him! He's kilt him, sure enough!"

Two local deputies jog up the path, guns drawn and keys clanging against ammunition. They freeze at the sight of the larger boy standing with the bat raised, and each assumes the shooter's position.

"Shoot-im!" the boy shouts. "Shoot-im before he kills someone else."

The larger boy recognizes the voice and spins around with fire in his eyes. One of the deputies pulls back on the trigger of his pistol.

"Shoot-im, before it's too late!" the boy screams again.

The moment hangs in the air with the Spanish moss.

"Easy there, Dub," the older of the two deputies says to his locked-and-loaded partner. "We ain't-a-gonna shoot nobody just yet."

The younger deputy slowly eases off the trigger, his hands trembling.

"All right, son," the older officer says, slowly lowering his weapon to his side. "There's been enough bad happened here today. Why don't you put that bat down and lie on your stomach there, so we can see about tending to your friend."

"God can make this all go away," the big boy says, his voice tapering as he lowers the bat. "If you give Him just a minute, He can make it all go away."

"Ain't nobody wanting to get in the way of God here, son. But I think He'd prefer if it you'd lie down on the ground so we can see to your friend."

The large boy drops the bat from his hand, but he is determined to press his request to give God a little more time. "I tell you, the Lord can do some mighty powerful things," he says, starting towards the deputies.

In a panic, the younger deputy fumbles with his gun and drops it from his sweating hands. It goes off with a ear-rattling bang.

"Jesus, Dub! What the hell you trying to do over there?" the older deputy shouts.

The gunshot stops the big boy in his tracks, while the younger deputy quickly falls to his knees to fish for his revolver amongst the kudzu.

"Leave it!" the older deputy commands. "Just get your handcuffs out."

As Dub fumbles with the handcuffs hanging from the back of his belt, his more experienced partner turns his attention back to the large boy.

"You see there? Unless you want my partner to find some way to kill himself, we gotta put an end to this."

"Yes, sir," the large boy says, lowering his chin to his chest.

"That's real good. Now, how about we start with you turning around and lying down on your belly for me like I asked?"

The large boy nods, then drops to his knees and flops on his stomach. He hits the ground with a thud.

"What ya doing?" the smaller boy shouts. "He's a killer. You gotta shoot-im!"

"Shut-up, boy!" the older deputy snaps. "Get on back down that path and wait there with your friend."

After a pause, the boy shuffles backward down the pathway. "My daddy's not gonna like this," he says.

"We'll all have us a chat with your daddy soon enough. Now git!"

The boy takes off running, as the younger deputy struggles to get the handcuffs around the bigger boy's wrists.

"For Pete's sake, Dub, can't you do nothing right?" the older deputy says, holstering his gun and bending down to help his partner. He notices something as he come in closer. "My God ... did you wet your britches?"

Dub looks down with shame while his partner finally clicks the handcuffs onto the boy. "Come here," he says, pulling Dub back down the path a few steps. "You better rub some dirt on that spot or something. I will not be embarrassed by such a thing, and I'm telling you right now—"

As the older deputy applies a stern lecture to his partner, the larger boy raises his head out of the Kudzu and looks back in the direction of the body. "I'm so sorry, Marcus. There weren't nothing I could do," he whispers.

On the brink of full tears, suddenly his eyes light up, and a happy, satisfied smile breaks out across his face.

Chapter 2

Of all the people to work for in the newspaper business, Carl Odette is one of the very best. As an editor, he may lack a few of the characteristics assumed essential for the job; but as a human being there is none finer. As it turned out, this was a very good thing for me. If he was even one scintilla less than the man he is, these days I would not only be unemployed, but very likely locked away in a mental ward somewhere. Another flame-out quietly added to the list of synonyms for unfulfilled potential. For being the single most tolerant and understanding person I have ever come across, Carl will forever have my personal loyalty and sincere gratitude. My biggest hope is that someday he and I might even be able to speak again.

When Carl first took over the national news desk at *The New York Times*, most of us grunts cranking out copy saw it as a chance to finally be out from under the thumb of a tyrant. Carl's predecessor had been a desk-thumping, vein-popping, shout-at-you kind of a guy; which was the main reason that when Carl became our editor, every single one of us prima donnas in the national newsroom was determined to do whatever it took to make him successful. I think we all wanted desperately to prove that yelling wasn't the only way to get good copy in on time. And while in the beginning we kept ourselves in line, it could never have lasted if Carl hadn't earned our respect and admiration.

I may have flip-flopped a couple of times over how I felt about Carl, but deep-down I know he's a good man all the way to the core. And though I'm fairly certain he would not be so kind in his words about me, I'll never let anything cause me to question the character of my former boss again. We did hundreds of stories together over the years, very few with any measurable degree of conflict between us. But sadly, I let the last one wreck our relationship altogether. I allowed conflict to devolve into outright warfare between us, and in the end I must accept that our friendship was the biggest casualty – and that it was my fault. It wasn't the only bad-ending I brought down on myself with that story, but in many ways it had the most impact.

It was just about this same time one year ago that Carl first introduced me to the folder on the proposed re-trial of a convicted murderer – some sixteen years after the crime – and from the very start my world was slightly off kilter. Over the past year, I have been convinced that my involvement in what was to become a three-part series entitled "Hate and Racism are Alive and Well in the New South," was an assignment I would forever curse Carl for laying at my feet. There were a lot of good things that flowed from my work on the "Hate" story, such as sharing a Pulitzer Prize; which by itself should have been the ultimate highpoint in my life as a newspaperman. That it wasn't even close is the best evidence to show how drastically I have changed; how totally upside-down my short list of priorities has become. There is literally not one single value-judgment I could make today that would match the answer I would have given *before* doing that story – which is something I now believe may just be one of those good things.

It's taken a while for me to come to that conclusion, as the better part of the past year ground by before I was able to allow myself to even think about the whole affair again. And while for me, it was by far the worst year ever, now that it's all behind me I'm glad to have gone through it. I understand now that all the questioning, soul searching, and nearly manic bouts of depression I suffered through as a result of that original story were for a purpose. I have been truly blessed. Not by the members of the Pulitzer committee, but by the simple act of getting to know an even simpler man – a man that will one-day whisper the quiet words of an angel.

During the very intense two weeks we spent together last spring, I became one of the world's leading authorities on Bosephus Buckminster of Chases Corner, South Carolina. From his highest hopes to his deepest fears, I believe I have come to know him as well as anyone can – and that's the real blessing I'm talking about. It's the one thing that makes all the emotional garbage I've had to wallow through since then worth something.

In the process of coming to that fresh outlook on things, after an absence of nearly a year, the writer in me is back at his craft. The new Mark Daniels has another story to tell about his time in Chases Corner, South Carolina. And while ultimately I have Bo to thank for that, it is to Carl Odette that credit must be given for getting us together in the first place. For some reason, Carl fixed on me to do the story and wouldn't let go.

The day Carl first brought Bo my way, it was a rainy Sunday afternoon, and I was in the office just killing time while my fiancée spent the day with her parents. Carl came in shortly after I did, and although he waved across the newsroom, he went straight into his office without so much as a hello. Later, as I was sitting at my desk listening to a tape of a disgruntled lobbyist named Hodges throwing his former benefactors under the bus, over my right shoulder came a thick, tattered manila folder. It was wrapped with rubber bands at the top and bottom and there was enough material crammed into it for the file to bounce the other items on my desk when it hit.

Turning in my chair, I asked, "Did you just drop that on my desk, Carl?" There was no one else around, but the question was asked out of a sense of incredulity rather than a need to know.

"I did," Carl said in a matter-of-fact fashion. "It's a story I need you to cover, and it's not something I want to debate."

That was not the way Carl passed out stories. His normal method was to send an email asking politely if you could stop by his office, followed by a mandatory chit-chat about things at home or the Yankees' ridiculously bloated payroll. Eventually, Carl would gently slide a folder across his desk and say something like, "Tell me what you think about this one."

It may have something to do with his football-player frame or his near movie-star good looks - a thing he downplays with five-dollar haircuts and a Walmart wardrobe - but Carl is one of the few people I've met who possesses enough quiet confidence to give anyone speaking the upper hand in a conversation. When he handed you a story, he always gave you plenty of time to peruse the material, and sat patiently while you read. If you asked a question too soon, he'd say something to the effect of, "Go ahead and finish looking over the whole thing, and we'll talk." Then he'd lean back in his chair, waiting like an umpire between innings until he was sure you were done. At that point he'd sit up straight and throw out a handful of open-ended questions, like "Tell me what's going through your head." He was brilliant that way.

That's why the day Carl assigned me to Bo's story, I was more than just a little taken aback by *how* he did it. No small talk; no sagacious guidance – just a big fat folder tossed over my shoulder, followed by an un-Carl like pronouncement.

"Mark, I know you're getting married in two months and that's probably got most of your attention right now," he said with an out-of-place determination written across his brow. "But this one *has* to be you."

With a closer look, the puffy bags under Carl's eyes hinted that the decision was harder on him than it should have been. "Can I ask why?"

"No. I can't get into that right now."

I considered a stiffer resistance, but was knocked so far off-track by his demeanor that I couldn't get the words out. The one thing Carl had gotten right was that I had other things on my mind. Getting married had been keeping me preoccupied for some time, and with the day fast approaching cold feet were getting most of my attention.

"Carl, do you expect me to cover these proceedings in person?" I asked.

"Yes. You'll have to be there."

"Boss, there's no way I can just pack up and head off to chuck-a-luck, South Carolina," I said, anxiety ratcheting up the frustration in my voice. "Damn it, Carl, when Karen hears that I'm going a thousand miles away ..."

"I know. She's going to be pissed. But, Mark, I swear to you, if you do this one right, I'll nominate you for the Pulitzer myself."

I'd seen a couple of the original story summaries coming over the wire, and there wasn't a shred of evidence to suggest the file in front of me was good enough to win an award.

"What exactly do you see in this thing that makes you think a Pulitzer is even remotely possible?"

"I can't put my finger on it. You'll have to trust my instincts on this one. There's something there. Something big."

I rubbed my forehead between two fingers. By the way he was hanging around, it looked like Carl meant to have an answer right away and saying no didn't seem to be a possibility. "Even if I say yes, it'll have to be a tentative answer. I have to talk this over with Karen."

"I understand."

"No. I don't think you do. Things have been rocky enough between us lately."

What followed were the first truly uncomfortable moments Carl Odette and I had had in nearly six years of working together. After a couple of minutes of looking down at his shoes, Carl just turned around and headed back in the direction of his office.

As he settled into his seat behind his desk, I could see him through the glass partition. He was just staring straight ahead. It was like he'd fallen into a trance, and I remember feeling worried for him.

I sat alone with the file for a while, struggling without precedent to know what the next step is after Carl forces a story on you. The first of the clippings inside was a small *Times* story. The headline read: "Retarded Black Athlete Killed in Scuffle."

The article reported on the death of one Marcus Brown of Pixley, South Carolina, killed by multiple blows to the head with a baseball bat. The incident had taken place following a practice session for a Dixie Youth Baseball team, when a fight reportedly broke out between teammates. I suppose that's how the story made it into *The Times* in the first place. A fight among teammates has a slightly different angle to it, especially when one of them winds up dead. Still, it must have been a slow news day to make it all the way north and into *The Times*.

The local paper had a few more details. Three boys were being interviewed regarding the incident. One, the son of a local politician, was a pitcher; the second was the team's catcher; and the third boy a reserve outfielder. Their stories differed widely as to exactly what had happened, and the local sheriff confessed to the reporter that "one of the boys is a little slow in the head, and it's hard to match up what he thinks he saw with the others." The third boy, I would come to learn, was Bosephus Buckminster; but the paper hadn't reported the names of any of those involved yet. The sheriff would only say that his officers would get to the bottom of things in a day or two, and that he fully expected charges would be filed against one or more of the boys.

Three days later, charges were filed. The local headline read: "Buckminster Boy Charged with Killing Friend." The story claimed the motive for the killing was simple jealousy. The sheriff spelled it out in a short quote:

"We don't think the boy meant to kill his friend, Marcus. He was the one who talked Marcus into joining the team in the first place. Seems like the Buckminster boy just snapped."

The official statements taken from the other two boys told their side of the story.

Official Statement of Trey Hunter:

On Thursday, September the thirteenth, Corey Aycock and me was cutting through the woods after practice on our way home. We saw Marcus Brown walking ahead of us, and we ran to catch up to him so we could all walk together. We was walking along like that when all of a sudden Bo Buckminster come running up on us, hollering and cussing at Marcus. He was saying things like, "Why you walking with them? Ain't I good enough for you no more?" Marcus told him he was welcome to walk with us. That we was teammates and we could all walk together. That's when Bo called him a cuss word and hit him hard on the back of his head with his baseball bat. Marcus fell to his knees and Bo hit him another lick. That's when me and Corey took off back out of them woods to get some help. A couple of deputies was hanging out by the ball field when we left, so we went on back to fetch 'em. When we got back, old Bo had killed that black boy dead as nails. He was just standing over him with that bat in his hand, looking crazy enough to do it again.

Trey Hunter was the politician's son. The statement from Corey Aycock matched Trey's almost to the word, with the exception that Corey did not mention Bo using the cuss-word before hitting Marcus. The odd part of the official record was that no statement was recorded for Bo's version of the story. The sheriff himself had admitted there were discrepancies between the three boys as to what happened, yet the official record had just the one version, told by two separate witnesses.

I made an entry in my notebook about finding what the other story was, official or otherwise. It was the first of many notes I made that day, and it was just about all that was needed to hook me. Had Carl just let me read the file first, I'm sure I would have jumped at the chance to get off the Hodges story and move on to one that actually required notes. I was fairly certain Carl would have known that too, which made the question of why he didn't all the more mysterious.

Chapter 3

There was still the issue of my fiancée being okay with my new out-of-town gig, which was certainly no slam-dunk. After spending the weekend with her parents, Karen and I were supposed to meet at seven that evening for a quiet dinner she'd planned at our favorite Italian restaurant, Il Vagabondos. We both loved the place. I got to the restaurant early, figuring I could settle in, get comfortable, and prepare for the rocky conversation ahead. To my surprise, Karen was already seated when I arrived; a full forty-five minutes ahead of schedule.

"Karen?" I shouted across the room when I noticed her.

Hollering her name startled her, and as I drew closer to the table I noticed that she may have been crying; though with Karen it's not always easy to tell. Because she absolutely refused to push herself from naturally pretty to beautiful by wearing makeup, there wasn't the usual mess to give away her emotions. And of course, there was the whole pride thing – something she has more than her fair-share of.

"Mark? I didn't expect you for at least another half-an-hour," she said, covering something with a forced tone in her voice.

"I snuck into the office this afternoon to get some work done, but Carl was there and he took me off the Hodges thing. There really wasn't any reason to hang around, so I figured I'd get a glass of wine while I waited for you."

"Oh, I'm sorry to hear that. Should I be sorry?"

"I wasn't. It was a pig of a story, anyway. I don't think I could have dressed it up enough to take it to the dance."

"Well, then I'm happy for you."

"Yeah, me too. There's more to it, but we can get into that later. How was your day with your parents?"

"It was good. Things are good."

"You look troubled." I slid into a chair at the table, and motioned for the waiter to stop by. When I looked back Karen's lip was trembling. "Alright," I said, grabbing her hand across the table. "Something is wrong. Tell me what happened today."

After a couple of sniffles, Karen dabbed a Kleenex at the tears that were beginning to collect in the ocean-blue eyes I had swam so deeply in the night we'd first met. "Nothing happened today. It's not about today."

As is always the case, the waiter found the worst possible time to jump in. "How can I help you two love birds?" he asked in his most cheery voice.

"A glass of Merlot, please."

"And for the lady?"

Karen shook her head without looking up. For the first time the waiter realized something was amiss, and he gave a pained, sympathetic expression before stepping-off lightly.

"This must be big," I said after the waiter had gone from earshot.

Karen shook her head again, and then withdrew her hand from mine and off the table completely. I tried to be calm with her. I even thought about feigning a gentleness that was not really a part of my character. But as usual, I became frustrated far too soon.

"Okay, look. Did someone die or what?" I snorted after a few minutes.

My lack of tact and compassion seemed to steel Karen for whatever was ahead.

"No one is dead. Someone *is* dying, however."

"Who?"

The sadness in her eyes was replaced by a touch of fire, as she looped the golden brown hair falling across her face back behind each ear. "How about me? How about, I'm dying inside? Every day just a little bit more of me is sacrificed for the sake of our relationship."

I don't know how women do it. How they're able to go from zero to sixty in a relationship conversation in a matter of milliseconds. Men – me, first and foremost I suppose – always seem to get thrown back in their seats by pure g-force when that happens. It's a serious disadvantage.

"I mean, my God, Mark. What are we doing here?"

This was bigger than big.

"Well, I thought we were getting married this summer," I said, still a little lost.

"Getting married? Why? Why are we getting married, Mark?"

I desperately wanted to leave. Inside my head, I heard myself shout "check please," and imagined myself running for the relative safety of the mid-town Manhattan sidewalks. I'd rather have a woman hit me square in the face with a large piece of lumber than have her hurl emotional riddles at me. "The reason most people do it. They love each other," I mumbled.

"Love has nothing to do with it, Mark."

At that moment my blood began to boil. Somewhere around the six-month milestone in our relationship, almost overnight, the pressure to come out with that magic four-letter word had built to mountainous proportions. Every day that went by, every day past the "I think if you *did* love me you would certainly know by now" conversation, the pressure just kept getting turned up. It was the single most important and all consuming concept in our lives for quite awhile. Did I or didn't I? Once the burning question, now apparently an irrelevant afterthought.

"Waiter," I said, reaching for my wallet. It was a brilliant response. Simple and clear in its message. The suddenly hyper-attentive waiter came right over.

"Yes my dears, how can I be of service?" he said with a feminine reassurance.

I wanted to punch him in the nose. It was the tone I should have been able to use in that circumstance, but I would never have been able to pull it off. "Bring us the check," I said.

"You won't be dining with us?"

"We won't be dining."

"I *understand*. The glass of wine is on me, honey."

I could see my hands around the waiter's neck, wringing the life out of him for his sensitivity. I couldn't bring myself to look over at Karen, but I felt her glare.

"So that's it? Conversation over?" she asked.

"What the hell do you want from me? Do you want to cancel the wedding?"

I knew it was unwise to jump so far ahead, but from my experiences with Karen – or with any other woman who had ever occupied a place in my life, for that matter – I also knew there was a train-wreck coming that I wasn't going to be able to stop.

"That's something that *has* crossed my mind, Mark. I was hoping we could talk through some of the things that are ..."

"You know what, just shoot me. Please, put a gun to my head and just pull the damn trigger. We don't need to go through an inquisition over this. Be a big girl and tell me what you want to do."

Karen stood up and thrust her balled-up little hands on her slender hips, staring at me in disbelief for a few seconds. She was calmer than I thought she would be after such a splendid volley. Slowly she slid in her chair, put away her Kleenex, and took in a deep, cleansing breath. "Fine. I'll call the caterers and get up with anyone we've sent deposits to. Maybe with the pressure off, we can finally have a real conversation about what's going on between us."

"Maybe so."

I didn't know it at the time, but with that, Karen McDonough was gone from my life. We never did have that one, purging conversation to clear the air. We didn't really need to. We'd had it many times in pieces and parts over the few months leading up to that night at Il Vagabondos. And while sharing just that one final peek into our time together could give the impression my former fiancée was a bit of a shrew, the fact is that over the years I've turned many a good woman into a frustrated ball of disappointment and anger. The truth: Karen was the best thing that ever happened to me. Much more than I ever deserved; which of course is the reason I could never have held on to her. She was a simple, passionate, devoted, and deeply caring human being. I can't say I was happy about what happened, but considering how her future husband stacked up against those core values, it was understandable.

And so it was that in one day, one solitary trip of the sun from east-to-west, I lost the woman I had planned to spend the rest of my life with, and an eighteen-year career in journalism began a painful slide straight into the crapper.

Chapter 4

The next morning I tried to focus on the positive aspects of spending the rest of my life with an ex-fiancée. That might sound strange to anyone that hasn't watched the first forty-years of their life fly by without being betrothed at least once, but it is much more meaningful for those who have ever had to stumble through a response to questions like "You mean you've never even been engaged?" At least after our breakup I had something to throw out as an answer, something that wouldn't immediately render my sexuality suspect or have folks wondering what deviate personality flaw I possessed that was keeping the keepers at bay.

"Yeah, I came close once." That would be my response going forward, and for that at least I knew I could take some solace from my split with Ms. McDonough.

I got to the paper early that morning, and headed straight for Carl's office to give him the news that I was officially available for his story after all. He seemed to know I was coming.

"Come in, Mark. I picked up an extra coffee at Starbucks on the way in. You want it?"

"Thanks. I'd love it."

Carl was still acting somewhat outside his norm, but that morning he was different from the day before. He seemed nervous.

"So, it looks like my schedule is clear for your South Carolina gig," I said after a couple sips of the dark, rich Hawaiian Kona.

"Yeah, I heard. I'm sorry about all that, Mark."

"You heard? You mean word is already on the streets?"

"Well, you know ... Karen and my Susan have gotten pretty close the past few months. They talk a lot."

It was all starting to come together. "You knew yesterday, didn't you?"

Carl went from nervous to scared. "I didn't really ... not that she was going to ..."

"You son-of-a-bitch. You knew she was going to dump me last night, and you didn't say a word about it."

"No, you're wrong. I didn't know she was going to actually dump you. The only thing that I—"

"Un-frigging-believable. Is that why I've been banished to the boondocks of the Carolinas?"

"No, the two aren't related," Carl said with a sudden burst of surety. "Be mad at me if you like, but you have to separate the two."

"Seems awful convenient."

"Yeah, well I knew that's what you'd think," Carl said, suddenly on the defensive. "You have to get over it though. I'm telling you, this South Carolina story has legs!"

"Relax. I'm gonna do the story. Fact is, it's probably a good idea to get out of town for awhile. Give myself something to think about other than women."

"Good. That's real good."

After a while of nothing between us, Carl may have been wishing he'd brought along an extra donut rather than a tall cup of hot Starbucks for me to sip at.

"So, what do you think?" he said. "Are you and Karen going to be able to work through this?"

"I doubt it. I know it may seem sudden to you— on second thought, maybe not with your Susan connection, but it's not all that sudden. This has been building for awhile."

"Is there a compromise in there? A middle ground you two can meet on?"

"I don't see it if there is. Not unless you want me working out of a house a hundred miles north of here."

"Karen feels that strongly about taking the job upstate now that she has her master's degree?"

"Yes, she does. I guess she just finds it impossible to pass up the whopping thirty-six thousand dollar a year salary they offered her. You know, what with her gazillionaire parents so strapped for cash and all."

"Maybe she doesn't want to have to keep depending on them, Mark. There is something to be said for independence.'

His words were so close to the exact same ones I had heard come from

Karen's very own mouth, they were laughable. I don't know how I ever missed the back-channel connection through Susan.

"Yeah, well, it hasn't bothered her all that much up till now. The woman's going to be thirty-two years old next month, and her dear daddy's been supplementing her social worker income for her entire adult life. She lives in Manhattan, for crying out loud. Let's not even discuss the seven-years of full tuition at NYU."

"I can't argue with you there. Wish I had that kind of a safety net. I'd still be in school."

"What the hell would you want to go back to school for? You already run the biggest frat house in New York."

"Ain't it the truth?"

Thankfully, we'd found a way out of the conversation. There was a lot more to be said, but neither one of us wanted to get into it. We probably never would.

"I suppose I better get a travel request in," I said. "No sense waiting around here with a vacation paradise like Chases Corner, South Carolina waiting on me."

"You really don't have to take off right away, you know. You could hang out for a few days and not miss anything important down there."

"What for?"

Carl shrugged his shoulders. We shook hands across his desk, a confirmation that things were back to normal for both of us.

Back at my desk, while I waited for my computer to fire up and connect to the paper's Intranet, I remember distinctly that I had a genuine moment of sadness. The night before, I'd been frustrated and angry over the quick outcome of my near-dinner with Karen, but as I watched Windows go through its start-up routine, I felt a sensation that could only be described as melancholia. It didn't last very long, but it was real.

I have come to understand why the women in my life become so disgruntled by what I'm not capable of, but what I have never understood is why the spotlight can't be put on what I *can* do. You know, a little balance between the yin and yang. Once, I even took the huge step of trying to communicate that thought directly to a woman with whom I had an exceptionally good start. It didn't have any effect on the outcome, however. It's like the story of the scorpion that stung the turtle halfway across a pond, after the turtle had agreed to give the scorpion a ride because he couldn't swim.

"Why did you do it?" the turtle asked. "Now we're both going to die!"

"I couldn't help it," the scorpion replied. "It's just my nature."

In all these years, I have never figured out whether I'm the turtle or the scorpion. It doesn't really matter though. To me, going against the natural order of things has never seemed the smart road to take.

I will say this about Karen: she tried. Not to change me, but to accept me for who I was. We were happy for a very long time, almost two years. In the end though, I was ready for our conversation at Il Vagabondos, and to tell the truth maybe even grateful that it came so cleanly. I would have hated for the final part of our time together to drag on, hiding all the really terrific times we had together in a fog of bitterness. It was encouraging to know that when the end came, I still loved her. And despite her obvious frustration, I'm fairly certain Karen still loved me too. That was something to hold on to; something to build on for future relationships.

Within a few minutes of submitting a travel request through the Intranet, the phone rang at my desk.

"Mr. Daniels, it's Kathy, downstairs in the travel office."

"Kathy, how are you this morning?"

"I'm fine, thanks."

"That's pretty quick service. It may even be a new record."

"Yes, sir. Mr. Odette called ahead and asked me to be on the lookout for your travel request. He said you were a priority."

"He did, did he? He must really want to get me out of here."

"Oh, no, sir. He just wanted me to have his approval ahead of time, so as not to hold up your travel plans."

"Yeah, I'm sure that's it. Listen, before we go any further, I need to ask a favor of you."

"What's that, Mr. Daniels?"

"Don't call me *sir* anymore this morning. It's a bad time for me to be feeling old."

"You're funny, Mr. Daniels."

"And no more Mr. Daniels. My name is Mark."

"Okay, Mark. Will there be anything else?"

"Yes. Flirt with me a little bit."

"I'm sorry?"

"You know, let's have some playful banter back-and-forth; the kind that two people have when they're teasing about the idea of a dating ritual."

"I know what flirting is. Though I must say, you writers always seem to find so many complicated ways to explain things. I'm afraid I can't comply, however."

"Why not?"

"You're engaged. Remember?"

I debated whether to share the news, but the idea of a sympathy flirt wasn't very appealing.

"Yes. Well then, tell me what my options are for travel to Chases Corner, South cack-a-lackee."

"For starters, you'll have to fly into Charleston. There's plenty of direct flights going in and out of there, but the best I can tell, you've got about a two-and-a-half hour drive from there into Chases Corner."

"Is it close to an interstate at least?"

"Depends on what you call close. It looks to be about forty-five miles from the nearest exit off I-95."

"You're kidding. I don't think I've ever been forty-five miles away from an interstate exit in my entire life."

"Yeah, well from what I understand, there are people down there that haven't ever *seen* the interstate."

We both laughed, but I could easily imagine her light-hearted assertion might be more on the money than she thought. At least it would fit within the stereotype we Yankees have of all Southerners. A sense of superiority helps us get through the brutal winters, which our cousins below the Mason-Dixon Line don't have to put up with. It's our only answer to the seemingly logical January question of "why do you stay there?"

"Okay, then. Make sure you get me a decent rental car for the drive. No compacts. A mid-sized at the very least."

"You've got it. What day would you like to leave?"

"Tomorrow morning."

"Early, or ..."

"Get me the first flight out."

There was a delay while Kathy checked the system on the other end – an interlude where I considered jumping back in to give myself another day. Another day to see if maybe Karen had a change of heart.

"It looks like the first flight out tomorrow is at seven fifteen from La Guardia. Is that too early for you?"

I hung on to the Karen idea a bit before answering.

"Mark? Are you still on the line?"

"Book it, Kathy. No need to delay the inevitable."

"Consider it done. Now, the only hotel I recognize is a Marriott Courtyard, but I'm afraid it's back at the exit off the interstate. That's a pretty good sized commute if you're going to go back and forth to Chases Corner every day."

"I'll take it. There's no way I'm going to roll the dice on the standards of the local establishments. I've developed a real quirk about having my own bathroom when I'm on the road."

"I understand, completely," Kathy said, enjoying my quip.

It took just a minute or two to get everything finalized, and before she came back on the line I heard the ping of an email landing in my mailbox.

"You're all set, Mr. Daniels. I just sent you the itinerary and confirmation numbers. Is there anything else I can do for you today?"

"No, you've been great, Kathy. Thanks."

"Oh, you're very welcome. Mark ... can I give you one small piece of advice before we hang up?"

"Um, sure. What've you got?"

"Don't flirt with any of the woman down there. I've heard horror stories involving angry fathers and shotgun weddings."

I laughed loudly. "Good safety tip."

"If the urge to flirt gets a little too overwhelming, call me back on the toll-free line and I'll do what I can to help out."

A small dollop of salve to apply to a wounded heart. "I will absolutely keep that in mind. I'll talk to you soon."

"Have a good trip."

After buttoning up a few loose ends for the intern who would be taking over the Hodges story, I took the rest of the day off to get myself prepared for the ridiculously early flight Kathy had booked for me. I always seemed to do that to myself: book the first flight out, and then regret not asking for something at a more civil hour. I think that somewhere drifting in my subconscious is a bent for wanting to use the words "get me the first flight out." It's so dramatic. It seems like anyone taking the first flight out of New York must be awfully important, because to catch it you really have to start for the airport the night before.

By early evening, I'd finished the job of getting ready. After laying out the clothes I was to wear for the trip, I set my fully packed bags next to the door for the cab driver to help carry downstairs in the morning. That was probably a mistake – the symbolism was pretty powerful. With nothing left but to knock around a little and take it easy, I sat down in the corner chair in my living room to watch TV. The thing was, I never sat in the corner chair to watch TV. It had the worst angle for viewing and for all intents and purposes was there for decorative purposes only. It *was* closest to the phone, however, and I think some small part of me was waiting on a phone call that would never come.

Chapter 5

My trip to the great State of South Carolina the next morning was uneventful. Since it was just after noon when I arrived at the Marriott Courtyard, I didn't bother to drive all the way into Chases Corner, choosing instead to work the front-desk attendant for an early check-in. It was a brand spanking new hotel, with an acre of hay covering the green sprouts of new grass struggling to take the shape of a lawn. The guy at the front desk was accommodating enough. A big smiley fellow, still spouting off the script he'd learned at front-desk school; but a little difficult to understand. He had the thickest accent I'd ever had to decipher. There was nothing about it that would put someone off; his soft twang actually added to the feelings of hospitality and welcome a hotel would want from its staff. Once he got past the script though, it was hard to make sense of the colloquialisms. I'm mean, just how far away is something that's "a good bit of road from here"? That's what he told me when I asked how far it was to the county courthouse – a good bit of road. Whatever the exact distance, I chose not push for further explanation, satisfied that it was evidently not close, and that I was going to have to adjust my ear for the English language.

The suite he gave me was perfect. I'd meant to ask him how long the hotel had been open, but from the condition of my accommodations I knew it had to have been within the previous month or so. There was not one single trace of other people. No stains on the carpet; no chips or scratches on any of the furniture. The one drawback was a lingering smell of fresh paint, but within a couple minutes my sense of smell was able to filter it out.

By the time I'd finished my road ritual of unpacking all of my bags and finding a drawer or shelf for each and every item, the travel anxiety diminished enough to relax. I was exhausted from the ridiculously early start to the day and the idea of taking a cat-nap crept in, but I felt the need to check in with Carl first; a need that I'm sure was based on the hope that some kind of word from Karen might have made its way along the Susan Odette connection. I was surprised but pleased to learn that my cell phone was sporting four bars of coverage. It was just after lunch when the call went through to Carl's desk.

"Carl Odette. New York Times."

"Hi, Carl. It's Mark."

"Oh, hi, Mark. Where are you? Have you made your way to Chases Corner already?

"Not quite. I'm at the hotel. I'm still a good-bit-of-road away."

"What's that?"

Apparently Carl didn't know what it meant, either.

"Never mind. I haven't gone over to the courthouse yet."

"Well, at least you made it that far. Any trouble with the trip?"

"It took a while for me to get out of the airport in Charleston, but the directions to the hotel were right on. Not a lot of traffic coming this way."

"Yeah, I can't imagine there would be."

A hole appeared in our conversation. I wanted to ask about Karen, but my maleness wouldn't let me just blurt out the question.

"Oh, hey, you know what, Karen stopped by a little while ago," Carl said, working hard to make it sound like an afterthought.

"Did she?'

"She sure did. I was on my way for coffee when I bumped into her at the elevator."

"Really. She must have thought I was still in town. We haven't talked, so I don't guess she knew that—"

"She knew you were gone, Mark."

"She did?"

"Yeah, I think I had mentioned it to Susan."

"Of course. Susan would have told her, wouldn't she?"

"That's it, I'm afraid."

"So, what was she doing there? What did she want?"

"She left some stuff for you."

"Stuff? What kind of stuff?"

"You know, like the key to your apartment. Some clothes. Little things."

For some reason Carl's description hit me like a ton-of-bricks.

"You still there, Mark?"

"I'm still here. Just hold on to it for me. I'll get it from you when I get back."

"You bet. I'll put it right here in my bottom drawer."

I had to blow out a long breath before I could speak again. It was loud enough so that I'm sure Carl heard it. "You know, I think I still have the key to her place," I added. "Did she seem anxious to get it back? I could probably Fed Ex it to you from the hotel, and you could ..."

"She did mention something about that. She said you can just turn it in to the apartment manager. I guess they change the locks when someone leaves the building."

"Leaves the building? She's moving out?"

"Looks like it. I guess she decided to go ahead and start that new job. I think she said she's leaving tomorrow."

"Wow, that was quick."

"I thought the same thing. But, you know Karen. Once she has her mind set ..."

"There's no stopping her. I know that only too well, I'm afraid."

"Exactly. Well, listen, let me know if you need anything down there."

"I will."

"And check in from time-to-time as things develop."

"Absolutely."

There was one last pause where Carl's goodbye should have been.

"And, Mark?"

"Yes."

"I'm sorry about all this."

"Sorry? Do you mean for giving me this wacky assignment or sorry about Karen."

"I mean about what's happened between you and Karen."

"Don't be. I told you, it's been coming for a long time. It's just not that big a deal."

"You did say that. Anyway, I've got to go to a meeting. Let's talk soon."

"Get going. We'll talk later."

I was lying through my teeth and Carl knew it. Thankfully, Carl's in-step with the male ego and he let me go without calling me on it. If we had talked more, I would have told him that I was fairly certain *I* was the reason behind Karen's quick flight out of the city. She and I talked a lot about my many relationship phobias – the worst of which was my hatred of long, drawn-out break-ups.

"Listen, Karen," I used to say. "Please do me a favor. If you ever grow tired of me, leave without looking back." Must have said it a hundred times

The trip had exhausted me physically, but the news about Karen had sapped the life right out of me. I fell back for a nap, which instead turned out to be the earliest I'd gone to bed in my entire adult life. I didn't even rouse enough to go to dinner. I think I was trying to sleep her out of my system.

Chapter 6

Rural South Carolina may be the noisiest morning spot I've ever awoken to. There's not much of it, only the occasional rooster or the sound of a tractor rumbling by. But that's the point – there's not enough things happening to create a stream of background noise. Every single sound seems to pierce a delicate layer of perfect silence. Of course, with fourteen-hours of sleep under my belt, there was no way I was going be able to sleep-in on my first morning in South Carolina. I can't remember ever not needing a cup of coffee to get myself jumped-started for the day, but on that morning I was cranked and ready to go long before the sun broke.

By five thirty I was dressed and hanging out in the lobby with the night-shift security guy, who, as it turned out, had been to New York City once – though only to change planes. I was glad he hadn't stayed longer, because the tale he told of his adventure probably took longer than the actual event. My reward for standing and nodding through his New York City story was a fairly detailed set of directions to the Chases Corner County Courthouse. The thing was, he didn't seem to care a bit about what I was doing there. He wasn't curious in the least. I think somewhere in my gut I got the impression that he already knew; a sensation I would come upon quite a few times while staying there. In fact, it was Hank the night-watchman that had brought up my need for directions in the first place.

"I reckon you'll be needing to know how to get to the courthouse," he said.

I'd known about this trip to South Carolina for less than forty-eight hours, but old Hank seemed to have gotten word of it ahead of time. I chuckled when I considered the possibility that maybe Hank was a part of the Susan Odette, back-channel connections. Not likely, but after the odd way the previous couple of days had played out, it wouldn't have shocked me.

The ride over to the courthouse took more time than I'd calculated based on Hank's directions. His estimation that it was "no more than forty miles" was accurate enough, but the trip took over an hour to make. There were no major thoroughfares between the Marriott Courtyard at exit 97 and the town of Chases Corner, South Carolina. At least, not the kind I was used to: the type of roads you can tick off a mile a minute on. And when I finally did get to town, I nearly drove right through. I had to backtrack a little after coming upon a Tasty Freeze, when Hank's final piece of advice came back to mind.

"Do you care much for soft-serve ice cream, there, Mr. Daniels?" he'd asked.

"Yeah, I suppose I do."

"Well, if you come up on a Tasty-Freeze on your left, you might just as well pull over and getchya one, cause you've gone too far."

The courthouse was the biggest building in the square, and though it was obviously old, it seemed to have been well taken care of over the years by the local townsfolk. It was very much out of place for the size of Chases Corner, but I could tell from the washed granite facade that it was a source of pride for the people there.

Outside the courthouse building there was a carnival atmosphere. There were media of course, though maybe not as many as I'd expected. Tables were set up all about the place, selling everything from soft cider to corn on the cob. One enterprising young man had found a way to get T-shirts made up that said simply "Justice Was Done in Chases Corner". No sense splitting your market potential by taking a position either way. I was just about through the crowd, ready to start up the steps of the courthouse, when a boy on a bicycle came screeching to a stop just in front of me.

"You Mr. Daniels?" he said.

"I am. Who wants to know?"

"There's a lawyer from Charleston come up to represent old Bo. He says that if I see you coming to the courthouse this morning, I should fetch you over to Molly's so he can have a word with ya."

"A lawyer, huh."

"Yes, sir."

"And did this lawyer pay you some kind of fee for bringing me to him?"

"Not just yet. Ain't-a-going to neither, less I can get you to come with me."

"I'll tell you what. Here's ten dollars."

When I handed the boy the ten-dollar bill his eyes nearly popped out of his head.

"Who you need kilt?" he asked, quickly stuffing the money into the pocket of his blue jeans.

"Nothing like that. Just tell your lawyer friend I don't have enough background yet for him to start lobbying me for positive press. Tell him I'll find him when I'm ready."

"I'll do it. Anything else I can do for ya?"

"You can tell me your name."

"Billy Thornton's my name."

"Well, Billy Thornton, make sure you track me down again tomorrow morning to see if I have any other jobs for you."

"I sure will do that, Mr. Daniels. You can count on seeing me first thing tomorrow."

Just five minutes in town and two good things had already happened to me. First, a lawyer was ready to talk. But even more importantly, I'd lined up a local gopher to work with while in Chases Corner. The first was inevitable, the second absolutely essential.

I knew I would have to get a press-pass to get into the courtroom, but as it turned out I didn't need to make an inquiry about where to get one. While being patted down by the lone deputy sheriff manning the security line, he took the liberty to offer assistance.

"You that fella from *The New York Times*?" he asked while running his hands around my ankles.

"As a matter of fact I am."

He looked through my bag. "Go through them double doors just ahead of you there, and make a left. The ladies will help you with your pass and the like."

"Oh ... many thanks."

I moved to follow his instructions, but after taking a single-step towards the double doors, I just had to turn back with a question. "Can I ask you something?" I said to get the deputy's attention.

"Yes, sir."

"How did you know I was with *The Times*?"

"Well, now, that ain't no big mystery."

"Humor me."

"Your socks. Them socks look like they cost more than what most folks around here spend on a whole outfit."

We were both smiling. "Right. The socks," I said. "Thanks."

I'd just pushed open one of the double doors when the deputy shouted to me one more time.

"Say, Mr. Daniels," he said, and I stopped in the doorway. "No offense, but ain't you supposed to be an *investigative* reporter."

I laughed a little, appreciating a dig as much as the next guy. "That's right. I am indeed."

"Alright then. I was just checking."

My first impression of the people of Chases Corner was that they were friendly people, with a tendency for a little good natured ribbing. That part, at least, held up over my entire stay with them.

When I found the ladies handling the press passes, I didn't have to wait. One handed me a form to sign, another came around the counter to tag my bag and put a badge holder around my neck, and a third lady whisked me down a long hallway.

At the doors to the courtroom I was passed to the bailiff. "This here's that fella from *The New York Times*," the woman said to the bailiff.

"Thank you kindly, Martha. You must be Mr. Daniels, then."

"That's me."

"Welcome to our little courthouse. I've saved a seat for you up near the front. Will you follow me, please?"

"Lead the way."

After taking my seat in the very front row of the courtroom, right smack behind the defendant's table, I have to say I was feeling something close to a celebrity. Deep down my instincts might have been urging me to be skeptical; but that's another of the many things about my journey last year that I can't really describe well. It was as though there was a different feel to this town; a welcoming feeling that went beyond the courtesy and friendly disposition of the people. It was as though, in passing over the town limits, you did more than just cross a geographical boundary; you entered a warmer more peaceful place – a place where you got the sense things were just going to work out for the best.

The expedited process of getting through the system at the courthouse meant the time I'd allocated for that task would be spent sitting and waiting for the courtroom to fill up. For a guy like me that's never a problem, as long as I have a pen and my notebook along with me. I was still furiously scribbling away when the bailiff came in to call the courtroom to order.

"—the Honorable Preston K. Jefferson presiding."

The honorable Judge Preston "KKK" was a familiar name, even for someone from as far away as New York City. Preston K. Jefferson was infamous north of the Mason-Dixon Line; somewhat celebrated south of it. His was a dinosaur of a judge, an ancient relic of days gone by. Jefferson had sat on various benches across the State of South Carolina since 1972, but his position on the wrong side of the civil-rights movement of the 1960s had gained him a dubious reputation across the rest of the country. Some folks claimed he kept the "K" in his official signature as a signal to others of his real sympathies; hence, the nickname. Years on the losing side of the social battlefield had left his expression wrinkled and sour, and he looked like he should be standing in a driveway somewhere, yelling at neighborhood kids to stay off his property.

As he took his place behind the bench, I couldn't help but think that finding oneself a defendant in Judge Jefferson's courtroom must seem a mighty imposing start. Whether innocent or guilty, you were in for the fight of your life. While that thought lingered, the old man's first words scared the dickens out of me.

"I understand that Mr. Daniels from *The New York Times* has joined us this morning." The judge said to open the proceedings. He kept his eyes on the papers in front of him while he made the announcement, but then, ever so slowly, his icy stare shot straight over his reading glasses in my direction. It was as though two bullets had come flying from his Derringer eyes and struck me hard in the chest. "Mr. Daniels, I trust you've found our little county accommodating so far?"

I swallowed hard. "Yes, Your Honor. Very much so."

"Good. That's real good," he said, obviously a set-up for something yet to come. "Then I'm also sure you've figured out by now that we do things a bit differently down here."

"I have, Your Honor, but it's not so—"

"But that different doesn't necessarily mean it's a bad thing."

After his interruption I wasn't sure if I was supposed to speak again. The whole courtroom seemed stuck on their last breath, and when the stillness became too much to bear, I blurted something out to keep from exploding. "It's very nice to be here, Your Honor."

Every muscle in my body went slightly limp, as the old geezer held me in his tractor-beam glare a few seconds before moving to the business at hand. Forget about being a defendant in the man's courtroom, I sensed that being a Yankee reporter was probably worse. His words had had their desired effect; I was on my toes.

"Bailiff, read the first case please."

"Yes, Your Honor. Upon appeal to the State Supreme Court of South Carolina, the conviction in the case of Orangeburg County versus Bosephus Buckminster has been returned to this jurisdiction for further review."

"Are the attorneys for the defendant present?"

A man dressed smartly in a light blue seersucker suit stood up from the defendant's table.

"We are, Your Honna."

The man looked like a younger Matlock, sporting pre-maturely white hair that was still unable to convince me he could be more than forty-years-old. To my northern predisposition, it seemed to me he was trying to be funny with his wardrobe, but I knew he wasn't.

"Good to see you again, Mr. Galax," the judge said, shifting gears slightly.

"Good to see you also, Your Honna. I trust you are well."

The judge didn't reply, but from the tone of their first exchange it appeared the two had a history that was at least pleasant.

"Is the district attorney ready to proceed?"

"We are, Judge Jefferson."

"Bailiff, bring in the defendant."

There was a bustle in the left corner of the courtroom as people in the gallery began to stand or lift-up out of their seats to have a look. A deputy sheriff came through the door first, followed by a second deputy holding the very large arm of a man in an orange jumpsuit. The man had the most unusual, warming smile I had ever seen stretched across his face, and when he entered the room his presence seemed to push the tension created by old judge Jefferson up against the walls.

"Go get 'em, Bo," someone yelled from the back, which set-off of a flurry of encouraging shouts followed by a raucous round of applause.

When Bo turned and gave a tentative, queen-like wave to the onlookers, the cheers grew wilder. The grin across his face seemed to widen in proportion to the size of the applause, as if it were feeding on the attention. Sensing the connection, the crowd nearly blew the roof off the place.

The judge's gavel banged hard against the bench. "That'll be enough of that!" he demanded.

Whether they were seated, half-standing, or standing, everyone in the courtroom froze in their last position. Some still had hands ready to come together.

"I simply will not tolerate such outbursts in my courtroom." The judge flipped his gavel around so that the handle was pointed directly at the defense attorney. "Mr. Galax! You will instruct your client to refrain from stirring up the gallery, do you understand?"

"Your Honna, Mr. Buckminster was simply trying to—"

"Mr. Galax! Have I made myself clear to you?"

There was a pause from the defendant's table. "Perfectly, Your Honna. I shall speak to him about such matters."

No one moved until the judge put down his gavel, as if it were a handgun rather than a block of wood with a handle sticking out of it. Satisfied, the judge pushed his reading glasses back up his nose and went back to studying the papers in front of him.

"Please be seated in the courtroom," the bailiff announced.

With military precision, every bottom left standing fell back into their chairs.

Unfortunately, Bo had only made it halfway across the courtroom, and before the deputy holding his arm could get him moving again he spun to say something to the judge. "I remember you. Good morning, Judge," he said.

"Good morning, Bo" the judge replied, adjusting his tone as if understanding the need to do so. "You'll need to take your seat now, we're about to get started."

There was a softness in the judge's voice when he spoke directly to Bo. A shift in tone that made him seem more like a kindly old grandfather than a grumpy old man.

"Yes, sir, I'll do it," Bo said as a second deputy grabbed his other arm, and the two tried to lead him to the table. They got him turned in that direction, but Bo's big feet weren't ready to move yet. "Thank you kindly for having me here today," Bo said, stretching his neck back around to keep eye contact with Judge Jefferson.

"That's no trouble, Bo. Now please, have a seat over there next to Mr. Galax."

"Yes, sir."

With that Bo shifted the weight from his big frame and allowed the deputies to take him to his place at the defendant's table. The deputies seemed relieved.

There was only one picture of Bo included in his file. It was the head-shot taken during his arrest, and in it he'd been just a teenager. His height and weight were reported along with his photo, so the fact that Bo was big was known to me. What wasn't easily deciphered from the booking sheet was the size of his individual parts. It was striking how much bigger his parts were. His hands and fingers appeared to be twice the size of the average man's, and the same scale seemed to have been used to construct all the other pieces. Head, eyes, nose and mouth – all a good bit larger. It made for a most imposing physical presence, made all the more queer by the kindergarten-like pattern to his speech.

There were other clues to his true mental age, but they didn't kick in until I had heard him talk. Tip-offs – like disheveled hair that always has the same fly-away clumps sticking out on the side of his head, or the problem he has keeping the back of his shirt tail in. His teeth are well brushed in the parts one can see when he's just smiling, but when he lets go with one of his very broad, happy grins, a deep layer of plaque tells you he isn't as thorough as he should be. He's oblivious to all these things of course, not unlike the way a kindergartner would be. It's as though anywhere in the book of personal hygiene where a mom might need to stay after her young son, Bo came up short.

Just as the judge looked up, ready it would seem to get things underway, Bo squinted his eyes and turned his head, as if a thought had suddenly crossed his mind. He spun around in his chair to look directly to me. "You must be Mr. Daniels," he said with a full voice. "My name is Bo. My real name is Bosephus Buckminster, but that's not what people call me."

There was a knowing chuckle from the rest of the courtroom and a long sigh from Judge Jefferson.

"Hello, Bo," I whispered. "I'm pleased to meet you, but I think the judge is ready to start now."

Bo nodded his head as his attorney slipped his hand over his mouth to keep him from saying anything further. Somehow, through his big smiling eyes I heard what he was going to say anyway.

"Does the district attorney's office have any motions they would like to make before I proceed?"

"No, Your Honor. None at this time."

"Mr. Galax, anything from the defense?"

"Yes, Your Honna. Defense moves that my client's conviction be immediately overturned, and furtha, that his record be expunged."

"Of course you do, Mr. Galax," the judge said. "But I'm afraid it's not going to be that easy. Motion denied."

"Then I move that bail be granted for Mr. Buckminster, and that he be released in the custody of his aunt until these proceedings are completed."

"Mr. Prosecutor, do you wish to request a specific bail amount?"

"No, Your Honor. The County does not see Mr. Buckminster as a serious flight risk and offers no recommendation as to bail."

"You make my job easy then."

The judge took a few minutes to write on the papers he'd been shuffling then handed them to the bailiff. "This court orders that Bosephus Buckminster be released into the custody of his aunt, Ms. Evelyn Nutter. Bail is set in the amount of one-dollar."

In spite of the previous warning, the news caused a couple of deep whistles and a happy hush across the courtroom.

"Thank you very much, Your Honna,' the defense attorney said.

"Do you think you can scrape up that kind of money, Mr. Galax?"

Galax pulled a one-dollar bill from his pocket. "It just so happens I have the entire amount right here, Your Honna."

"Good then. Bailiff, collect up Mr. Galax's life savings. The first hearing on this matter will be scheduled a week from Friday. Mr. Galax, I will remind you that this is not a trial."

"I understand, your Honna."

"I will need your initial brief by Monday next, and if need be, you should be ready to present your case for a new trial at the next hearing."

"We shall be ready, Your Honna. We surely shall be."

"Bailiff, see what you can do to find something other than that great orange pumpkin suit for Bo to wear. He's conspicuous enough as it is."

"His aunt has brought him some clothes, Your Honor."

"This case is adjourned, then. Good luck, Bo."

Bo didn't answer. He seemed to be struggling with what was happening. He sat there awhile, still and confused. From my vantage point I could hear his attorney as he leaned-in to explain things. "Bo, the judge has decided to let you go home while we get your case together," he said softly.

"Home? What do you mean? I ain't going back to prison?"

"That's right, Bo."

"Mr. Galax, I ain't got no home."

"Your aunt has agreed to take you in, Bo. You're gonna stay with her a while."

"Aunt Evelyn?"

"Yes. Your auntie Evelyn would like you to go live with her. She's made up a fine room for you there."

Bo processed the latest twist with difficulty, as if things hadn't gone his way. The smile that is permanently dug in across his face was still in place, but it seemed to be fighting against a deeply wrinkling brow. "Mr. Galax, it seems like it would be a whole peck easier if I just stay put where I am," he said.

"That could be. That surely could be. But it would be much better for our case if you were to go with your auntie. There's people 'round here that love you, Bo. We need this town to show the judge just how much they care about you, and how much they'd appreciate you coming back."

As Bo struggled with the logic, the bailiff took a large brown paper bag from an old woman seated in the gallery and brought it over to the defendant's table. "Bo, I have some clothes for you to change into here. If you'll follow me, we can get you out of that jumpsuit."

Bo fixed his gaze on the bailiff, and then turned it back to his attorney, who nodded approval.

"Go with the bailiff, Bo. We'll talk some more when you get into your new clothes."

Bo slowly pushed his chair away from the defendant's table, and then lumbered across the courtroom with the bailiff. After he'd passed through the side exit, his attorney spun around in my direction.

"Mr. Daniels, it's mighty fine to finally meet you," he said, thrusting his hand across the rail that separated the gallery.

"Mr. Galax," I said, nodding uncommitted.

"May I say that I have read your stories over years with great diligence. I am truly a fan, sir."

"You're very kind."

"I am so sorry you were unable to join us for a taste of Molly's fine southern delicacies this morning. Her biscuits and gravy are well known."

"Perhaps another time," I said.

"The invitation will stay open for as long as you choose to consider it."

"Thank you. I may just take you up on that."

Galax leaned over the back of his chair, striking a more casual pose. He took the liberty of a Southern pause before he spoke again. "Mr. Daniels, I would like to make Mr. Buckminster available to you for a direct interview at whatever time you may feel is appropriate."

"I very much appreciate the access, Mr. Galax."

"Oh, please. Call me Trevor, Mr. Daniels. I dare say we will become very familiar before the next few weeks are through.”

“Okay, Trevor. What sort of conditions will you impose on this proposed interview?”

“None, sir. They’ll be no manner of restrictions asked or imposed. You may speak with him on whatever terms you like.”

Unrestricted access through an attorney to his client is rare, and the blank-check Galax was writing caught me by surprise. “I suppose the one requirement I should assume would be your presence at said meeting?”

“Why, not at all. You may speak with him privately, if that is your desire.”

Access without representation is totally unheard of. Galax was either incompetent or had knowledge of something I did not. For a moment, my face remained unaffected. “I’ll accept your gracious offer eventually, Mr. Galax. I’m sure we can work out the where and when in due time.”

A surprised Galax smiled and nodded graciously as I prepared myself for an overly polite goodbye.

“May I suggest this very afternoon, sir? That is, if your schedule permits. I would be more than happy to make arrangements for Mr. Buckminster to meet with you at your hotel.”

As I’ve learned to do when lacking a good answer, I said nothing.

“You are staying at the Marriott Courtyard near the interstate, are you not?”

“I am, but I’m not sure ...”

“I’m certain Ms. Nutter would be more than happy to carry Bo to meet with you there.”

My instincts were pushing back hard, but considering the terms he was laying out for the meeting, I couldn’t come up with a serious downside. I maintained my very best poker face before finally answering. “Can he be at my hotel at two this afternoon?”

Galax once again seemed surprised to have succeeded. “I’m quite sure that he can. We shall set the time for two o’clock at the Marriott Courtyard. You can count on it, as you would our government’s taxes.” He jumped to his feet and stuck out his hand, as if wanting to seal the deal before second thoughts crept in. We shook hands like old friends.

“Mark— May I call you Mark?”

“You may.”

“Might I ask a well meaning, but perhaps rather personal, question of you?”

"That would depend on the question, counselor."

"It's quite innocent, I assure you."

"The caveat remains, counselor."

"Very well. Though they are quite limited, there are from time to time certain social functions, even in this far-off part of the world."

"Social functions? Such as?"

"You know, dinner parties and such. They can be very much a part of the way things are done around here. The way the system works, if you will."

"So, what's the question?"

"If it's not too delicate to inquire, will your fiancée be joining you at any time during your visit with us?"

Having still not determined whether Galax was a bit of a buffoon or a wily fox, his question was either meant to assist with social planning, or it was a shot across the bow to let me know he too had done his homework.

"She will not," I replied plainly.

"I'm sorry to hear that. I do hope you shall not become too lonely while you make your way through this affair with us."

I slipped my notebook back into my bag. "Goodbye, Trevor."

"Good day to you, sir."

As I turned my back to leave the courtroom, I could almost feel Galax sporting a wide victory grin. Whether it was deserved or not would be up to me that afternoon.

Chapter 7

I hadn't noticed it when I drove in, but driving out of town I made out the lone, paint-peeled sign that announced Molly's "world famous eating." A bold boast for a place that, except for its weather-beaten placard, was hard to make out as a restaurant. Unsure if Molly's served breakfast so close to lunch, I went on with the long drive back to my hotel.

At the hotel, the message light was flashing on the phone in my room. There were two calls, both of them from Carl Odette. The first had been left at just before eight o'clock, the second twenty-minutes later.

"Mark, call in. I need to talk to you," the boss said in the first message.

In the second he seemed a little more anxious. "Mark, I *really* need to talk to you. Call me."

At first I wondered why Carl hadn't just called me on my cell phone, then I realized I hadn't switched it back on since shutting it down to take my nap the day before. When I checked the cell phone voicemail, there were four other messages, all from him. I hit the call return for the last one, a call from Carl's own cell phone at seven thirty-eight that morning.

He obviously saw the caller ID before he picked up. "Geez, Mark. I've been trying to reach you since last night. Where the heck have you been?"

"Right here. I took a little nap yesterday after we talked and forgot to turn my cell back on."

"Do me a favor and don't shut it off for a while. Things are starting to break back here on your story."

"Really. What's happening?"

"The Reverend Leyland Johnston is on his way to your neck of the woods."

"Reverend Lee? What does mister civil rights himself have going with this story? Is he coming down here to protest the retrial?"

"Hardly. It seems he's on the other side of the argument."

"Really? Are you saying he's coming down to argue *for* a new trial – a new trial for a white boy convicted of murdering a black boy?"

"So he says. He held a press conference late yesterday at the Association for Social Justice in Manhattan."

"Was there video?"

"The whole thing played live on CSPAN2."

"Damn! I wish I could get my hands on that video."

"Way ahead of you. I had Shelley in IT convert it to digital and stick it out on the Intranet."

"Why you old fossil. You're finally starting to embrace this whole new digital frontier."

"Yeah, well I wouldn't have a clue how to get to it, I'm afraid. I forwarded the instructions she sent me that explain how to watch it. Do you have broadband access there?"

"Believe it or not, I do. It may be the only place within a hundred miles, but they have high-speed satellite feeding the rooms here."

"Good, then. Watch the tape and call me back. My guess is that the Reverend Lee's is probably close to you. He left New York this morning."

"I'll do it. And I'll keep my phone on."

"That would be nice. Call me in a little while."

The sudden urgency surrounding the Reverend Johnston's visit meant a rundown of the morning's court proceedings for Carl would have to wait. After reading through what turned out to be fairly simple instructions for connecting to the satellite Internet provider, Media Player began the CSPAN capture from the point of Reverend Lee's introduction. As the reverend approached the microphone, the first thing that caught my eye was that he was considerably less rotund than the last time we'd met, and he had shorn most of his long, artificially straightened locks.

"Ladies and gentlemen, I'll keep my prepared remarks brief this evening, in order to give you as much of what little time we have for questions."

The reverend began by reading from a prepared sheet. "The ASJ has reason to believe that a second miscarriage of justice is about to be perpetrated on the people of South Carolina and of this country. It is our intention to send a delegation to Chases Corner, South Carolina, to monitor events and do whatever is necessary to ensure the full light of day is shone on those proceedings. I'll be happy to answer as many questions as I can."

"Reverend Johnson, can you give us more details about what you perceive the injustice to be," a reporter asked.

"Obviously, we don't believe the person convicted in the murder of Marcus Brown sixteen years ago was the person that did the crime. We believe Mr. Buckminster was railroaded into prison, and that there are powerful people who know why."

"What makes you think that, and who do you think is responsible?" another reporter asked.

"Those questions will be answered in due time. Let's just say that this travesty could not have been accomplished sixteen years ago, or attempted again now, without people in very high places actively participating."

A man standing next to Reverend Johnston grabbed his arm and whispered something in his ear, before the second reporter asked a follow up question. "Reverend Lee, your explanation is rather cryptic. Can you give us more about just what exactly you mean by high places? Something to—"

"Not at this time," the man next to the reverend said.

"Reverend, the last time you took off on a crusade for justice, it turned out to be a hoax. Why should the American public believe you this time?" a third reporter shouted from the back.

Reverend Johnston seemed to start off the podium, but stopped suddenly and stepped back to the microphone. *"But you shall receive power when the Holy Spirit has come upon you; and you shall be my witnesses in Jerusalem and in all Judea and Samaria and to the end of the earth."*

After he had finished with his bible quote, one of Johnston's cronies stepped in front of the reverend to put a quick end to the question-and-answer session. The hasty interruption fit with recent events in Johnston's turbulent career as a social advocate. He'd used biblical quotes extensively in his defense of a black man who had been accused of killing a white woman in Mobile, Alabama. After the reverend had united the black community and fundamentalist Christians in a bizarre coalition to support the man, the defendant took a deal from the prosecutor and pled guilty to the crime. Many had thought Johnston's efforts were going to get the man off, but when the State lowered the charges to second-degree manslaughter, the chance to assuage his guilt and still get out of jail in six to ten was enough for the district attorney to get the man's confession. The right turned on Johnston for leading them down a path, and in the aftermath, the once mighty Reverend Lee had been made low. He had become, in short, a joke.

If the Reverend's intercession into the Bo Buckminster affair was an attempt at rehabilitating his reputation, it would have helped explain the considerable drop in weight and the loss of his trademark hairdo. As Reverend Lee's power and influence had grown over the years, so too had his size and controversial coif. Shedding himself of a great deal of each seemed to be an acknowledgement that his support base was no longer what it had once been.

After closing out the media player on my laptop, I noticed it was nearly twelve thirty. If Reverend Lee had been truly anxious to get to Chases Corner, it occurred to me that he may well have been nutty enough to take a flight out as early as I had. That meant he might even have made it down to the courthouse already.

My cell phone rang.

"Did you see it?" the voice said, before I could even get the phone to my face.

"I did, Carl. This could get interesting."

"Interesting? There's nothing old Reverend Lee gets his mitts on that doesn't turn into a circus. What do you think his angle is?"

"Your guess is as good as mine. Maybe he's just plain old interested in seeing to it that justice is done?"

"Right. And maybe the next time I take a crap, a monkey will fly out of my butt. Mark, you gotta get on him. You two have a history, don't you?"

"Yes. Not a good one, but we do have a history."

"Did you piss him off so bad the last time around that he's going to freeze you out down there?'

"Time will tell. Do you know when he was planning to leave New York?"

"His people said he'd be on the first flight out."

"He must like to hear those words too."

"What's that?"

"Never mind," I said. "I've got to get started back to Chases Corner. If he left early this morning, he may already be down at the courthouse, stirring the pot."

"Absolutely. And listen, if he seems bitter about the last time, take the soft approach. Tell him you were only editorializing and that I *made* you take a hard tact."

Carl didn't understand that even people on the outside saw him as anything but the stereotypical tyrant. His approach was a loser, because he wasn't.

"Sure thing, Carl."

After splashing some water on my face and slapping on a second layer of cologne, I started out the door at a trot. It took a while for the elevator to get to the second floor, so with a spring in my step I bounded down the stairwell. When I pulled open the heavy fire door that led to the lobby, there was a very large and menacing looking black man blocking the way.

"Hello, sir. Are you a guest of the hotel?"

Distracted as I was, he gave me quite a scare standing there. Then I noticed the lapel pin he was wearing: a fish symbol balancing on a set of scales – the logo for Reverend Lee Johnston's group. He was at the hotel.

"Yes, I am," I replied, a knowing smile rolling across my face. "But if you could just tell—"

"Do you have your key with you, sir?"

"I do, but I'm a reporter with the—"

"Could you show it to me please?"

The guy was starting to anger me, but considering his size I gave in to his request and produced my room key. For good measure, I whipped out my press badge as well.

"Mr. Daniels, I'm afraid the lobby is going to be closed for about ten minutes while an important guest checks in," he said after handing me back my credentials. "If you need to get to your vehicle, you can access the parking lot through that door just behind you."

With the reverend at the Marriott and not in Chases Corner, I no longer needed to get to my car. I thought about making a case to get through to the lobby anyway, but decided it would be futile. I'd made it up to the first landing when I heard loud voices coming toward the stairwell from the lobby.

"Make way, please. The reverend needs to get to his room."

The big man noticed my pause. "Sir, please keep going up the stairway."

"Your boss and I are acquainted. I was hoping ..."

"Sir, get moving. Now!"

I froze, and as the big man from Reverend Lee's entourage started up the stairs after me, and I nearly wet my pants. Just as he was about to snatch me up by my collar, a man's voice hollered from the doorway leading to the lobby.

"Well, if it isn't Mr. Daniels from *The New York Times*," said the friendly voice, the tone of which caused the bodyguard coming for me to pause in mid-snatch.

I took in a deep breath, then exhaled long and slow. "Reverend," I said with a nod.

"I am truly sorry if Malcolm disrupted your comings and goings. He is in charge of my security and is perhaps overly protective."

The big man stood aside on the stairwell as if willing to let me by.

"That's quite alright. You may have just saved your man here from a thorough thrashing," I said, as I squeezed by the big man with some difficulty.

"I'm quite sure your mighty pen would have been more than enough to overtake his sword, Mr. Daniels. It has dealt a blow or two to my own person from time to time."

"Never in anger, Reverend. Never in anger."

I stuck my hand in the Reverend Lee's direction, which made two men standing behind him tense up. The reverend greeted my hand with both of his and pulled me in closer to him. "You know, Mark," he said in a softer, quieter voice. "I somehow suspected you would be here. You may be surprised to learn that I have dreamed of you recently."

A bizarre statement from an even more bizarre man. That's all I thought at the time.

"I hope in your dream we were civil. That we let bygones-be-bygones and didn't let the past overtake the present."

It was my appeal for access. The reverend just smiled.

"In fact," he said. "We became allies in my dream. I am quite convinced that you and I will be working on the same side."

He finally let go of my hand, and I felt a little dirty. When those riding the crest of public attention fall, actions and words that seemed as though they could be the work of genius while they were on top, become downright odd when they hover near the bottom.

"I try not to take sides in my line of work, Reverend Lee. But if it turns out that we're both on the side of truth when this thing winds down, I'll be as happy as any man."

The bodyguard directly behind the Reverend Lee stepped through from the lobby and positioned himself in-between us.

"Reverend, we have to get to your suite for a conference call."

The reverend took his eyes away from mine for the first time. "I'm afraid Terrell here is in charge of my time, Mr. Daniels. We'll talk again."

No sooner had I nodded than the entire group started up the stairs as one unit. When the reverend reached the landing, he raised his right hand slightly, and the whole cabal stopped on a dime.

He turned back in my direction. "Mr. Daniels, perhaps we can share a lunch together tomorrow and have a conversation about why *both* of us have come here?"

"Sure thing. You name the place."

"Do you have a suggestion?"

"How about Molly's? It's close to the courthouse."

"Molly's? Sounds like a place that would serve food to tempt a man such as myself."

"That may well be. I've heard good things about the biscuits and gravy there."

"Ah, you've chosen well then. Lunch tomorrow at Molly's it is."

With that, the entire group scooted up the stairs and was gone. Things were going too easy. I should have seen that, but sometimes you just want an easier time of it for yourself.

When I got back to my room the message light was flashing again. Figuring it must be Carl, I hit the speed dial on my cell phone. The phone quit ringing at three rings, followed by a couple of erratic clicks and a cuss word from the other end.

"Carl?"

"Oh, hey, Mark. Sorry, I was trying to switch over from another line."

"The new phones still giving you fits?"

"Forget about it! I don't know why they can't just make these things so normal people can us them."

"They do, Carl. You're just not what they had in mind as normal."

"Okay, smart guy. What did you want?"

"I don't know. You called me."

"No I didn't. I may not have mastered the new phone system, but I know when I make a call."

"Really? My fault then. I saw the message light in my room and figured it must have been you."

"Wasn't me. But as long as I have you on the phone, are you on your way to the courthouse?"

"I just finished speaking to the Reverend Johnston."

"You did? I thought you were still at your hotel when you called me before?"

"I was. I bumped into him and his entourage down in the lobby as I was heading out."

"How convenient for you. And you talked with him?"

"Yup. Mighty bizarre. Like everything else about this case so far."

"Is he still holding a grudge about the piece you did on him last year?"

"Not enough to keep him from inviting me to lunch tomorrow. He said I came to him in a dream."

"Oh, boy. Here we go."

"Yeah, I hope I wasn't wearing horns or something in his dream. You know, burning at the stake while he praised the good Lord for his righteousness."

Carl paused a moment. "Seriously, don't get all wrapped up with that guy. He's a little desperate for attention these days."

"Don't worry about me," I said with a more reassuring tone. "I can handle old Reverend Lee."

"So what's he doing there? Any hints as to motive."

"Nothing yet. I'll find out more tomorrow, I'm sure."

"If you get something, post it right away. He's a story within a story."

"Sure thing; but I'm going to have to let you go now. I need to get ready for my afternoon meeting with Mr. Buckminster."

"Wait. Did you just say you're meeting with the defendant this afternoon?"

"I did. I thought I told you that when we spoke earlier."

"You left that little detail out, Mark. You're moving pretty fast."

"Sorry about that. Must have got lost in all the bustle over Reverend Lee's arrival."

"That's fine, but get me out a daily by the end of the day. If there's something there for the morning edition, I'd like to get it in."

"Count on it."

It was good to get back to an assignment that required a daily. They were the vehicle Carl used to keep up with all the major stories his reporters were working on. He had them sent to him at the end of each day, and from them he could keep himself up to date at his own pace.

When Carl had denied responsibility for the message light flashing, butterflies flew across my stomach. I'd almost asked him if he'd given Karen the number to my hotel, but I hadn't wanted to travel back to the topic. I thought it might have sounded desperate.

I punched the message button within seconds of hanging up with him.

"You have one message. Push seven on your key pad to—"

I hit the button hard.

"Hey, old buddy. Where the hell are you? It's Bart, and I'm back from the dark continent. I'm gone for two weeks and you totally screw everything up. What the hell happened? Call me!"

Bartholomew Kennedy – a.k.a. Dirty Bart – was sadly my best friend in the whole world. I was never exactly sure how he got that distinction, but over the years we connected somehow. We met in college, back in the day when living on the edge was an expected rite of passage. Unfortunately, his rights never passed. Some of the stuff the guy did could be so damned infuriating, what with his insistence on living his life as if it were the sequel to the movie *Animal House*. But he was my best friend, and good friends were just not something I had an abundance of.

I wasn't sure if it was disdain for Bart's raunchy banter, or disappointment over the voice in the message not belonging to Karen, but I decided against calling my pal back right away. It was nearly one o'clock in the afternoon and there wasn't much time left before my first visit with Bosephus Buckminster. I definitely needed some quality time to prepare an outline of questions to ask. Dirty Bart would have to wait, which if nothing else meant my ears would be spared a while longer from the usual barrage of cuss words he threw around like pronouns.

Chapter 8

While jumping back into the material on Bo's first trial, something triggered the addictive-compulsive part of my personality; the trait that had so often led me down a path to trouble. Since my first year in college, I'd battled against feelings of anxiety. It came and went, depending on what was happening during any particular slice of time in my life, but for the most part it had been on the decline as I grew older. About fifteen minutes into a more thorough reading of Bo's file, I could feel the blood pumping across the top of my stomach. By the time another half an hour had passed, my breathing had become shallow – a sure sign I was on the path to a full blown episode. I knew I needed to take a break from the material, long enough to focus on a few of the relaxation techniques I'd learned along the way.

It was from a deep trance-like state that I heard the phone ring.

"Mr. Daniels," the caller said. "You have a guest in the lobby."

Before the front desk person could finish I heard a second voice in the background. "Tell him it's Bo. My real name is Bosephus Buckminster, but that's not what people call me."

"It's Mr. Buckminster," the front desk guy added.

"Thanks. I'll be right down."

Waiting for the elevator, I couldn't help but feel as though I were on my way to meet a small child. Except for the deep baritone rumbling behind his words, Bo's exchange with the man at the front desk supported the premise. As I got in the elevator, I could see in the reflection of the polished metal doors that I was smiling broadly. When I stepped out into the lobby there were a half-dozen or so hotel employees milling about, and every single one of them were wearing the exact same smile.

One of the employees said something to Bo and pointed in my direction.

Bo seemed to be studying me as I approached. "Yes, sir. I sure enough remember you," he said. "We met there at the courthouse." His face lit up as he let go of the minor battle with his memory.

"You did indeed, Bo," I said, reaching my hand out to him. "I was sitting behind you."

His big hand wrapped around mine so that only the top part of my thumb was showing. At one time or another, someone must have convinced him to be careful when he shook hands, because rather than squeeze, he held onto my hand as if he had just caught a butterfly.

"My aunt is a waiting on me to tell her it's okay to go ahead on, Mr. Daniels," he said, pointing at an old pickup parked in front of the hotel entrance.

"I'll go talk with her, Bo. You can wait right here."

"I'll do it. I'll just stand right here and wait on you while you speak with Aunt Evelyn."

As I approached the beat-up truck, it was hard to see inside. Up close I could see the cab was filed with cigarette smoke, a dingy film covering the windows.

"Ms. Nutter?" I asked.

The woman seemed agitated as she leaned over with some effort to tug on the handle to the passenger side door. "That window ain't worked in years," she said, sounding as if I were the one who had broken it. "What time you want me to come back and collect Bo?"

Without the smoke and dirty window to blur the image, Evelyn Nutter was a scary sight. Her yellow upper lip and overly wrinkled face were a perfect match for the cigarette she'd stuck in the corner of her mouth to free her hands for the door latch.

"We shouldn't be more than an hour."

"Fine," she snapped, and pulled the door shut. With that, she jammed the clunker in gear, ground the transmission a few times, and then rolled out of the driveway. It was hard to tell whether the cloud of smoke billowing out from under the truck came from a rusted through muffler, or if it was letting off the proceeds from the old woman's habit.

When I arrived back in the lobby, Bo looked worried.

"I was supposed to ask you what time my aunt needed to come back by, Mr. Daniels," he said.

"No problem, Bo. I took care of it with her. She'll be back in an hour or so."

"You'll have to tell me when that is, Mr. Daniels. When the hour is up I mean."

"You can count on it. Just leave that part to me."

"Thank you kindly. It's probably best that way," he said, as if he were making an apology.

"Mr. Daniels, would you like us to call up in an hour?" one of the employees asked from behind the counter.

"You know, that might not be a bad idea." I said. "What do you think, Bo? Would you like to head upstairs and talk in my room?"

"I surely would. I ain't never seen a hotel room first hand. Least not one I can remember."

"Follow me then. I've got a pretty big one for us to talk in."

We'd started back across the lobby when Bo had one of his frequent afterthoughts. "Oh, and I'd like to say thank you kindly to all you people working here at this hotel," he said, spinning around to talk to the group still mingling around the front desk.

After everyone in the group had called some sort of reply, Bo nodded, and we were underway again. He had more questions as we made our way to my room.

"Does anyone stay here at the hotel full-time?" he asked.

"Not really. Most folks just stay a couple days."

"That's one thing different about that prison I been at. Almost everyone there stays on for years at a time. Do you have a roommate?"

"No. Everyone has their own room."

"That'd be another difference, then," he said.

When we finally got to the suite and stepped inside, Bo seemed in shock. His mouth dropped wide open in wonder. "Oh, my! This here ain't nothing like prison," he said. "You could fit a whole peck of prison rooms right inside this one and still have space left over."

"It's called a suite," I said.

He wandered around a bit, hitting every light switch in each room he went into. "I can't see why folks don't just live here permanent," he said. "Why, you even have a kitchen for cooking and such."

"Bo, what do you say we settle down in the living room area and have a little chat about things?"

"That'd be real fine. You want me to sit on that couch over there?"

"Whatever you like. Wherever you think you'll be the most comfortable."

Bo made his way to the living area, stopping to touch a few things along the way, running his big hand across them like a blind man might do. He plopped down on the couch. "The good Lord has truly blessed you, Mr. Daniels," he said.

"I suppose you're right. It is a little hard to be away from home, though. No matter how nice a room they give you."

"I reckon you're right about that, Mr. Daniels. I hadn't really thought much on that part."

I grabbed my laptop case before joining Bo in the living area, and after taking out my trusty composition book and a pen, I hesitated before bringing out the next item. "Bo, sometimes reporters like to record the conversations we have. You know, to make sure we get everything down exactly right."

"Yes, sir. I reckon that's a might good idea. Wish I had one me of them recorders, sometimes. I ain't real good at recollecting most things."

"Then, would you mind if I use a tape recorder for our talk here today?"

"Nope. Wouldn't mind that at all."

I put the tape recorder on the table, and the first session with Bo was underway. In many ways, it was the classic introduction to Bosephus Buckminster.

TRANSCRIPT
Tape # 1 (first interview)
Interviewer: Daniels
Responder: Buckminster
Date of Interview: Wednesday, April 3rd
Location: Marriott Courtyard Hotel

2:16 PM

DANIELS: Bo, I want to thank you for taking the time to talk with me today.

BO: That's no bother, Mr. Daniels.

DANIELS: When we met this morning at the courthouse, you seemed to know who I was. Do you know what I do?

BO: Think so. Mr. Galax told me you was a reporter from up North. Said I should make it a point to say hey to you.

DANIELS: That's right. I'm a reporter for *The New York Times*. It's a newspaper, and I write some of the stories that go into it.

BO: Yes, sir. Can't say as I've ever read it though. I don't think we get that one in these parts. I reckon it might be because it would be mighty hard for them young fellas to ride their bikes all the way down this way every morning. You know, to deliver it and all.

DANIELS: That could be part of it. A lot of people do read it, though. A lot of important people that are interested in seeing how your case comes out.

BO: I guess I have to thank them for that. Can you make sure they know I said so, Mr. Daniels?

DANIELS: Yeah, I'll make sure they know. But, Bo, I want you to be very careful with what you say here today. Once a thing is said, I'm not allowed to ignore it. Once something is in the public record ...

BO: You trying to tell me I shouldn't tell no lies?

DANIELS: Well, yes that's part of it. But, you also need to be careful of—

BO: Cause I don't tell no lies, Mr. Daniels. Hard enough for me to keep track of what most folks know to be true. Can't see as how I could ever keep up with telling whoppers.

DANIELS: Okay. That's a good foundation for us to have our conversation. I'm going to ask you some questions and you just tell me what you remember. I suppose the best thing for us to do is get right to the question at hand. Did you kill Marcus Brown?

BO: No, sir. I sure enough did not kill Marcus.

DANIELS: Then, can you tell me what happened that day?

BO: I can't say as I recall much from that day. It's hard for me sometimes.

DANIELS: How is it you're so sure you didn't do what they say you did?

BO: Marcus told me so himself. Marcus and me are like two peas in a pod, ya know. He can't much keep track of whoppers either.

DANIELS: Did you speak with Marcus that day in the woods before he passed away, Bo?

BO: Oh, no, sir. Like I said, I probably wouldn't much remember it if I did.

DANIELS: What do you mean then when you say Marcus told you so himself?

BO: He told me after he was gone. He's an angel now, ya know. He gets to cross back-and-forth whenever he needs to.

PAUSE:

DANIELS: Bo, I want to believe what you said about whoppers before. So, let me make sure I understand what you're saying. Are you saying that you get visits from Marcus's ghost?

BO: Oh, no, sir. He's not a ghost! I don't believe in such things. To tell you the truth, I'm surprised that you do, though. What with you being a reporter and all.

DANIELS: No, that's not what I said, Bo. I don't believe in ghosts either, but what I thought you were saying...

BO: Do you believe in angels?

PAUSE:

DANIELS: Well, I was raised a good Catholic, so I suppose I believe in them to some degree.

BO: There you go, then. That there is what Marcus is. He's an angel. I don't think he's one of those Catholic ones, though.

PAUSE:

DANIELS: Did Marcus tell who *did* kill him?

BO: Oh, no. He ain't allowed to do that. That would be getting someone into trouble. His job is to help people get out of trouble, not into it.

PAUSE:

DANIELS: Alright, let's put Marcus aside for a minute. What can you tell me about the other two boys who were with you the day Marcus was killed? Do you remember anything about them?

BO: You talking about Trey and Corey, Mr. Daniels?

DANIELS: That's right. Do you remember them?

BO: I kinda remember Trey. Don't recall much about him, but I know we was teammates and all. On that baseball team, I mean.

DANIELS: What about Corey?

BO: Yes, sir. Corey and me got to be fine friends. I like Corey a great deal.

DANIELS: You and he were close before all this happened?

BO: Oh, no, sir. He didn't much talk to me before it all happened. He was good friends with Trey, you know. Trey didn't much care for me and Marcus, that much I remember,

DANIELS: How is it you and Corey became friends, then? Did he visit you in prison?

BO: You could say that, Mr. Daniels. More like he came to live with me there.

DANIELS: Corey spent time in the prison with you?

BO: Yes, sir.

DANIELS: How long was he there?

BO: Seems he was there a good bit. Can't really say exactly, cause I don't do real well with calendar time.

DANIELS: Do you know what he was there for?

BO: He did something wrong, most likely. You can't just go to that prison anytime you want to. It ain't like this hotel. A judge has to send you there.

PAUSE:

DANIELS: Did you two ever talk about what happened to Marcus?

BO: Not really. In the beginning, he told me a bunch of times how sorry he was for what happened. That's about it, though. He got real sad if Marcus came up while we was talking, that much I recall. Think he must have liked old Marcus a lot more than people thought he did.

DANIELS: How long has it been since Corey got out of prison, Bo?

BO: I can't say exactly. Been a while though.

PAUSE:

DANIELS: Bo, do you understand what's happening now? Why you've been brought back here to Chases Corner.

BO: I think so. Seems some folks don't want me to live up at that prison no more. Guess they think they've found out something about what happened to Marcus that proves I didn't kill him.

DANIELS: That's right. How do you feel about that?

BO: Oh, I don't know. Not sure I feel one way or another about it.

DANIELS: Wouldn't you like to see your name cleared? For people to know it wasn't you that killed Marcus?

BO: Mr. Daniels, they's two people that already know that for a fact. The two that matter the most already know I didn't do such a thing.

DANIELS: One of those being Marcus.

BO: That's right.

DANIELS: Who would the other one be then?

BO: God, Mr. Daniels. God knows I didn't kill Marcus. I suppose if he wanted everyone else to know, it wouldn't be such a hard thing for him to do.

LONG PAUSE:

DANIELS: Bo, I think I've got what I need for now. I'm sure we'll get a chance to talk some more later on, but is there anything you would like to know from me? Is there something you'd like me to explain about what's going on with your hearing?

BO: I don't suppose there is, Mr. Daniels. Least ways nothing I need to know that Mr. Galax ain't already explained. There might be one question you could answer for me, though.

DANIELS: What would that be?

BO: Well, it ain't got nothing to do with court. Is it okay to ask you a question that ain't got nothing to do with court?

DANIELS: Of course. Go ahead and ask your question, Bo.

PAUSE:

BO: What's making you so sad, Mr. Daniels? They's something real sad sitting right there behind your eyes. Something that's keeping your face from being as happy as it could be.

DANIELS: Sad? I don't think there's anything making me sad just now. In fact, I'm pretty content.

BO: Well, I'm not real sure what that word content means, Mr. Daniels; but I sure enough thought I saw something troubling you behind your eyes.

DANIELS: Nothing that I'm aware of, Bo.

BO: Alright, then. I suppose it could just be from your being so far away from home and all. Maybe you're just missing someone back home.

PAUSE:

DANIELS: That could be. For now though, what do you say we put away the questions and head on back to the lobby?

BO: Whatever you'd like, Mr. Daniels.

DANIELS: I don't think your aunt will be back yet, but the hotel keeps snacks and drinks out for the guests to nibble on during the day. Are you hungry?

BO: I don't guess I've ever had a reason to turn away from a snack.

DANIELS: Good. Let me just put this stuff away and we'll see if we can get us one while we wait on your Aunt Evelyn.

Knowing we hadn't even come close to the full hour yet, I took my time putting things away. Bo's last question had caught me off guard, and touched a nerve that I wouldn't have guessed in a million years would have been vulnerable during our conversation. As we made our way back to the lobby, it was obvious by Bo's pace that he was focused on finding out what kind of snacks were waiting on us. I've noticed that when his mind is occupied by something, he doesn't much say anything. He has just the two modes: quiet and asking questions. I'm sure he has to ask about most things more than once, so it would seem to assure a never-ending flow.

I, on the other hand, was quiet for different reasons. I was pissed first and foremost, and my ire was focused squarely on the wily Mr. Galax. He would have known I was going to ask the big question, and just as certainly he would have known what Bo's answer was going to be. I didn't understand what his angle was exactly, but he'd put me on the spot for sure. If he had been trying to lay the groundwork for an insanity defense for Bo, it would have been helpful for him if I had slipped Bo's response into the paper. But the only way he could have expected such a result, would have been if he held a very low opinion of me as a journalist. If that were the case, Galax was very shortly going to learn first-hand how he'd misjudged.

As the elevator opened to the lobby, I looked down at my watch. There were still twenty minutes before Bo's aunt was to return, but when I glanced outside the entrance to the hotel, the old truck was chugging on idle and smokier than ever.

"Bo, it looks like your Aunt Evelyn is already here. Why don't you go over there and pick out a snack and a drink, and I'll go let her know we'll only be a couple minutes."

Bo was already on his way over to the spread before I could finish my sentence. I took a couple steps towards the front door.

"Mr. Daniels," Bo shouted to get my attention.

"What is it, Bo?"

"They's a whole bunch of things to choose from. You think they'd mind if a fella took more than one snack?"

I looked over at the front desk guy, who smiled and nodded.

"You could get yourself one of each, Bo. I don't think anyone's going to mind."

As the automatic doors at the entrance slid open, I could make out the gritty glare I'd seen earlier. Rather than risk the wrath again, I walked around to the driver's side to speak with Ms. Nutter. Apparently, the driver's side window didn't work either, because Bo's aunt pushed the door open on her side as well.

"You finished with Bo?" she snapped.

"Ms. Nutter, I'm sorry if I was unclear earlier. I wasn't expecting you back for at least an hour."

"Where in the devil was you expecting me to go? We live an hour and fifteen minutes from this place!"

This was not a happy woman. I don't think she was mad; but rather a matter of not being happy. Probably for many years. "Right," I replied. "I'm sorry. I should have just asked you in."

Ms. Nutter's eyes flared up big. "Mr. Daniels, I am a married woman! I ain't about to go sitting around in a no hotel lobby just so people can gossip and spread untrue lies about what I was doing there."

I assumed she was talking about folks wondering if she was having an affair – the thought of which nearly turned my stomach. "I can respect that, Ms. Nutter. Please accept my apology."

The old woman didn't reply, but I could tell by a slight relaxation of her shoulders that she wasn't mad enough to hit me any longer. "Perhaps next time I can come to your home, if that would make things more comfortable for you."

"Next time? Why you need a next time?"

"I want to learn more about what Bo was like before all this happened," I said. "I'd like to have some time to speak with you about that, too. I mean, with a proper chaperon and all."

"You don't need to talk with me. I ain't got nothing to say. And if it's Bo you need more talking with, you can just take that up with Mr. Galax."

Ms. Evelyn Nutter was the first genuinely nasty personality I ran into on my trip to South Carolina. Her bitterness and contempt stood in stark contrast to her nephew's disposition, which – by itself – set off alarms as to what her motives were for taking him in.

Bo came through the sliding glass doors just in time to end the awkwardness that had developed between his aunt and me. He walked gingerly, balancing an assortment of muffins, small cakes, and turnovers in his hands and up his arms.

"Looks like you got them all, Bo."

"Yes, sir. One of each, just like you said."

I couldn't help but laugh a little, and for just a moment I thought about trying to rustle up a large zip-lock bag to put his goodies in, to keep them from getting all smoky from the long ride home with his aunt.

"I won't shake your hand, Bo. I wouldn't want to see you drop any of those fine cakes. I'd like to get up with Mr. Galax and set up another time for us to talk, though."

"Sure thing, Mr. Daniels. Any time you'd like. I sure enough enjoyed our talk today."

I held the door open for Bo to gently settle in with his snacks for the drive. The way he was looking at the goodies, my worries about the cakes acquiring a smoky taste before he got them home wouldn't be a problem.

I wasn't back in my room more than a minute when the phone rang.

"So, when were you planning to call me back, you rat-bastard?"

The unmistakable language of one Dirty Bart. "Bart. I got your message earlier."

"So why the hell didn't you call me back?"

Jumping the chasm between Bo and Bart was a lot to deal with. "Bart, do you think you can chill out a bit with the gutter mouth. I'm not in the mood to be cussed at every other word."

"That's all you have to say to your best man after canceling the wedding? 'Please don't swear at me'?"

"That'll do for starters."

Bart paused a minute like he was actually considering my request. "You asshole. Don't give me that shit."

"Bart, I swear to God, I'll hang up the phone."

"Alright, don't get your panties all in a wad," he said, laughing freely on the other end. "All I really want to know is what you did to make Karen mad enough to dump you, old buddy?"

"I'm not really sure. It might have had something to do with her asking me to not see *you* anymore."

"Nah, that's not it. We both know you would've thrown me clean overboard if that were the thing."

He was right, I would have. "Let's just say it's as good a reason as I can come up with," I said.

"Ah, you poor guy. I thought this one was going to beat the curse."

"Well, it didn't. But life goes on."

"It sure does, my friend. I guess it's back to wild nights out on the town with Dirty Bart. When are you getting back?"

"I'm not sure right now. I wouldn't count on me for the wild nights, either."

"Yeah, right. Say, how far are you from Charleston?"

"A little over two hours."

"Oh, man, that's something we could do. I love that town. We could play a little golf during the day, and get into some trouble at night."

I knew that saying no to one of Bart's many great road trip ideas wasn't really necessary, because he rarely followed through on them.

"We'll have to see. Things are pretty hot here right now. Maybe when things slow down."

"You just let me know, and I'm there."

"I will. But I promised to get a daily to Carl by five so I need to get to it."

I didn't really, but as a fellow newspaper man Bart could at least identify.

"Get to work then, but you call me when the load lightens. We'll meet up in Charleston and wash this whole Karen thing out of your system with some of that Jameson's whiskey you're so crazy about."

"I'll do it."

"And listen, old buddy. Seriously, I'm sorry about—"

"Thanks, Bart. We'll talk later."

The one good thing about the timing of Karen's decision was that she'd waited until Bart was out of town. I made a mental note to thank her for that, if we ever talked again.

I did manage to get a daily out to Carl by five. I never would have admitted it to him, but the truth was that preparing the dailies did help me to get a focus on how all the pieces of the puzzle fit together. I also sent him a request via e-mail to get me more information on Corey Aycock. Specifically, why he'd been in prison with Bo.

Chapter 9

With my body clock still out of sync from the marathon sleep session the night before, early to bed and early to rise was inevitable. My second morning in the deep South began with a severe craving for some biscuits and gravy, but it wasn't just the unanimous recommendations of the Chases Corner townsfolk that drove me to it. While finding out why those served at Molly's were so "well known around these parts" was as good as any reason to start my day at her place, there was another motive for paying Molly a visit. Giving Attorney Galax a piece of my mind had weighed heavily on me the evening before, and I was counting on him being a creature of habit. By morning, I was ready to partake of an old Southern breakfast specialty, overlapped by the chance to knock one of her esteemed native sons down a few pegs for good measure.

As I pulled up to Molly's Restaurant, Billy Thorton caught sight of me and followed me into the parking area at full speed on his bike. I got out of the rental car, and tiny bits of rock and gravel flew everywhere as Billy fish-tailed his bike to a stop.

"Morning, Mr. Daniels."

"Good morning, Billy."

"I was just fixin' to head over to the courthouse to find you," he said, a tinge of apology hanging on his words. "Just like you asked me to."

"Thanks. I decided to get a bite to eat first."

"You should try the biscuits and gravy."

"That's what I've heard. Is Mr. Galax inside?"

"I reckon he is, Mr. Daniels. You want me to go tell him you need to speak to him?"

"No, that won't be necessary. I think he'll find me."

I started toward the old place. Up close, it looked considerably more beaten down than when I had just caught a glimpse of it driving by.

"Say, Mr. Daniels," Billy hollered to get my attention. "You think you're gonna need me for something this morning?

"Don't you have to get to school?"

"Nah. Ain't going today."

"What do your parents think about that?"

"They're the ones that told me not to go. We got us a barbecue stand over there at the courthouse. They want me to help work it."

"They want you to do that instead of going to school?"

"Yes, sir. That is, if you ain't got no errands for me and such."

The ten-bucks I'd given Billy the day before must have made a favorable impression on his parents.

"There is something you could do for me, Billy. You ever heard of Reverend Lee Johnston?"

"Oh, yes sir. There's people coming into town from all over just to see him. That's the reason my daddy wants me to hang around and help with the barbecue."

"Really?"

"Yes, sir. People go in mighty big for a man of the Lord around here."

"Can you go over to the courthouse and sniff around to find out if he has any official events planned for this morning? Maybe a press conference or a photo-op."

"I'll do it. You want me to come back here and tell you what's happening?"

"That'd be perfect."

With that Billy Thorton took off, pedaling as hard as I'd ever seen anyone pedal a bicycle. The kid was one big ball of energy.

Stepping into the "world famous" Molly's was like stepping into a time warp. There didn't seem to be anything in the place that hadn't seen its best days somewhere in the 1950s or 60s. The floor in particular, which I'm sure was a lovely layer of linoleum when first laid down, had lost all remnants of its original color and pattern over the years. It had become a dirty gray, with the high traffic areas just slightly darker than the rest. There was an old woman, in an even older smock, perched behind a counter on a high stool off to my left as I walked in.

"Good morning, Mr. Daniels," she said.

I was starting to get accustomed to people knowing who I was ahead of time, but decided to take a stab at understanding why that was. "I'm sorry, have we met before?"

"Oh, no, sir. My cousin Martha works over at the courthouse. She's one of the ladies that got you your badge and such."

"Yes, Martha. I remember her. I can see the resemblance."

"Most folks do say we favor each other." The woman let go with a semi-toothless grin.

"You are both quite lovely women, I must say."

She smiled even bigger as her face flushed with color. "They say you writer folks have a way with the words'" she said as she handed me a plastic menu. "Will you be alone this morning?"

"I will."

The woman slid her considerable backside off the stool, and as I followed her to a table I thought of Kathy's quip about flirting while in Chases Corner. Out of the corner of my eye, I noticed a large group having breakfast. I'd heard them talking loudly when I came in, but as I made my way through the dining area a hush fell across the place.

The hostess lady lingered a moment while I sat down at the table. "Maggie will be your waitress. You really should try our biscuits and gravy."

"They're world famous, I understand."

"That's what they say."

There wasn't much reason to look over the menu, because I was sure that *not* ordering the biscuits and gravy would cause a local scandal. Nevertheless, I gave myself a preview of the lunch menu. As I read, I heard someone shuffle up behind me.

"Good day to you, Mr. Daniels. I trust you are well."

The voice was both masculine and from the Charleston area. "Mr. Galax," I said turning in my chair.

"Mr. Daniels, you need not sit here eating alone. It would be my pleasure if you would agree to join us over at our table just there in the corner."

"Thank you for the offer, but I'm fine right here."

For effect, I turned my attention back to the menu. I'm certain I surprised Galax by declining his offer, because he started back toward his table without another word. He hesitated, then turned to retrace his steps.

"Mr. Daniels, if I have in some way offended you, or otherwise caused you to think poorly upon me, I must sincerely apologize."

"That would be a good start, counselor. You did piss me off pretty good yesterday."

"Did I, indeed? I assure you, I truly did not mean for such a thing to happen. Might I inquire as to how?"

"Well, for starters you let me meet with—"

"May I join you here at your table?" Galax asked, knocking me out of combat mode.

"Sure."

As he sat down, Galax waved to the waitress, who came over immediately with two cups of coffee.

"Have you decided what you're gonna have yet, Mr. Daniels?" the waitress asked.

Yet another person already familiar with who I was. I played right along with it this time. "Yes, I'll have the biscuits and gravy please."

"A very wise choice, I assure you," Galax said.

"Anything else to drink, sweetie?"

"No, just the coffee, thanks."

The waitress made an odd giggling sound before retrieving the menu and heading-off to serve other customers.

"You must forgive her, Mr. Daniels. It would appear that word has made it to the women in town that you are a single man."

I tried to pick up my anger where I'd left off, but it wouldn't come back with the same intensity.

"You started to say something earlier, Mr. Daniels. Please continue."

"Look, Trevor, let's get something clear between you and I," I said, less agitated this time. "I'm here to find the facts. That's what they pay me for."

"Absolutely. Your reputation would have me believe none other."

"Letting Bo come see me alone, just so he could tell me his story of invisible friends; this will *not* help you lay the groundwork for a diminished capacity plea."

"I assure you, we have no plans to—"

"That sort of thing will never make it into print."

Galax paused before trying to answer. "As I was saying," he said calmly. "There are no plans to make use of an insanity defense for Bo."

"Really?"

"That is correct, sir. That would be somewhat akin to putting the proverbial cart before the horse."

"How so?"

Galax took a sip of his coffee while searching for just the right words, then he leaned in close across the table. "You must understand that a new trial for Bo is by no means a sure thing," he said in a near whisper. "While his case has been referred back to these courts for furtha review, it is a mistake to assume that Judge Jefferson will comply with our request to throw-out Mr. Buckminster's earlier conviction."

"But I thought the State Court ruled Bo's attorney's had provided an inadequate defense during the trial."

"They did indeed. And they were very much correct in that ruling."

"I don't get it," I said incredulously. "How could the judge even remotely consider not tossing the verdict?"

"I'm afraid the yardstick you are using to measure our system of justice here in the Palmetto State, does not take into account certain *undulations* in the terrain."

"What the hell does that mean?"

"Let us just say that there are political forces to be considered. Politics in our part of the world are very much different from what someone like yourself may be used to."

I wasn't sure from his tone, but the content of Galax's remarks was definitely condescending.

"Is that going to be your defense? Politics?"

"No, sir. I shall not come within a country mile of the politics surrounding this matter."

I was growing weary of the counselor's riddles. "Trevor, speak your mind. What are you trying to say to me?"

"In due course. I'm afraid that more on this topic will have to await another time and place."

"Whatever. I can't say that you've got me hooked, but I'll play along for now."

"Thank you, sir. I could ask no more of you."

As if choreographed ahead of time, the waitress arrived back at the table with a plate in one hand, a gravy-boat in the other, and a basket of extra biscuits balanced between her forearm and her chest. Steam was still coming off the biscuits.

"I shall not keep you from your feast," Galax said, as he stood up from the table. "If you are like me, it may well turn out to be the best part of your day, sir."

Galax was waiting for me to acknowledge his last comment, but apparently he knew to be patient with a man's first introduction to the biscuits and gravy at

Molly's world-famous restaurant. I wanted to dig right in, but knew it would be impolite to do so without exchanging the proper parting pleasantries. I was prevented from doing either by the arrival of a winded Billy Thorton at my table.

"Mr. Daniels, I got some info for you on that Reverend Lee fella," he said, before bending over to catch his breath. While stooped over, he must have noticed Galax's shoes. "Oh, sorry, Mr. Galax. Hope I didn't barge in on nothing."

"Not at all. Mr. Daniels was just about to get after his first plate of Molly's biscuits and gravy."

"That *is* something, then," Billy said. "I'll just tell you real quick-like what I found out, and you can commence to eatin'."

"Don't worry about it. What'd you find out?"

"Seems the reverend's gonna speak from the steps of the courthouse this morning at ten sharp. People's gathering already to have a good spot to listen to him."

"Thanks, Billy," I said, reaching into my pocket for another ten-dollar bill.

"Thank you, Mr. Daniels," he said stuffing it into the pocket of his jeans. "I'll just let you get after them biscuits, then. Same time tomorrow?"

"Yes. Check with me in the morning."

With that Billy was gone. Galax, however, lingered.

"You are driving up the cost of good gophering, Mr. Daniels."

"Yes, and I know how important it is for you attorneys to be vigilant with the expenses you charge back to your clients." I reached for the gravy boat, hoping he would go away.

"Unfortunately, the services I am providing Mr. Buckminster are pro-bono," he said to clarify his position. "I know you are ready to have at Molly's specialty, but may I ask if you are planning to attend Reverend Lee's talk today?"

"I am. Why do you ask?" I said, drizzling gravy over the top of the eggs staring up at me from the plate.

"To avoid what I suppose may be a bit of a shock for you, I must inform you that Bo will be in attendance as well."

I slid my chair out and away from the table. "Tell me he's just going to watch the good Reverend Lee from the crowd with everyone else."

"I can't do that, I'm afraid. He shall join the reverend on the steps. They are very well acquainted."

I shook my head in disgust. A few things were finally starting to tie together. "Let me guess, it was Reverend Lee that helped Bo figure out his dreams were actually visits from an angel."

"Your guess would be incorrect. I happen to know for a fact that it was Marcus himself who told Bo about his celestial status, long before Bo and the reverend became acquainted."

"What are you saying, counselor? Are you telling me you believe Bo has little chats with Marcus, the man he's convicted of killing?"

"It doesn't matter what I believe. Mr. Buckminster believes so."

"Then I suppose you've brought in old Reverend Lee as an expert witness to support Bo," I said, growing ill with the topic. "You're following a doomed strategy if you think he can help you. He has zero credibility left."

"That may be the case where you come from, Mark. You may not find so much incredulity around these parts, however. At least, as it pertains to the esteemed Reverend Leyland Johnston."

"You're a piece of work, counselor," I said as I slid my chair back in place and grabbed a knife and fork.

"As I know not whether that is meant as a compliment or a canard, I will leave you to enjoy your fine breakfast. Good day to you, Mr. Daniels."

I didn't bother to answer, as all the excuse I needed was sitting on the plate in front of me. From first bite, I was deeply in love. It was by far the best food I have ever tasted before lunch time. I still wasn't so sure about Molly's claim of being world famous, but I could easily see how with the right marketing, she had a legitimate vehicle to make it so.

Chapter 10

Although Molly's breakfast specialty lived up to the hype that morning, after finishing I felt as if I'd swallowed a small brick. The drive back to the Marriott would have taken more time than I had available before the reverend was scheduled to speak, so with the extra weight to hold me in my chair, I decided to sit it out at Molly's.

Without access to e-mail I wasn't able to check if any information about Corey Aycock had arrived, so I decided on a call to New York from my table.

"I'm glad you reached out, Mark," Carl said. "I just finished reading your daily."

"Why do you have us do those at the end of the day if you're not going to read them until the next morning anyway?"

"I usually do read them at night, smart guy," he snapped. "I had a charity thing I had to attend with the brass last night."

I knew how much Carl hated the social functions that came along with his position, so I let him off the hook. "So, what did you think?" I asked.

"Well, for starters, I'm not real thrilled about you meeting with the defendant without a member of the defense team present."

"Yeah, I agree. I had a talk with his attorney this morning."

"What's his angle?"

"I don't know. But he's not after an insanity defense."

"Really? In your daily you said you were leaning that way."

"I was. But now I'm not so sure. He has something up his sleeve, but I haven't pinned it down yet."

"Well, you're the man to do it. Just be careful in the meantime."

"Don't worry, I'll keep my distance. Have you been able to get anything on Corey Aycock or find out the reason he went to prison?"

"Not yet. But the Librarian is on it."

Jim Ghirardelli, a.k.a. the Librarian, was one of the research associates at the paper. He was also in very high demand.

"Great! Thanks for giving it to him," I said. "I want to take a good look at this Aycock guy before I get in much deeper."

"I'm sure he'll have something for you before lunch. Is there someplace for you to get access to the Internet?

"Come on, Carl, I'm sitting in Chases Corner. This is cow-country."

"I gotcha. I'll give you a shout just before lunch so I can fill you in on what Jim came up with over the phone."

"You do remember that I have lunch with our favorite reverend today?"

"Yeah, I remember. I'm guessing you know how to handle Reverend Lee by now."

"I do. He's speaking on the steps of the courthouse this morning."

"You're going to be there, right?"

"Of course."

"If he says anything of interest about why he's down there, call it in right away."

"I'm way ahead of you, Carl."

"Good. Let's talk before lunch. Sooner, if I get something from the Librarian."

"Looking forward to it. And thanks again for the Librarian."

It was a little before nine when I hung up with Carl, still over an hour before Reverend Lee was due to speak. Knowing I was coming back to Molly's for lunch with the reverend, the idea popped into my head to just leave the rental car where it was and maybe walk off the biscuits and gravy. After cashing out, I checked the distance with the cashier lady.

"It's not so bad a walk, sweetie," she said warmly. "If it weren't for my having to stay here to help get ready for lunch, I'd just walk on over there with you." She smiled at me as if she'd just slipped me the key to her apartment.

"What a pity," I said with some difficulty. "Can you point me in the right direction?"

"It's easy. Walk on up that way about a mile or so," she said pointing north. "When you get to Market Street, take a right and it will run you all the way in to Main. After that, just look for the crowd."

"Thanks," I said, trying not to let her lock in on me eye-to-eye.

"That's no problem, honey. We'll see you when you come on back for lunch. I'll have a table set up for you and the Reverend Johnston."

I thought about asking how she knew about my meeting with Reverend Lee, but the risk of deepening the flirtatious banter scared me out of it.

The walk into town was relaxing, friendly, and warm. That simple description also matched perfectly with the plain-spoken people of Chases Corner. I knew from my TV trivia that Mayberry was supposed to be in North Carolina, but it seemed like anywhere I went in Chases Corner, I'd bump into Aunt Bea or Andy Taylor. They are, to the man and woman, happy to see you when you meet them on the street. Before I made it to the corner of Market and Main, my arm had grown tired from returning the many waves I got from total strangers. And even though I didn't know a single one of their names, by the way they freely used my own, by the time I got to the courthouse I started to get the sensation that I had actually grown up in the place.

At the courthouse, things were already starting to get crazy. The crowd was dense enough to keep me from getting anywhere near the steps of the place, but it looked as though they had roped off an area for the media. After pulling my press credentials from my sport-coat pocket and hanging them around my neck, I started to make my way around the crowd to see if I could come in through the side of the courthouse. That's when Billy came dodging through the mass of people on his bicycle.

"Hey, Mr. Daniels. How was them biscuits and gravy?"

"Billy, you're going to hurt someone with that thing," I said.

"Nah. This here bike's as much a part of me as my own legs. I ain't-a-gonna hit nobody."

"You might scare them to death, though. The biscuits were terrific, by the way."

"You save room for lunch with Reverend Johnston? I hear Molly's got fried chicken on the menu today."

"Billy, I need to ask you a question."

"Yes, sir. Ask away."

"How is it that everybody in this town seems to know my business?"

"Your business?"

"Yeah. How does everyone know what I'm doing next?"

"People just talk, I suppose. This here's a small town."

"Does everyone get together at night at the town hall and share gossip or something?"

"No, sir. Not exactly."

"Not exactly?"

"Well, there ain't nobody goes to the town hall at night," he said, and then paused briefly. "Most folks do wander by the church, though. It's open every night of the week."

I couldn't even imagine why someone would have to spend so much time talking to God. In the Catholic church, all your business with the Lord can get done in forty-five minutes of mass, once a week, and a trip to the confessional every month or so.

"Tell me, if I walk around to the side of the courthouse, can I get over to that roped off area for the press?"

"Ah, you ain't got to go walking around, Mr. Daniels," Billy said in disbelief. "You just follow on behind me."

"Wait—"

Before I could stop him, Billy had already started into the crowd, calling out for people to make way. I jumped quickly into his wake, walking straight through the middle without so much as bumping shoulders with anyone.

"There you go, Mr. Daniels," he said, lifting the rope for the press area from his bike. I slipped under. "You want me to come back and fetch you after Reverend Johnston finishes his talk?"

"No thanks, Billy," I said laughingly. I reached for my wallet to give him a bonus, but he would have nothing of it.

"No, sir! I can't take no more money from you today. It just wouldn't be right."

I was definitely in a parallel universe. In New York, if someone refuses a tip they would be immediately whisked away for a mental evaluation.

As Billy rode away, I felt a tap on my shoulder. "Mark? That you?"

I turned my head just in time to get a face full of cigarette smoke blown from the mouth of one Trip Singletary, a freelance photographer that often did work for *The Times*.

"Trip. What the hell are you doing here," I said, waving away the smoke cloud rather than sticking my hand out to greet him.

"Sorry about that," he said, helping to chase the smoke with his only free hand. The other hand was permanently attached to the shutter button on his camera. In the ten-plus years we'd known each other, I'd never seen him without the camera hanging from his neck or the photographer's vest draped across a dirty T-shirt.

"Shouldn't you be in some God-forsaken corner of the world?" I asked.

"Someplace where there's a good war on?"

"Don't get me started," he said, a tinge of disappointment in his words. "I got married a few months ago. The new wife made me promise to stay out of war-zones for a while."

I was a little slow responding. The only thing more out of place than Trip Singletary in Chases Corner, South Carolina, was that there was now a Mrs. Trip Singletary.

"You took the plunge? With who?"

"You wouldn't know her. She's actually a friend of my mother."

"Your mom introduced you to the woman you married?"

"Don't go there!"

"Listen, fella, I don't know who you are; but I want you to tell me right now what you've done with my friend Trip."

"You have *no idea* the pressure the woman can lay on you."

"You mean your wife?"

"No. My mother! It's like she just can't be happy unless she has grandchildren before she dies. I spent eighteen months in Iraq without blinking an eye. Then I take ten weeks off back home to regroup, and she cracks me like an egg."

I started to laugh. Trip is somewhat infamous for the jams he's gotten himself into around the world. Those who know him simply can't get together without bringing up a Trip story; like the time he passed out on a bus in Liberia and wound up in rebel-controlled territory, or the time he kept three hookers with him for a week while on R&R in Madagascar. He was a mess; but a mess that everyone loved to talk about.

"No offense my friend, but I don't see you as the fatherly type."

"None taken," he said, dragging hard one last time on his cigarette, before crushing it out between his yellow fingers. "Don't worry. That's not going to happen."

"Really? And what about your mom?"

"I'm going to wait the old bag out," he said. "She can't live forever."

"That may be a little tough on the wife. A woman has needs, you know."

"Hell, let the mailman do it then. I just don't want to be responsible for bringing a kid into the world from this gene pool," he said, checking the settings on his camera. "You ready for the right honorable Reverend Lee?"

"I guess so. I'd kinda hoped he'd played his final hand the last time out, but he's like a cat with nine-lives."

"Yeah, I wonder how many more he has left though. People around here seem to think he's better than sex underwater."

"What?"

"Oh, sorry. Did I say that last part out loud?" Trip reached for his pack of Marlboro lights. "I meant to keep the underwater thing to myself."

"You probably should have. I get your point, though."

"Well, let's just hope the guy conjures up the image of Mary, or makes this poor Buckminster fella levitate above the crowd or something. Nobody's going to buy a picture of this knucklehead quoting from the same old scriptures."

"That's the price of being a freelancer, old friend. I wouldn't expect much that's fresh and new from Reverend Lee. He's still only got one song."

Just then the crowd started a mild applause. A few of Reverend Lee's entourage stepped out from the courthouse and took their positions on a hastily constructed dais. When the well-coiffed reverend, dressed in a fine dark-purple, double-breasted suit, came through the doors, the applause swelled to low roar. He made the most of his latest fifteen minutes, waving to the crowd and shaking hands along the way to the podium. He seemed to linger a bit once or twice, reveling in the attention that was severely lacking for him in other parts of the world. Suddenly, he raised his hands, palms down, to hush the crowd.

"Ladies and gentlemen, thank you for that fine welcome," he began, the crowd rewarding him with a taste more applause. "Coming back here reminds me that I am now, and will always be, a *Southern* man of God!"

The place erupted and Reverend Lee reveled in it. After a few seconds, he raised his hands again. "But while I've been away all these many years, there is another southern man of God that has kept faith with his Creator. A man who, no matter the trials and tribulations, has continued his unwavering faith in the Lord." He paused to build the tension. "Ladies and gentlemen of Chases Corner, I give you one of the truest servants of our savior Jesus Christ. I give you Bosephus Buckminster!"

As Bo came lumbering out of the courthouse the entire town broke out in wild wave of noise. Bo seemed unsure of how to take all the attention at first, his normal smile somewhat subdued and uneasy. He stopped dead about ten paces from the dais, before one of the entourage came to his side and whispered something in his ear. He smiled broadly and took the last few steps to join the reverend.

"Let's hear it for Bo!" Reverend Lee shouted into the microphone, reaching out and raising Bo's hand as high in the air as he could.

As he did, the whole county felt like it was rocking. Bo let loose with his widest possible grin. Then, as if unable to keep still, he reached around the Reverend Lee's waist and lifted him high in the air.

"There's your picture," I shouted to Trip over the crowd.

He was already snapping off shot after shot, sensing as I did a potential cover. To the left of the dais, somewhat hidden from the view of the crowd, I noticed Bo's attorney taking in the action. He looked neither pleased nor concerned.

It took a good ten minutes before the crowd had calmed enough for the reverend to continue.

"Ladies and gentlemen, for the past sixteen years, your very own Bosephus has been shut away inside a prison, kept from you while he served out a sentence for killing another man."

The crowd interrupted with a chorus of boos and hisses.

"Now, now," the reverend continued. "These are just the unfortunate facts associated with Bo's past. There is nothing we can do about that now."

The crowd made a low rumble.

"But there *is* something we can do about the future..."

The noise turned up a notch.

"There *is* something we can do about not letting them take Bo back to that place."

Frenzy began to build.

"God has spoken to me and I tell you all, we *must not* let Bo go back to that prison. Not now. Not ever!"

The crowd lost control of itself, everyone standing, shouting, some even crying hysterically. Bo, on the other hand, looked as if his emotions had gone the other way. He seemed confused and concerned. The smile on his face had lessened considerably. The Reverend Lee allowed the pandemonium to continue a while, pumping his fists in the air whenever the tide seemed to be rolling back, before finally stepping to the podium and motioning for the crowd to settle down. In spite of his recent troubles, the reverend still knew how to fire up an audience of believers. There is a power available to those with that kind of ability – a power that can be very dangerous in the hands of someone with something to prove.

"God has asked me to come here to be with you, my friends. He has sent his messengers here to be with us as well. They are here today – right on this dais – here to help guide us in the coming battle against evil."

The crowd began cheering again, and when the Reverend Lee made a sweeping motion with his arm, which covered the dais from end to end, the frenzy renewed with a vengeance. Bo looked absolutely terrified by the return of the wild applause and seemed to be trying to say something to someone over the noise.

"*You* know they are here," the reverend shouted into the microphone. "And praise Jesus, *I* know that now, too!"

The Reverend Lee signaled to a man at the top of the steps, and through the courthouse doors came a six-piece Salvation Army band playing "Onward Christian Soldiers".

"Hey, man, this is starting to get a little out of hand," Trip said, nodding in the direction of four burly security guards who were struggling to keep the crowd from collapsing the roped-off press area. "This isn't the best place in the world for an agnostic shutterbug to be hanging around."

Trip looked genuinely scared, and he fumbled a bit while stuffing his camera and lenses back into his backpack. Especially odd, considering this was a man with a reputation for continuing to click away in the middle of falling shells and sniper fire.

"I think your best bet is to head up those stairs and get into the building," I said. "If you try to go back through that crowd, you'll never make it."

"You coming?"

Just then the Reverend Lee snatched a toddler being held up to him in the front row, tucked the child safely in his right arm and began making his way over to the lone TV camera positioned in front of us. The crowd seemed to shift with him.

"Yeah, man, get going," I shouted. "I'm right behind you."

We hadn't made it but a few steps up the stairs to the courthouse when Reverend Lee's security people gave up the fight to keep people out of the press area. Those that remained were swallowed up like sandcastles in high tide. When we reached the doors to the courthouse, the deputy that had patted me down the day before was on watch.

"I was thinking you were a goner for a minute there, Mr. Daniels," he said.

"I thought I was going to lose a couple thousand dollars worth of camera equipment," Trip said, out of breath.

"Nah. Nobody would have bothered with you over that stuff," the deputy said to Trip. "You might have lost those socks of yours though, Mr. Daniels."

The deputy and I chuckled, while Trip looked left out.

"Anyway, can we sneak through the building to get out of here?" I asked the deputy.

"Sure thing. I'll clear you through, then just turn right after the double doors and head all the way to the end of the hallway. There's an emergency door that'll let you out in the employee's lot."

After patting us down and looking into Trip's camera bag, the deputy let us through. When we stepped outside and into the employee's parking lot, Tripped was relieved. "Man, I wish I'd taken that assignment to Baghdad."

"You looked like you were going to pee your pants out there," I said. "What happened to the Trip I know with nerves of steel?"

"Buddy, there's nothing that scares me more than a town full of Bible-thumpers," he said. "You just know they're looking for a sinner like me to give a thrashing to."

"I think that's your conscience talking to you, my friend. Not the good people of Chases Corner."

"Yeah, well, at least the insurgents in Iraq only wanted to kill me. These folks would rather send me straight to the fires of hell."

Yet another Trip story to share when I got back to New York.

Trip started to scan the parking lot. "How far away is your car?" he asked.

"Oh, damn. I've got bad news for you."

"What's that?"

"I walked here from Molly's restaurant. I'm afraid my car is about two-miles back in that direction." I pointed back the way we'd come.

"Good luck with that," Trip said. "I'll take my chances this way."

My odd-ball photographer friend started out across the parking lot.

"Hey, Trip. I'm staying at the Marriott Courtyard back off the interstate," I shouted. "Give me a call if you want to hook-up later."

"I'll do it," he said, never turning back, and without so much as a hint about where he was staying himself or how he was going to get there. But that was Trip – the well regarded loner. There was no way on earth I could ever picture the guy as a married man.

Chapter 11

It took me a while to wrangle my way back to Molly's; the couple-mile walk stretching out as I tried to get around Reverend Lee's gathering. After a few bad decisions, I finally managed to get back to the road Molly's was on.

"Welcome back, Mr. Daniels," the cashier said. "How was Reverend Johnston's little talk?"

"For starters, not so little." I said.

"Yeah, men of the cloth have that way about them. I can sit you down, but I'm afraid you're gonna have to wait a while to put in your order."

"That would be fine."

"Maggie caught a ride over to the square with the cook to hear the reverend."

The cashier started to roll-off the stool, but I stopped her.

"Don't get up. Where will Reverend Johnston and I be sitting when he gets here?"

"You see them French doors over there, next to where the bathroom signs is?"

"I do."

She handed me a one-page menu with the day's lunch specials. "That's a private room Molly has set aside for important guests. The governor himself ate lunch in there a couple years ago."

"Really? Did she set it up today for me, or for the reverend?"

The cashier smiled. "I guess you can decide on that for you own self, Mr. Daniels," she said. "Least ways, there's a place for both of you in there."

"That's all I need to know."

The VIP room wasn't much different from the rest of the place, except that the floor had retained a little more of its original color. There were no windows, and from the symmetrical rows of holes up and down the plaster on the back wall, it appeared that the VIP room had probably been some kind of storage area in an earlier life. There were eight chairs squeezed in around two tables, which had been pushed together and covered with a slightly frayed, off-white table cloth. Hanging at one end of the room was a neatly framed picture of a man in a sharply pressed suit, surrounded by a group of people crowded around the cash register. I recognized the cashier and my waitress, Maggie, and wondered which of the other ladies leaning into the photo was the world famous Molly.

"Sorry to keep you waiting, Mr. Daniels," Maggie said, sticking just her head and shoulders in through the French doors. "Can I get you something to drink?"

"What would you suggest?"

"Maybe a glass of ice cold tea?" she added. "You look a bit over-heated."

"You've talked me into it," I said, then wiped the sweat from my forehead.

"Coming right up!"

Glancing across the room, I noticed another picture hanging at the opposite end. As I drew closer, I recognized the VIP room as the location for the shot, and saw a familiar face in the picture. It was a younger Bo Buckminster, sitting at the table with a distinguished looking man and a somewhat less well-attired woman. Bo was smiling his trademark smile. He couldn't have been much older than twelve or thirteen, but he already had a good deal of the size that he would grow into as an adult. Underneath the picture, someone had typed a caption on a two-inch square piece of paper and stuck it between the photo and the glass of the picture frame: "State Senator Winston Hunter, Ms. Beverly Buckminster and her son Bosephus."

The senator wore a smile as big as Bo's, though his was a bit smarmier. Bo's mom looked like the balance point of a teeter-totter sitting between the two, with neither a grin nor a frown written across her face. Her eyes looked sad, as if she either didn't want to be there or just didn't want her picture taken. I studied her face a while.

"You admiring that picture of our Bo as a youngster?" Maggie asked, stopping at the doorway with the tea.

"It's an interesting picture," I said.

"The girls here say that you could erase everything about Bo on that picture except his smile, and you'd still know it was Bo."

"Like the Cheshire cat."

"Yes, sir, just like that cat," she said. "He's just got the warmest smile anyone ever put on a face, I reckon. Oh, and I have your tea here for ya."

"Thanks," I said, taking the tall, cloudy glass from her hand. "Tell me something, Maggie. The man in that picture, is that—"

"Yes, sir, it sure is. That's Trey Hunter's daddy," she said, seeming to know what my question was going to be. "Trey was one of the fellas that was with that black boy the day he was killed."

I took note of the fact that she didn't say "the day Bo killed that black boy."

"Bo looks so young in this picture," I said.

"That picture was taken just a few years before all that terrible stuff happened."

"And that's Bo's mother with him?"

"It is indeed. Poor thing passed just a few months after that picture was taken."

I took another look at the picture, thinking maybe that was what I'd seen in her eyes.

"Seems like an odd gathering. What was it that brought them together in the first place?"

"It wasn't such an odd thing back then," she said. "Years ago, Beverly Buckminster worked for Senator Hunter. She was a maid over at his family's place before Bo was born. After her husband left, Beverly and the senator would get together every couple of months or so for lunch. He sort of kept an eye out for them two."

"Really?"

"Yes, sir. The senator and Beverly were friends growing up. Her momma worked for the senator's daddy too, and they played together when they was little."

"Was Bo's mother working for the senator when she passed away?" I asked, trying to make the probe sound more like an afterthought.

"Oh, no, sir. Bo needed a lot of attention growing up. After her husband left Beverly and the boy all alone, she had to quit the senator's place."

Just then the burly henchman that had blocked my way in the staircase back at the hotel came into the room. He brushed passed the waitress like she wasn't there, studied the small room a bit, and then retreated back to the dining area.

"Looks like your lunch guest has arrived," Maggie said. "I probably oughta get the reverend a glass of tea as well."

"That would be great."

Shortly after Maggie left, a round of applause broke from inside the restaurant, followed in short-order by the arrival of a beaming Reverend Lee in the doorway to the VIP room.

"Good day to you, Mark," he said warmly, sticking out his hand. He wore an air of confidence that I had not seen from him since his early days in public life.

"Reverend. That was quite a speech today."

"Thank you. It's easy when the good Lord is feeding you the message."

"I'm not quite sure I understood what your message was. Maybe you can fill me in on it over lunch."

"I'll do my best," he said, adding his other hand to our shake and pulling me in closer. "I have always thought that somewhere inside you, there is a believer waiting desperately to be let out."

"You might want to save your ammo. I'm a professional skeptic."

"Everyone has to believe in something."

"I do. The truth."

"And the truth shall set you free."

The reverend was in rare form and I was already starting to feel icky. "Reverend, would you mind if we sat down and focused on you a little bit?"

"By all means. Let's have a seat and see what Molly has cooked up for the mid-day meal."

It was only then that the reverend finally let go of my hand. The one good thing about his long, two-handed shakes was that you knew where both his hands were.

"My apologies, Mark. I'm afraid I'm a little pressed for time," he said, picking up the menu right away. "Would you mind if we place our orders before we begin any intense discussion?"

Maggie the waitress returned with the reverend's tea.

"We can do that," I said. "I'm just going to order the special."

"And what would that be?" the reverend asked.

"I think its fried chicken."

Maggie chimed in to explain that the lunch special was indeed fried chicken and confirmed that it was the best choice. "You could order anything you like off the menu," she said, before scrunching her eyes and forehead. "Not sure why you would, though. Considering that Molly's fried chicken is world famous."

Molly was one renowned fry-cook.

"I thank you for the tip, young lady. I'll have the chicken as well," the reverend said. He waived-off the one remaining member of his entourage, who promptly left, pulling the door closed behind him. The reverend turned his attention to me. "I understand you've had the opportunity to sit down with our mutual friend, Bosephus Buckminster."

"Only briefly. Looks like you two have become buddies, though."

"Oh, yes. He's a fine young man. In his thoughts he is as pure as the driven snow."

"Being so pure is an easier thing for him than for you and I," I said. "Considering his handicap and all."

The reverend looked surprised. "Handicap? Then I would guess your meeting with him was, in fact, brief."

"Why do you say that?"

"If you were to spend a little more time with Bo, what you now see as a handicap might come to be thought of as something else entirely."

"Such as?"

"A great blessing from the Lord."

"A slow mind? That's a blessing these days?"

"In the case of Bosephus Buckminster," the reverend said with a pause. "I would say your statement is not only accurate, but dead-center through the bull's-eye." He had dropped his usually affected manner when he spoke the last sentence, adding a tinge of sincerity that was rare in the man.

"Reverend, why are you here?" I asked, trying to cut to the quick.

"To be with Bo during this difficult time of course."

I struggled a little, looking for a delicate way to be more blunt. "Listen, we're off the record, here," I said. "It's just you and me, Lee. Come on. What's your angle?"

The reverend absorbed my question without any reaction. "Mark, you want the truth - but if it comes from me you won't be able to accept it."

"My mind is wide-open. Trust me on this one."

I thought he was about to give in, but was surprised when he stayed on the sidelines. "This one's not about me, Mark," he said with uncharacteristic humility. "You're here to find things out. I believe that *you* are more a part of God's plan here in Chases Corner than I am. "

Reverend Lee Johnston was a lot of things, but I'd never known him to *not* have an opinion on any topic. The only thing I could think of to explain his behavior was that the scandal he and his organization had endured had taken a bigger toll on him than I'd imagined. I'd always thought of the Reverend Lee as a bit of a self-centered jackass, but he was also a fighter, and I could admire him for that at least. That day at Molly's he was acting like a turtle pulling his head back into his shell.

"Reverend, you mentioned in your speech today that God has sent you here to Chases Corner," I said, trying to stir the pot a little. "Did the Lord also tell you who killed Marcus Brown?"

He laughed. "That would be good for you, wouldn't it?" he said. "I'm afraid you've got some work ahead of you if want to find that out."

"But he *did* tell you it wasn't Bo?"

"God hasn't told *me* anything," he said, his face as honest as a portrait of George Washington. "Praise be, He's led me here to this place to listen; but I'm not waiting on him to speak to me directly."

"What is it you're listening for?"

"For the words of his mighty messengers. They are everywhere in this part of the world, if you'll only have the courage to accept the gift."

"The gift?"

"That's right," he said, his eyes suddenly as peaceful as a summer pond. "You of all people know the trials and tribulations I've come through these past couple of years."

"That's your gift? God took you down a couple of notches to bring you back among the meek."

"While that may well be a true statement," he said, "it's not the gift I'm talking about."

This was definitely a different reverend in front of me. The old Reverend Lee would have preached out everything on his mind within minutes. This one seemed to want me to pull his words out of his mouth like healthy molars. After a few uncomfortable minutes sipping my tea, the smell of spicy fried chicken knocked on the door ahead of our waitress.

"I hope you gentlemen are ready for some good eatin'," she boasted as she entered.

"My, that does indeed smell like my momma's kitchen, young lady," the reverend said.

The chicken did nothing to damage Molly's reputation. The reverend made a comment about it being what he called "gravity chicken" – meat that slips off the bone just by holding it above the plate. In spite of still being slightly full from breakfast, I found myself getting after lunch with a purpose. I try to pay attention to the social graces, but I knew Reverend Lee didn't feel slighted because the few times I did look up from my plate, he was sporting such a mouthful it would have prevented him from answering questions anyway.

"Well, now, that was worth every ounce of energy put into the job," the reverend said after he'd gnawed the last piece of chicken down to the bone. "Sometimes the reward-to-effort ratio is balanced much more heavily on the reward side."

"That was the best chicken I've ever had in my life," I said. "I think Molly could make a fortune if she took her biscuits and gravy and this fried chicken up North."

"Ah, but that would be a big mistake. The fact is, cooking in the Southern air is what truly makes a meal special in these parts."

"Is that right?"

"Sure enough. Have you ever eaten anything that even comes close to this chicken north of the Mason-Dixon?"

"You've got me there. I have not."

"I rest my case," the reverend said, sitting back in his chair and pulling a toothpick from his pocket.

I also leaned back, minus the toothpick, and gave a tug or two at my belt to make a bit more room for my burgeoning belly. "Reverend, you were saying something about Bo having some great gift earlier," I said. "Tell me more about what you meant by that?"

His wry chuckle made a comeback. "It's not a topic I can speak to with the details I know you are digging for. I *can* tell you this: before you are through, I believe you will have a lot more to say on the subject than I ever could. That much God has made clear to me."

"That's sounds very reassuring," I said, dripping with sarcasm. "But do you think you might slip me a little hint in the meantime?"

The reverend pondered my request a bit, as if he were looking for a clue he could give to where the Easter eggs were hidden without giving away the exact spot.

"I can offer only a small piece of advice," he said finally.

"Very well, pastor. I can't say that I'll take it, but by all means, advise away."

"Don't fight against it."

"Don't fight against what?"

"Your own gift," he said leaning in to whisper. "In order to understand Mr. Bosephus Buckminster, you're first going to have to look inside yourself."

He leaned back in his chair as if not expecting an answer to his riddle. He was right to do so, because if I'd tried to reply, I don't think I could have hidden the humor I found in his enigmatic little slice of wisdom. I knew from previous experience that when the Reverend Lee starts in with the metaphysical stuff, there isn't much of value to be had by hanging on to the conversation.

On her next trip into the room, I asked Maggie for the check and made something up about needing to get to a meeting. The reverend would have nothing of my paying for even half of the tab, and though I'm usually pretty rigid about accepting the proverbial free-lunch, the idea of quickly putting some distance between us won out. It wasn't until I reached the parking lot that I even considered how I was going to spend the afternoon. With a plate of Molly's fried chicken layered on top of her fine biscuits and gravy, I decided on another nap back at the hotel. As I drove away I could see Reverend Lee come out of Molly's behind his entourage. When I glanced in my rear view mirror, I saw raise his hands to heaven.

Chapter 12

With two heavy meals weighing me down like an anchor, I slept hard that afternoon at the Marriott, but woke from my nap abruptly. During my little siesta I did something I rarely do – I had a dream. Like everyone I suppose I dream quite a bit, but I had always been one of those folks that just couldn't remember them afterward. That afternoon was the exception to that rule. I could remember all of it, and it scared the stuffing out of me. It was who had turned up in the dream that had rattled me awake, that being none other than the late Marcus Brown himself.

There hadn't been a picture of Marcus in the original file, so I supposed that my imagination had made up most of the details surrounding his cameo appearance in my dream; but it was a vivid picture. If I'd been back in New York with my sketch artist friend back from the NYPD, I would have been able to give him more than enough to put together a complete composite. Eyes, hair, body type – right down to a small but prominent scar over his right cheekbone. It was a little creepy.

What he said to me in the dream was equally disturbing.

"Look inside yourself," were the only words he'd used.

He said it more than once, and it didn't take a psychiatrist to understand that it was most likely the Reverend Lee's comments during lunch that had influenced my subconscious. Still, it was enough to give me a case of the willies.

While I splashed water on my face, the cell phone rang. With the water running I almost missed it.

"Hello."

"Hey, Mark, I hate to bother you, but I have some info for you from the Librarian."

I didn't have the gumption to confess to my boss he'd caught me after yet another afternoon nap. "Not at all. Just doing a little research of my own. What do you have?"

"A couple things. First, your boy Corey Haycock is a real piece of work. He's been arrested a dozen times. Six of those were felonies."

"How big were the charges?"

"The two that got him put away were for assault. The first was a bar fight that sent the other guy to the hospital with a cracked skull, and the second was an attempted homicide charge."

"Sounds like he's got quite a temper."

"You might say that. He walked on all the other charges, but none were for jaywalking."

"Did the Librarian find out anything on his current whereabouts?"

"Nothing contemporary. The last time he had to check in with his parole officer he was at an address in Charleston, but that was four years ago. It looks like he's been a bit of a gypsy, but it might be worth a shot if you get down that way."

"We'll see how things go. I'd definitely like to have a talk with him," I said, almost adding something about Carl not telling Bart about my potential trip. "And what about the senator's son, Trey Hunter?"

"That's one you're not going to get a chance to have a conversation with, I'm afraid. Seems he shot himself in the head ten years ago."

"On purpose?"

"It was an accident. At least, that's the official word on it."

"Why, was it suspicious?"

"The Librarian seems to think so. He supposedly did it with a shotgun while on a deer hunting trip. At the family hunt-club."

"What does the coroner's report say?"

"Let's see ... 'The deceased was partially decapitated while cleaning a firearm.' That's all it says."

I paused to take in the latest chapter in the growing saga.

"There was a great outpouring of sympathy for the senator in the media back then." Carl threw into the silence. "He was right in the middle of his first campaign for state office."

"Damn, his son's death helped jump-start his political career?"

"It didn't hurt."

Carl was pumping out more information than I would have been able to remember without my trusty notepad, but as I started to jotting down notes the boss jumped back in. "If you're writing notes right now, I have all of this in a summary from the Librarian," he said. "I can just email it to you."

In some ways, technology was taking the fun out of this job.

"That'd be fine," I said, flipping my pen across the bed.

"The Librarian put the supporting documents and backup in a file on the Intranet marked *Palmetto Perturbation.*"

"Palmetto Perturbation? I don't think anyone without an English degree is ever going to be able to decipher that one."

"I think that's the point."

"Yeah, well if you ask me, the Librarian is way too in love with the words."

"From the way he keeps himself, that's probably for the best," Carl said. "Words don't care about how you smell or the last time you put a razor to your face."

There was something gnawing at the back of my mind, something I was supposed to ask Carl.

"So ..." Carl asked. "How did your meeting go with Reverend Lee Johnston?"

"It was, to say the least, different."

"You mean like the usual Reverend Lee kind of different, or something else."

"Definitely something else. There were times I was thinking about that movie with Donald Southerland."

"*Invasion of the Body Snatchers?*"

"That's the one. He's definitely acting strange, even by Lee Johnston standards."

"Well, get it all written up for—"

"I know. Put it in the daily."

"Right."

"So you can read it tomorrow."

"Do you always have to have some kind of smartass remark at the end of a conversation?" Carl asked.

"Oh, I don't know. Sometimes I like to—"

The click I heard on the other end was Carl's response to my second attempt to get in a dig. After I set the phone down I remembered what it was I'd wanted to ask him, but decided just to include it with my daily. It took about an hour to get the rather bizarre events of the day written up so that they didn't come across like the opening of a Kafka novel, but satisfied with a rough synopsis, I went online to access the paper's network. When I opened my email box, a message with the little red flag came up in my in-box.

Mark,

I tried to reach Carl, but his admin told me he was gone for the day. I just got the log of visitors from the prison your guy has been in. Need to talk to you. Call me as soon as you get this.

The Librarian

When I checked the clock by the nightstand, it was still just a little after five – way too early for the Librarian to have left the office. I put in the call.

"Ghirardelli," the voice said.

I can never remember the Librarian's real name, so I was slightly reserved at first. "Librarian?"

"Yes. This is Jim Ghirardelli."

"Oh, hey. It's Mark Daniels."

"Hi, Mark. How ya doing?" On the phone, the Librarian sounded a lot like Joey Tribbiani from *Friends*, which by itself was another one of the things about him that you couldn't piece together from the type of work he did.

"I got your email. What's up?"

"I have something here for you, but it came over in a hard-copy fax format, so I won't be able to get it out on the Intranet until I can get it scanned."

"That being the log from the prison?"

"That's it. There's something here that I thought you might want to know about. You got a piece of paper and something to write with?"

My trusty notebook was back in use. "Sure. Go ahead."

"There's a Catholic priest that's been going to see Bo Buckminster."

"A Catholic priest? That's odd in this part of the world."

"Yeah, that's what I thought. He's been visiting him at least once a week for the past fourteen-years. He doesn't seem to have missed a week since his first visit."

"That doesn't make any sense. Is he like the prison chaplain or something?"

"Not that I can tell."

"What's his name?"

"Father Michael Hanaway," he said, "But here's the mystery – about six years ago, he stopped signing in as Father Michael Hanaway."

"He changed his name?"

"No. He dropped the 'Father'. I'm checking on it now, but I think he might have left the church."

"What would a Catholic priest be doing visiting inmates in this part of the world? Do they even have Catholics down here?"

"Mark, when you use *inmates* in the plural, it assumes he was visiting others," the Librarian said, stopping to correct the record. "From what I can tell, that's not the case."

"He goes there just to see Bo?"

"That's correct. As for your question about local Catholics, he may be the only papal devotee in town, but he's there with you."

"Here in Chases Corner?"

"Yes. At least that's the address he's provided for the last six years on the guest-log at the prison."

Yet another man of God thrown into the mix. "Can you send me—"

"Way ahead of you. I'll have a new summary with the street address in your email box within the hour."

"Thanks, man. You are definitely the best."

"Yeah. Just remember me at Christmas time. Call if you need anything."

I was starting to feel as though Carl might have been better off turning this assignment over to the folks who handle the religious section of the Sunday paper. God was popping up everywhere, in all the different varieties and flavors man has created for him. While I always had a healthy respect for those who believe deeply in anything, religion was never a topic I felt comfortable with. Mine was certainly a lazy man's religion. The conviction that God and I were getting along very well all by ourselves, led to a sort of enmity toward anyone who would claim that joining their particular club was the only way to salvation.

After absorbing the latest twist from the Librarian, I tightened up the daily report for Carl, adding a cynical "good morning" to the body of the email. When I'd finished, rather than the usual sensation of having things just a bit more under control, the summary of the day's events left me feeling as if things were starting to get away from me. Over the previous couple of years, whenever I'd felt backed into a corner by events, there was someone around who would listen and not accuse me of over-thinking. I think Karen knew instinctively that no matter how far-out on a limb I went, I would eventually come back all by myself. She would listen; occasionally guide; but never once did I hear her say I was going too far.

That evening, the more I thought about that part of our relationship, the more I wondered just how I was going to fill the huge void. I laid around a while, trying to shake the malaise that thoughts of Karen were dumping on me. I decided to head down the interstate to grab some dinner, but Karen came with me. She was still hanging on after I made it back to the hotel, even though I'd traveled far enough to find a place to get a couple cocktails with my meal.

I was starting to think the melancholia over my former fiancée was growing into something more dramatic, and that maybe the listlessness I was feeling was the first sign of a growing depression over the whole thing. To distract my mind from reminiscing over Karen any further, I grabbed the remote control for the TV and flipped around for a while. It was a two-hour special on the History Channel about the *Secret Enigma Machines of World War II* that finally put me out for good.

Chapter 13

Set down in the middle of a field full of newly-blossomed cotton, a weeping willow tree blew slightly with the wind. Its malleable branches swayed effortlessly, changing direction slightly with each shift in the breeze. The old tree was at least two hundred yards from where I was walking along the edge of the cotton field, but the lure of its rustling leaves was strong enough to coax me into a detour. As I stepped awkwardly through boulevards of knee-high cotton plants, the prickly edges were a sharp contrast to the pillowing cotton balls popping out. The closer I got, the faster my feet moved, and by the time I reached the tree I'd broken out into a full trot – as if running through the bristles would somehow lessen their damage to the flimsy double knit covering my legs.

Growing up a city-boy, I didn't have much experience with the great outdoors, so I wasn't certain that sitting under a willow tree was possible. But I did remember reading a poem in high school, and I was fairly sure it included the line "resting 'neath a weeping willow" or something similar. With each new rush of wind, the willow tree seemed to whisper a welcome in my ear, slipping in a kind reassurance that a spot for me had already been prepared.

As I bent down to peek under the bowing branches, a wisp of cool air brushed up against my face and raised goose bumps on the back of my neck. The harshest of the sun's rays weren't getting through the tree's cover, so it was semi-dark, and after stepping under the canopy and resting my back against the tree, I let my bottom slide to the ground. For the first time in quite a while, I felt every single muscle in my face relax.

I fell asleep right there under the tree. I don't know how long I might have snoozed, but after easing back to consciousness, my eyelids took their time coming around. The way they might do on a lazy Sunday morning. While sleeping, I'd slid all the way down the trunk of the tree and was lying flat on my back. As I slowly raised my arms up over my head to stretch away the grogginess, an unseen force tugged at the corners of my mouth and raised them up into a satisfied smile.

After sliding my hands under the back of my head like a pillow, my eyelids finally raised enough to start letting the world back in. I struggled to clear away the sleepy blur, but as I looked up into the tree a curious form began to take shape. As the details filled in, what I saw there caught hold of my next breath with an iron grip. There was a man hanging in the tree, and when I realized there were no branches beneath his feet to support him, I jumped up with such a sense of panic that my heart nearly exploded. Moving quicker than I had ever moved, I pointed my feet toward the cover of dangling willow branches and launched straight for the canopy. As I burst through to the other side, I felt a sting to the side of my neck, before I stumbled and landed spread eagle; my face planted firmly in the dirt.

"What the hell is going on?" I shouted, jumping back to my feet.

In an instant, I'd gone from a lazy afternoon nap beneath a cool, shady willow tree, to standing in the hot sun; sweating, panting, and scared half out of my wits.

"Alright, Mark, get control," I said to myself. "You gotta get a grip, man."

The world continued to spin, while I tried to slow things down enough to make sense of what I'd just seen. Followed in natural order by questioning myself on whether I had actually seen it in the first place. It was fairly dark beneath the tree, after all, and I had been wavering somewhere between being asleep and awake when it happened.

When I felt the blood rushing through my veins slow down enough to allow me to walk, I made the move back toward the mysterious willow tree. At the edge of the dangling canopy, I hesitated, and then felt even sillier for my reluctance. "Stop being such a baby!" I said out loud to steel my nerves. "Pull back the vines, stick your head in, and prove it was all just a nightmare."

Which is exactly what I did. Unfortunately my theory fell apart right away, and with better light from the willow vines being pulled back, I could see the unmistakable ridges of a hangman's knot coming out from the back of the man's collar.

"Damn!" I shouted, more frustrated now than afraid.

I pulled back hard with an armful of the vines, grabbed a single strand with my free hand, then wrapped and tied it around the first bunch. It created a pie-shaped slice in the canopy, large enough to act as a doorway. As I stepped through, my emotions made the full circle from fear to pity.

"You poor fellow," I said, speaking to the man's back. "Just how in the heck did you wind up like this?"

The wind began to pick up a bit, and as the branch holding the man started to sway, the motion caused the dangling body to begin to turn slightly under the rope. Slowly the man's front side came into view, and wanting to spare myself the sight of what gruesome distortions a hanging might have on a man's face, I quickly trained my eyes downward. That's when I noticed a clue to the man's identity. A suggestion of just who it might be that was hanging from the willow tree.

"Please, dear God," I said, crossing myself and squeezing my eyes shut. "Please, please don't let it be him."

When I opened my eyes again, the clue was still there. It was a camera, the same make and model as the one I'd seen my friend Trip Singletary clicking away with at the courthouse. At first I couldn't bring myself to look up again, and even after I'd made the decision to do so, it took a real physical effort to overcome the reluctance still holding my head down.

"Ah, Trip," I said, my vision gratefully blurred by the sadness welling up under my eyes.

I'd never seen the lifeless body of someone I knew before. At least, not before the funeral home got a hold of them. Death is an ugly thing, and as I looked at Trip, my only thought was that I didn't want to remember him that way.

Suddenly, I heard the wind begin to hiss through the trees again. Out of the corner of my eye, I caught the faint image of a dark figure moving behind the tree trunk.

"Who's there?" I shouted, leaping back towards the edge of the canopy.

"Mr. Daniels, you don't have to be sad," a young black man said as he came toward me. "This hasn't happened yet."

It was Marcus Brown.

Marcus raised his hand in the direction of Trip's lifeless body, turning his palm toward him and making a few controlled motions. As he did, the body hanging from the willow tree slowly dissolved away – as if Marcus had simply rubbed the image from a pencil sketch.

"You can still prevent this, Mr. Daniels. It doesn't have to be this way."

Both Marcus and the willow tree stood quiet and calm, as if the whole world were on pause.

"How?" I finally asked.

"Give in to it, Mr. Daniels. Accept the gift you've been given."

With that, Marcus shot me a warm and peaceful smile, before he too simply faded slowly from view.

Chapter 14

Outside of my first year in college, I'd never really been a big drinker. During those initial lost months as a freshman, I drank enough to come to know that befuddling and sometimes embarrassing sensation that can only be described as "where the hell am I". The gradual road to semi-sobriety that I chose was driven by a paranoia I developed over not being in control. I could handle the headaches and embalming effects that excessive alcohol consumption had on my body, but the mental strain was way too much for me to continue the habit unabated.

I woke up face-down on a pillow that felt as damp as a wash cloth thrown from the bathtub, and in total darkness that very same sensation returned with the power of an all-nighter. Fumbling around in the dark for a light switch, I truly had no idea what I was going to see when I found one. One of my wandering hands finally touched on a lamp, but I hesitated tripping the switch.

"Who's here?" I yelled.

There was no answer, which put me slightly more at ease, but I still didn't turn the light on until I'd cocked the telephone handset I'd found with my other hand. With the light switched on, the reflection I caught in a mirror across the room scared me – at least until I realized it was *me* that I was frightened of. A quick scan of the room jogged my memory enough to put me back in my hotel room, but the images of the willow tree were still leaking across the dividing line between reality and imagination.

As I slid to the edge of the bed, my body felt as though it had made the trip through dreamland bouncing around in the back of a pickup truck. My mouth was as dry as the desert, but when I picked up the glass on the bed stand and tried to bring it up to my lips, I couldn't keep the water from shaking out of the glass. The clock on the stand said it was too early to make my next move, but the overriding fear of what might be coming drove me beyond that piece of logic.

"Keep still!" I grumbled, struggling to pin my right elbow against my side while I tried desperately to scroll through the directory on my cell phone.

I hit a long unused speed-dial number.

"Hello?" a groggy voice answered.

"Dr. Keller?"

"Yes, this is Dr. Keller."

"It's Mark Daniels, Jim."

"Mark. Oh, hi," he said in a bedroom whisper. "Listen, can you give me just a second to switch phones?"

"Sure thing, Doc. I'm not going anywhere."

The brief delay while Dr. Keller moved to another room was enough to ratchet the anxiety to the next level and cause me to have to stand.

"Okay, Mark. I'm back," his normal, soothing voice returning to a level that is not very loud to begin with. "I'd ask something silly like 'is everything alright'; but since it's three-thirty in the morning, I'l just assume things aren't perfect."

"Not by a long shot, Doc. I've got my cell phone scrunched between my ear and shoulder because I can't keep still long enough to hold it."

"Oh, no. I'm sorry, Mark," he said, knowing my dilemma right away. "I thought after so much time we'd put that behind us."

"Me too."

"Have you been drinking?"

"No. Nothing significant."

"Mark, with your medication there isn't anything insignificant when it comes to alcohol. Mixing the two chemicals ..."

"I haven't been taking my medication."

There was a pause on the other end after my confession. "How long has it been since you stopped taking it?"

"A year and a half, maybe two years. I just didn't need it anymore."

"Well, don't beat yourself up over it," he said to ease my guilt – an emotion I wasn't feeling. "It was never our intention to keep you on the stuff for the rest of your natural life anyway. Are the symptoms pretty much the same as previous episodes?"

"There are a couple of new twists."

"Like what?"

"Dreams."

"Dreams? That wasn't part of your signature, was it?"

"No. You tried a few times to get me to remember some, but this is new."

"Are they good dreams or nightmares?"

"Well, they're scary enough I suppose. But I can't really say nightmares."

"How would you describe them?"

"Real."

The doctor took another head-shrink's pause. "Mark, have there been any dramatic changes in your life recently? Shifts in the status quo?"

"Like what?"

"A death in the family. A relationship ending."

"I did break up with my fiancée."

"*You* broke up with *her*?"

"Well, not technically."

"Hmm."

"Don't go there, Doc. It really wasn't that big a deal."

"Mark, what doesn't seem like a big deal on the outside won't necessarily dictate how we cope with things on the inside."

"I'm telling you, it's a dead-end."

"How long were you together?"

"About two years."

Doctor Keller was quiet again; I'm sure in order for me to kick around my last answer and make the connection. "Listen, can you come by the office later this morning?" he asked, obviously not wanting to take me on about Karen over the phone.

"Actually, I'm out of town. Way out of town."

"Will you be back in the next few days?"

"Possibly. I'm thinking about it, anyway."

"When you get back into town, call me. I'd like to see you as soon as possible. Would you like me to call in a prescription for you?"

"No, not just yet," I said, mostly concerned that a call to the local pharmacy would get around the Chases Corner chat-line before I could even pick up the pills.

"Okay, then. In the meantime, do you remember the exercises we learned to help cope with the anxiety attacks?"

"I do."

"Take some time out to pamper yourself a little. Do the exercises and give yourself a reward."

"I'll do it."

"How are you feeling right this minute?"

"Better. I'm actually feeling a little better."

"Good. I'm glad. You call me if anything else comes up."

"I will."

"And come see me first thing when you get back into town."

"You'll be the first person I call."

"Alright. Good night, Mark.

"Yeah, good night. Thanks Jim."

Talking with Dr. Keller had a soothing effect all by itself, just as it had back in my most difficult times. He was the one port in the storm that kept me from sinking completely, and after giving it a few minutes I was finally able to get the glass of water to my mouth without spilling it all over myself. The half-full glass wasn't nearly enough to quench my thirst, and after making my way to the sink to fill it up again, I got a close-up look at myself in the mirror. I looked like death warmed over. The man in the mirror was familiar, but his return was like an annoying relative who turns up at your door unannounced.

I nearly drowned myself splashing cold water on my face, and after toweling-off I was as wide awake as I could've been. I thought about taking a trip downstairs to see if Hank the night-watchman had a pot of coffee brewing, but it wasn't even four o'clock. Instead, I decided to spend some time with an old friend. That one low-tech though always dependable reporter's companion: my black speckled, English composition book.

I have always enjoyed writing in my notebook, though the feelings I had for that activity went far beyond utilitarian benefits. It had been the one constant in my life – the one thing that has crossed the bridges of puberty, adolescence, and manhood unchanged. From the time I was first able to put words into full sentences, I was finding places to write them down.

After the most troubling dream of my entire life, I sat down with my most favorite cathartic release. I did what I always do when I'm trying to make sense of things: I wrote. When I'd finished, I felt better. Not because I had an understanding of what was happening to me, but my writing reminded me that I'd overcome much worse episodes in the past. None of those were based on dreams, but the dreams weren't the challenge anyway. It was the anxiety that needed to be handled, and after a couple of hours of pen and paper therapy, I had it under control.

It was five-thirty when I figured it was safe to head downstairs and see about some coffee. Hank was there, and ever the observant onlooker he commented honestly on what he saw.

"You don't look so good this morning, Mr. Daniels," he said. "Did you have trouble sleeping?"

I hesitated. "A little," I said.

"You know, they's a history of that very same thing running in my family. We've gotten pretty darned good at finding ways to cope with it."

Hank was giving me the chance to volunteer to hear about his family's insomnia cures. "I'm sure they have, Hank. This was just a minor case of indigestion, however."

"Yup. That's one of the causes alright," Hank said. "My cousin Albert used to have horrible bouts with the heart-burn at night. Couldn't even lay himself down on the bed come evening. What finally cured him of it was ..."

As Hank's words blended together in a steady droning, I felt myself go slightly numb at the prospect of standing there and waiting for him to talk himself out.

" ... and his wife was the one that came upon the idea to—" Hank stopped and stared as if I had a booger hanging from my nose. "You been in a fight there, Mr. Daniels?"

"What are you talking about?"

"That's a pretty nasty welt you got on your neck."

I reached up and felt a warm, raised area on the side of my neck.

"It looks as though someone took you out back and lashed you with a willow branch."

Chapter 15

As I pulled into the parking lot at Molly's, the gravel crunching under the wheels of my rental car reminded me that I'd run out of time to settle on a cover story. Even with a high-collared dress shirt, the mark on my neck was still visible. I had little doubt the keen-eyed folks of Chases Corner gathered for breakfast would pick it out as soon as I walked in. I was still struggling to come up a story when young Billy Thorton startled me by knocking on the driver's side window.

I rolled the window down. "Hey, Mr. Daniels," Billy said. "Did you get that scratch on your neck from your seatbelt?"

I adjusted the driver's side mirror and saw that the two more or less lined up with each other, close enough to be plausible. I took Billy's lead.

"Yeah, I forgot to unbuckle when I went to step out of the car."

"You must've been in a mighty big hurry."

"As a matter of fact, I was."

"You oughta slow down a little bit."

"Look who's talking," I said as I got out of the car. "Is that Billy-the-pot calling the kettle black?"

"What's that?" I saw Billy scrunching his brow and realized I was creating more questions.

"Never mind. Do you have time to do an errand for me this morning?"

"That's why I'm here."

"I'm trying to get my hands on something. Do you have any contacts inside the local police department?"

"If you mean the sheriff's office, my aunt works there. She's the dispatcher."

"Good. I was counting on something like that."

"You want to talk to my auntie?" Billy asked.

"I don't think that'll be necessary. I do need *you* to speak to her, though."

"Sure thing, Mr. Daniels. What do you need me to find out?"

"The background file I have is missing a few items from Bo's original arrest. The statement they took from Bo the night that Marcus Brown was killed isn't in there."

"Yes, sir. You need me to try and get a copy for you?"

"Bingo!"

"Bingo?"

"Sorry, I meant, that's exactly what I need."

Billy shot me a queer look. "I'm on it, Mr. Daniels. They's probably gonna be a fee for that," he said as he readied one foot on the pedal of his bicycle.

"Oh, I'm sorry, Billy!" I said as I dug out my wallet. "Here's twenty dollars. Do you think that will cover it?"

"Ah, heck, Mr. Daniels. The copy charge ain't gonna be more than a buck or two."

"You keep the change then. If you can get me a copy of that statement, it'll be well worth it."

Billy looked slightly embarrassed, something I should have expected.

"We'll just consider it an advance for the next time I need you for something."

"Well, if you put it like that, I guess it's alright."

"Good. Now get out of here and get me that copy."

Billy's legs got to pumping the pedals on his bicycle, and as he rode off he turned his head back in my direction. "But I'm gonna owe ya a free one next time," he hollered.

I truly wanted to adopt the boy.

A soon as I stepped inside Molly's, the hostess stared at me with a question in her eyes.

"I forgot to unbuckle the seatbelt in my rental car," I said.

"What's that, Mr. Daniels?"

"The welt on my neck. I got it from my seatbelt."

"Welt? Oh, yeah, that's a nasty one," she said, as if noticing it for the first time. "I was looking at your eyes, though. They're mighty puffy this morning."

"I see."

"You sleep okay last night?"

"A little indigestion is all."

"Oh, my," she said as she started off her stool. "You might not be used to good southern cooking. I hear ya'll don't spice your food much up north."

"That could be it. I'm sure my stomach will adapt, however."

"Geez, I hope so Mr. Daniels. I'd hate to think you'd have to give up Molly's cooking. We'd sure enough miss you around here."

I managed a smile for the hostess.

I had been hoping to talk to attorney Galax, and after slipping into my seat at a table, it didn't take long for the mountain to come to Mohammed.

"I see, like the rest of us, you have become addicted to Ms. Molly's biscuits, Mr. Daniels."

"That may be true, Mr. Galax, but is there really any alternative?"

"No, I suppose you are right about that. But may I say, a more appropriate question might be *why* would an alternative be necessary?"

Galax had approached from behind me, and as he settled into the chair directly across the table, he took on his first full view. The smirk fell from his face.

"My goodness, Mark. Have you been ill?"

"A little case of indigestion kept me up last night."

Galax looked as though he had more to say, but said nothing.

"And the scratch on my neck came from the seatbelt in my car," I snapped preemptively. "So do me a favor and get that out on the rumor wire so I can quit answering so many questions."

"I assure you I did not mean to pry. I was simply concerned that—"

"Forget it."

My grumpy retort left Galax sitting like a statue, the silence he allowed between us eventually causing me to re-think my response.

"Hey, look, I'm sorry about that, Trevor. I'm a little on edge this morning. Let's start over."

"Very well then. Good morning, Mark."

"How can I help you this morning, counselor?"

"Actually, I was wondering if there was any way that I could be of service to you, sir. Mrs. Nutter informed me you would like to sit with her to discuss her nephew, and that you perhaps might even want to have another conversation with Bo as well."

"True. Not right now necessarily, but eventually."

"Yes, well, as I have promised to act as a chaperon for her, and in light of your displeasure over meeting with Bo the first time outside of my own presence, I must tell you that my services for either will not be available for some time after today."

"How's that?"

"I am returning to Charleston tomorrow morning. I am afraid I shall not be back in this area until the evening before Bo's hearing."

"Ducking out on your client already, counselor? Are you that sure of your position, then?"

"No to both questions. However, I must return to finish compiling the brief Judge Jefferson has requested for Monday. After which, there is really nothing left for me to accomplish here until Bo is required in the courtroom."

I thought for a moment about the things I was hoping to get done during the day, one of which I needed Galax's help with anyway. "I may be able to sit with them today," I said. "That is, if you can help me with another item."

"You have simply to name it and I will oblige however I can."

"Have you ever met with the parents of Marcus Brown?"

"I have, indeed. Or, at least I have met with his father. His dear mother is deceased."

"How far is Pixley from here?"

"Not far, but Mr. Brown no longer resides in Pixley."

"Damn," I said, throwing my head back.

"You are indeed testy this morning, Mark. There's no need to be so over that bit of news, however."

"Where does he live, then?"

"Why, right here in Chases Corner, sir."

"You gotta be kidding me."

"I assure you I am not. From what I understand, he moved here just after the trial some sixteen-years ago. The community has taken him in, so to speak."

Once again, a bit too convenient for a hard-nosed skeptic like myself. "This place is wild," I said.

"I don't believe I ever did hear Chases Corner described as *wild* before, Mr. Daniels," the waitress said as she came by the table. "Sleepy, maybe; but never wild."

"Good morning, Maggie. Sorry, that word can sometimes be a bit pejorative."

"Yes, well just as soon as I can hunt-up a dictionary, I'll come back and tell you how I feel about that."

Galax got a kick out of my predicament. "He meant no harm, Maggie."

"I'll take your word for it," she said. "The usual, Mr. Daniels?"

I thought about asking Maggie how I'd come to have a "usual" in such a short time, but decided not to ruin it. "Yes, that would be perfect," I said.

"You need to be careful with your expressions, Mark," Galax said after Maggie had left.

"Yes, I've had that blow up on me few times since I got here," I said. "Getting back to Marcus Brown's father, can you arrange a meeting with him?"

"That won't be necessary."

"I don't get it."

"What I mean to say is that if you'll wait here a short while after you finish your biscuits and gravy, Mr. Brown will be along presently."

"Here? He comes to this restaurant?"

"He arrives each day at precisely nine o'clock for breakfast."

I shook my head in playful disbelief. "Trevor, have you ever had things go so easily in your job that you began to worry over it all."

"No. But if I ever did have the good fortune such as you describe, I would simply accept it graciously and give the Lord a wink or two."

"I suppose you're right. So, if I hang around and meet with Mr. Brown, that would leave this afternoon open for a cozy chat with Mrs. Nutter. Are you available then?"

"I can be. Shall we use your suite at the hotel as the meeting place?"

"It's as good a place as any. I've got a personal matter to attend to, but I should be finished by three."

"Then if it suits you, I will collect Mrs. Nutter and Bo and bring them by the Marriott Courtyard at, say, four this afternoon?"

"That works."

Galax pulled a small notebook from his pocket and wrote something down. "I know that you enjoy your privacy during breakfast, so if that concludes our business, I will leave you to it," Galax said.

"There is one other thing you could help me with."

He finished pushing in his chair and stood proudly behind it. "By all means. Tell me in what way."

"A research rat that works back at my paper tells me that Corey Aycock was last living down there in Charleston."

"He would be correct."

"He's correct? You mean you know where he is?"

"I do. I can make arrangements for you to meet with him, but I can say with a near certainty that he will not travel here to Chases Corner."

"I was afraid of that."

"My offer to host you on a trip to my city still stands. Shall we pick a day now?"

"Not just yet, counselor. But I'll probably take you up on your offer soon enough."

"You need only say the word. Good day, sir. I shall look forward to our meeting this afternoon."

"Have a good one, Trevor."

Maggie passed the silver-haired fox as she brought me my breakfast. They stopped to whisper for a second, before Maggie nodded acceptance of something and finished the trip to my table.

"Here you go, Mr. Daniels," she sang as she set down food. "Is there anything else you need?"

"No, I think you've got it all."

"Good. I'll let you be, then. I'll bring Mr. Brown by your table when he gets here."

"That would be great. Thanks!"

The more time I spent around Trevor Galax, the more respect I had for his abilities to make the music play the way he wanted it. He was definitely the conductor type, if not an original composer.

Chapter 16

Breakfast disappeared in record time. I finished a full thirty minutes before Mr. Brown was to arrive, and I took the opportunity to do some breathing exercises with a little discreet meditation. While doing the breathing thing at the table, I tried to be inconspicuous. I was sure the good folks of Chases Corner were already starting to think that I was as odd as I knew they were. After about twenty minutes of sitting there, still as a mouse, I could hear a few whispers back at the cash register. I felt better though, which was all I really cared about anyway. The short-fuse I'd tried to light with Galax was not a good mode for a reporter to be in. Feeling more relaxed, I even thought about making a call to Carl. It took a few minutes to convince myself, because I wasn't really up to the hundred questions game. But, I had a great excuse for cutting the call short if it were to go poorly.

"What's going on, my friend?" Carl answered after the first ring. "How are things?"

"Good. Things are going well."

"How did you sleep last night?"

"What?"

"I know you have trouble sometimes when you have to sleep away from your own bed. So, how did you sleep?"

I hesitated, paranoia holding me back some. "I slept well."

I knew that if somehow Carl had gotten wind of my difficult night at the Marriott, he'd stay on the topic and keep probing me until I caved. I also knew he would tell me to come home immediately.

"Good. I'm glad," he said. "Any late-breaking items on the agenda today?"

"I'll be meeting with Marcus Brown's father here in just a few minutes. And

I have another get-together with Bo and his aunt set for later this afternoon."

"What do you hope to get out of the dead boy's father?"

"I'm not sure. I might start by digging into why he moved to Chases Corner after his son died."

"He lives there, too?"

"He does."

"What is it about that place that drives people to want to live there? Do the locals get free beer or something?"

"No, actually you can't buy a beer here," I said. "There *is* something about this place, though."

"Such as?"

"I don't know. A warmth. A certain gentleness about the people, I guess."

Carl paused. "This is Mark Daniels, isn't it?"

"I think so."

Carl paused again. "You sure everything is okay down there?"

"Yeah, everything is fine."

"You'd tell me if it wasn't, wouldn't you?"

"Carl, Mr. Brown just arrived. I'm afraid I'm going to have to cut you short."

A third pause from Carl told me he'd locked in on something. "That's fine, but give me a call later."

"Right. The first free minute I have," I said, ending the call.

Marcus Brown's father hadn't shown up yet, but Carl was on to me. If we'd stayed on the phone any longer he would have cracked me like an egg. There were benefits to getting so close to your boss that he knew you forward and back, but there were some serious drawbacks as well. We'd been through a lot together, and there was no way I could ever repay him for the way he stood by me during the hard times; but I did sometimes wish he were a little more distant.

I glanced around the restaurant to see if I could spot Maggie for another cup of coffee. When she saw me looking for her, she came right over with the pot in hand. "I'd have brought you over a warm up earlier, but I didn't want to disturb you," she said as she filled my cup. "Is that what they call meditating?"

"Kind of. More like a relaxation technique."

"Relaxation technique," she said, as if pondering the notion. "I don't guess folks around here need much of that. I reckon most people in Chases Corner are already relaxed enough to be mistaken for dead."

"Yeah, that's a nice quality for a place to have."

"I suppose so. Anyway, that's old Mr. Brown just came through the door. You want me to see if I can fetch him for you?"

I turned in the direction of the entrance and saw an old black man standing at the hostess station. With white hair covering both sides of his head, he looked more like he would fit the role of Marcus' grandfather. When Maggie grabbed him by the elbow to lead him over, I realized that he was also somewhat frail. The two of them took their time shuffling over to my table.

"Mr. Daniels, this here's Atticus Brown. Marcus Brown's daddy," Maggie said in a big voice.

"Good morning, Mr. Brown. It's a pleasure to meet you. Can you join me at my table for a few minutes to talk about your son?"

Mr. Brown nodded, slightly confused but seemingly willing. Maggie helped him get seated, then poured him some coffee and added cream and sugar.

"There you go, Mr. Brown. I'll hold off a little before I put in your breakfast order. That okay with you?" Maggie was speaking loudly, as if he were hard of hearing. I was worried that I might have to shout my questions to him.

"Mr. Brown, thanks very much for putting off your breakfast," I said, repeating Maggie's volume level. "I'll try not to keep you from it for very long."

"You don't have to yell," he said softly.

"I'm sorry?"

"I said you don't have to yell. I ain't deaf."

The old man surprised me with his declaration, but I did get a little kick out of it. "Forgive me," I said. "I thought from the way Maggie was talking to you that you might have trouble with your hearing."

"Nah, she's been a yelling at me like that ever since I started coming here," he said. "I'm a low talker. Have been all my life. I guess she just figures that if she has trouble hearing me, I must have trouble hearing her as well."

It took real effort to keep the smile on my face from becoming offensive. "Well, listen Mr. Brown, I'm a reporter for the New York Times. I'm doing a story on Bosephus Buckminster and his retrial and I was hoping to get your take on things."

"Fine," he said. "He didn't do it."

"You don't think Bo was responsible for your son's death?"

Mr. Brown closed his eyes for a couple of seconds before answering. "I know he didn't," he said, a tinge of sadness starting to color his soft voice.

"Okay," I said shifting gears. "Before we go any further, would you mind if I take out my tape recorder so that I can keep track of the things we say today."

"Ain't gonna make me no never-mind."

"Thanks."

I bent down to take the recorder out of my bag, and as I brought it to the table I saw that Mr. Brown had pulled a handkerchief from his pocket and brought it to his nose. I fiddled with the recorder until he'd finished. I knew I was going to have to be delicate with my questions.

TRANSCRIPT
Tape # 2
Interviewer: Daniels
Responder: Atticus Brown (father of Marcus Brown)
Date of Interview: Friday, April 5th
Location: Molly's Restaurant

9:08 AM

DANIELS: Mr. Brown, if you don't mind me asking, how old are you?

BROWN: Eighty-two years.

DANIELS: That would have made you, let's see, fifty-one or fifty-two when Marcus was born. Is that right?

BROWN: That's right.

DANIELS: Pretty late in life for a child. Did Marcus have any brothers or sisters?

BROWN: Nope. Me and the Misses only had the one.

DANIELS: How old is your wife?

BROWN: Marcus' momma passed on. She followed Marcus by about a year.

DANIELS: I'm sorry, Mr. Brown. I think I knew that already.

BROWN: Thank you, kindly. It were a hard year, that one. She'd be seventy-seven next month had she stayed on with us.

DANIELS: So, she was in her forties when Marcus was born?

BROWN: She was.

DANIELS: I hope I'm not prying too much, but was Marcus, shall we say, expected?

BROWN: We expected him a lot sooner, I'll say that much. We'd mostly given up hope by the time he came.

DANIELS: A late blessing in life.

BROWN: Oh, yes sir. A mighty powerful blessing. We saw straight off how he was gonna be our little angel. We know'd that from the very beginning.

DANIELS: Was he a lot like Bo Buckminster? By that I mean in his disposition and all?

BROWN: They was like two peas in a pod. Them two was as same as they could get, excepting the color of their skin, that is.

DANIELS: Were they always friends growing up? They did live in different towns, right?

BROWN: Yes, sir. They met at the Arden School, after them teachers at the regular school realized Marcus was having trouble keeping up.

DANIELS: How old were they?

BROWN: When they met? Or when they went off to that other school?

DANIELS: Both, I guess.

BROWN: Well, now, Marcus was in the second grade when they sent him off to the new school. Seems to me they didn't get around to sending Bo over there till he was up to the fifth or sixth. Can't swear to that though. That's when they met.

DANIELS: Was Bo more advanced than Marcus with his thought processing?

BROWN: I don't believe so. Least ways, if by that you mean was he smarter.

DANIELS: They got to know each other through school. Did they hang out together after school?

BROWN: Oh, yes, they was together constant. Since it were tough to get around – we didn't have no car back then – they'd spend the night over at each other's house quite a bit. Weekends, school nights, it didn't matter. That momma of Bo's was a fine woman, and she seemed real happy to have Marcus around. Same with us and Bo.

DANIELS: You knew Mrs. Buckminster pretty well, then?

BROWN: Yes, sir. Like I said, she was a real fine woman. Can't say as much for his daddy, but he took off soon enough anyhow.

DANIELS: You can't say much for his father. I take it you didn't care for him?

BROWN: Hard to like a man like that. Stayed mad all the time. Had a special dislike for old Senator Hunter.

DANIELS: They didn't get along?

BROWN: Wouldn't give the senator the time of day. Guess he held bad feelings towards him in his heart.

DANIELS: Why would he feel that way?

BROWN: You know, he may have his own faults, but the senator did his best to help that family however he could. I suppose Bo's daddy might have resented that at times.

DANIELS: What was Bo's mother like?

BROWN: Quiet. Sad sometimes, but not about having Bo for a son. She loved that boy more than anything on Earth. She said Bo was put here for a purpose, and that it was her job to see to it that he got his angels wings.

DANIELS: Do you think he will?

BROWN: How's that?

DANIELS: Do you think Bo will get his wings one day?

BROWN: Oh, yes sir. Sure as I'm sitting here in front of you. I know he and Marcus will be together again doing the Lord's work. Marcus' already made his, you know.

PAUSE:

DANIELS: Bo says Marcus comes to see him in his dreams. Do you believe Marcus can visit people in their dreams?

PAUSE:

BROWN: You one of *them*?

DANIELS: What do you mean by *one of them*?

BROWN: Did Marcus come to you?

DANIELS: I'm not sure I know what you're asking. I was only trying to—

BROWN: You having dreams with Marcus in them?

PAUSE:

DANIELS: No, I'm sorry, Mr. Brown. I'm not one of *them*, as you say.

PAUSE:

BROWN: Excuse me, then. It ain't my place to ask something like that, anyway.

DANIELS: I understand.

BROWN: Thank you kindly.

PAUSE:

DANIELS: Before we get off the subject entirely, what exactly did you mean when you asked if I was one of them? Who are *they*?

LONG PAUSE:

BROWN: It ain't my place to say.

DANIELS: You were looking at my tape recorder just then. Would it be easier for you to talk about it if I shut it off?

BROWN: No, sir. I was just throwing things out before. I didn't really mean nothing by it. Nothing at all.

PAUSE:

DANIELS: Okay, let's just move on then. Why is that you decided to move here to Chases Corner of all places. It might seem unusual for some people that a parent would to want to move to the town where the child was murdered.

PAUSE:

BROWN: I just ... I was just ...

DANIELS: I'm sorry if that came out too bluntly. Forgive me for being so cold.

BROWN: I just wanted to be around him.

DANIELS: Around who?

BROWN: Marcus.

DANIELS: Is he buried here in Chases Corner?

LONG PAUSE:

DANIELS: Listen, let me just shut up here, Mr. Brown. I'm sorry that I seem to have upset you. We can stop this now.

Shutting off the recorder, I felt an ache in my heart looking at Mr. Brown. Tears were rolling down his face like rain on a statue. Such a proud man; it tore at me to see him after I'd obviously touched a very vulnerable spot. Even after the tears had stopped, the only reply he could muster to my words of apology was a nod. I felt awful as I watched Maggie help him up and start to walk with him to his usual seat, so much so that I couldn't bring myself to look back in his direction.

"Mr. Daniels," he said after a few steps, in as loud a voice as he could manage.

I turned toward the old man. "Yes?"

"If you do see Marcus sometime, make sure and tell him his daddy said hello."

Chapter 17

After making my way back to the Marriott that morning, with another full breakfast from Molly's sitting on my stomach like a sumo wrestler, it took every bit of strength I had to keep from flopping down on the bed for yet another nap. There was plenty of time before Bo and his Aunt would arrive, but I was determined not to give in. At least not until I'd taken care of a personal matter. It was another of Dr. Keller's tricks – one that involved forcing everything out on the table. Instead of catching a little shut-eye, I sat at my computer, quickly chugging the first of the two Styrofoam cups of coffee I had carried with me from the lobby, and got to work on an open letter.

"Remember, you don't have to mail your letters," Dr. Keller used to say to our group. "They're really just letters you're writing to yourself, a little note passed between your subconscious and conscious mind."

It took me a good part of the afternoon to write out my goodbye letter to Karen. The letter was more than six pages long, but when I'd finished one passage stuck out: *Karen, deep down you and I both know we're two very different people. They say opposites attract, but no one ever said opposites stay together forever.*

After reading those two lines for about the hundredth time, a meeting reminder popped up on my laptop. I saved the letter to my hard drive under the file name of *Goodbye Karen*; and as it closed out on my computer, a satisfied sense of finality settled in. A little closure that I hoped might somehow get my subconscious off my back.

There was still time left to call Carl back as I'd promised earlier, but I simply didn't want to. Instead, I sent him a quick email to tell him I'd get him a daily by the end of the day. I had just tucked my laptop in the bag when the hotel phone rang.

"Mr. Daniels, Mr. Galax is waiting for you here in the lobby."

"I'll be right down."

I don't like winging it when it comes to interviews, but I'm not sure what I would have prepared for my next meeting with Bo, even if I'd had the time. I really didn't know why I'd asked for another get-together in the first place, other than that we hadn't spent much time together first time we met.

Bo was standing over near the snacks when the elevator opened to the lobby.

"Good afternoon, Bo," I said to get his attention.

Bo's head spun in my direction. "Mr. Daniels, you think they'd mind if a fella had a snack?"

"No, not all."

"One of each? Like last time?"

"Mmmm ... maybe you better stick with two this time, Bo."

"Sure thing, Mr. Daniels. It's gonna be mighty hard to choose, though."

While Bo debated which of the goodies looked the most tempting, Trevor Galax stood up from a couch across the lobby.

"Mr. Daniels, as always, it is a pleasure," he said.

"Trevor. Do you see anything you'd like on the snack tray?"

"Thank you, but I shall resist the temptation."

I looked around the lobby for Mrs. Nutter.

"I'm afraid Bo and I are alone. Ms. Nutter has chosen to remain behind."

"She wouldn't come? Even with a chaperon?"

"It seems that the only suitable chaperon for Ms. Nutter would be her husband."

"That would've been fine with me."

"I dare say there was no way to convince Mr. Nutter to come with us," Galax replied. "Nor do I believe you would have wanted him to, if you had ever made his acquaintance."

"A piece of work, is he?"

"A very fine description. Certainly, Mr. Nutter is a piece of *something*, that much I can assure you."

"So be it," I said. "We'll just consider it a blessing and move on. Shall we make our way to my suite?"

"Lead the way, sir."

Bo had chosen two large cookies, and as we walked the hallway to my room he carried one in each hand, palm up, as if he were balancing two containers of nitroglycerin. I knew I wasn't going to have his full attention unless the first order of business was to let him get after the cookies, and once inside I gave the go-ahead.

"Bo, why don't you take a minute and enjoy your snack at the table over there before we get started?"

He didn't say a word, but delicately laid the cookies down on the table, and then suddenly began stuffing them into his mouth with very large bites, as if he hadn't eaten in days.

"Trevor, make yourself comfortable in the living area while I get my bag."

"Thank you. Is there any place in particular you would like me to—"

"Sit anywhere you like."

When I came back with my bag, Bo was picking a few crumbs off the front of his shirt. He used his shirt sleeve to brush the remaining remnants from his face.

"Bo, how about we join Mr. Galax?"

"Sure thing, Mr. Daniels. You want me to sit where I sat the last time?"

"You can if you like." I was little surprised Bo could remember such a minor detail.

"You recall where that was exactly, Mr. Daniels?"

"I believe you were on that big couch over there."

"Right. I thought that was it. Just couldn't say for sure."

With the three of us settled in, I unloaded the tools of the trade from my bag and set them on the large coffee table.

"That's your recorder thing-a-ma-bob, ain't it Mr. Daniels?"

"It is indeed."

"You used that last time we was talking together, right?"

"I did. I used it in order to keep track of the things we said together."

"You listened to that talk again yet, Mr. Daniels?"

"I haven't, Bo. Not yet anyway."

Bo focused hard on the tape recorder, like he was studying some kind of top secret machine.

"Sure would like to have one of those things, Mr. Daniels." he finally said. "Seems like remembering is the one thing that's always kept me from staying up with the other fellas, if you know what I mean."

I understood right away that for me the tape recorder was a convenience, but in Bo's mind, it had the potential to be a magical solution to a life-long challenge.

"Bo, I may have something for you." I said, a thought darting across my mind.

As I dug around in one of the compartments of my bag, Bo had the look of a small child watching someone open a present on Christmas morning. "You got another one of those cookies in there?" he said.

"No, but I may have something else you might like."

I finally managed to pull a small, square pen-length device from the bag – a gift from my former fiancée that had never really found a use in my work routine. Knowing I used my old tape recorder like a crutch, Karen had bought me one of those super hi-tech micro jobbies that fit into your coat pocket. It was lightweight and digital, so there was no need for me to carry tapes either. It also wasn't my old tape recorder, and though I made sure to carry it with me at all times after she'd given it to me, I'd never used it.

"You may not believe this, but this little device I have in my hand right here is also a tape recorder."

"That little thing? That there can record what we say?"

"It sure can. It doesn't need a tape to do it, either."

"Go on now! How does it work if it ain't got no tape and all?"

"Truthfully, I haven't a clue," I confessed. "It's hi-tech stuff that I don't know all that much about. It does work though, and it's a pretty easy thing to use."

"You think I might be able to try that thing out, Mr. Daniels."

"How about I do you one better? What would you say if I just gave it to you?"

Bo looked at me like he didn't understand. "Nah, I couldn't take that from you, Mr. Daniels," he said. "A thing like that's probably pretty darn expensive."

"It was a gift, Bo. I didn't cost me a penny."

Bo started to reach his hand out to take the micro-recorder from me, and then pulled it back quickly. "You know what," he said, "They don't allow things like that back at the prison I stay at."

"They don't?"

"No, sir. Some fellas sneak stuff like that in every now and again, but I could never do that, Mr. Daniels."

"I see how that could be a problem," I said. "How about this? Why don't you hold on to it for now, and if you wind up having to go back to the prison, you can give it back to me."

Bo hesitated, but then as if the idea had suddenly taken hold of him, he reached out and snatched it from my hand. "Alright, that's what we'll do then," he said. "I'll just hold on to it till I have to go back to that prison. Then I'll sure enough give it back to you."

He immediately began pushing the buttons.

"If you want to record something," I said, "push the red button. To play it back again, push the one with the arrow, and then the black one."

Bo pushed the red button.

"Go ahead, say something."

"My name is Bo Buckminster. My real name is Bosephus, but that's not what people call me."

After talking him through how to play back what he'd recorded, Bo's smile was prideful − a slight smirk at the corners telling the world he'd just accomplished something big.

"You need me to record our talk here today, Mr. Daniels?"

"Thanks, Bo, but I think I'm going to use this one," I said. "No use in recording it twice, if you know what I mean."

Bo nodded and slipped his new tape recorder in his pocket.

TRANSCRIPT
Tape # 3
Interviewer: Daniels
Responder: Buckminster (Attorney Galax also present)
Date of Interview: Friday, 5 April
Location: Marriott Courtyard

4:17 PM

DANIELS: So, Bo, how are you doing getting settled in at your aunt's house?

BO: Pretty well. Been mighty tired since I left the prison, though.

DANIELS: Are you having trouble sleeping?

BO: No, sir. Getting to sleep is no problem. Just seems like whenever I nod off, people keep a coming by to wish me luck.

DANIELS: When you say people, do you mean regular people, or ...

BO: Oh, no sir. They's angels. Fact is, real people don't hardly ever stop by to see me late at night. Except the one time when my Momma died. They woke me up for that. I guess they figured I'd want to know about it before morning came.

PAUSE:

DANIELS: Are you worried about what might happen in court when you go before the judge again?

BO: Ain't much I can do about it either way. Things is gonna happen the way they was meant to happen.

DANIELS: You do understand that when it's over, you might have to go back to prison? They'll probably want to take you right from the courtroom if the judge rules against you.

BO: Yes, sir. I understand that.

DANIELS: And the possibility of that happening doesn't bother you?

PAUSE:

BO: Not sure I know any other way to answer you, Mr. Daniels. Things is gonna work out the way they was supposed to. You worried?

DANIELS: I'm a little worried for you. I'm concerned about what having to go back to prison might do to you.

BO: Well, that's real nice of you, Mr. Daniels, but I wouldn't waste no worry lines on me. It's really not so bad in that prison, when you look at it right. Plus, it's springtime you know. Time for a new start.

DANIELS: Going back wouldn't be all that new. You'd probably be sent back to the same place. Same people, same rules, same everything I'm afraid.

BO: I don't know. That's kinda like saying it's the same old tree every year. That's what most folks see when winter's over, just the same old tree. It ain't like that though. New leaves and new little branches sprouting out. Every year a tree gets to take a whole new shape against the big, blue sky. Different from the year ago one.

DANIELS: That's a pretty keen observation. Is spring your favorite time of year?

BO: Oh, yes, sir. In the springtime it's like God is starting over. I say that whenever it comes around, 'cause people seem to think it makes me sound smart. I remember the first time I said it my grandma was still alive, and she made a real big deal about it. It was during one of those times we was giving my momma a break. That's what Grandma used to call it whenever I visited her – giving Momma a break. And when my momma came to pick me up from Grandma's house, it were the first thing she told her about when she got there. I was staying up at her house a good long time, and of all the things that happened that was the very first thing she told her about. Even though on that trip I broke a bunch of the old bottles my papa had collected because I was spinning myself dizzy in the living room.

DANIELS: So what did your grandma say to your mother?

BO: "You better think twice about that boy," is what Grandma said to Momma. "He ain't no retard. Any child that can see the work of the Lord first hand ain't got no problem thinking straight." Those was the sweetest words I ever did hear. She was always real proud of me. Sometimes for no reason at all. Her words that day made me smile so big it made my face hurt. I still get a smile when I think on it. Not as big as I used to, 'cause right after it, I remember that my grandma's gone to heaven to be with Jesus.

PAUSE:

DANIELS: Can you tell me what caused your grandma to say what she did?

BO: Sure. That's one of those things that's stayed in my head pretty clear. Not many things do, you know. That one did, but not much else does.

DANIELS: Why do you think that is?

BO: Why's what, Mr. Daniels?"

DANIELS: Why do you think it is that you have such trouble remembering some things, but others stay with you so long?"

BO: Guess if I know'd the answer to that, it might be something I could use all the time. I just know that some things stay with me almost like they was waiting for me to play them back again inside my head. Kinda of like that tape recorder of yours, only with pictures added in.

DANIELS: You mean like a movie?

BO: Yes, sir.

PAUSE:

DANIELS: Are you playing it over again in your head right now?

BO: Yes, sir.

DANIELS: Whenever you're ready.

PAUSE:

BO: It happened when I was at my grandma's house.

DANIELS: Right. You were giving your mother a break.

BO: That's it. I was up real early one morning, just a doing some wandering before Grandma and Papa got up for breakfast time.

DANIELS: Do you mean *wondering*, Bo? You were just sort of taking some time out to think about things?

BO: No, sir. Wandering. Papa used to call me the wandering gypsy 'cause I was always getting up before them. Whenever they'd go off a looking for me I'd be wandering around outside.

DANIELS: Did you like to go exploring in the morning. Is that why you wandered around?

BO: No, I don't suppose so. I just know'd that if I stayed in the house, sooner or later I'd make some kinda noise that would wake Papa up. He could get mighty ornery when he didn't get a full night's sleep.

DANIELS: So what happened on this particular morning's wander?

BO: Well, it were a glorious morning. I sure enough remember that. I do love springtime you know. But this was just one of those mornings that everything seemed perfect-made. The sun had just come up over the tops of the trees that ran across the big hills along the other side of the valley. I know'd it was going to be a hot one that day, cause the sky started to glowing a great orange color straight off.

DANIELS: Red sky at night, a sailor's delight. Red sky in the morning, sailors take warning.

PAUSE:

BO: What's that?

DANIELS: It's an old saying that goes with a red sky. It has something to do with how sailors see the—

BO: It were an orange sky, Mr. Daniels.

DANIELS: Right. I'm sorry, I keep interrupting you. Please continue with your story.

BO: That's okay, Mr. Daniels. I know it's your job to be asking questions. Aunt Evelyn said you'd probably be asking all kind of silly questions, so I guess that's just one of those. Anyway, while I was looking at how the tree growing outside my Grandma's window was shaping up for summer, against that big orange sky, I saw a momma bird and one of her young'uns perched in a nest on one of the high-up branches. The little bird was just a squawking and holding her mouth open, trying hard as he could to get the momma bird to give him some food. There wasn't enough light yet to see what kind of birds they were. All you could see was them two birds up against that sky – almost like they was a couple of shadows. It was a mighty beautiful sight to behold, Mr. Daniels. I sat there a good while, just a looking and a marveling at how tender God's hand can be. Feeling downright lucky to be witnessing for Him.

PAUSE:

DANIELS: Are you feeling all those feelings over again now, Bo?

BO: Yes, sir. It was a little cool that morning. I'm getting a chill right now just thinking on it. Anyway, those two was just a going back and forth like that for a good while, and I was starting to get worried for the little fella. Seemed like either the momma didn't have any food to give him, or just didn't think it was time yet for him to be eating. Then I got the idea to start searching around to see if I could come up with a worm or two to help out. That's what them birds eat, ya know, worms and such.

DANIELS: I don't think that's the meal I'd choose to start my day? I prefer blueberries on my Cheerios.

LAUGHTER:

BO: That's 'cause you ain't no bird, Mr. Daniels. If you was, you might see them worms as just the thing.

DANIELS: I suppose that's true. So what happened when you went to see about finding a worm to help the momma bird?

BO: I come across a couple soon enough. The ground was still mighty damp from the morning dew, so it only took a couple turns of the soil in Grandma's garden to bring 'em up. I got me a handful of dirt and the worms just sorta sifted out.

PAUSE:

DANIELS: What happened then?

BO: The next part's kinda hard, Mr. Daniels.

DANIELS: Just take your time, Bo. We're not in any hurry.

PAUSE:

BO: When I got back over to the tree them birds was in, I saw something powerful sad. That momma bird wasn't ignoring her young'un anymore. She was trying best she could to push the poor thing clean out of their nest.

DANIELS: What did you do then?

BO: At first I tried to get the momma bird to stop. I was holding up that handful of dirt and worms, doing my best, ya know, to get her to come get her baby one. It didn't work though – she just kept a pushing. She wasn't gonna be satisfied till that poor thing came a tumbling out of that nest.

DANIELS: Did you feel sad for the baby bird?

BO: No, sir. I got mighty angry with that momma though. Seeing her treating that baby of hers that-a-way caused me to lose track of Grandma and Papa being asleep, and I commenced to hollering at her pretty loud. She still wasn't paying me no mind, so I started to climb up that tree after them. I was about halfway when that poor little bird lost the battle and came a-tumbling head over foot right out of the nest. He hit the ground so hard I was just sure it must of been kilt.

PAUSE:

DANIELS: What happened after that?

PAUSE:

BO: (sniffles) I started into crying, I reckon. Must have been pretty loud about it too, cause grandma came a running out in her night coat. (sobs)

PAUSE:

DANIELS: Let it out, Bo. You don't have to keep things in around me. Would you like a tissue?

BO: I thank you much, Mr. Daniels (sniffles). It'll pass here in just a minute or two.

PAUSE:

BO: Course, my grandma knew straight off what had happened. She saw that little bird a lying there at the bottom of the tree, and pieced together right away what had gone on. She was mighty smart, that grandma off mine. She could see things for what they were.

DANIELS: What did your grandma say to you?

BO: Well, first she coaxed me out of the tree. I said "Grandma, that momma bird's kilt her baby. The devil got into her and she kilt her very own little one to keep from having to feed him." But grandma knew better. She knew it weren't the devil that was in that momma bird. "Oh, Grandson, that ain't the devil moving that momma bird to do what she did. She's doing exactly what God intended her to do."

DANIELS: Did you understand what your grandma meant by that?"

BO: Not at first. But she went on to explain it a bit more. Told me how there comes a time when momma birds have to give them young'uns a little push to get them to leave the nest. That if they didn't, their baby's might stay there with them forever. That's not natural of course, 'cause God wants for all baby birds to strike out on their own, eventually. Grandma said that's how He keeps the chain of life moving.

PAUSE:

DANIELS: Bo, did that baby bird ever get up off the ground?

BO: Oh, yes, sir! That's the real glorious part of the story. When I got down out of that tree Grandma pulled me in close to her. We sat there a while, just a leaning up against the tree trunk and watching. "Let's just sit here a spell and see whether that baby bird has enough sense to pay a mind to what his momma's trying to teach him," Grandma said. After a little while that baby bird just sorta shook a couple times, then stood up on them skinny little legs. It started in to looking around, kinda like it was amazed at what the world looked like from outside that nest. Then after a just a few seconds, it started running. There it was, just a running around in circles, trying to flap them little wings.

DANIELS: It was trying to fly on its own.

BO: That it was. It didn't have much luck right away. But then all of a sudden – just like it had done it a thousand times before – that little bird lifted itself right up into the wind. It circled that tree a couple of times, and with me and grandma watching in wonder that bird sailed high up into the sky. Every now and again it would fly straight in between that big orange sun and us, making for the prettiest sight your ever gonna get right here on Earth.

PAUSE:

BO: That morning's what started my *worry time.*

DANIELS: Your worry time? What do you mean by that, Bo?

PAUSE:

GALAX: Perhaps this is where I might be of assistance, Mr. Daniels. I believe I can explain what Bo means.

BO: I thank you kindly, Mr. Galax. It'd sure make things easier if you did the explaining on it. That okay with you, Mr. Daniels?

DANIELS: Certainly. Go right ahead, counselor.

GALAX: As Bo may have told you, he has some difficulty keeping track of calendar time. At least the way you and I might be accustomed to.

DANIELS: Yes, I think I knew that.

GALAX: He does, however, have a certain ability to keep up with extended periods in his life by associating them with emotions. Feelings, if you will, that perhaps dominated during specific spans of time.

BO: That's it, Mr. Galax. You said that real good.

DANIELS: Okay, I think I understand. Bo, are you saying that the morning with the baby bird started a long period of worrying for you?

BO: Yes, sir. It were a good long time of worrying for me after that.

DANIELS: How is that? How could such a morning be the cause for you to worry for so long?

BO: I was worrying on the natural order of things.

DANIELS: How do you mean?

BO: Well, like Grandma said, comes a time when a momma bird just has to give her baby a push to get him to take off on his own.

DANIELS: Right. Otherwise it might never leave.

BO: What started the worry time for me, was that I couldn't help but worry that one day my own momma was gonna have to give *me* a push.

DANIELS: Ah, Bo!

BO: Fact is, I know'd I couldn't just fly off like that baby bird, Mr. Daniels. I guess I always know'd I wasn't one to be able to fly off like that.

PAUSE:

BO: You okay, Mr. Daniels?

DANIELS: Yeah. I'm okay.

PAUSE:

BO: You want this box of tissues back?

DANIELS: Thanks, Bo, but I'm fine.

BO: I hope my story didn't upset you. Everything turned out alright for the bird, Mr. Daniels.

DANIELS: I think you're right. I think it all turned out according to God's plan, didn't it?

BO: Yes, sir. It sure enough did.

PAUSE:

DANIELS: Bo, do you have any idea how old you might have been during that trip to your grandma's house?

BO: Can't say exactly. But as I recollect, I only had about a few more springtimes left after that. You know – before I went into that prison. That's one thing I did miss about going off to that place. You can't much tell one season from the next cause there ain't much to look at when it comes to trees.

DANIELS: Were you still in your *worry time* when you went to prison

BO: Oh, no. Going into that prison commenced my *free* time. I was as free as a bird in there, not a worry in the world. Ain't nothing to worry about really. They tell you when to go to bed, when to get up, when to eat a meal. A fella ain't really got nothing to worry about in there. They just kinda handle everything for you.

PAUSE:

DANIELS: Was it hard getting along with the people at the prison?.

BO: You mean like the guards and such?

DANIELS: No, I mean the other inmates. I'm guessing there are some pretty tough characters in there.

BO: You know, I don't guess so. They's some that have a tendency to get after each other from time to time, I suppose. Mostly though, they's all been real nice to me. There was one fella that seemed to have it in for me pretty bad when he first got there. Called me names and such. I can't recall exactly what.

DANIELS: Did you have a confrontation with him?

BO: How's that?

DANIELS: Did you to get into a fight with him over something?

BO: Oh, no, sir. Nothing like that. Fact is I think some of the other fellas must've helped him to move to another part of the prison, cause the next day my friend Stick came by and told me him and a few of the guys took care of things. Said they took him out.

PAUSE:

GALAX: We may not want to pursue that line here, Mr. Daniels. There are incident reports in Bo's prison file if you would like to learn more, but I think it best if Bo says nothing more on it at this time. You do understand, don't you?"

DANIELS: Not totally, but that's your call counselor.

PAUSE:

BO: Mr. Daniels?

DANIELS: Yes?

BO: You remember me talking about Marcus?

DANIELS: I do.

BO: You remember me telling you how Marcus comes to visit every now and again?

DANIELS: Yes. He comes to you sometimes in your dreams.

BO: Well, sir, it ain't always that he comes in a dream. Sometimes he comes to pay a visit when I'm full awake.

DANIELS: Like when for example?

BO: Like right now, Mr. Daniels. He's standing there just behind you.

PAUSE:

DANIELS: I don't see anything. You say he's in the room with us?

BO: Yes, sir. Right there behind you. I hate that you can't see him. I kinda had the feeling that you might be one that could.

DANIELS: No, I'm sorry, Bo. If he's here, he's invisible to me.

BO: That's alright. He's the same way to Mr. Galax. He's come around a few times when we was—

GALAX: Mr. Daniels, we may want to adjourn our session for now. I don't think you're going to get anything further today.

BO: Wasn't I supposed to say anything about Marcus, Mr. Galax?

GALAX: Not at all, Bo. I just think we should be getting back to see your aunt and uncle. They'll be expecting us shortly.

BO: I'll leave that up to you, Mr. Galax. I ain't much good at keeping up with time you know.

PAUSE:

DANIELS: That's fine, Bo. I've enjoyed our conversation.

BO: Me too, Mr. Daniels. I sure enough enjoyed our conversating as well.

END OF INTERVIEW:

The abrupt end to our interview had me once again a little miffed at the esteemed attorney for the defense. I supposed Galax was trying to protect Bo's credibility, but the topic of Marcus coming to pay Bo the occasional visit had already been put out on the table. That Marcus visited him in the middle of the day was new to me, but it wasn't such a huge revelation that we had to quit the interview.

When Bo stuck his hand in his pocket he found the recorder I'd given him earlier and began to focus on it once again. I used the opportunity to ask his attorney for a side-bar in the kitchen area.

"What was that about, counselor?" I asked.

"There are some things that I believe are better for Bo's case if they are left unsaid."

"Do you think I would put any of the stuff about Marcus being in the room with us in the paper?"

"I do not know. I am more concerned about how I can find a way to get it across to Bo that not everything should be said out loud."

"So you're coaching your witness."

"Call it what you like. If I should decide to put Bo on the stand at his hearing, what do you think would happen if Mr. Marcus Brown should turn up in the gallery?"

"I'm not so sure you're going to be able to keep that genie in the bottle. It seems to me that not saying a thing is as much a lie to Bo as telling a 'whopper'."

"Then you see my dilemma."

I didn't acknowledge it openly, but I did feel certain empathy. "Well, I'll leave that to you. Tell me something, though. Why do you think it is Bo can't remember anything at all about the day Marcus was killed, yet the story he just told about his grandma and the baby bird has enough details to it that you get the feeling it happened to him just this morning?"

"Do you think I've somehow convinced Bo that he should lie about that topic?"

"Well ... no, I don't think that. I just don't understand how something that happened eighteen or nineteen years ago can be so crisply etched in his memory banks when he can't remember where in the room he sat a couple of days ago."

"That's one of the mysteries that is Bo, I'm afraid. Like his struggles with time and the calendar, I think it has something to do with the emotions he feels at the time. There also appears to be some tie-in to his grandmother as well."

"He has a lot of memories of her?"

"You know, not so much of her specifically. More like things she was trying to teach him."

"Interesting."

"I suppose it might be to a psychologist or mental health professional, but truthfully I can't figure it out. I'm just his attorney."

"Right. Well you've got your hands full in that capacity."

Galax nodded and look down at the tips of his shoes.

"Bo, we must be getting along now. Your auntie will be waiting on us."

"You bet, Mr. Galax. Hey, listen to this!"

Bo fumbled with the buttons on his tape recorder. "*Bo, we must be getting along now. Your auntie will be waiting on us.*"

"What do you think of that, Mr. Galax?" Bo said with giddy excitement. "They ain't nothing I can't remember now!"

"Your gift may have opened Pandora's box," Galax said quietly.

"The good news is the device doesn't have a whole lot of memory. Five or six minutes, max."

"I would dare say that is ample enough time to be troublesome in the wrong situation. I shall have to have a discussion with him about when it is appropriate to play with his new toy."

The three of us moved to the door. Bo paused after Galax opened it for him.

"Mr. Galax, I know you don't want me to speak much about Marcus and all," Bo said. "But there is something I think I need to say to Mr. Daniels. A thing I think is powerful important."

Galax hesitated. "Very well, Bo. But please make it brief."

"Mr. Daniels, Marcus had a message for me to give you just now."

Galax moved his hand to his forehead, bracing himself.

"He did?"

"Yes, sir. I'm not real sure what he meant by it, 'cause you did say you can't see him and all."

An icy chill shot up my spine. "What was his message?"

"Marcus said he'll meet up with you later. Says he needs to show you something."

Chapter 18

The old courtroom was frosty cold. It was empty, and the wear and tear of over a century of use was much more apparent. With what little light there was flickering like the glow from a candle, it was still very dark. At some point the room grew brighter, and I was no longer alone.

"Hello, Mr. Daniels."

"Hello, Marcus," I replied, surprisingly calm. "Your father asked me to pass along his greetings."

"I thank you kindly for that, Mr. Daniels."

"No trouble at all. Why are we here?"

"I'm afraid there's something I have to show you."

"You're not going to scare the bejesus out of me again, are you?"

"Well, sir, what you're about to see is a mighty powerful vision. You might want to prepare yourself."

The middle of the courtroom began to illuminate with a bright, white light. The benches in the gallery disappeared, and in the middle of the room the light began to condense into a tornado-like tunnel. The circle it made on the floor glowed in radiant hues of orange and red, like the coals of a fireplace.

"Marcus, what's happening?" I asked.

"Just keep watching. It's coming."

As he finished speaking, wisps of white smoke appeared around the edges of the red circle on the floor, and with a loud crash it gave way, leaving behind a dark and very ominous looking pit in the middle of the courtroom.

Suddenly my viewpoint changed so that I was looking out from behind the judge's bench. Marcus was looking back at me, and when he swept his arms back toward the gallery, Bo appeared on the edge of the still smoking hole in the floor. He wasn't smiling. He seemed scared and upset, as if he were about to cry.

"Help me, Mr. Daniels!" he pleaded.

Another man appeared at the entrance to the courtroom.

"This one is guilty, Your Honor," I heard a voice shout, as the prosecutor stood up from behind his desk.

An unseen force seemed to pin the man's arms to his sides and slowly lower him to the floor, onto his back. His feet pointed directly towards the hole.

"Please, Mr. Daniels," Bo implored. "You can stop it."

The man slowly slid forward, toward the smoking hole in the courtroom. Bo tried to catch him, but the man slipped easily through his grasp and into the dark abyss. The man let out a horrific scream after falling in; a sound that ended abruptly with a flash of red flames that shot up from the center.

"Mr. Daniels, I must insist that you do something to put an end to this," Trevor Galax said from the defense table.

"For God's sake, what do you want me to do?"

Before I could finish, two more men appeared at the door.

"Mr. Daniels, you have been most thoroughly prepared for the necessary action," Galax shouted. "You must forget your predilections and do something now!"

The two men were once again locked to attention, and as before they were slowly lowered to their backs. As they slid toward the hole, Bo was able to use his heavy frame to pin one of the men under him while struggling desperately to keep a grip on the second man's collar. As his outstretched hand began to lose its hold, his weight shifted and the first man slipped out from under him and into the black hole. This time the flash of red flame sent Bo reeling back, causing him to let go of the second man who also tumbled in. Bo's head reared back and his mouth opened wide, but the roar of the flames drowned out what would have been a deafening yell.

Marcus was standing behind me now, looking out from the judge's bench. "Mr. Daniels, Bo needs your help," he whispered.

Four more men appeared at the entrance to the courtroom. One of the doors behind them began to turn smooth and deep black, as if a taut piece of rubber had replaced the door.

"Mr. Daniels," Bo screamed again. "We don't have much time."

When Bo finished, the outline of a face began to press against the black opening where the door used to be, as if trying to press through. The face wore a terrifying expression of rage, and seemed to grow angrier as the rubbery blackness began to shake violently. It was as if two fist were beating against the darkness from the other side trying to bust through.

"Marcus, what is that? Who's trying to get in?"

"Oh, that's not good Mr. Daniels," Marcus said, a tinge of alarm disrupting the usual calm tone of his voice. "We can't have him getting through. I'm going to have to see to that my own self."

"Just tell me what to do, Marcus" I said, panic beginning to fill every blood vessel.

"Mr. Daniels, you have to look inside yourself. The answer has been with you your whole life if you'll just let it out."

As Marcus spoke, the four men were already sliding toward the hole. Despite desperate effort, Bo was unable to slow a single one of them. The four slid in together, and the flame that flew from the hole shot straight to the ceiling and out along the walls. The heat rocked me back in the judge's chair.

"Marcus, enough with the clues." I shouted. "Please just tell me ..."

Marcus was gone. The flames that had struck the ceiling were harsh enough to set it on fire. It burned quickly, spreading across the room and down the walls. Through the smoke, I could see Bo still standing on the edge of the pit, raising his hands to the sky, staring up through an opening in the flaming roof of the courthouse.

"God, they weren't that bad! They was good fellas inside!" Bo pulled his hands back to his face and began to cry into them.

"Bo!" I screamed to get his attention. "I didn't know what to do!"

Bo looked up at me through the flames and smoke that engulfed the courtroom. "It weren't your fault, Mr. Daniels," he said with a sudden tranquility. "You best get on out of here while you still can. This ain't no way for a man like you to spend eternity."

With that, Bo calmly turned toward the center of the pit and with one great leap threw himself into the abyss. The resulting conflagration blew the roof and walls clean off the courtroom, and sent me flying out onto the front lawn, flat onto my back.

Chapter 19

"Mr. Daniels, are you in there?"

Through a thick, sleepy fog I heard someone banging on the door with determined fists.

"Mr. Daniels, if you're in there you have to wake up!" the man hollered.

"Break it down," I heard a second voice command.

The idea of someone busting in on me in such a confused state roused me to respond. "Hold on a minute!" I yelled out from the darkness. "What's going on?"

"Oh, thank God, Mr. Daniels! It's Hank. Are you alright in there?"

"I think so," I said as I noticed a stream of light flowing up from the middle of the room.

"Stay where you are for a minute. Don't go moving around in there until we get the door open."

"Okay. I'll stay right here."

I could hear people in the room beneath mine, their voices clearer than they should have been. I also heard someone come running down the hallway before stopping abruptly outside my door.

"Hank, I have the key!"

"Give it here," I heard Hank say. "Now, Mr. Daniels, we're going to open up your door. Are you near the bed?"

"I'm still in it."

"Good. Just stay put, then."

Within a couple of seconds the door swung open and the light pushed into the room from behind Hank. It left him a dark, shadowy outline standing in the entrance.

"Mr. Daniels, there's been a little problem with the sprinkler system downstairs," he said. "If you would, please, how's about you reach over carefully there to the night stand and flip on the lamp?"

With the light coming in from the hallway, I got a better bearing on the room and where I was in it. After reaching over to lamp, I slid my feet off the bed and moved to stand up.

"Hold on there!" Hank yelled. "We don't want you to walk around in there just yet."

"What the hell is happening?" I asked.

"Mr. Daniels, you must be one mighty sound sleeper," he said. "There's been a leak in one of the pipes that runs to the sprinkler system in the room just below."

"And?"

"And a piece of the ceiling dropped out. Which, of course, would be your floor."

I crawled to the edge of the bed to get a better look. The light I'd seen was coming from a great hole that had opened up in the middle of my room, and water was still dripping from it and into the room below.

"Jesus, Hank!"

"I don't think you're in any jeopardy, there, Mr. Daniels. Doesn't look like any of the support beams were affected," he said. "All the same, we got a plan to get you out and not take any chances."

"What's the plan?" I asked.

Just then I heard a clanging coming from the hallway, as if someone were running with an aluminum ladder.

"Just a minute, Mr. Daniels," Hank said. "Bring that thing over here. Your end first," he barked into the hallway.

A man in a blue maintenance uniform came to stand next to Hank, and hanging from his right arm was the bottom end of a ladder.

"What's that for?" I asked. "Do you expect me to climb down to the room below us?"

The men in the hallway chuckled.

"No, sir," Hank said with a smile in his voice. "When we slide this here ladder across to you on the floor, it will run opposite to how the floor beams is laid out. If you walk across on them ladder rails, it'll just make extra sure you don't wind up in a new room before we want you to."

The nightmarish image of men delicately balancing on the edge of the abyss reclaimed my thoughts as I gently made my way across the room on the ladder rails. I wondered whether or not I might still be dreaming.

"Bet you never thought you was going to have to walk the high-wire to be able to stay with us, hey, Mr. Daniels?" Hank said as he reached to grab my forearm to guide me the last couple of feet to the hallway.

"It's not a talent I ever thought a need to develop," I said. "How long were you guys banging on my door?"

"A good while. I don't think I could have banged any louder without waking up the dead."

Hank was staring at me with an odd bent to his eyes, as if he still hadn't completely ruled out that I had something to do with the collapse of the floor.

"Now what!" I snapped, which seemed to put Hank off of his suspicions.

"We're gonna put you in a new room for now, Mr. Daniels. We'll be clearing this end of the hotel just to make sure, but we got you another room down the hall, away from all this mess."

"What about my things?"

A couple of the men had already begun to step delicately towards the hole in the floor, as if testing the thickness of the ice over a country pond.

"We'll collect all that up for you, Mr. D. You just get along and see if you can pick up on that dream you was a having when we woke you up."

That was the last thing I wanted to do.

"Fine. How do I get the key?"

"I got it right here. After we get your things gathered—"

I snatched the key out of Hank's hand as soon as he'd pulled it from his pocket, which caught him unaware. I'm sure it struck him as rude, even under the circumstances, but as I walked away I couldn't have cared less. I needed to think.

By the time Hank and his crew had gathered up my belongings from the water damaged room, I had nearly worn a path in the carpet from the edge of the bed to the bathroom sink in my temporary room. I must have splashed enough cold water on my face to irrigate the entire corn field that butted up against the hotel property, as I used the shock of the icy wetness over and over again to confirm my state of consciousness. When Hank finally made it to my new room with my hastily packed bags, I'm certain he wasn't prepared for what was on the other side of his now gentle knock.

"Mr. Daniels, I got your gear."

Hank's eyes bugged out of his head as he took in the full view of me. "Good Lord, Mr. Daniels. How'd you get all wet?"

"I splashed a little water on my face."

"A little? Looks like you been sprayed down good with a—"

"Hank!" I snapped to cut him off. "Leave the big bag, but take the others downstairs, please. I'll be checking out."

Hank lingered a moment, the look on his face suggesting that he was trying to decide between complying with my request or dialing 9-1-1. The door shut, and I looked down and saw that my shirt was soaked almost to the belt line. As I ran my hands back through my hair, water squished along my fingers like ten tiny squeegees. I toweled off as best I could, a full rush of angst filling every vein in my body. I was on the verge of a full-blown episode.

At the front desk, the attendant was overly apologetic.

"I'm sure enough sorry for the troubles with your room, Mr. Daniels," he said before I could speak. "Hank says you're wanting to check out. I hope you'll accept our sincere—"

"Do I need to sign something?"

"No, sir. I've cleared your balance with us. If you'll just hold on a minute, I'm printing you up a receipt that shows—"

"Mail it to me."

I knew my abrupt responses were probably taken as displeasure over the incident with my room, but the truth was I felt responsible in some way. Like, if I hadn't had that crazy dream, the floor in my room would still be intact. It was a little secret I carried with me as I walked out into the parking lot at the Marriott Courtyard, an extra piece of baggage that could only be opened in the presence of one other person. Getting to that person was now my only goal. Everything else had to be put on hold, including the exchange of pleasantries with the hotel staff.

Chapter 20

Driving to the airport that morning my head buzzed with so many thoughts I could barely see the road. Not once, not even while backing out of the parking space at the Marriott Courtyard, did I ever muster the courage to look in the rear-view mirror. As I got closer to Charleston, the white knuckles clenching the steering wheel eased enough to let a little blood back to my fingertips. The more miles I put between myself and Chases Corner, the easier it was to breathe, and by the time I pulled up to the rental car drop-off point in the Charleston airport it was almost back to a normal rhythm.

When the plane finally touched down at La Guardia airport I let out a loud sigh of relief.

"I take it you're a New Yorker," the young woman next to me said.

"I am. What made you come to that conclusion?"

"I don't know, you just seemed a little wired-out," she said. "That is, until we landed. I figured you must be glad to be home."

I caught a cab into Manhattan from the airport, and after arriving at the address I needed, I gave the driver the lucky news that he was about to get a two-fer.

"Look, the bags I put in the trunk need to go on to another address," I said to the cabbie. "Can I trust you?"

"Sure thing," the cab driver replied in a bouncy Middle Eastern accent.

"I need you to take the bags here," I said, handing him a small piece of paper. "When you get there, just leave them with the bellman and tell him the resident in four-twelve will pick them up later today."

I knew from memory that the cab fare would be between ten and eleven-dollars, so I gave the cabbie a twenty. The cabbie's forehead lifted up toward his hairline, indicating he knew it was more than enough.

"You can count on me, sir."

I didn't know for sure if I would ever see my bags again, but it wasn't important. Standing outside my destination, I took the time to call – something I probably should have done before I'd left South Carolina.

"This is Doctor Keller," the voice on the other end said.

"Hey, it's Mark Daniels. Are you working today?"

"I am. At least for the next hour or so."

After hearing his voice on the other end, I started into the building and headed straight for Dr. Keller's office.

"So, can you make time on your schedule of shelling nuts to see me?'

"I don't have any appointments for today if that's what you mean, Mark," he said. "It's Saturday, so I really just came to catch-up on paperwork."

"So, can you see me today or not?"

"Sure. I mean, if you can get here within a decent amount of time."

I'd tackled the flight of stairs to the floor for Dr. Keller's office while we were chatting, and arrived at the door just as he finished.

"Just a minute Mark," he said. "Somebody just came into the reception area here at my office."

"Doc, you really oughta start locking the front door when you're not open for business," I said. The good Dr. Keller caught sight of me about halfway through my chiding.

He slid his cell phone back into the leather clip hanging from his belt. "Mark, it so good to see you," he said, his arms opening for an embrace.

"It's good to see you, too," I said. "You have no idea *how* good."

"When did you get back into town?"

"About forty-five minutes ago."

"That's about the time it takes to get from the airport this time of day."

"Exactly!"

"Oh, I'm sorry. Has it turned bad for you?"

"Oh yeah. It's turned bad alright."

"How are you compared to when we talked the other night?"

"Doc, look at me here," I said raising my arms up in the air.

"Okay, then let's just go on into my office and roll up our sleeves."

That's just what we did. Sleeves, outward appearances, inward fears – we rolled it all up, just like we had back when our meetings were three or four days apart, rather than three or four years. Dr. Keller is the best darn onion peeler I'd ever come across. Layer-by-layer, he pulls it back – subtly at times, so you barely feel it happening, but other times it's more like he's ripping off a band aid that's been stuck across the hairiest part of your leg.

"So, here's what I think we might do," Dr. Keller said after listening to my rambling Chases Corner story. "First, we have to get you back on your medication."

He waited to see if I was going to object, but I'd already given in to the idea long before I left the Marriott Courtyard.

"And considering the latest twist – the dreams – I'm also going to give you something to help you sleep."

"Sleeping is what got me into this mess, Doc."

"I'm not as sure of that as you are," he said. "It sounds like your sleep schedule has been pretty erratic."

"It has."

"Besides, what I'm going to prescribe is more to make you sleep soundly, rather than help with when or for how long."

There was a pause after we got the drug discussion out of the way. Which, from experience, I knew meant we were heading back to the psychotherapeutic dissection.

"Now, Mark, it seems to me we need to talk some more about Karen."

"Okay, here we go."

"There's no reason to close up with me. If there's nothing there, we'll move on. But just sticking your head in the—"

"Doc, I just don't see how she has anything to do with what's been happening."

"And you wouldn't. These things don't work on the surface."

"So you're saying that my break up with Karen is causing me to have bizarre dreams featuring a dead black boy.'

"I didn't say that. Something has your subconscious rumbling, however. There doesn't have to be a direct connection, you know. The dots don't always line up so perfectly."

I considered putting up a fight, but knew Dr. Keller's analytical mind would only take it as proof we needed to go down that road.

"Look, Doc, I'll talk about her with you if that's what you want," I said giving in. "But if you start by making the lovely Karen McDonough the focal point of your diagnosis, you're gonna miss a whole lot of important stuff here."

"I understand."

"Karen calling off our engagement was *not* a surprise to me!"

Dr. Keller nodded his head in silence before moving on with his agenda anyway. "Let's go at this from another angle. How long were you and Karen together?

"Almost two-years. I told you that on the phone"

"Yes, you did. That's a long time for you," the doctor said, with an emphasis I suppose I deserved. "What was it about Karen that attracted you to her in the first place?"

"So, let's see. The chosen strategy for this part of our session is to get me waxing melodically about how wonderful Karen was, and then you'll see if you can break down my emotional barriers and get me to open up more about my feelings."

Dr. Keller sat expressionless for a moment. "Yes, I suppose that's exactly what I had in mind. Can we proceed?"

"Sure. I just wanted to make sure I understood my role."

We spent the next hour or so rehashing my relationship with Karen, and when we were done I was fairly confident I hadn't cracked. I really didn't think I could. There had been the one moment of weakness when I'd decided that I needed to get Karen out of my system and had written the goodbye letter back at the hotel, but the idea had been put in my head by the good Dr. Keller in the first place. And the fact was, the little purging exercise hadn't done a thing to put an end to the nightmares.

It was then that the good doctor caught me off guard.

"Mark, tell me about your very first love."

"What do you mean, like the first woman I ever had feelings for?"

"It doesn't have to be a woman."

"Whoa! If that question is meant for me to explore my true sexual orientation, let's stop right there. I don't need to come out of the closet, believe me."

"No, no. I mean that it doesn't have to be a mature woman. For most folks, their first love is a young girl."

"Oh, right. You scared me a little bit there," I said, pausing to consider the new angle on the question. "Let's see, I suppose that would be ..."

He sat patiently while I ran through the memory banks, before ever so slowly a face began to come back.

"I can almost see her," I said. "But you know, I can't remember her name to save my life."

"That's a little out of the ordinary," Dr. Keller replied.

"It was twenty-some years ago, Doc."

"Yes, but for most people it's like remembering where you were when Kennedy was assassinated or when the planes struck the towers on 9/11," he said. "Memories of a first love are often some of the strongest that people store away."

What he said made sense, which made the whole exercise that much more frustrating. I stayed at it a while, as the good doctor left me to struggle with it on my own. Eventually, sensing a growing exasperation on my part, he started to throw an occasional probe at me.

"Was she pretty?" he asked.

"I think she was."

He let me stew on the answer.

"You say you remember her little bit?" he tossed in after a few minutes.

"I do. Kind of."

"What color hair did she have."

"Black," I said, surprising myself. "She had black hair ... and it was really short."

Sensing something, Dr. Keller backed away again, almost as if he knew that the dam holding back the memory was beginning to break apart.

"She was Italian." I added. "I remember thinking that she should never let her hair grow long, because it would get in the way of her huge smile."

"That's a nice thought," Dr. Keller encouraged.

The details had started filling in like a crossword puzzle, before suddenly coming together in one glorious picture. "Her name was Jill!" I said proudly. "Her name was Jill DeAngelo." A smile rolled across my face as the details of Jill DeAngelo began to give way to memories of us together, busting out from some locked room in my head. "There is one really fantastic moment I can remember with her," I said after a few minutes.

"Tell me about it," Dr. Keller said right away.

"It was in the middle of summer. I was fourteen, maybe fifteen. Jill was a year younger."

"Okay ... go on."

"Well, I went over to her house one night – I can't remember why – but her folks would only let her come out to the front stoop to sit with me. It must have been late."

"So you were sitting on the front stoop with her, and ..."

"We were holding hands, leaning back up against the stairs and looking up at the most clear and crisp night-time sky I had ever seen."

"Lots of stars and such?"

"Yeah. They seemed to be jumping right out of the black background at us. As if you could almost reach out and grab one."

"It sounds idyllic. Did you and Jill talk about the sky that night?"

"Yeah, we did. I remember coming across the Big Dipper. I'd never really been able to pick it out before; I'm not sure I ever tried. I'd seen it in pictures but never real-time like that."

"And did Jill see it, too?"

"Of course. I pointed it out to her. You know, like I always knew where it was. I think she was impressed."

"Okay," Dr. Keller said with a chuckle. "Then what happened?"

"I did something – well, romantic I guess."

"You? Romantic?"

"Yeah! Believe it or not."

"So what was this romantic thing you did,?"

"I picked out the last star in the Big Dipper."

"Yes, And?"

"I told her that star had been there for billions of years, and that it would be there for billions more."

"Very smooth beginning."

"I thought so."

"But there's more, right?"

"Yes. I told her that the only difference between the first few billion and the billions that were yet to come, was that from that point forward the star on the end of the Big Dipper would always be *our* star."

"Ooh. Very nice."

"I also told her that no matter how long I lived – even if it were a million years – every time I looked at that star I would think of her."

"Geez. It sounds like you already had the makings of a writer there, Mark."

"You know, I wish I had written it down back then. Truth is, I didn't even remember it until just now."

"And did she melt into your arms?"

"You could say that. It was one hell of a moment. We stayed there on her porch for hours that night, never saying another word. Her father literally had to come out and chase me off."

Dr. Keller sat quietly with me for a while, both us just soaking in the imagery and enjoying my memory. He maybe even more than I.

"She sounds like a wonderful girl," he finally said to break the silence. "Whatever happened to Miss DeAngelo?"

I pondered his question for a bit, digging around in closets full of old memories. Eventually, I stumbled into the one that held the answer, and the sweet taste attached to my fabulous reminiscence of Jill DeAngelo came to a bitter end.

"What's the matter, Mark? Your face just went white."

"Things didn't turn out very well for Jill and me," I said.

"You broke up?"

"Not really," I said, a sudden sadness welling up behind my eyes. "She died."

I had stunned even my very experienced listener. He paused a minute with his mouth half-open.

"I'm so sorry, Mark."

"Me too."

"How did she die?"

"She was hit by a car."

"Oh, how awful."

"Yeah, but the worst part is that I think I knew about it ahead of time."

Dr. Keller was again caught off guard, and seemed to be shopping carefully for his next question. Almost as if he didn't want to ask it. "It was an accident, right?"

"Yes. It was an accident."

"I don't understand, then. How could you possibly have known about it ahead of time?"

I waited a minute before answering; not sure if I wanted to. "I had a dream."

"You had a dream about the accident? A premonition?"

"Not really."

"I don't understand."

I almost couldn't let it out, but after a while I guess I just decided that if not him, who else could I tell? "Someone came to me in the dream and warned me that Jill was in danger," I said softly. "Said it was up to me. That I was the only one that could help her."

Chapter 21

Dr. Keller didn't get the chance to catch up on his paperwork that Saturday. If anything, I might have created a whole new stack for him. Touched-off by the sudden remembrance of the lovely Jill DeAngelo, a rushing river roared its way through the early years of my life, washing long forgotten memories downstream. They collected like silt in the delta that was Dr. Keller's office, and after Jill came back into my life that afternoon, Dr. Keller and I spoke for hours.

The odd thing was that Jill didn't remain the topic of our conversation for very long. Instead, we seemed to meander through my childhood, reaching all the way back to the imaginary friends I'd invented as a child. It was new ground for Dr. Keller and I to cover, and after so many years of rehashing the same personality quirks over and over, my therapist seemed to draw new energy from it. Eventually, he focused in on how my parents had convinced me to say goodbye to all of them.

"Sweetheart, an imagination is a wonderful thing to have," my mother used to say. "But I'm sure Kevin Mooney would enjoy having someone to play with. Why don't you go over and see what Kevin's doing?"

Kevin Mooney was the dorky kid next door, whose mother also fought a never-ending battle to get him out of the house to play. Most times Kevin would sneak a book with him when he would come out to play, and then he'd sit in a corner somewhere reading; leaving me to get back to playtime with my imaginary pals. But as long as we were together, both his mom and mine were satisfied that we were developing the social skills we were going to need as adults.

My dad, on the other hand, was not as delicate about the subject of my imaginary friends. By the time I was ten, he'd had enough. "Look, this crap is going to end!" he said one day, after catching me talking to myself in my bedroom. "You're ten years old, for God's sake. People are going to think you're crazy as a bed-bug if you keep talking to yourself. I will *not* have a son of mine running around making people think he's not right in the head."

His words had been building for awhile, so I'd mostly hidden my pals from him before getting caught in the act that day. I wasn't really surprised by his reaction, but *he* was surprised when he found out my friends were still hanging about.

"Now you get rid of those imaginary friends of yours right here and now, or I swear I'll be back to snap their little necks and put such a welt on your behind you won't sit for a week."

By that point in my childhood I'd developed a tough enough layer of skin across my butt that his personal threat didn't really shake me all that much. I did recall being very concerned for my pals, however, and though it wasn't immediate, shortly thereafter they all began to heed my warnings and didn't come around any longer. For reasons he chose not to elaborate on that Saturday, Dr. Keller focused in on that part of my life, and to a large degree on my relationship with my father. I'd always thought shrinks were supposed to be obsessed with the maternal relationship, but for the balance of our session the good doctor seemed bent on digging through the fraternal side of my upbringing.

It was sometime after five o'clock that afternoon before I finally made my way out of Dr. Keller's office and back into the streets of the city I loved so much. I hadn't noticed New York on my arrival, but with over five hours of soul searching behind me, the world slowed enough for me to take it in. Like a guest to a house-party that I forgot to say hello to, the Big Apple seemed to be waiting awkwardly for me to acknowledge it.

"Hello, New York!" I said, raising my hands and sucking in a deep breath of the stale city air.

A cabbie pulled up right in front of me, and I smiled.

"Where to?" the driver asked.

"I need to go to West 32nd Street and 7th Ave, but I have to hit a pharmacy along the way."

"There are plenty of them between here and there. Did you have a particular one in mind?"

"Not really. Pick the one that's easiest for you to wait while I dash in a drop-off a prescription."

Dr. Keller had offered to call in my drug order, but in the years that had elapsed since filling my last prescription, the pharmacy I'd always used had shut its doors. The one the cabbie chose was far enough away from my apartment to be discreet, but close enough for me to walk home after the pharmacy had agreed to deliver when ready.

As I strolled through my neighborhood, for the first time in a few days I was feeling like Mark Daniels again.

"Good evening, Mr. Daniels," Marty the doorman sang. "I have your bags inside behind my counter."

He scrambled for the bags and returned to place them at my feet, before casually holding out his right hand.

"Marty, you have no idea how good it feels to be back in a place where people clip you for even the most mundane of tasks performed on your behalf," I said, peeling off a twenty.

"What's that, Mr. Daniels?"

"It's good to be home."

"Well, you look pretty tired."

"You have no idea. And just as soon as the pharmacy delivers a prescription I'm having filled, I'm going to hit the sack. Can you bring it up when it gets here?"

"Sure thing. It's good to have you back."

The elevator pinged just as Marty was finishing his welcome, and he reached in to push the button for my floor while he stood against the elevator door.

"I'll bring your medicine right up, Mr. Daniels. Do you think you'll be ordering out for dinner tonight?"

I hadn't given a single thought to food all day long, but when the doorman mentioned dinner I felt a hunger pang in the pit of my stomach.

"What do you feel like?" Marty asked, deciphering my hesitation as a yes.

"I don't know. Maybe some New York Italian."

"The usual from DiNovio's?"

"Yeah," I said with a satisfied smile. "The usual from DiNovio's would be great."

Fresh from a marathon therapy session and safe in my detached little apartment, by the time Marty delivered my pills and food, all signs of anxiety had left my body completely. What those symptoms left behind was an exhausted shell of a man, and it took great effort just to finish my plate of DiNovio's lasagna. It was good, but not quite as delightful as it might have been had I been able to sip a glass of hearty Chianti with it. But I was back on the meds, and after taking one yellow pill and one blue pill, my long return from Chases Corner was officially over.

I slept like a baby. Not a break, not a twitch, and not the slightest hint of a dream.

Chapter 22

My first morning back in New York the sun made its usual run between buildings, and as the inside of my eyelids went from deep black to bright orange it began to feel as though I'd never left the city at all. As if the trip to Chases Corner itself had been a dream, and that the Hodges story would once again be waiting for me when I went into the office. It would have been the perfect solution to the bizarre events of the previous week. But when I did finally roll over to turn away from the sunlight beating in, seeing the two bottles of pills on my nightstand forced me to re-wind everything back from that point. I was back on my meds; things had gotten bad enough to bring Dr. Keller back into my life; and worst of all, and there really was a Chases Corner, South Carolina.

I also had a story to get back to. Although it was a Sunday the news never stops, and the national desk at the *Times* never closes. After I'd ordered up breakfast and read through my copy of the Sunday paper, there didn't seem to be any huge stories breaking that would keep the whole staff working through the weekend. That meant that the odds were good that Carl wouldn't be in the office either, and since I hadn't bothered to tell him I was coming back, I didn't really want to bump into him. The first thing he would have wanted to know was why I had returned, and I knew full-well I would not have been able to blow smoke up his backside.

After a long, hot shower and shave, I was starting to feel more like me than I had in the previous couple of days, and I figured my karma was changing. After rustling up a cab and breezing through the easy Sunday morning traffic, it was just a little after nine o'clock in the morning when I signed in at the security desk at *The Times*. I rode the elevator alone, another sign that nothing much was happening in the world, and as I stopped on the floor for the national desk my walk was as light as a feather. But as I passed through the reception area and into the open bay of the news room, I suddenly felt as though I were wearing fifty-pound shoes.

The instant he saw me, Carl waved in my direction, then curled his index finger back toward his face a few times — one of two very distinct gestures he used to get you to come by his office.

"Carl?" I said, speaking first. "I didn't think you'd be in on such a slow news day."

He was already standing by the time I made it to the door to his office. There was someone sitting in the chair opposite him, but at first I didn't recognize the back of the head.

"I'm sure you didn't," Carl said. "Considering you didn't even bother to tell me you were coming back in the first place."

"Sneaky little bastard, isn't he," the man sitting said.

Bart Kennedy turned in his chair to look in my direction.

"What the hell is *he* doing here?" I asked, irritably.

"I don't know about you, but I'm screwing up a perfectly good chance to sleep till noon," Bart said. "Where have you been, you piece of crap?"

I was too angry to look away from Carl. "Am I the reason you're missing church this morning, Carl" I sniped. "Not to mention keeping the sloth over there from lying in till noon nursing a hangover?"

"Hey, I don't have a hangover!" Bart complained. "At least, not one that needs nursing."

Carl's eyes locked on mine for a few moments of silent combat. "Your return seems a little stealth-like," Carl finally said.

"Don't *even* talk to me about stealth," I shouted. "Since I've only spoken to one person since I've been back, I'm guessing your little spy is still on the payroll."

"Don't go getting all huffy with me, Mark. *You* signed the waiver allowing Dr. Keller to talk to me."

"Signed the waiver? That was four friggin' years ago?"

"Yes, and it was a condition of your continued employment. It remains so today."

"What? No statute of limitations? No time off for good behavior?"

"I'm afraid not."

"So, let me see if I have this right. Until I retire, or just plain old quit, you're going to be all-up in my personal business, like some never ending cycle of probation."

"Unfortunately, that would be correct!"

"That's a bunch of baloney!"

After a while, I plopped down in the chair next to Bart, defeated.

"Just tell me this, then. Was it you that put old trash-mouth here up to calling me at the hotel in South Carolina?"

"I asked him to check in on you, yes."

"Why? I'd only been gone for one day?"

"I didn't hear from you for almost twenty-four hours, Mark. When you didn't return any of my calls, I started to worry that—"

"I told you. I forgot to turn my cell phone on!"

I could tell by his unflinching eyes and zombie-like expression that Carl had slipped into his immovable-rock role. While he may very well have let me rant for a while longer, I knew from experience that the effort expended would be wasted. Sensing that I knew I was beaten, after a few minutes Carl began to build a bridge between his rock and my hard place.

"Hey look, we care about you, Mark," Carl said. "Believe it or not, that's really what all this is about."

"You care about me?"

"That's right, we do," Carl insisted. "You said it yourself: I'm missing Sunday service and the lush here came in early on a weekend. That's gotta count for something."

Arguing further would have just been rhetoric. The ending wasn't going to change.

"Okay," I said after a pause. "So why the ambush? Why not just call me or send me an email telling me you were worried so that I could explain?"

Carl and Bart looked at each other with eyes that were suddenly bouncy and nervous.

"Come on, Carl," I said. "What is it you have to tell me that you had to catch me like a rat to be able to say it?"

Carl worked on steadying himself while Bart just scratched his neck and looked out the window.

"I'm thinking this might not be the best time for you to be out of town," Carl said.

"I see. So, how is it that you're expecting me to be able to cover this story? You said yourself I have to be there."

Bart stood up and walked over to the window, as if trying to get further away from the coming explosion.

"You're kidding me!" I said.

"I wish I was," Carl said.

"You're taking me off the story?"

"I feel very strongly that with everything that's going on right now, you would be best served if you and Dr. Keller could—"

"Damn it, Carl! Just say it. You're taking me off the story."

"Okay - I'm taking you off the story."

I wasn't sure I had a right to be shocked by Carl's decision. If he'd caught me twenty-four hours earlier, he would have had all the evidence he needed, but by that time Dr. Keller had restored the fighter in me. After a little cooling down, I picked up the gauntlet and threw it right back at him. "Well, screw you. I'm not giving this thing up. Especially not to a drunk."

"Hey!" Bart snapped. "I resemble that remark."

"Did Carl tell you that it's dry down there in Chases Corner, Mr. Party Animal?"

"No. He didn't mention that."

"So, Carl, you'd rather have a guy down there covering the story with the DTs, is that it?"

"I don't think it will kill Bart to go a few weeks without a drink," Carl said.

"A few weeks?" Bart snapped

"There you go, Mr. Editor," I said. "Looks like you have a choice between an alcoholic without access to booze, or a potential nut-job that came back specifically to get his medication."

"You're back on your meds?" Carl asked.

"I am," I replied. "What's the matter? Didn't the good Dr. Keller feed you that little piece of intelligence?"

"Actually, no, I don't think it came up "

"There you go then. I'd like it put into the record that I voluntarily came back here to get my prescription refilled. No one had to come get me and drag me back."

Carl sat quietly as he took in the latest twist. It seemed as though I had created an opening.

"I'm proud of you for that," Carl finally said. "I know it took a lot. That's a big step for you."

"Well, thank you. I may be crazy, but I'm not a fool."

Carl thought things over a while longer, as if playing out all possible scenarios in his head before speaking. Bart seemed to relax a bit, probably sensing he was going to get off the hook.

"I'm still going to send Bart down with you to help out," Carl said. "This thing is starting to feel like it could blow up pretty big."

"I could live with that," I said. "But let's just make sure vodka-boy over here knows I sit first chair."

"You could sit first, second and third chair for all I care," Bart said. "By the way, Charleston's not a dry county, is it?"

"No, it's not," I said. "And if you're really going to come down to be of help, that might be a good place for you to start."

"Are you talking about following up on the Librarian's trail to the Aycock boy?" Carl asked.

"I am. Before I left Chases Corner, Attorney Galax informed me that he knows how to get in touch with him."

"Did he?"

"He did. He even offered to broker a meeting at his offices."

"Well, then, I'm your man for that gig," Bart said. "You head down to Bumpkinville, and I'll go check out what the Southern belles wear when they go to the beach."

"Look, if you're going to do some actual work, then by all means come on along," I snapped. "But I've got a lot to get done myself, and I don't need to be worrying about having to bail you out somewhere."

"Oh, relax you stiff," Bart said. "No one has ever accused me of not getting the job done."

Bart was right about that. In spite of his penchant for the high-life, he always had managed to do the work, and do it well. He was always a top-notch reporter when you got past all the nonsense. Bart let his rare moment of seriousness hang in the air a few moments before chasing it away.

"Besides, I've covered tougher stories than this from a bar," Bart said. "You get more good information from the inside of a gin mill than any other place I know of."

It's hard to stay mad at Bart for very long, mostly because Bart never stays mad back. It's just not in his nature. "Fine." I said. "Do you need me to call ahead to Attorney Galax?"

"I do not."

"It's settled then," Carl said. "Bart will head to Charleston on Monday to look for this Aycock fellow, and the two of you will keep each other – and me – updated."

"Do you want me to book you a seat on my flight tomorrow?" I asked Bart.

"Depends. Which one are you taking."

"The first flight out," I said.

"I'll pass," Bart said. "I prefer to put my hours in on the other end of the day."

"Whatever."

"So, Bart, thanks for helping out on this," Carl said. "Can you give Mark and me a couple of minutes here?"

"Sure thing. I'll head back to my place and snuggle up with that hangover nurse." Bart stood and thrust his hand out to me. "See you in paradise, old buddy."

"I'm excited beyond words," I said. "Just see if you can stay out of trouble until I get over to Charleston."

Bart just smiled and took his leave.

"Okay. I was going to wait to do this, but since you're back on your meds..." Carl said after Bart had shut the door behind him.

"Do what? What are you talking about?"

Carl reached down and slid out the bottom drawer to his desk. "I have the items Karen left for you."

He pulled three items from the drawer. A plastic shopping bag that appeared to hold sundry items, such as shaving cream, razors and the like; a blue and red tie with the Yankees logo patterned across it; and finally, an interoffice envelope – the type with the clasp at the top to keep papers in. When he put the envelope on the desk, I could tell from the bulge in it there was a key ring with a couple keys.

"I promise you, I haven't looked inside," Carl said.

"I don't think it makes any difference."

"I know. I just wanted to make sure that you knew that even with our little waiver, we do have boundaries."

One little metal clasp on an envelope represented the boundaries between my life and Carl Odette. It seemed silly. "Right. Boundaries. I'm not even going to touch that, Carl."

"Let's not go down that road again," Carl said. "What were you hoping to accomplish here today."

"A little more research. I was going to dig a little deeper for info on the Catholic priest that's been visiting with Bo."

"Well, don't go duplicating effort," Carl said. "The Librarian left a file on the guy here on my desk. He must have come in yesterday to work on it."

Carl reached out across the desk to offer me the file. "Keep it," he said. "I know the Librarian wouldn't have left me original documents."

I could have worked a month of Sundays doing my own research, and still would not have come up with the type of quality info the Librarian can provide in an hour surfing the web.

"That's one thing off my list,' I said, as I took the folder from Carl.

"What's the next thing?" Carl asked.

"Since its Sunday, I think I'm going to go to church."

Chapter 23

Later that morning, in unusually brisk weather I walked six blocks from a subway stop in Brooklyn. Thick clouds had crept in and kept the day from warming as it should, and the cold added a quickness to my step. As I came upon the home of the Soldiers of Zion, where Leyland Johnston was the pastor emeritus, I was as eager to get inside a church as I had ever been. *Pastor emeritus* was the title the reverend had taken when the winds of controversy had been swirling around his bigger-than-life persona. While that meant he no longer had to bother with the day-to-day chores of ministering to his flock, he still maintained a platform from which to speak his mind at any time. Something that for the man I'd come to know down in Alabama, was as essential as the air he breathed.

They just don't make churches like the Soldiers of Zion anymore. The building was the former home of the Our Lady of the Assumption Catholic congregation, something I knew from my days of playing basketball against them as kid. As I approached the reborn version, it seemed from the sounds of the activity inside that the old church had found a new life; albeit, under the banner of a slightly different theology.

Services were already underway and I could hear unrestrained praising of the Lord seeping out of every crack and crevice in the old building. As I opened one of the big, ornate doors left over from the church's Catholic days, a loud rush of the choir clapping and singing its way through a fast-paced spiritual number spilled out into the streets. Pausing in the back, I watched as the congregation behaved as if this was what they'd been waiting for all week long. It was such a huge contrast to my upbringing inside St. Luke's Cathedral; a solemn place where God showed up on Sunday to look inside our hearts, and help us feel guilty for what we'd been doing Monday through Saturday.

After I had slipped into the last pew in the church, the choir started into its third refrain of an old gospel song, and I found myself clapping along, even trying to mouth a few of the words. I spotted Reverend Lee right away, seated just in front of the choir in a splendid purple and gold robe. When he began to make his way to the podium, the verse was intermittently overlapped by shouts of "hallelujah" and "go get 'em, Reverend." At the precise moment the choir had reached the end of the last refrain, with impeccable timing the reverend gently laid his bible on the rostrum. He kept his eyes trained on the book as the congregation replaced the song with wild cheers and many more hallelujahs. Slowly, he raised his hands up over his head, and the crowd responded with a quiet hush.

As he looked up from his bible, Reverend Lee's eyes went straight to mine. "To those of you that are new to our services this morning, I welcome you to the Soldiers of Zion church," he said, still staring directly at me. "God has brought you here this morning for a reason. He has given you a purpose to your life, and we hope that we can help you along the way to understanding *what ... that ...purpose ... is!*"

Taking their cue from his bold emphasis, the congregation erupted again. The reverend had never taken his eyes off me, which caused half of the screaming crowd to turn back in my direction to have a look. As conspicuous as I already was, I didn't know if he had singled me out to make a connection or to make me feel uncomfortable. He accomplished both.

"Now, now," he said, raising his hands and quieting the crowd again. "I know that some of you think that our God is a stand-offish kind of a god."

Reverend Lee waited through shouts of: "No, no, Reverend," and, "Not us, Reverend Lee," – as if they were choreographed to be part of his sermon.

"That He sits back on that big throne of His and simply watches things play out down here."

"Not our God, Reverend," someone shouted from the front row. "Our God ain't no couch potato."

The reverend chuckled along with the congregation. "No, indeed. Our God is not a coach potato. He likes to be a part of the *action!*" A preacher's tone and rhythm had begun to take hold of the reverend's words, and his flock was responding. "We may not see it firsthand. Most of us are not as blessed as that."

"That's not true, Reverend. We see his work every day," someone called out, and the crowd agreed.

"Oh, brother," the reverend said turning directly to the man. "You see his work, sure enough. But do you see his heavenly workers?"

"Tell us what you mean to say, Reverend," came another voice from the congregation. "Tell it, Reverend Lee. Give us the word," added another.

Reverend Lee paused for a few beats, adding to the anxious expectations of his flock. "It is the *angel* that God uses to do his work amongst us," he said in a much more conversational voice. "Beautiful and innocent, pure and wonderful, He blesses us with angels to do his work down here."

"You'd be one yourself, Reverend," a woman shouted, followed by a chorus of amen's.

"Sister, now you know full well you are *not* looking at an angel up here at this podium," the reverend replied. "Why, *The New York Times* can give you all the evidence you need to take down that myth."

There was a chorus of boos at the mention of *The Times*, which Reverend Lee put an end to by raising his right hand. "Now, now," he said to settle the group. "We all know that Reverend Leyland A. Johnston ain't no angel."

The congregation seemed unsure how to respond to the reverend's admission.

"The fact is, I am a man. No better or worse than any one of you out there."

"You're a good man, Reverend," someone finally replied, followed by a dozen or so affirmations from the rest of the group.

"That is for you and for God to decide," he said. "But I am a *man*, sure enough. A flawed man: a man that has sinned. A man humbled by those who are anointed by the same blood that washed across Israel, flowing straight from the cross of our Lord and Savior, Jesus Christ."

The crowd cheered at the mention of Jesus, but seemed to know collectively that there was still another shoe to drop.

"I can't point to the angels I speak of," he added when the cheers had died down enough. "I know they are here with us. I can't see them, but I know for certain sure they are here."

The reverend paused, probably waiting for the group to prod him along, which they eventually did.

"By all that is holy, I wish I could see them," he said. "It must be a glorious sight to behold – to look directly into the face of an angel." He looked back in my direction. "And while I may not be able to see them, I'm here to tell you that there are those among us that *can*, those who have a very special gift – one that allows them to see and even to *speak* with God's heavenly angels."

The crowd erupted, though still slightly restrained, sensing this was not yet the reverend's crescendo.

"I don't know why some of us can and some of us can't. Don't know why God chooses those He does to be blessed with such a gift." The reverend had taken his eyes off me as he waited for the latest round of hoopla to fade, but then found me again, for a third time. "But I do know this: a gift is not a gift until it is *received!*"

"Then give us some more," someone shouted. "We'll take all you got!"

The Reverend Lee smiled and chuckled, setting off a slow wave of laughter that rolled from front to back.

"Very well, then," the reverend said. "I'll offer you this one slice of wisdom, words straight from the mouth of God himself. In Genesis 31:11 we find these words: *And the Angel of God spoke unto me in a dream...and I said 'Here am I'.*"

Both the congregation and I got a little uneasy as Reverend Lee continued to stare in my direction. By the time he finally moved off me and onto another topic, I'd already decided to make a graceful exit as soon as possible. When the congregation jumped to their feet for a new song by the choir, I beat a path out the same way I'd come in.

There was a small problem with that move. With nowhere to go until services ended, I would have to wait it out in the mean streets of Brooklyn – and the Bedford-Stuyvesant area at that. After bounding down the concrete stairs on the way out, I hung around on the sidewalk a moment or two, suddenly uncomfortable with my surroundings. I slowly retreated a stair or two closer to the entrance, caught between the proverbial rock and hard place. By the time service had come to a close, I'd inched my way back up to the top stair of the church. The big door nearly hit me in the forehead when the congregation began to file out.

The reverend was the first through the door, to be in position for glad handing and baby hugging as the faithful strolled out.

"There is our most honored guest!" he said, reaching with two hands in the same way he had back in Chases Corner. "Mr. Daniels, I can't tell you how surprised and satisfied I was to see you in the back of my church this morning."

"Really? It felt like you were trying to put a bulls-eye on me in there, Reverend."

"I assure you, my comments this morning were prepared well in advance," he said. "I had no idea you would be joining us."

"Then should I just assume that *accepting one's gift* is your latest hook?"

"Oh. I don't know about any *hook* as you call it," he said before acknowledging the first of the congregation in line with yet another two-handed shake. "But those are the words the Lord has put into my head as of late."

A line had formed to the reverend's right, and since I was standing off his left shoulder the parishioners were awkwardly reaching out to shake my hand as well.

"Malcolm, Mr. Daniels is probably not as used to having his hand wrung by so many good people," he said to his big assistant. "Before they pull his arm off, can you please take him into my office in the rectory while I finish my duties here?"

"Sure thing, Reverend," Malcolm replied, grabbing the back of my arm at the triceps muscle and guiding me back into the church. Once inside, he let go off his firm grip and walked slightly ahead of me to clear a path through the stragglers that still mingled. Inside the rectory, the big man stopped at a door to an office and stood to the side.

"You can wait in here, Mr. Daniels," he said with a sweeping arm motion.

"Thank you," I said. For some reason my voice cracked with a tinge of nervousness.

Malcolm waited for me to sit down, as if to send a message that this was all I was allowed to do. "Mr. Daniels, I never got a chance to thank you for not giving me a 'thorough thrashing' back there at the Marriott," he said, wearing a somewhat menacing look as he reminded me of my comment back in Chases Corner.

I swallowed hard before trying to stumble through a response. "You know, I was only trying to ... I didn't really mean that I could ..."

When a huge grin finally pulled itself across Malcolm's face, I realized he was having a little fun at my expense.

"Good one, Malcolm. You had me going there."

"The reverend will be right with you," he said with a chuckle. "Now you stay put!" He wagged his big finger at me before taking leave. I heard him snort with laughter as he made his way back down the hallway.

Despite the now obvious humor in his words, I stayed put as he had suggested. I did feel a little like the lamb in the lion's den. As a barely-believer, it was somewhat intimidating to be sitting amongst all the signs of religion that were plastered throughout Reverend Lee's office. Jesus was everywhere, depicted in all the many scenes Christians have come to remember him by:

Jesus in the manger, Jesus on the temple mount, there was even a painting of a black Jesus hanging from a cross behind the reverend's desk.

The one thing that was absent from the walls of the office were pictures of Lee Johnston himself. The Reverend Lee I had come to know over the years was a megalomaniac. If Jesus were seated at the right hand of the Father, I'd always figured Reverend Lee saw himself as the guy to the left. But aside from an oversized wood-block nameplate someone must have carved for him, there were no other signs that this office belonged to the Reverend Leyland Johnston. In a million years, I never would have guessed that about him. But there was a lot about the new Reverend Lee I couldn't match up with the one I had come to know in Alabama.

Next to the leather Queen Ann chair I was sitting in, there was a round, maple coffee table with a high-poled lamp built through the center. Around the lamp pole were various religious magazines, neatly spread in an overlapping circle with just their titles showing. Sandwiched in between a copy of *The Christian Life* and *The Weekly Monitor* was something that looked more like a pamphlet. Unlike the glossy covers of the magazines, it was printed on plain, matte finish paper. In simple black lettering the title read: "The Blessings of Angels and the Fragile-X Gene: How God is Bringing His People Back to a State of Acceptance."

I reached across the table to snatch up the pamphlet, and just as I'd settled back into the chair to get after it, Reverend Lee made yet another timely appearance.

"That is perhaps the single most important paper I have read in many years, Mark," he said. "I see it has quickened your curiosity as well."

"Actually, I haven't read a word of it yet, Reverend," I said. "Except for the title, that is."

"By all means, then, please take it with you. Perhaps it is a gift I can give." He was standing in the doorway, sporting a satisfied smirk, and seemingly waiting to see what I would do with the paper.

Giving in, I slipped the paper into my bag. "Thank you. Since as you say, a gift is only a gift if it is *received*. I don't see how I can turn it down."

"That is an excellent habit to get into," the reverend said as he closed the door and made his way behind his desk. "To give is holy; to receive, divine."

"Okay. I think you may have that a little bit jumbled, but I get the message … *again*," I said. "Reverend, I've come a long way this morning."

"Yes, of course you have. My apologies. How can I help you on this fine day God has made?" He settled in behind his desk as he spoke.

I reached for my tape recorder. "Reverend, do you mind if …"

"I do."

"You do mind? Or is it all right to—"

"I do mind."

I paused a beat, but the truth was I would've been surprised if he'd said yes. I pulled out my composition book instead. "Reverend, I'm heading back to Chases Corner in the morning and I wanted to get up with you for a little follow-up to our conversation at Molly's."

"Follow up?"

"We didn't really get into much depth about your involvement with Bo's case during lunch last week, and I've still got a few questions."

"Yes, just the mention of our lunch together brings back the taste of Molly's fried chicken. I think we both can be forgiven if we were distracted by such a meal."

As he spoke I actually had the same sensation, but pushed on. "Let's start from the beginning, and forgive me if ask for a break from the metaphors," I said, eliciting a small nod from the reverend. "Can you tell me just exactly how you became aware of the Buckminster case?"

"That's easy enough. It was a very old and dear friend that exposed me to Bo's predicament."

"How long ago was that?"

"Two years ago. Perhaps I knew about his case for longer than that, but I didn't really pay much attention until I agreed to visit with Bo in prison."

"So, this old friend asked you to go to South Carolina to speak with Bo?"

'In a manner of speaking. And I have been blessed ever since."

'How so?"

The reverend massaged the back of his own neck while he looked to the ceiling for the right words. "Mark, you of all people would know that there was a period in my life where I struggled a bit over God's purpose for me," he admitted. "Let's just say that meeting Bo started the process by which I realized He really *does* have a purpose for me."

I was determined to keep Reverend Lee from getting metaphysical on me. "Who is this dear friend you speak of?" I asked.

"A former pastor here. A fellow *man of the cloth*, if you will."

"One of the associate ministers from your church?"

"Oh, no. We were not contemporary."

It took me a few seconds to decipher the reverend's riddle. "But you founded this church, isn't that right?"

"I did indeed."

"Are you saying this *colleague* of yours is a Catholic Priest?"

"He was at one time."

Bizarre flashbulbs were going off in my head. "Would his name happen to be Father Michael Hanaway?"

"It is indeed. Father Hanaway and I became acquainted as he was completing his duties as the last parish priest for Our Lady of the Assumption church."

It was an odd connection to say the least, but it got my blood pumping. "You met Father Hanaway fourteen years ago?"

"Or thereabouts."

"And he reached back to tell you about his work with Bo?"

"Not exactly. He reached out to me as a *friend*," the reverend said with a certain softness. "He was, you might say, a sort of spiritual guide for me during the trying times I faced after the Alabama incident."

"And that's how you became aware of his work with Bo?"

"No. He invited me to Chases Corner for a visit. Father Hanaway regards his adopted town with a special reverence. He thought I might find a measure of peace there."

"And did you? Did you find the peace you were looking for?"

"Yes, and much more," he said. "Chases Corner is where I discovered that God still has a purpose for me."

"And what exactly would that be? What's your new *purpose*."

The reverend smiled. "I promise you that I'm not being coy; but I really can't say."

"You won't share it with me?"

"No, I said I *can't* say. I haven't figured that part out yet."

In a moment of confusion, I paused to study the reverend's face a little, but found nothing to help me. I decided on a new approach. "Reverend, forgive my language for a Sunday, but you're starting to piss me off here."

"That's not my intention, I assure you."

"Intentional or not, you keep forcing me to dig away at you with question after question, while you throw out a little nugget here and there that only leads to yet another question."

"I'm not the reporter, Mark."

"No, I'm the reporter, and you're the one with the story to tell. So how about we cut through all the back and forth grilling and just get to whatever it is you're trying to position me for here."

His expression never changed. There was no fire in his eyes, no wrinkle across his brow. "I can certainly understand why you might suspect me of trying to use you for a spot in the limelight," he said. "But the truth is, I'd prefer it if you'd leave me out of whatever story you wind up writing about Bo."

"Leave you out of it?"

"That's correct."

"Is that an official request for anonymity?"

"Yes. Please keep my contribution to your research into Bo's case confidential."

In my attempt to cut to the chase, I'd only succeeded in making the labyrinth more complex. "You *have* acquired a certain degree of unpredictability," I said after a short staring contest.

"Unfortunately, your technique of trying to stir my ire is not so unpredictable anymore, Mark."

I let go and afforded the reverend a smile. At that precise moment I think I actually started to like him – or at least not dislike him as much as I had.

"Really, you shouldn't be talking with me anyway," he said.

"I'll grant you that."

"No, seriously. You should have a talk with Father Hanaway."

"That's already on my agenda. Can you make an introduction on my behalf?"

"That won't be necessary, Mark. I believe Father Hanaway is expecting you."

Chapter 24

The phone rang in my apartment that evening at the precise moment I experienced an intense desire to reconnect with a former lifeline; one that I could always count on to help pull my head back above the swirling water. I was disappointed.

"Okay, butthead, I'm booked out to Charleston in the morning."

"Hello, Bart. Did Carl ask you to check on me?"

"Don't give me that crap. I'm still pissed at you."

"You're pissed at me?"

"That's right. You got Carl all riled up. All you had to do is call him every now and then and he would have of stayed off your back."

Bart was taking the high road again, trying to deflect. "It was nice talking to you, Bart. Give me a call if you get anything down there in Charleston."

"Wait, wait. Don't be that way," Bart said changing his aggressive tone. "You know damn well you're not going to stay mad at me forever. Let's start fresh."

"All right, then. How about we start with an apology?"

"Can it be just a general apology? I don't think I can nail it exactly the way you'll want it presented."

"A general apology will do. If it's *sincere*."

"I'm *soooo* very sorry. So deeply and incontrovertibly sorry. There just isn't enough sorrow in the world to fill up—"

"Okay, jackass, that's enough," I said, pulling the curtain down on his dramatics. "Just tell me one thing: why didn't you at least give me a heads-up?"

"I know. I should have," he said. "Carl just seemed so sure you were on your way to some kind of bottom."

"But you and I talked while I was down there!"

"Not really, old buddy. If you'll recall, you shut me down pretty quick the couple times I reached out to you."

Like Carl, Bart had stood by me during the darkest time in my life. After burning-out just about every friendship I'd ever had, Bart was the only link in the friendship chain that remained unbroken. For that, I supposed I would always have to give him the benefit of the doubt when he claimed to be genuinely concerned. "I'll grant you that. But tell me you know I'm *not* going bananas now."

"I don't know about that, pal. There's still the issue of you chasing off a fine woman like Ms. Karen," he said. "There's more than a little bit of crazy in that act."

"Really, Bart, there wasn't a thing I could have done." I was lying, of course. The idea that I hadn't done enough to hold on to Karen that night at Il Vagabondos strengthened each time my mind wandered her way.

"I'll just have to take your word for that," Bart said. "But I suppose there is one good thing to come from all this. At least now you won't have to feel like you're cheating on her when we hook-up with a couple of baby dolls down there in Charleston."

"You better not count on me as your wing man, my friend."

"Why not? They do say you have to get right back on the horse."

"I'm too old and worn out from the last pony ride, I'm afraid."

"Suit yourself. I'm guessing a pretty smile from one of those belles might change your mind, though. When are we going to connect down there?"

"It depends. I've got to go see a priest as soon as I get back to Chases Corner."

"More therapy, or are you paying a visit to that defrocked priest the Librarian tuned up visiting the prison?"

"The Librarian's guy."

I considered telling Bart about the connection I'd uncovered between Father Hanaway and the Reverend Lee, but for some reason I still didn't feel quite ready to bring him all the way in.

"Good luck with that," Bart said. "Your man Galax has me getting together with the Aycock boy late Tuesday afternoon."

"He's not a boy anymore, you know. It's been sixteen years. He's in his thirties by now."

"You know what I meant. Are you going to try to make it over to Charleston for that meeting at least?"

"I don't know, maybe. A lot will depend on when I can get in front of the good Father Hanaway."

"Wow! Does that mean you actually trust me to handle Aycock all by myself?"

His tone suddenly he had me questioning the idea. "I did say maybe," I said, deciding to rethink it and not allow him the victory just yet.

"Either way, you mope," Bart said. "I've got to run now; I'm meeting some people out for one last taste of the big city. You want to come?"

"It's Sunday night and I've got an early flight."

"That's right, the first flight out."

"That's it, I'm afraid."

"Power to you, brother. You'll probably be heading off to the airport before I even get in, so we'll talk again when we're both down below the Mason-Dixon."

There was at least a small piece of me glad that Bart had become involved. I didn't like the way it had all come about, and I wasn't exactly crazy about having to put up with his antics, but it was good to know that someone who knew me well was going to be in the general vicinity.

Before Bart had called I'd settled in for the evening, and was just about to plop down in my big leather reading chair with a glass of tea and the pamphlet that Reverend Lee had given me. I'd been anxious to read it since sliding it into my laptop case, but had resisted in favor of that exact moment.

It wasn't until I'd started reading the publication for the third time that I noticed the name of the author. It was not anywhere to be found on the cover, and because Reverend Lee had been so adamant about my having a copy, I'd assumed it had been written by him. But there on the second page, tucked away inside a paragraph with very small italic type, was an acknowledgment married to a disclaimer.

The theories and ideas posited by this paper are the sole responsibility of the author, Father Michael Hanaway, and are in no way meant to represent the teachings or beliefs of the Catholic Church, its leadership, or any other member of the universal clergy.

It was less a claim to authorship and more a denial that a couple million or so others had anything to do with its contents. By the time I'd finished my third run through of the thirty-two pages of the pamphlet, I was pretty sure I understood the reason for the disclaimer – and perhaps even why the good Father Hanaway was no longer a member of the clergy.

There were plenty of answers put forth in the paper; answers that could only create more questions for any Catholic that read it. As a Catholic by indoctrination myself, the biggest question I had after reading it thoroughly was why the answers put forth were so definitive? In spite of the disclaimer there hadn't been even the slightest attempt to cover things with the softer blanket of supposition or theory, it read like a book of facts. And because so many of the purported truths it delivered flew squarely in the face of the doctrine and dogma of the church of my upbringing, I could imagine that Father Hanaway had set himself up for something more than a couple of hard whacks across the knuckles with a ruler.

By the time I'd finished reading and re-reading his paper a half-dozen times, I was glad I'd booked the first flight out the next morning. The desire to sit face to face with Father Michael Hanaway had become so intense, I would have left in the middle of the night if I could have.

Chapter 25

The next morning, I was already up and making coffee when the alarm went off. I had no trouble sleeping; I was just eager to get back to Chases Corner. An odd condition considering the shape I'd been in just forty-eight hours earlier when I'd left the place.

As with my first trip, the flight back to Charleston was uneventful, and the ride from the airport to the Marriott bereft of any of the restlessness of the Saturday-morning ride in the opposite direction. After checking into the hotel and stumbling through a couple of uncomfortable apologies from hotel employees, I once again had to work hard to not to flop down on the bed in my room. Determined not to be slowed down, I grabbed the items I was going to need for the day and headed back out to the parking lot. One of those items was an address pulled from the Librarian's email.

It was nearly lunch time when I rolled back into Chases Corner. I had a pretty good idea where to start looking for the address the Librarian had sent. I remembered crossing the street when I had walked back to Molly's from the Reverend Lee's speech at the courthouse. With just two right turns from the main road – both partial guesses – I came upon Picket Street, and pulled up to the house number I had written in my notebook.

The small Southern-style mill home was like hundreds I'd passed on the winding road from the Marriott. The house was washed in white paint, with a layer of dirt and dust covering over the chips and wear spots. The oddest part of Father Hanaway's home was its location. The house sat next door to the town's only church, *The First House of God for All People*. From its position to the church, it looked as though the house might once have been the pastor's home, though the church building appeared to have been washed and painted many times over the years while the house looked on.

As I got out of the car, I noticed there were two men planting flowers around a sign on the church's lawn. Another man stood in the doorway, doing something to the hinges. All three stopped what they were doing, put down their tools, and threw me a friendly wave.

"Good day to you Mr. Daniels," one of the men planting the flowers shouted in my direction.

Though certain I'd never seen any of the men before, I smiled back and returned their waves. All three paused and continued to grin as I made my way to the porch, returning to their chores only after I'd knocked on the front door.

I was expecting a priest to answer, but through the rusted mesh of the old screen door I was greeted by something else entirely. "Mr. Daniels," the man said through the screen. "I knew you'd make your way here eventually."

Father Hanaway had given up more than just his priestly garb. His face was covered by a beard with years of growth behind it, and his hair was as uncut and un-kept as his beard. The good father was miles away from the clean-shaven, close-cropped, well manicured padres of my youth. Apparently his rebellion against the Church had been complete. He was hunched over slightly, probably from the effects of scoliosis, which, combined with the deeply cut wrinkles etched into the corners of his eyes, reminded me of one of my university professors we 'd nicknamed *Professor Hermit* back in college.

"Are you Father Hanaway?" I asked.

"Not anymore. But you can still come on inside."

I'd used the title because I wasn't sure if it was one of those lifetime things; like when a congressman or a judge leaves their post. As he held open the screen door for me, the mystery of an odd smell lurking beneath the incense was solved as I slipped passed the old priest.

"Welcome to my humble abode," he said. "You'll have to forgive the mess."

Describing his place as a 'mess' was an understatement. A mess is how housewives with a few of the kid's toys scattered about describe their homes. This looked more like a tornado had gone through, blowing around whole stacks of papers, books, and pamphlets – except a tornado would have at least blown away the quarter-inch layer of dust. As I followed him into what I assumed was once the living room area, the old man started digging out one of the stacks on a sunken chair to make room.

"You can sit here if you like," he said after swatting at the cushion to knock some of the dust off. "Careful though. I think there are a couple of springs sticking through on that one."

The layer of dust particles he'd disturbed with his swatting hung in the air over the chair, as if waiting for me to sit. I hesitated before plopping down and quickly regretted not taking his advice about the springs more seriously.

After making a space for me, the former priest took on the more difficult task of clearing one for himself on a couch directly opposite. He delicately shifted a couple of stacks of books and papers from the middle, removing just enough to squeeze in between. As he sat down, the stacks on either side collapsed inward onto his lap. He quickly stood up to shake them off, only to have others come down on him when he tried to take a seat again. After a couple more tries he finally gave up.

"Let me just grab a chair from the kitchen table," he said as he swept the books off his lap one last time and made his way to the other main room in the house. He returned with a wobbly chair plucked straight from a sixties-era kitchenette. "This will do much better," he said, "I always leave at least one chair free to be able to have a place to sit and eat my dinner."

He spoke as if this were evidence that he was not totally disorganized. He set the chair just a few feet from where I was slowly sinking deeper into my own, the springs digging ever harder into my backside. I pushed my elbows into the arms of the chair and tried in vain to relieve the growing discomfort.

"You know what," I said. "I thought I saw a couple of chairs on the front porch. Why don't we take advantage of the weather and just talk out there?"

Father Hanaway looked defeated, as if on that rare occasion for him to demonstrate hospitality, he had failed. "I'm truly sorry," he said. "I'm afraid I don't get many visitors."

"Listen, don't worry about it," I said. "It's really no big deal."

I lied. It was a big deal. The little voice in my head that nags at me to keep things in perfect order was screaming for me to get out of there.

I stood with some difficulty and grabbed my bag. Father Hanaway quickly shuffled ahead of me to hold open the screen door, and as we stepped out onto the porch the men at the church stopped their work once again. "Good day to you, Father," one of them shouted.

"Good day to you as well," he hollered back. "We're just coming out here onto the porch to take advantage of the wonderful spring weather God has provided."

"Amen to that, Father," the man replied. "The weather surely is a blessing today."

Only after we'd both chosen a porch chair to sit down in did the men go back to work again.

"Yes, this is a much better idea, Mr. Daniels. I sometimes forget how drab and dreary it has become inside there."

"Not at all, Father. Where we talk makes no difference to me. I've been anxious to ask you a few questions."

"And I've been waiting for just the right person to ask them, I assure you."

"And you think I'm that person?"

"That's my sincere hope, Mr. Daniels. Others have come, but none I could talk with openly."

"These others ... were they reporters?"

"*They* might claim so. The most persistent of the lot was from the *National Enquirer*."

"Ah ... they were from the rags."

"I don't have any desire to see my story running next to something about aliens vacationing on Miami Beach, you understand."

One usually reliable sign that a story you are working is heading down a dead-end road is the presence of reporters from the seamier side of the business. If these types were pestering my priest, it was because they had caught the smell of something outrageous in the wind. I'd had the same sensation since reading through Father Hanaway's treatise.

"Father, I'd pretend I didn't know what the folks from the scandal sheets might want with you; but to be honest, I think I can understand their interest."

"Yes. I suppose you've read some of my work then?"

"I have. Reverend Johnston lent me his copy of your paper on angels."

"I see. And which one was that?"

"You've written more than one?"

Father Hanaway stood up and walked back over to the rusted screen door. "Go on in and grab the first paper you find with my name on it," he said as he pulled the door open.

"That won't be necessary," I said. "I have the paper in question right here in my bag."

As I pulled out the pamphlet, Father Hanaway took it from me and sat back down. "Ah, yes. The penultimate work of my career."

"Really?"

"Yes, and also the one that directly preceded my leaving the priesthood." He handed it back to me. "You might say it was the proverbial straw that broke the camel's back."

"Father, I have to admit that some of the things you've written about here would certainly upset me if I were the pope."

"And that they did, Mr. Daniels," he said. "He told me of his disappointment personally."

I almost gave in to an instinct to probe for more of his pope story, but decided instead to put it on the shelf for a while.

"I'd love to hear about your conversation with the pope, Father, but maybe we're getting ahead of ourselves here," I said. "Do you mind if we back-up a bit."

"Not at all. My time is yours."

"Since I'm here covering the Buckminster hearing, why don't we start with why you've been going to see him all these years he's been in prison."

"You've done your homework."

"I have someone who does that sort of thing for me."

"Then you know I began seeing Bo while I was still in the priesthood."

"Yes. And I know that you continued to see him even after you left. Every single week, without a break."

"Bo is a remarkable young man."

"Was it a quest to save an innocent man that motivated you to visit Bo so regularly? I know socially involved priests can have a tendency to get themselves knee-deep in the cause of justice."

"Socially involved, you say," he said, contemplating the words. "No, I don't think that would fit me. I didn't come here on a mission to get Bo out of prison, if that's what you mean."

"You don't care whether or not he's guilty?"

"If you were to ask Bo that question, he'd tell you God knows he didn't do it. That's a pretty good answer for me, Mr. Daniels."

"He also says the murdered boy knows that as well."

"Ah, yes. Marcus knows that too, doesn't he?" the old priest said, smiling at me like we were sharing a secret.

"So you believe Marcus talks to Bo?"

Father Hanaway stopped smiling. "You've spoken with him, haven't you Mr. Daniels?"

"You mean with Bo?"

"No, I mean with Marcus."

Once again, as with so many times during my stay in Chases Corner, the hair stood on the back of my neck. I briefly considered the propriety of holding back on a priest, but as he was no longer a man of the cloth, I let go of the guilt. I did decide that it was time to stop avoiding the topic, however.

"All right," I snapped, sitting a little straighter. "Why is it that so many people around here seem to think I can chat with the dead anytime I want to?"

"Oh," the priest moaned knowingly. "So you haven't accepted it then."

"Accepted what? You know, I've had a belly-full of this *accepting the gift* nonsense. You're the third person to try and get me to bite on that riddle, Father. So what gives?"

Looking a little confused at first, the old priest slid back in his chair. Then he sported a wide grin. "I'll assume one of those who approached you was Reverend Johnston?"

"Yes it was. He practically devoted his entire sermon to the idea yesterday."

"And the third, Mr. Daniels?"

"What's that?"

"The third person you just mentioned – besides the reverend and myself. Who was the other to bug you about accepting your gift?"

Beneath the hair standing on the back of my neck, a warm flush spread across the skin.

"It's all right, Mark," the priest said in a soothing tone. "If you truly want to understand things, the best place to start is within yourself."

I was stunned by the predicament I found myself in. My reporter training caused my brain to search frantically for connections. Obviously the priest had spoken to Reverend Lee, but I'd told no one except Dr. Keller about my dreams of Marcus.

Father Hanaway allowed me tread water, waiting for my arms to tire. Eventually he threw me a rope. "Mark, I'm sure you didn't come here to talk about yourself," he said. "Since I suspect you're more a man of science, why don't we get back to my research?"

Staring at the old priest, I felt as if I'd just been let out of confession. If he'd put a white collar on that morning, I suspect at that very moment I would have blurted out everything I'd experienced as I romped around in dreamland the week before. Father Hanaway seemed to understand that, but it was as if he'd accepted that it wasn't his job to coax it out of me.

"Yes, I was fascinated by your work," I said after an uncomfortable pause. "Maybe we can start with you explaining how a spiritual man such as yourself got so deep into the science of DNA and genealogy?"

"Two of my favorite topics. Where should we begin?"

I remembered my tape recorder. "Would you mind if I use this?" I asked as I pulled it out of my bag. "I'm sure I didn't do well enough in the sciences back in college to be able to keep up with you."

"By all means," he said without hesitation.

TRANSCRIPT

Tape # 4

Interviewer: Daniels

Responder: (ex) Father Thomas Hanaway

Date of Interview: Monday, 8 April

Location: His Home in Chases Corner, SC

2:16 PM

DANIELS: Tell me, Father, how is it that a man with a religious background such as yours came to be a student of the sciences? Especially something like DNA?

FATHER HANAWAY: Same way as any other, I suppose. I read as much as possible on the topic, went to seminars and conferences when I could.

DANIELS: But you're not just any other, Father. You were a priest in the Roman Catholic Church.

FATHER HANAWAY: If, by that, you mean the Catholic Church is somehow uninterested in science, you begin with a flawed assumption.

DANIELS: I always thought a seminary education stressed more of the creationist version of the world.

FATHER HANAWAY: Science and faith are not mutually exclusive. In fact, if we begin by saying that God is responsible for getting everything started in the first place, that premise seems to answer the one question that science has never been able to solve.

DANIELS: If we did evolve from apes, God was the one that got evolution started ... that sort of thing?

FATHER HANAWAY: Well, I don't think I can go with you on that one particular topic, but you get the idea.

DANIELS: So at some point in your career, you set out to become an ordained DNA scientist. Was your work sanctioned by the Church?

FATHER HANAWAY: At first it was, though DNA wasn't my original focus.

DANIELS: What was your original focus?

FATHER HANAWAY: I was granted a two-year sabbatical to study angels. To be specific, I set out to look for answers as to why they are not as prevalent in today's world as they perhaps once were.

DANIELS: You mean, you were allowed to study why it is angels don't visit as often as they used to in, say … biblical times?

FATHER HANAWAY: Yes, you could say that.

DANIELS: And what was the conclusion you came to? Why don't they show themselves these days?

FATHER HANAWAY: Ah, well, that's where my original thesis got flipped completely on its head.

DANIELS: Because?

FATHER HANAWAY: Because what I learned was that they *do* visit us often. If anything, they seem to be appearing to people more often than ever these days.

DANIELS: And you claim this is a result of the whole right-brain, left-brain theory you have written about?

FATHER HANAWAY: You really did read my paper, didn't you?

DANIELS: I did. You know … the whole research thing.

FATHER HANAWAY: Well, I'm impressed. And the left-brain, right-brain theory you speak of is also referred to as the bi-cameral mind.

DANIELS: Right, I couldn't remember the name you gave it.

FATHER HANAWAY: Oh, I didn't give it that name. None of the theories or conclusions I've written about are my own. I simply pull them from published science.

DANIELS: I do recall something from high-school science class about the two sides of the brain. One side is responsible for imagination and creative thinking, the other for deductive reasoning or calculating mathematics and the like.

FATHER HANAWAY: It's perhaps a tad more complicated than that – but for the layman, that probably sums it up well enough. By the way, if you're looking for more research, there's a book called *The Breakdown of*

Consciousness and The Bi-Cameral Mind, by Max Harmon. It really is quite good.

DANIELS: I'll keep it in mind.

FATHER HANAWAY: To take it a step further and use your summary as a starting point, some scientists believe that as civilization advanced, there was a shifting of sorts in the center of our cognitive thought.

DANIELS: A move from the left-side to the right.

FATHER HANAWAY: That's correct. Or let us just say that an increasingly predominant portion of Western society has experienced the shift. If our theory holds up, there are still parts of the world – non-Western societies, to some degree – wherein, either through social training or some biological difference resulting from the evolutionary process, members of those societies still react to environmental stimuli primarily with the left hemisphere of cranial processing.

DANIELS: Okay, Father, you've gone way beyond high-school science class. How about we back up and say that again in a way my readers and I might understand.

FATHER HANAWAY: My apologies, Mr. Daniels. I'm afraid the right side of my own brain sometimes takes over. Let me see if I can come up with an allegory or metaphor for you.

DANIELS: I like either.

FATHER HANAWAY: Yes, that would seem to fit what we've learned about you. Let's say a man – a left-side-brain man, we'll call him – comes across a single burning bush on a mountain top. What do you suppose his first thoughts might be?

DANIELS: I'm not following you.

FATHER HANAWAY: Of course you do, Mr. Daniels. You know the story of Moses, and so you also know that the first thought Moses had was that it was a sign from God.

DANIELS: Okay, so the bush spoke to him … and eventually it gave him the Ten Commandments. So the bush is the metaphor?

FATHER HANAWAY: In this case it is, at least for an ultimate left side of the brain guy like Mosses. But, what would have happened back then if we had put a right side of the brain guy on that mountain. Someone like the ultimate right-side guy, Sir Isaac Newton?

PAUSE.

DANIELS: He would have looked for the source of the fire.

FATHER HANAWAY: Right! He probably would have begun checking the barometric pressure, looked for signs of increased weather patterns …

DANIELS: And his first reaction might have been that the fire was caused by a bolt of lightning.

FATHER HANAWAY: You've got it. For Newton there were no mysteries in the world, only riddles that needed solving.

DANIELS: But what about the voice of God? Certainly the Lord speaking to him directly would have shaken Newton up a little.

FATHER HANAWAY: Ah, but there is the crux of our question.

DANIELS: And what is that?

FATHER HANAWAY: Would he even have been able to hear it?

DANIELS: You mean God's voice.

FATHER HANAWAY: That's exactly what I mean. The entire premise upon which my thesis is built is that God's voice – and miraculous visions, appearances of the Virgin Mother, and even the occasional visit by the army of angels that watch over us – is impossible for those of us for whom thinking is primarily a right-side-of-the-brain activity.

DANIELS: So you're saying that if Newton had made the trip up Mt. Sinai, instead of the Ten Commandments we'd have a scientific discourse on the effects of lightning, or how electrical disturbances can be caused by the changing weather patterns.

FATHER HANAWAY: Well, you are pre-dating the findings of Mr. Franklin by a few centuries, but the idea is spot on.

LONG PAUSE.

DANIELS: That would confirm what I thought you were saying in the first part of your paper then.

FATHER HANAWAY: And what was that?

DANIELS: That more people are able to converse with angels these days, because as a whole, we're reverting back to using the left side of our brains to think with.

FATHER HANAWAY: You are correct. That is the first of my underlying theories.

DANIELS: But, Father, forgive me for saying so, but your most important premise doesn't seem to hold water these days.

FATHER HANAWAY: And why do you think that?

DANIELS: I mean … this is the age of computers, Father. We live in a binary world.

FATHER HANAWAY: And your point is?

DANIELS: Well, I mean, being holed up here in lovely Chases Corner for the better part of the last couple decades, you may not realize that the world has been taken over by geeks and digit-heads.

FATHER HANAWAY: That fact hasn't been lost on me, Mr. Daniels. Even here in far away Chases Corner.

PAUSE:

DANIELS: Those folks are not the type of people who I would say use the left side of the brain for primary thinking patterns.

FATHER HANAWAY: Because you see math as the underlying foundation for all computers, right?

DANIELS: Well ... yeah.

FATHER HANAWAY: I struggled with that one myself for some time. But I keep coming back to how creative someone like a programmer has to be. The stuff they come up with is amazing.

DANIELS: There are also an awful lot of *agnostic* programmers out there, from what I can tell. To me, they're more like Newton than Moses. Let's not even talk about the army of scientists trying to find the formula for *string theory*, hoping to finally reduce the whole universe to one mathematical equation.

FATHER HANAWAY: All good examples for the argument against my premise.

PAUSE:

DANIELS: And you don't feel the need to dispute them?

FATHER HANAWAY: I don't have to. I think my science is stronger.

PAUSE:

DANIELS: Which would bring us back to the DNA data?

FATHER HANAWAY: It would. At least in part.

PAUSE; SOUND OF PAPERS SHUFFLING:

DANIELS: Help me to understand it a little better, then.

FATHER HANAWAY: In what way?

DANIELS: For starters, could you explain a little more about this mutated Fragile-X gene? It sounds like something out of a cheap science-fiction novel.

FATHER HANAWAY: Yes, the name it's been given is unfortunate. But it is very much a non-fiction topic, I assure you. Work on the Fragile-X gene heated-up during the 1980s, but it really thrust itself into the research spotlight in 1991 when a test was developed to identify the gene in its mutated form.

DANIELS: And that mutation is the marker to identify whether or not a set of parents will have children with some degree of mental retardation?

FATHER HANAWAY: Yes and no. First, the chances of that happening are controlled somewhat by gender. For instance, a father with the gene will never pass it along to a daughter born to him, but he will always pass it to a son.

DANIELS: Is it similar for the mother.

FATHER HANAWAY: Not really. There is a fifty-fifty chance the mother will pass it along to either sex.

DANIELS: But if the mutated gene is passed, then the child will suffer some degree of mental retardation.

FATHER HANAWAY: Again ... that's not necessarily true.

PAUSE:

DANIELS: Father, you did say this was science, didn't you?

FATHER HANAWAY: It is. It's just a little more complex than you're trying to make it. There are two categories of mutation. The first is what is known as a pre-mutation. In this form, the gene is stretched but can still produce the protein needed for normal development of the child.

DANIELS: It's not damaged enough to cause problems.

FATHER HANAWAY: Right. A person with this level of mutation is not at risk of having a child that is not fully developed mentally. However, over time and generations, the gene will repeat itself and can eventually develop into a full mutation; which is when protein production is shut off entirely.

DANIELS: So, a grandfather who is a pre-mutation carrier could have a grandson that will pass the fully mutated gene along to his children.

FATHER HANAWAY: Theoretically, that is correct. It is the number of repeats – which by the way are completely measurable – that the gene has in the DNA chain that determines *carrier* versus *active* mutations. That's an important point to be able to completely comprehend my theory.

DANIELS: And why is that?

PAUSE:

FATHER HANAWAY: You know what, let's put that question on hold for a few minutes. The answer may require a leap of faith for you to stay with me, and I think we should get through the science first.

DANIELS: Okay, you're on a roll. Keep going.

FATHER HANAWAY: How much do you know about autism?

DANIELS: You mean the learning disorder in children.

FATHER HANAWAY: It's a little more than just a learning disorder. It's a form of mental retardation, and I'm afraid people have it for life. Calling it a children's disorder is a misnomer.

DANIELS: How does autism connect with the Fragile-X gene, then?

FATHER HANAWAY: A good question! Let me set the stage for you first. Are you aware of the data surrounding the explosive growth in reported cases of autism over the past two decades.

DANIELS: I've seen the data in your paper, but even you commented that the numbers may be impacted by improved testing and diagnosis techniques.

FATHER HANAWAY: This is true, of course; and it is once again the crux of an argument against my theory. Add in other intangibles such as increased awareness, possible substitution of the autism label for less palatable designations such as mental retardation, as well as a lack of universally accepted standards for diagnosis, and you have a very wide margin for error in the data.

DANIELS: Are you talking me out of your own conclusions?

FATHER HANAWAY: Not at all. Just putting the facts out on the table. In 1989, a respected survey by Riveto et al. found that four in every ten thousand children tested showed symptoms of ASD, the term given to the various forms of autism disorders.

DANIELS: And now?

FATHER HANAWAY: In 2006, a similar survey showed that the number of instances had increased to *sixty* in every ten thousand.

DANIELS: That's a big jump, but honestly, sixty out of ten thousand is a pretty small number.

FATHER HANAWAY: So let's look at the numbers another way. First, we're looking at an increase of nearly 1,500 percent in under twenty years.

DANIELS: That does make it look a little bigger.

FATHER HANAWAY: Let's give it even more perspective then. Twenty years in the reproductive cycle of our species is just about *one generation*. When we talk about such things as genetics and repeats in DNA, that's really the time frame we should be using. Remember, the Fragile X gene is passed from one generation to the next. It's not passed every year.

PAUSE:

DANIELS: That's pretty alarming when you look at it that way. What's being done about it?

FATHER HANAWAY: Nothing, really.

DANIELS: Nothing? Why not?

FATHER HANAWAY: Why isn't anything being done about global warming? Both are pretty difficult topics, and both could have such an enormous impact ... but it's human nature to find ways *not* to think about them.

PAUSE:

DANIELS: Are we ready to go back to my question about how autism and the Fragile X gene are connected?

FATHER HANAWAY: What do you think is the number-one cause of autism?

PAUSE:

DANIELS: The Fragile-X gene?

FATHER HANAWAY: There you have it.

DANIELS: There I have what?

FATHER HANAWAY: The first of my conclusions, of course. Disputed data or not, the reported cases of autism are on the rise. Maybe even at epidemic proportions. The number-one cause of autism is the fully mutated Fragile-X gene, something that because of the degradation that occurs from increased repeats from one generation to the next, is likely to continue to rise as well.

PAUSE:

DANIELS: So if you will allow me the liberty, if we bring your hypothesis back to the bicameral-mind idea, with an increasing percentage of the population afflicted with mental handicaps of one form or another, then mathematically the population is shifting back toward using the left-side of the brain for primary thought processing.

FATHER HANAWAY: Again, there is more to it perhaps, but you have the gist of it.

DANIELS: Father, I have to be honest. That's a pretty big stretch.

FATHER HANAWAY: I would agree.

DANIELS: And yet you said you think your science is stronger.

FATHER HANAWAY: Ah, but you forget, my science has one important ingredient that the data we've just discussed does not.

DANIELS: And that would be?

FATHER HANAWAY: Faith, Mr. Daniels. I'm not trying to use the data to understand autism, the Fragile X gene, or what the future might hold for either. I'm looking for bigger answers than that.

DANIELS: Why some people can see angels?

PAUSE:

FATHER HANAWAY: And how God is using them to bring us all back to a simpler time. A time when his love and presence was all we needed to make sense of the world.

DANIELS: And your science tells you that as well?

FATHER HANAWAY: No. That is where we must turn to the bible for the final piece to the puzzle.

DANIELS: Father, I was raised in the Catholic school system, so I've had time enough with the bible. I don't remember it saying anything about autism in there."

FATHER HANAWAY: How familiar are you with Corinthians?

DANIELS: Enough so that my knuckles still hurt when it rains.

PAUSE; FATHER HANAWAY LAUGHS

FATHER HANAWAY: My apologies on behalf of my overzealous colleagues. Specifically, do you recall Corinthians 12: 24-26?

DANIELS: Isn't that something about how God has arranged something or other?

FATHER HANAWAY: Very good, Mr. Daniels! I am impressed. But what it says exactly is – *'God has so arranged the body, giving the greater honor to the inferior member...'*

LONG PAUSE:

WORKER FROM THE CHURCH: Father, I hope you haven't lost track of time over there?

FATHER HANAWAY: I may have, my son. Are we going to be late?

WORKER FROM THE CHURCH: Not if we leave pretty quick-like.

END OF INTERVIEW

The official transcript of my first interview with Father Hanaway ended abruptly, after one of the men working over at the church had made his way across the grounds to us.

"Mr. Daniels, I'm terribly sorry but Curtis here is my ride to my weekly appointment."

"You're going to see Bo?"

"Yes, and I'm afraid that Mrs. Nutter is somewhat less flexible about being on time than Bo's former prison guards were."

"I can relate," I said with a laugh. "But we're shutting things down just as they were getting interesting. Can we meet again soon?"

"Of course, anytime. As bad luck would have it, you've come just before my only scheduled appointment for this week, or any other week for that matter."

"I'll try to give you a heads-up before I come next time. Is there a number where I can reach you?"

"I'm afraid I don't have a phone, myself. But you can try over at the church." At the mention of the church, he stood up and looked over at Curtis, who nodded as if to say he would be happy to pass along a message.

"I'll do it," I said. "But, Father, can you answer one more question before we part?"

"I can, if you will follow me inside. I've got to gather a few things for my meeting with Bo."

"Lead the way."

Father Hanaway opened the screen door and held it open for me to follow behind him. My hand partially missed the wood frame as he passed it to me and landed on the rusting screen. A scraggly piece of metal punctured the palm of my hand. "Ouch," I said, pulling my hand away.

"Oh, my! I'm very sorry, Mr. Daniels," the old priest said as we stepped inside, knowing straight off what had happened. "I've been meaning to replace that screen for some time. Are you injured."

I turned my hand over. A small trickle of blood was oozing out of a pin-hole sized wound on the palm. Though tiny, it was deep enough for a considerable amount of blood to immediately begin collecting.

"This is my fault," Father Hanaway said with an apology in his voice. "Stay right here and I'll get something to put on that."

"Really, it's nothing. Don't bother with any—" I was already speaking to the back of the priest's head.

He returned within a few seconds with a wipe and a band-aid. "Here," he said, handing me the wipe. "Clean off the wound and we'll stick this band-aid on it."

As I blotted up the blood, the priest opened the band-aid. "That door is pretty rusty," he said waiting on me. "You may want to see about getting a tetanus shot for peace of mind." He took the wipe from me with one hand and applied the band-aid securely with the other.

"Father, the one thing I'd hoped we could touch on before I—"

I was speaking to the back of his head again. He made his way into a back room and shortly afterward emerged with two notebooks and a small stack of papers.

"Yes, you were saying?" he said, heading straight past me toward the door.

I followed him back out onto the porch and tried to think of a way to phrase my question for a short answer. "Father, in your paper you seemed to insinuate that you believe the people of biblical times were mostly ... well, mentally handicapped. Did I get that right at least?"

Father Hanaway had already started across the driveway toward the church lot, but stopped and spun around at my inquiry. "Ah, but where you see a mental handicap, others may see something else entirely."

"Such as?"

"Innocence, Mr. Daniels," he said with a smile. "The one true qualification for all angels is the purest of thoughts. That's what I see is different during biblical times."

"Are you using a metaphor again?"

"Truly, Mr. Daniels, I really must be going," he said as he tried with difficulty to walk backward and still maintain eye contact with me. "But we will talk again soon, I'm sure."

Suddenly, he stopped dead in his tracks. "By the way, your argument for geeks taking over the world? The one you thought might cast doubt on the idea of a shift to left-side thinking?"

"Yes."

"One very well-known corporation's employees had such an unusually high outbreak of autism among new births, that the company felt compelled to amend their healthcare coverage to include special provisions for the disorder."

"And which corporation is that?"

"Microsoft. In 2004, they became the first company to officially recognize the increase of autism in their healthcare plan."

I watched him hustle to catch up with the driver for his meeting with Bo. The old priest had a spring in his step that made him look thirty-years younger.

Chapter 26

Saturated with information, that afternoon I backed the rental car out of Father Hanaway's driveway and knew exactly where I was going next. A late lunch at Molly's was the only thing my stomach would let me consider.

Billy Thornton was straddling his bike out in front of the restaurant and waved to me as I parked.

"I heard you was back in town, Mr. Daniels," he shouted, as I made my way from the lot in the back. "How was your time back in the big city?"

"A little too noisy and a little too crowded. Just the way I like it."

"We ain't got much of either around these parts, so I hope you got your fill of it while you was up there."

As I approached, he stuck his hand out in business-like fashion for a shake.

"Billy, I hate to keep bugging you about this, but shouldn't you be in school?"

"I just got out, Mr. Daniels. It's near three o'clock."

I looked down at my watch. "Well, so it is. I must have lost track of time."

"Can't say as that would be much of a surprise to folks around here, considering you was meeting with Father Hanaway and all. He sure does have a whole peck of big words to use, don't he?"

"He does indeed."

"You understand all those words he uses, Mr. Daniels?"

"I got the gist of what he's saying."

Billy paused a second or two. "Gist? Is that one of Father Hanaway's words you picked up then?"

"No, what it means is that I kind of understand what he was saying," I said. "Truth is, he lost me a couple times this afternoon as well."

"Good to hear it ain't just us country folks, then. My daddy says Father Hanaway's one of the smartest men he ever met."

"Is that so?"

"Yup. He also says he wishes he knew what he was talking about most times – so he could prove it were true."

I laughed and thought how Billy's daddy and I had something in common. "Billy, do they serve lunch inside at this late hour."

"I don't guess they'd serve you lunch so close to dinner, but I reckon you could still get something to eat. So long as you was paying."

"Well, the ethics of my profession don't encourage free lunches anyway, so that formula works for me."

"What's that, Mr. Daniels."

"I have money and I can pay."

"Good. You won't go hungry, then," Billy said. "I guess you'll be wanting this to look over while you're eatin'."

Billy reached around to the back pocket of his jeans and brought forward a rolled up and slightly creased manila folder. "That there's the copy you asked for – of the interview with Bo the night of the killin'."

"Oh, right. I'd almost forgotten."

"I been-a carrying it here every morning since you left, just to make sure."

On closer look, the smudge marks and what appeared to be a soda stain on one of the corners added credibility to his claim. "I'm sorry about that, Billy," I said, reaching for my wallet.

"Oh, no. I ain't-a gonna take no more money from you for this one, Mr. Daniels," Billy said as he backed his bike away and pointed it in the opposite direction. "Fact is, I still owe you a free one. You need me to do something for you today?"

"Nothing comes to mind. But considering you made the trip here the last couple mornings on my behalf, we can wipe the slate clean over that free one."

"Sounds fair," Billy said, looking relieved. "All the same, next time I'll just wait till you have the proper change. I don't much like being in debt to a man."

Billy started pedaling before I could respond.

"I'll check back with you from time-to-time," he hollered as he sped away.

I climbed the stairs at Molly's and, through the screen door, I saw a set of eyes staring at me, dancing with excitement.

"Well, if it ain't that good-looking reporter from New York City come back to pay us a visit," the big hostess sang. "We missed you, Mr. Daniels."

I was pretty sure she was hoping I'd say I missed her too, but I just couldn't do it. "Well, thank you," I said. "I have to admit, I missed Ms. Molly's cooking while I was away."

The hostess looked a little disappointed, but not enough to knock her out of her happy mood.

"Well then, let's just get you seated, and we'll see if we can do something about your new-found hankering for Southern food."

I followed behind her to my table. It looked like she had added a bit of a sway to her ample backside.

"There you go, hon," she said as she pulled a chair out for me. "Maggie will be along in a minute to take your order."

"Are there any lunch specials today?"

"There were ... but they're long gone, sweetie," she said, handing me a menu. "I'm afraid you're going to have to order *ella cart*." She spoke the last words with an odd sounding accent over the top of her Southern drawl and giggled as she walked away.

"Better watch out there, Mr. Daniels" a voice said from behind me. "When she starts speaking French, it usually means she's smitten."

"Was that French, Maggie?"

"Near as I can tell. Least ways, as close as someone from these parts can get."

We both chuckled a little, although mine was more of a nervous laugh.

"I hate that you missed the lunch special, Mr. Daniels," she said, pulling her pad from her apron. "It was meatloaf and it went mighty quick on account of so many folks wanting seconds."

"I hate it, too Maggie," I said, picking up the menu. "What should I order off this, then?"

"Anything you like, but..."

"But what?"

"I'm tempted to tell you that you might be better off if I asked them to put together a plate of leftovers from yesterday's special for you."

"And what was yesterday's special?"

"Fried chicken."

I thought it over for a second or two, but decided on something lighter. "Do you guys make BLT's this far south."

"We sure do. Is that what you want?"

"Yes, and a glass of iced tea to go with it."

"You got it," Maggie said before dashing-off, straight for the kitchen.

Almost from the instant Maggie had stepped from the table, I began second-guessing my decision. Though my first instinct was in favor of less over more, the memory of Molly's fried chicken wouldn't go away – even if it was in its leftover state. I waited for Maggie to pop back out of the kitchen, but something was delaying her. Not wanting to miss the window on canceling my BLT before it was made, I started for the kitchen myself. When I stuck my head in through the swinging door, an older woman wearing a white string apron cinched at the waist was standing in front of a large food-prep table.

"I'm sorry," I said. "I just put in an order for a sandwich."

The woman nodded and smiled at me.

"I don't mean to bother you, but is there a chance I can cancel my BLT in favor of the fried chicken leftovers?"

She nodded again with a slightly bigger smile, then turned around and pulled what appeared to be a plate drumsticks wrapped in plastic from a stainless steel refrigerator. Satisfied my new order was in, I feigned a tip of the hat; which caused the old gal to respond with a slight bow in my direction.

On my way back to my table, I noticed for the first time that except for the staff I was the only one in the restaurant.

"Here's your tea, Mr. Daniels," Maggie said, startling me as I slid back into my chair.

"Oh, thanks, Maggie."

"That BLT will be up in a jiffy," she said. "As you can see, we ain't real busy."

'Oh... yeah, well, I sort of changed my order, Maggie."

"I'm sorry, did you say you want me to change your order?"

"No, no. I stuck my head in the kitchen. An older woman switched out my BLT in favor of the left-over fried chicken."

Maggie paused as if I'd done something I shouldn't have. "This old woman, did she have a white apron tied around her waist?"

"She did," I said, sensing something was amiss. "I assumed she understood my request because she pulled a plate of chicken out of the refrigerator as soon as I asked."

Maggie was still thinking hard on something she wasn't sharing. "Did she say anything to you?"

"The old woman?"

"Yes, sir," Maggie said, determined. "Did you speak with her directly?"

"Well, no ... now that you mention it she didn't say anything to me. I'm sorry if I wasn't supposed to—"

"No, no, that's fine, Mr. Daniels," she said, perhaps realizing she'd given me something to worry about. "It's okay. I'm just making sure you're gonna get that chicken is all." She seemed to be forcing her usual friendly tone and tenor back to the front, as if wanting to push-off any concern she may have caused me by her probing.

"I think I'm set, Maggie," I said. "But maybe you better check with the old woman, though."

"I'll do that Mr. Daniels. I'll just check in the back to make sure."

Maggie had started to walk away when a question popped into my head. "By the way, Maggie, is that the world-famous Molly herself I switched my order with?"

Maggie stopped dead in her tracks, and the other staff within earshot of my loud question seemed to pause. She turned her head and looked back at me over her shoulder.

"Yes, sir, Mr. Daniels," she said, the same kind of knowing smile taking over that I'd seen on her boss's face earlier. "I guess it was Molly you saw back there in the kitchen. Ain't no one else goes back there this time of day."

Maggie spun her head back in the direction her body was pointed and walked off. It was an odd exchange. The idea that I was unknowingly breaking some rule or cultural norm popped up often at Molly's. With even the most mundane of actions, I could get a look from someone that seemed to say I was forgiven for not understanding. The trouble was, I rarely understood what I wasn't understanding in the first place.

Undaunted, I went back to work and opened Billy's dirty envelope. Inside was a handwritten note held by a paper clip. The note was from Mrs. Edith Thorton, informing me that, as I was on official business, she was not charging for the copies.

There were two one-dollar bills clipped beneath the note, a rebate Billy Thorton very easily could have kept for himself. The top copy was of the police report the night of the murder, and highlighted in yellow was the deputy's account of what Bo Buckminster had told him about what happened.

When speaking to the Buckminster boy, all he would say was that he weren't the one that did it, but that he was mighty glad for Marcus. When asked to explain why, the boy would only say that being an angel was what

Marcus was always intended for, and now he was one. The boy had been crying when my partner and me came on the scene, but he smiled the entire time we were transporting him back to the jail. The boy seemed as if he were in some kind of trance.

The second page was an official statement typed on a form identical to the one used for each of the other two boys in the file. There was very little written on it.

The following was repeated by the suspect several times. No further statement was offered.

God has a purpose for everyone. Marcus has found his, and now I reckon you can take me off to mine.

I don't know what I'd expected to find in Bo's official statement, but the very few words reported fit what I had come to know of him. I suppose by then I'd expected him to point the finger at one of the other boys; but although he did deny the crime, he gave no other explanation. In his behavior and comments afterward, I could see how the authorities would have been hard-pressed to come up with an alternative to the version offered by the other two boys.

After slipping the paper back into the envelope, my waitress rolled up with my lunch in one hand and the pitcher of iced tea in the other.

"Here's your plate of second-day fried chicken, Mr. Daniels," she said, as she set the plate front of me. "Most folks think it's even better the next day, but I guess we'll have to see if you're one of them folks."

"I'm sure it will be fine."

Maggie leaned over my shoulder to fill my glass of tea, and I caught a slight giggle from her in my ear. After finishing the pour, as she walked away she seemed to do it again, only louder. I thought about what might have caused it, but the familiar fried-chicken smell was drifting straight up from my plate, and it jumped ahead of a giggling waitress in the battle for my attention.

That afternoon I learned I was "one of them that likes it better the second day." Molly's trick for day-old chicken appeared to be a very delicate layer of gravy gently drizzled over the pieces before re-heating. It had a bit of a tang to it, not unlike the gravy she poured over her biscuits in the morning. No one came in or out of the restaurant while I ate my meal, and I had the feeling most of the staff were watching, waiting for me to finish

When I finally took my attention away from the licked-clean bones on my plate, every single member of Molly's crew was staring and smiling in my direction. I wasn't uncomfortable, but I figured they might have been waiting on me to finish so they could start some sort of work ritual to get ready for the dinner customers. With not a bit of room left for desert, I grabbed the check Maggie had dropped at my table with my chicken and stepped, still chewing, to the cashier.

"'I'm sorry folks," I mumbled before my last swallow. "I'm probably getting in the way of something you need to be doing."

"Oh, that's alright, Mr. Daniels," the cashier lady said as she took my check and twenty-dollar bill. "We ain't got nothing to do. People don't start coming in for dinner till after five."

When she handed me my change, I dropped a five back on the counter for a tip, which elicited a giggle from her. I thought it might have something to do with the tip, but the cashier set off a chain reaction amongst the others.

"Okay, then," I said a little lost. "Could you let Molly know how much I appreciate the trouble she went through putting a plate of chicken together for me?"

The cashier giggled harder. "Well now, Mr. Daniels, you might be better off telling her that yourself," she said, setting off another chorus of giggles from the others.

"Really? And why is that?" I said, trying to smile with the group.

"Well, sir, I don't get to see much of Molly these days," she said. One of the ladies who had just sipped some tea had to work hard not to snort it back out through her nose.

It felt like I was still in the fifth-grade, and just as I had done back then when faced with silly classmates, I smiled and walked away without another word.

Chapter 27

Back at the Marriott that evening, I struggled putting a daily together for Carl. I missed his five-o'clock deadline by a bunch as I in vain to summarize the science lesson I'd received earlier from Father Hanaway. Despite some additional web-based research, I was having trouble being succinct – mostly because I hadn't really come to a complete understanding of what the priest was getting at for myself. From his paper, I'd cobbled enough of the facts together to understand that, in his opinion, angels were making a resurgence of sorts in today's world. What I didn't understand yet was just what all this had to do with Bo Buckminster, his re-trial, or the story I was preparing. The one thing I was certain of was that I couldn't have Carl getting the impression that I was stepping off the deep end of some sort of mental pier. I tread lightly with my report, working hard to make anything controversial sound like an afterthought.

The network news was half-over when a call came in from my new story partner.

"Well, I'm here!" was all the voice on the other end said.

"When did you get in?"

"I just checked into my room on the beach. The view is spectacular."

"Did Carl know you were planning on making this a beach trip?"

"I doubt it, but he damn sure should have expected it," Bart said. "As you know, I work under the rule that a thing not expressly prohibited is allowed. Carl should be clued-in to that little fact by now."

"I take it he didn't warn you about beach-front hotel rooms."

"Nope. And by the time he finds out from my expense report, I'm thinking we'll have your story well in the can."

That too was vintage Bart. Better to ask forgiveness than seek permission. "I hope you're right, my friend," I said. "I'm just not so sure we're going to get through this one all that quickly."

"What are you talking about?" Bart asked incredulously. "Buckminster's either going to get a new trial or he's not. In the one case, he goes back to prison and we go home. In the other, a new trial takes months to get placed on the docket, and in the meantime we still go home."

I hesitated, trying to counter Bart's rationalization. "I hope you're right," I said instead. "Are you ready for your meeting tomorrow?"

"You mean, do I have my notes and such ready for the Aycock guy?"

"Exactly."

"You know better than that. I like to let my interviews meander where they may, like a river."

"You mean you're lazy."

"That's your take, Mark. Some say my style is brilliant."

"All the same, if it won't cramp your brilliant style too much I'm going to email you a couple of questions I'd like to have answers to. Would that be all right?"

"Sure," Bart said. "As long as you don't mind waiting until the morning for me to look them over."

"Why? I can have them to you in ten minutes."

"That's all fine and good, old buddy, but I told Trip Singletary I'd meet him in the lobby bar in five."

"What? Trip's in Charleston?"

"He sure is. I bumped into him downstairs as I was checking in."

"Man, that guy just pops up out of nowhere," I said. "I ran into him in downtown Chases Corner."

"It is a bit creepy sometimes, but old Trip's always up for an adventure. I like that about him."

Suddenly the thought of two road legends like Bart and Trip in the same town had me concerned. "Hey, look, Bart. The two of you together is an accident waiting to happen. Do *not* screw this up."

"Relax, Mr. Worrywart, it's business," Bart replied. "Trip says he's on to something. He said I might want to get in on it."

"On to something? Does it have to do with the Buckminster case?"

"I would assume. He asked me if that's what I was in town for."

"What's that supposed to mean? Did he say he was working on—"

"Look, my friend," Bart said interrupting me. "I'm not going to be able to answer any of your questions unless you let me go down to the lobby bar and meet with him."

Once again the elusive Trip had popped-up out of nowhere, and I suddenly wished that I had met Bart in Charleston after all. Though more difficult to predict than the weather, whenever and wherever Trip surfaces there's usually something about to break.

"Bart, if it's something big you gotta call me!"

"I will. If it has anything whatsoever to do with your case, I'll hit the speed dial faster than you can say Jack Robinson."

I hung on quietly for a bit, trying to decide if I should jump back in the car and get started on the two-and-a-half-hour drive to Charleston.

"So, are we done?" Bart finally asked.

"We're done."

"Ciao!"

Chapter 28

I picked a drumstick from the plate with two fingers, shook it slightly, then watched with amazement when every bit of meat, sinew, and skin fell completely off the bone.

"That's the most unbelievable chicken I've ever seen in my life," I said.

"That's not just any-old chicken there, Mr. Daniels," Marcus Brown said. "That there chicken's been touched by the hand of God."

Marcus was sitting across from me at a table inside Molly's restaurant.

"Ms. Molly here has a gift," he added, looking to the seat to his left. "One that only the Lord can bestow."

The old woman from the kitchen was occupying the seat, and she smiled and nodded as she held up her hands and wiggled her fingers without speaking.

"We need to be getting mighty serious here for a minute, Mr. Daniels," Marcus said with a shift in tone. "There's still a bit of time left, but your friend's in big trouble."

Marcus bobbed his head to the right a couple times toward Trip Singletary, who was occupying the seat next to Molly.

"Oh, Christ!" I shouted, jumping from the table and knocking the magical plate of chicken to the floor.

I lurched a couple of times, just barely beating back the urge to vomit. A noose hung from Trip's neck, and his eyes were bulging from his head. His mouth was stuck wide-open, as if he had been caught in one last scream, and a maggot slipped out over his pale lips and landed on the table.

"Good God..." was all I could get out before doubling over and blowing lunch.

"Sorry about that, Mr. Daniels," Marcus said. "I hate that you wound up having to waste Molly's best meal that way."

"Marcus, is he dead this time?" I asked, unable to look back in the direction of the table.

"Almost. Mr. Daniels," he said. "But you gotta act quick-like. I'd say right this minute wouldn't be too soon, sir."

"Act?" I asked. "What do I have to do?"

"The answer's same as before, Mr. Daniels," he said. "And you can turn around now ... I smoothed over the sight of Mr. Singletary fer ya."

When I turned around, the gruesome image of Trip had vanished. Marcus motioned for me to sit back down.

"I just don't know what you mean when you say I should 'accept my gift'! I would if I could, but I don't know what you mean!"

"Of course you do," Marcus said. "Giving in to one's own-self ain't like having to trust in what others tell you. God lives in each and every one of us, and so giving your life over to what's inside you is the same as trusting in God's plan."

"I'm sorry, Marcus, but more riddles just won't help me. Please just tell me what it is I need to do!"

"I wished I could be more direct-like, Mr. Daniels, but that's just not allowed. Besides, the answer's in you, not me."

Molly got up and moved toward the kitchen. I watched as she walked straight through a closed door, and when I turned back around Marcus was gone as well. Alone in the restaurant, I heard a commotion outside the front windows and strolled over reluctantly to take a look. Across the street was a scene from Manhattan – specifically, the entrance to St. Patrick's Cathedral. As six men carried a coffin up the front steps, two women dressed in black hugged and cried on each other's shoulders. I did not recognize the younger of the two, but the older woman I'd seen at Christmas parties from years past. It was Trip Singletary's mother.

Chapter 29

From the pitched darkness of my room at the Marriott Courtyard, I was once again awoken by a pounding at my door, and to the loud but strangely muted voice of Hank the night watchman.

"Mr. Daniels! I need you to wake up for just a minute," Hank said after each booming knock.

The scene playing out was oddly familiar in my head. I calmly leaned over the edge of my bed to look for light coming up through the floor. "Hank? Do I need to stay put, or is it okay to come to the door?"

"It's safe enough this time, Mr. Daniels. I just have a message to pass on."

I flipped on the light next to my bed. There didn't seem to be anything out of place around the room. Still, I made my way to the door with caution.

"It's downright unhealthy how hard you sleep, Mr. Daniels," Hank said, after I slid the lock on the chain.

"Sorry. I'm taking medication that knocks me out pretty good."

"Well, that does shed a little light on things. Luckily we ain't all that full just yet, or I'm certain I'd of woke up half the hotel."

"You said you had a message for me?"

"Oh, yes sir," he said, pulling a phone message slip out of his pocket. "This Bart fella has been calling you since about four o'clock this morning."

"What time is it now?"

"About four-thirty, Mr. D. We've been a ringing him through to your room about every five minutes."

"Well, again, my apologies for your trouble. I'll give him a call after I get some coffee. Is it ready down there yet, Hank?"

"It sure enough is, Mr. Daniels, but this fella seemed in a mighty big hurry to get a holt of you. Said it were an 'absolute emergency'."

"Right, I better get to it then," I said, not yet as worried about a Bart *emergency* as Hank had come to be. "I'll call first, and then I'll make my way down for the coffee."

Hank seemed relieved and left me to it. The number on the message began with the area code for Charleston. Knowing that crazy Bart had been rushing off to meet even crazier Trip Singletary in the lobby bar the night before, my best guess was that the number would ring straight through to the Charleston Police Department. It wasn't the first "absolute emergency" from Bart I had responded to, and I knew it was likely to include a need to raise bail for one or both of them. It was four thirty-five in the morning when the call went through.

"Trevor Galax," is what I thought I heard the voice on the other end answer.

"Trevor? Is that you?"

"It is indeed. Would this be Mark Daniels?"

"It is. I'm sorry, but I got a message from my colleague to call him at this number."

"Mr. Kennedy is standing just here beside me, Mark. I shall put him on the line for you now."

"Mark, thank God!" Bart said quickly. "We've been trying to get you to pick up the phone forever."

"Bart, what the hell is going on? "

"I'm sitting here in Galax's office."

"I got that much. What have you done that you need an attorney?"

"It's not me this time," he said soberly. "You have to get down here right away. We have a *huge* problem here."

"What kind of huge problem?"

There was a pause as Galax seemed to whisper something in the background. "I can't get into that right now," Bart replied. "Just get in the car and drive down here ASAP."

"If you think I'm just going jump out of bed in the middle—"

"Damn it, Mark!" Bart shouted over me. "We don't have time for this nonsense. I'll explain everything when you get here, but there is no time for that now! This is a matter of life and death, my friend."

I'd never heard Bart sound so firm or serious. He used humor and wit at even the driest of moments, so much so that Carl had taken to finding ways to get Bart out of the office on days we were going to have internal meetings with the higher-ups at the paper.

"I'm leaving right now," I said.

"Good," Bart said, relief coming across the wire with the sound of his voice. "Call us from the road when you get close to Charleston and we'll give you directions."

As I hung up the phone, my nose detected an offensive smell coming from the opposite side of the bed. When I leaned across to look, there was a large pool of vomit – and my mind immediately returned to yet another interrupted dream. Rather than scared, this one left me angry. I was mad that the feeling of normality I'd taken from my session with Dr. Keller had vanished so quickly, and I was incensed the medication I'd felt so confident in was apparently worthless. But more than all else, I was infuriated by the prospect that I was once again losing control – and that there didn't seem to be anything I could do to stop it.

The connections between that night's dream and the previous ones were obvious. Marcus turning up and telling me to accept some kind of gift wasn't new; neither was the warning about Trip. The one difference that night was my breakthrough recollection of the lovely Jill DeAngelo with Dr. Keller - and the newly refreshed memory of the consequences that were possible if I ignored it.

Chapter 30

After spotting a sign announcing that Charleston could be reached from any of the next eight exits, my cell phone rang.

"Where are you, Mark?" Bart said without a greeting.

"I'm just coming up on the first exit for Charleston,"

"He's just coming up on the first exit for Charleston," Bart whispered away from the phone.

I could hear mumbles from the other end as the second of the signs for Charleston came into view. I quickly grew impatient. "Bart!" I hollered. "Just put Galax on the phone!"

"Hey, look, I'm just going to put Galax on the phone to guide you in," Bart said.

"That would be—"

"Here he is."

Bart was either uncharacteristically jittery or had gone completely deaf. He seemed lost.

"Good morning, Mr. Daniels. It sounds as if you are near to us."

"I'm just coming up on the exit for Meeting Street."

"Yes, you are still a few exits from the one you will need to take to get to my offices."

"Please don't use one of those silly southern colloquialisms like '*a good bit of road away*'."

"No, you are not that far, Mr. Daniels," Galax replied, giving me my first clue of just how long a good bit of road might be. "Take exit number six and turn in the direction indicated for downtown. In precisely four traffic lights, take a right-turn onto Bedford Road."

"Then what?"

"There is no more to convey. We are in the third building on your right. There is a sign in front. I will wait for you in the lobby to give you access."

"I'm looking forward to it."

Galax didn't seem as harried as my journalistic partner. He sounded as if he were a guide at a museum, taking a group of out-of-towners through an exhibit he'd been through many times before. It helped to ease the angst I felt.

As I pulled into the parking lot behind the sign for Galax's offices, I saw Bart waiting on the porch, nervously smoking a cigarette. He recognized me behind the wheel and began to trot in my direction.

"Shit, man, am I glad to see you," he said, reaching me before I could step from the rental car.

"Bart, come on. I know you're worried but do you have to keep—"

"Oh, give it a rest, will you!" he screeched uncharacteristically. "The last thing I need right now is a grammar lesson."

"Actually, your grammar isn't the problem. It's your choice of words that—"

"Enough already! This is just not the time for this!"

It was not the light-hearted Bart in front of me. "Okay, okay. Settle down," I said. "Tell me what's going on."

"It's Trip. He's in trouble."

"What happened? Is he in Jail?"

Bart let out a nervous laugh as we reached the front porch of attorney Galax's office. Galax turned the key in the lock and opened the door for us.

"So, is he in jail or what?" I said pressing.

Bart waited for Galax to close and lock the door behind us.

After the lock clicked, Bart said, "He's a hostage!"

"A hostage? What the hell are you talking about?"

Bart looked over at Galax.

"I'm afraid that term is probably appropriate, Mark." Galax said.

Bart gestured toward Galax as if he were an expert witness that had just cinched the case.

"Look, you guys aren't really giving me much to work from here. Bart, why don't you start from where we left off last night. What happened after you went downstairs at your hotel to meet Trip?"

"Gentlemen, our receptionists will be along shortly to open the offices for business hours," Galax said as he moved from the lobby to a hallway. "May I suggest we adjourn to my office in order to maintain a level of privacy around our discussion?"

"Privacy? Why do we need privacy?" I asked.

"In due time, Mr. Daniels," Galax replied with an arm outstretched, pointing down the hallway. "In due time, sir."

Bart started down the hallway, and I grudgingly followed. Once inside Galax's office, the wily attorney calmly spun and turned the lock on his office door, then took a seat in the big leather chair behind his rather plain-looking and surprisingly worn, old desk. Bart flopped into one of the matching leather chairs in front of Galax's desk, as if he'd already had the opportunity to become well acquainted with it.

"Mr. Daniels, please have a seat and we will have Mr. Kennedy proceed with the story."

With those words it struck me that Trevor Galax was the only one in the room that wasn't anxious. Whatever was going on, Galax was acting as if he were the manager of a sports venue dealing with a couple of nuts who had forgotten their tickets to the big game. Despite Bart's dramatic pronouncement of Trip's status, Galax demeanor left me unprepared for the story that was to follow.

"Listen, Trip's gotten himself into a huge pickle," Bart said as I took my seat.

"From the beginning, Bart. What big piece of information did Trip have for you when you went downstairs to meet him in the hotel bar?"

"He'd come across the location of a meeting of the KKK."

"The Klu Klux Klan?"

"Correct. Or to be specific, the Knights of the Southern Resistance."

"A shadowy group, long rumored to exist," Galax interjected. "But a group for whom no one has ever acknowledged being a part – nor has anyone ever been able to prove are in fact a real organization.

"Until now!" Bart said.

Galax gently nodded his head.

"Okay, so let's back up. You mentioned that Trip had something to share with you about the Buckminster case. What does the Klan have to do with Bo Buckminster?"

"Trip got the meeting location from your boy, Corey Aycock."

"What?"

"You heard me right, my friend. He apparently caught up with him at a local bar yesterday afternoon and helped him along to a good drunk."

"He got him all liquored-up to pump him for information?"

"Something like that. Though Trip did say he was already well on his way to being snockered when they met."

"How?"

"What do you mean, *how*?" Bart snapped. "I suppose he bought him a bunch of shots. It's not all that difficult to get someone shit-faced – especially if they're already motivated."

"No, knucklehead. How did he know where to find Corey Aycock?"

"That would be a connection that I must take responsibility for," Galax said. "I provided Mr. Singletary with the name of an establishment where, at the appropriate hour, he might have the opportunity to meet up with Mr. Aycock."

I understood there was a connection, but couldn't make the pieces fit.

"So Trip pulls information about a KKK meeting out of the Aycock kid. But what does that have to do with the Buckminster case?"

"The guest-of-honor for the night, that's what" Bart replied.

"And who would that be?"

"A certain state senator. One that is currently campaigning to upgrade that title to the national level."

It was a huge development, and both Bart and Trevor Galax seemed to be letting me sit with it for awhile to get used to the idea.

"Wait a minute, are you guys saying that Senator Hunter was the guest of honor at a KKK meeting."

"One and the same," Bart confirmed.

"Gentlemen, I do feel I must point out that while Mr. Kennedy keeps referring to this as a meeting of the Klu Klux Klan, I am unaware of any direct ties between the Knights of Southern Resurgence and that organization."

"Shit flies are all related," Bart countered quickly. "Even when they don't happen to be sitting on the same pile."

My head was beginning to spin, and the image of Trip from my earlier dream was seeping back in front of my mind's eye. "So where is Trip now?"

"We don't know," Bart answered. "We only know that this organization is holding on to him until they get what they want."

"Which is?"

"The camera Trip used to take a picture of their meeting. He shot it through the window of a hunting cabin."

"You went there together?"

"We did. I tried to tell the crazy bastard not to get that close, but since he wasn't able to get a shot of the senator arriving without using his flash, he wanted to get to the window."

"So where is the camera now?"

Galax slid open one of the side drawers on his old desk and brought out Trip's camera – the same one I'd seen in my dream. My breathing began to get shallow, and I could feel the blood beginning to pump across my stomach.

"Do you have any water, Trevor?" I asked as I reached into my jacket pocket for my meds.

"Damn it, Mark!" Bart said. "Don't you go getting all cuckoo on me now."

"Shut up, Bart," I said.

Galax got up to retrieve a cup of water from a cooler we'd passed on the way in.

"I'm serious, man," Bart said under his breath as Galax stepped out. "We cannot afford for you to have one of your episodes here."

"Relax. That's what the meds are for." I popped a couple pills in my mouth

Galax came back in with the water and handed it to me. "Do you think you will need to lie down, Mr. Daniels?"

"Thanks, but I'll be fine."

Bart seemed to wait with me a minute, as if watching for my meds to kick in.

"So, Bart, how is it that you're here, and Trip is wherever he is?"

"Somebody must have spotted him through the window. I was about twenty feet behind him in the bushes, and when he saw a couple of the guys stand up and point in his direction, he turned and threw the damn camera at me like it was football."

"How did you get away?"

"I ran like hell. My rental car was parked back down a side road. They may not have known there were two of us – at least, not until they figured out that they had the photographer but not the camera."

A more important question had popped into my head while Bart was answering, but I took a minute to find the right phrasing for it. "And you, Trevor? How is that you are now knee-deep in this with Trip and Bart?"

"Thank God, he was waiting for me in the lobby of the hotel when I got back," Bart said.

"In the lobby of your hotel? At what – three or three thirty in the morning?"

"That is correct," Galax said. "It was approximately twenty minutes past the hour when Mr. Kennedy returned."

"And just how is it that you happened to be there at that hour?"

Galax paused, picking something from one of his fingernails. "Let's just say that you have come across one of those undulations I spoke of back in Chases Corner."

"Undulations?"

"For a lack of other explanation, yes. I'm afraid we must leave it at that for now."

"I'm not leaving nothing at nothing, Galax" I snapped. "How the hell are you wrapped up in this?"

"Mark, take it easy," Bart said. "He's helping here."

"Helping, huh? Sounds like you knew what happened before Bart even got back to the hotel. How is that?"

Galax leaned forward in his chair to speak.

"Mr. Daniels, things are not as black and white in our part of the country as they may be in yours," he said calmly. "While we too have our right and wrong or good and evil, the lines of communication between the two are perhaps more open than you might be accustomed to."

"More open? Are you saying that your superior sense of civility here in the South allows the good guys and the bad guys to remain friendly?"

"Not at all. What I'm saying is that here we are always on the lookout for a proper path to avoid confrontation. In some battles, the victor loses as much as the vanquished."

After a few seconds of mocking disbelief, I said, "That's bullshit."

"Mark, he got a call from the folks that have Trip," Bart said. "What was he supposed to do – hang up on them?"

I let Galax get a feel for my most menacing stare, before moving to the inevitable. "What'd they say?"

"They want the camera."

"That's it, they want the camera. And what's to keep us from downloading the pictures or printing out copies."

"You could, of course; but you must believe me when I tell you they will know."

"You bastard," I snorted. "Because you'll tell them, right?"

Galax leaned back in his chair with no response.

"Mark, is it so hard to believe they might have people at the hotel, or even here in Galax's office?" Bart asked.

"I don't know. Is it so hard for you to believe this clown's in on it? Jesus, when did you become so naive?"

"I don't even care!" Bart shouted. "Let's just give them the camera and be done with it. This is *way* more than I signed on for, for Christ's sake."

In the silence that settled in after Bart's outburst, there was a sick feeling of disgust building in my stomach over what was apparently inevitable.

"Gentlemen, we haven't much time,' Galax finally said. "A courier will be here in a few minutes to pick up the camera."

"And we just hand it over?"

"If that is your decision. I will leave that up to you."

"And if we don't?" I asked.

Galax stared straight ahead. "These are not men of conscience," he said simply.

"Mark, just give them the camera," Bart said. "We didn't come here for this."

"Do whatever the hell you want to," I said. "I don't want anything to do with this snake in the grass."

Just as I finished there was a buzzing from a box on Galax's desk.

Galax pushed a button. "Yes, Magnolia."

"Good Morning, Mr. Galax. You're here mighty early this morning."

"Good morning to you, my dear. We are at present awaiting the arrival of a courier. Can you please let me know the moment he arrives?"

"Yes, sir. I surely will do it."

"Thank you."

There was a tense, word-less pause.

"Will we still be able to meet with Aycock this afternoon?" I asked Galax with a sharp tone.

"All things considered, I cannot vouch for Mr. Aycock's attendance."

"Is he in some kind of danger?"

"Do you mean as a result of giving away the location of last night's meeting?"

"What else?"

"Yes, well, I think we can surmise that there are some who will not be happy if that information is known to them."

"And you haven't told them?"

"Mr. Daniels, surely there must be some way for me to assuage your suspicions of me. I am really not one of the bad guys."

I was on the verge of shouting when Magnolia buzzed back in. "Mr. Galax, your courier has arrived."

"Thank you, Magnolia. I shall be there directly."

Galax stood up without picking up the camera. "I'll give you this one opportunity to alter your decision," he said.

"Just take the camera out there," Bart said. He picked it up off the desk and thrust it at Galax.

Galax nodded his head slowly, and then turned to start for the door. I grabbed his wrist before he could make his first step. "How are we supposed to get Trip back after they have that camera?"

"The courier will place a call as soon as he has the camera. Mr. Singletary will then be released for us to retrieve at a location that will be provided."

"And how will we get that little tidbit of information?"

"I will receive a phone message directly."

"Really? So we're supposed to give the camera up and just wait for them to give you a little ring."

"Precisely."

I stood up and took the camera back out of his hands. Galax did not resist.

"You may think us Yankees to be idiots, but we're not fools."

"Oh, Goddamn it, Mark. Give him the camera!" Bart shouted.

"Mr. Daniels, it is not that anyone thinks you to be a fool,' Galax replied. "You must understand that though a man may be outside the law, in this small corner of the world his word is still as strong a bond as any you may receive."

I shook my head at the ridiculous statement, but as Bart was probably on the verge of using his superior size to take it from me anyway, I let Galax have the camera. He took it without a word and left the office.

"Look, let's just get through this thing and we'll sort out what we're going to do about it on the other side," Bart said, apology suddenly coloring every word.

"Seems to me there isn't anything on the other side," I said. "We don't even know if we'll really see old Trip ever again, do we?"

Bart appeared shamefaced and dropped back down in the chair, slumping as low as it would allow him without slinking to the floor. I had more for him, but there didn't seem to be much use in letting him have it.

Galax was gone from the office for just a couple of minutes. When he stepped back into the room, he immediately grabbed his coat off the rack near the door and spun around for an announcement.

"Gentlemen, we may pick up Mr. Singletary down by the docks."

"Okay, let's get this over with," Bart said as he pushed himself up out of the chair.

"Hold on there, Braveheart," I said, pushing him back down in his chair. "Somebody needs to stay behind – just in case the honorable Mr. Galax here is not so honorable after all."

Bart looked over at Galax, who never changed his expression. "You want me to stay here?"

"No, take my rental car back over to the hotel and wait for us in the lobby. If we're not there in forty-five minutes, go straight to the police."

Bart didn't struggle with my suggestion. In fact, he seemed to suddenly get the idea through his thick skull that we might be in as much danger as Trip.

"Lead the way," I said to Galax.

What had begun as a meeting that was surely going to push me to an episode, turned out instead to be one of the most sentient moments in my life. Whether it was the result of the fast action of my meds, or a deeper resolve to step on Galax, I had suddenly come across a very tangible level of courage. I was ready for anything.

Chapter 31

As Trip Singletary and I walked into the lobby of the Charleston Beach Front Hilton, Bart was pacing at the front desk. He had his cell phone in his hand and looked like he was about to dial. I saw him push three buttons on his phone and bring it to his ear.

"Bart!" I shouted as I quickened my pace and waved my arms in the air.

He looked around for the source, and when his eyes found me in the morning bustle of the lobby, his shoulders slumped and he let out a long breath.

"Jesus, Mark," he said as we got close enough to speak without yelling. "I was just calling the police!"

"I figured as much," I said, unable to keep a laugh from escaping.

Bart looked around the lobby, and before he could ask the obvious question a man came up behind him and stuck a stiff finger into his back, "Don't move or make a sound."

"Trip, he's been through enough," I said.

Bart spun around. "Oh, you mother!" he said as he hugged Trip's neck.

"Hey, man, get off me," Trip said. "No matter how much you may wish it otherwise, I'm not gay."

"Besides that, he's a married man now," I said.

"Damn, Daniels. You sure know how to suck the wind out of a happy moment," Trip lamented.

"Married?" Bart asked. "You?"

"Yeah, and I'm supposed to be staying out of dangerous situations for a while," Trip said. "Guess we can throw that one out the window."

The sense of relief and satisfaction hung on for just a few seconds, before giving way to immediate road ahead.

"Let's get a drink!" Bart suggested.

"It's only nine o'clock in the morning," I said.

"What's your point?"

"Well, for starters, I don't think the bar is open yet."

"There's good news on that front," Trip added. "I noticed yesterday that they were serving mimosas to the vacationers with the continental breakfast they set up in the lobby bar."

"It's not scotch and water," Bart said. "But it works for me."

The two set off arm-in-arm for the lobby bar before I could protest. Watching Bart fuss with Trip's hair playfully, and Trip push him away and punch his arm firmly in return, the image from my dream the night before finally let go of its iron grip. I wondered if Marcus were watching, and if he would now stop pestering my night's rest over it.

Bart and Trip walked straight past the hostess station to a table farthest from the rest of the crowd. The hostess had hustled over to the podium to retrieve a couple of menus when she saw them coming, and looked somewhat baffled when they didn't wait for her.

"There will be three of us," I said coming up behind her. "And I hope you don't mind if we take that table."

"Oh, well ... no ... I don't," she muttered as she retrieved a third menu.

"Thank you," I said, taking the menus from her and starting off toward Bart and Trip

"Boy, you two guys are oblivious," I said when I got to their table.

"Oblivious?" Bart replied. "Of what?"

"That's exactly my point. Do you two even need to look at the menus?"

"Not me," Trip replied. "I'll just have a muffin off the breakfast bar, and let's see ... a very large mimosa."

"Do you think they'll serve those things without the orange juice?"

A waiter arrived at our table just as Bart had asked his question. "We can do that, sir. One mimosa sans OJ. And for you gentlemen?"

"Wait," Bart continued. "Can I substitute the Champagne for Scotch?"

"I'm afraid not, sir," the waiter replied. "The liquor cabinet is locked in the morning."

"Right then, a juiceless mimosa it is."

"Make that two," Trip added.

"And the same for you, sir?" The waiter asked in my direction.

"No, no. I'll just take juice," I said.

"Coming right up," the waiter replied before quickly shuffling away.

Trip looked askance in my direction. "Are you not going to have a drink with a former hostage on the occasion of his liberation?"

"No, I'm afraid I can't."

"He's taking medication for his stomach," Bart said for cover.

"Ah, that's too bad," Trip said. "I don't guess this mess has done your stomach any good."

"No, it really hasn't, Trip."

The speedy waiter was already back at our table with our drinks. The three of us stayed silent while he set the glasses in front of us.

"How about we toast one whopper of a story," Trip said, raising his glass after the waiter had departed.

"You mean one *just missed* whopper of a story," I said. "Your picture *was* the story my friend."

"Yes, I know," Trip replied. "Now raise your glass and drink before you step all over the karma."

Bart and I looked at each other while Trip held his glass aloft.

"Trip, we had to trade your camera for you, my friend."

"I know," Trip said.

"We didn't get a chance to download your pictures, either."

"You didn't need to. It's all on the memory card."

Bart looked to me to break the bad news.

"We gave them the memory card as well," I said, bracing for the reaction.

"No, you didn't," Trip said, pulling a small memory card from the pocket of his photographer's vest and tossing it out on the table.

"You son-of-a-bitch!" Bart said. "Is that the picture?"

"It is. Now raise your glass."

I quickly covered over the memory card with my free hand and raised my glass along with Bart for a toast.

"How?" I asked with astonishment.

"My camera has dual ports for an extra memory card," Trip explained. "I knew Mr. Softie over here was sure to roll over and give up the camera at the first sign of trouble, so I dubbed it to the other one just before I tossed him the camera."

"How did you do all that so quickly?" Bart asked. "They were on us in an instant."

"Actually I have my camera set up to do it automatically. Sort of a fail-safe if you know what I mean. It only takes all of maybe three-seconds."

"That's still a mighty long three seconds," Trip said.

"Tell me about it, brother. I waited for them to see me toss it to you, then slipped the chip into my mouth. They didn't get suspicious in the least, even though I refused a drink of water about a half-dozen times."

"What if they had caught up to me?" Trip asked.

"Actually, I was counting on it. We could have been out of there in two minutes if you hadn't managed to slip away somehow."

"Damn it!" Bart said.

"So tell me, Mark," Trip said. "How is it that a dozen or so rednecks from the country could let a Yankee-assed city-boy like that one get away from them in the middle of the woods?"

I laughed heartily. "I don't know. I suppose there had to be a lot of luck in that."

Bart shook his head. "Let's be serious for a minute, guys. This is a huge story. How are we going to go about getting it in?"

"Hold on a second," Trips said, sliding his hand over mine, which still covered the memory card on the table. "There is no *we* just yet. I'm a freelancer, remember."

I slid my hand out from under Trip's, who picked up the memory card and dropped it into his vest pocket.

"*The Times* will buy that picture, Trip," I said. "You know that."

"You're probably right, but just the same I'll hold onto this baby until Carl gives the nod to a fifty K price tag. Not to mention the price of a new camera."

"That's pretty steep, but I don't think he'll have a problem with it."

"Let's say, for the sake of argument, that Carl's okay with the number. Then what?" Bart asked.

"Obviously we have a new angle to the Buckminster case," I said.

"New angle?" Trip replied. "I'd say you have a whole new story."

"I agree with Trip," Bart said. "We're talking about a candidate for national office that's tied into a hate group. Who knows how far that goes."

"I understand. But the senator is also one of the principals in the Buckminster case. I think we need to see where that thread runs first."

Trip and Bart sat back in their chairs, looking at each other as if two sides were forming.

"What do you propose we do?" Bart asked, already owning a touch of defiance.

"I've got some big things breaking back in Chases Corner. I've got to get back there ASAP."

There was another long pause as Bart and Trip looked at each other.

"I'm going to go get a muffin while you two sort this out," Trip said to excuse himself.

After Trip had left the table, Bart's demeanor became aggressive.

"What the hell is wrong with you. We've just been handed a ticket to the Pulitzer ceremony!"

"I agree, it's a big story; but I might be on to something even bigger."

"Bigger? What in God's name could be bigger than what is sitting in front of us right here and now."

"I don't really have all the pieces together yet. I can't … I mean, there's the possibility that—"

"Snap the hell out of it, man," Bart said, interrupting. "You're going to have to have a whole lot more than ramblings if you're expecting me to back you up with Carl."

"This story is supposed to be about the re-trial of Bo Buckminster, or have you forgotten that?" I said.

"Look, don't embarrass yourself or the paper any more in front of Trip," Bart said, disgusted. "I know you've gotten yourself wrapped up in this Buckminster case, but you've got to clear your head enough to see what's right in front of you my friend."

"What's that supposed to mean!"

"Nothing. I just think that maybe those meds of yours are starting to cloud your judgment a little."

"You son-of-a-bitch!"

"Not to mention they seem to be giving you a touch of Tourette syndrome."

I slid my chair out from the table, then stood up and slammed it back in again.

"Look, you're second-chair on this. Flush this thing out and start getting it down," I said. "Then we'll see where it goes."

"That much I can do."

"But do not, under any circumstances, even think about putting something in the can until I get through running the Buckminster story."

I was wagging my finger at Bart when Trip returned to the table. "Am I interrupting a lover's spat," he asked sarcastically.

"Yeah, well, just keep in mind that decision may not be up to me *or* you" Bart said, before polishing off his glass of champagne.

"Bart, if you screw me on this one ..."

"Then what? I think you better focus more on not screwing yourself my friend."

"You guys sure the two of you aren't married?" Trip asked. "This sounds just like my honeymoon."

I stared at Bart a moment or two, but he wouldn't look me in the eye.

"I'm going to drive back to Chases Corner," I said finally. "I've got some unfinished business with a priest to take care of."

"Let me guess," Bart said. "You're finally going get that hard evidence that proves we're all going to be retarded soon."

Chapter 32

I was madder than a hornet during the entire drive back to Chases Corner. I suppose I should have counted on Carl forwarding my dailies to my new partner, but from the way Trip had made his insensitive crack, I got the sense the two were critiquing them together. It was obvious my last post about my meeting with Father Hanaway hadn't impressed either of them.

Bart was right about one thing: this new story featuring Senator Hunter and his Klan pals was a big one. Trip's picture, even with nothing more than a caption below it, was enough to hit the front pages. And there was no telling what would be uncovered with some thorough digging. I knew that I had surprised Bart when I'd passed on such a juicy opportunity in favor of getting back to Chases Corner, but there was something driving me; a thing I was convinced was even bigger. Through it all there had been a constant, nagging feeling that I was *supposed* to be there in Chases Corner. It was either that, or I truly was going stark raving, out-of-my-head crazy – and by then I had not yet ruled that out.

My hasty exit from Charleston had blown one other opportunity: the chance to see if Corey Aycock turned up for the meeting Galax had arranged. Whether he would show or not was dicey, but I did want desperately to speak with him. He was the only person left on the planet who could say with a certainty who had killed Marcus Brown. When the meeting had first been set, I hadn't held out much hope of a dramatic shift in his story-line, but with the tip Aycock had provided Trip Singletary, it did seem that any ties with the senator and his family were now broken. If Bo Buckminster did not kill Marcus Brown, the only remaining suspects were Corey Aycock and Trey Hunter. With his pal Trey now deceased – and any protective cover that may have been provided over the years by Senator Hunter about to crumble – he might have been primed for a heart-to-heart cleansing. I knew I had to trust Bart to be astute enough to drill down on it for me, but with his new story angle breaking, I also knew there wasn't much chance my questions would be high on his list. The point-blank question of who killed Marcus Brown was going to have to come from me, and I almost turned back for Charleston to ask it.

Once again, the closer I got to the exit for the Marriott Courtyard Hotel, the sleepier I became. Very understandable after the day I had already put in, and considering the toll a morning full of high anxiety and stress tends to have on the body. I was stuck in a near trance-like state from the long drive when I heard the front desk guy yelling to get my attention.

"Um, excuse me, Mr. Daniels?" I heard him shout after I'd pushed the elevator button.

"Oh, sorry. How are you?"

"I'm fine, sir. There is a message for you, though."

"Thanks very much. I'll listen to it when I get upstairs."

"No, sir, I have the message right here. Mr. Buckminster wasn't comfortable with me transferring him to your voicemail. He asked that I write it down for you, word for word."

The elevator arrived just as he finished.

"I could have someone bring it up to you?"

'No, no. I'll take it now," I said and scooted back towards the front desk.

After handing me the folded note, the front-desk attendant had hung around, as if he were waiting for my reaction.

> Mr. Daniels,
> I'm powerful sorry, but if you was still wanting to meet again you'll have to come on up to that prison to talk more. Auntie is taking me back up there today, but don't you worry none. They's plenty of places we can sit and talk there if you like.
> Your Friend,
> Bosephus Buckminster

It was dated that day, received at 8:37 AM.

"Did he say anything else?" I asked.

"I'm sorry, Mr. Daniels. There was nothing else."

I stood there a few moments trying to decipher some hidden meaning, when the front-desk guy steered me to more answers. "You know, if you speak to

Hank, he might have more to tell you about that note," he said, as if not wanting to dabble in rumors personally. "Would you like me to call him on the radio?"

'Sure," I said. "If you think he's close by."

A couple minutes later, Hank trundled through the lobby.

"Hey, there Mr. Daniels," he said with a wave. "I didn't expect to see you back here so early in the day."

"I had to get back."

"You mean to say you made it all the way to Charleston and back already?"

"Yes."

"That would explain it then."

"Explain what"

"Why you look so darn tired," he said as he drew closer. "Mr. D., don't take this wrong, but you're looking plum tuckered-out just about now."

"You have a keen eye, Hank."

"I don't reckon it takes a keen eye to see a fella that's wore himself down. You oughta get some rest."

"I might just do that. But first; what can you tell me about Bo Buckminster going back to prison?"

'Oh, yes. I hear tell he just got one big hankering to go back there to wait out his hearing. If you ask me, it would be mighty tough to live with that aunt of his – least ways, if you was needing a clean breath of air every now and again. But folks say it weren't so much his auntie as he kept saying there was something he needed to be doing up there at that prison."

"Something he needed to do?"

"That's what they say. Appears he kept a bugging his auntie about it so much, she finally just took him down to the courthouse and gave up his custody."

"Has he already been taken back to the prison?"

"No, I don't reckon he's left just yet. I hear tell they're holding him down at the courthouse till the judge makes a decision on what to do with him."

I left Hank standing at the counter and bolted back out the entrance.

"You oughta get yourself a nap first, Mr. Daniels. A man can't just keep running—"

The sliding glass door cut off his last sentence, though I knew he was right with what he was saying. I wished I'd grabbed a cup of coffee, because the battle against my eyelids took a full effort as I drove the winding roads into Chases Corner. At one point, I think I actually did fall asleep at the wheel, but a couple large humps along the side of the road temporarily scared me out of the brief slumber. When I got to town, I was running on pure adrenaline.

"A very good morning to you, Mr. Daniels" my security-guard friend said as I entered the courthouse. "I had a suspicion *The New York Times* might be showing up here today."

"I can imagine you would," I replied, lifting my arms for a pat-down. "Is he still here?"

"Yes, sir. They put him in the holding area till the judge can get here."

"What time are they expecting the judge?"

The security guard finished patting me down before answering. "Well, sir," he said standing upright again. "It's almost noon now, so I reckon he'll be along in an hour or two. He's a circuit judge, you know – had court in another county this morning."

"Are they planning some kind of court appearance?"

"You mind if I look inside that case of yours, Mr. Daniels?"

"No, go ahead."

The guard gave a perfunctory look through the case. "I don't guess they'll be all that formal," he said, zipping the case back up again. "I believe the judge is more likely to handle things in chambers."

"Is anyone from Bo's attorney's office coming in to be here?"

"Now, that I can't say. Seems like they could do it all by conference call, but I'm not in a position to say either way."

"Who would I need to see to get permission to speak with him?"

"You mean old Bo?"

"Yes. To speak with Bo."

"Ah, you don't need no permission for that. Bo ain't being held against his will, at least not yet anyway."

"How do I get to the holding area?"

"Hold tight and I'll get you an escort," the guard replied, taking a walkie-talkie from his waist-belt. "Hey, Margie, anyone in there with old Bo?"

"I don't believe so," a voice came back.

"Say, how about you come up here to the front and take Mr. Daniels from *The New York Times* back there to see him," he asked. "That is, if old Bo don't mind having his company."

"I'm sure he won't mind," she said. "I'll be along shortly."

In a few moments, I heard the quick clatter of heels coming toward the front. The woman from my first day at the courthouse stuck her head through the glass door. "It's a pleasure to see you again, Mr. Daniels," she said. "If you'll come with me I'll take you to see Bo directly."

As we walked through the hallways, I thought I heard the woman giggle to herself a couple of times. When we got to the large, maple doors to the holding area, the bailiff was there waiting for us.

"Here you go, Fred. You remember Mr. Daniels, don't you?"

"I sure enough do. How are you today, Mr. Daniels?"

"I'm fine thanks."

"Well, this is where I leave you," Margie said, thrusting her hand in my direction. "You think you might be heading over to Molly's when you finish up here?"

"Maybe. It depends on when I finish up with Bo, I guess."

"Well, I'm sure everyone over there will be happy to see you," she said, this time not even trying to cover over the silly little laugh.

"Yes, I'm sure."

Margie giggled a couple more times as she walked away from us down the hallway. "Don't pay her no mind, Mr. Daniels" the bailiff said. "Them women will conspire against any man that ain't got a ring on their finger."

"Do you know any place I can buy a ring in a hurry?"

The bailiff laughed. "No, sir, but I can get you out of harm's way by letting you in to see old Bo."

"That would be good enough for now," I said with a smile, my first of the day.

As the door opened, I could see Bo sitting abnormally erect in a plain chair, rocking slightly forward and back.

"Bo, Mr. Daniels is here to see you," the bailiff announced.

Bo bolted to his feet at the bailiffs words and plastered a huge smile across his face.

"Mr. Daniels?" he said. "Well that is one mighty fine blessing."

'Hello, Bo. Do you have a few minutes to talk?"

"I reckon I have plenty of minutes, Mr. Daniels. That is if you're willing to keep track of them till we get to a few."

"I'll do it. How are things going?"

"Pretty well, Mr. Daniels. Least ways, I can't complain."

"I'm glad to hear that. Do you mind if we sit down?"

"No, sir. I've been sitting right over there in that white chair. Would it be okay if I sat back down there?"

"That would be good. I'll sit in the one right across from you."

Bo nodded his head, then went back over to the seat and assumed the same nervous, rocking position he'd been in when I arrived.

I took my time settling in and opening my laptop case, waiting to see if he would relax. "Bo, you seem a bit anxious. Is there something wrong?"

"I reckon that's right, Mr. Daniels. I am a might anxious just now."

"What's got you feeling that way?"

"I need to get back to that prison, Mr. Daniels. I'm in a real anxious way over that, I suppose."

"Why do you need to get back there?"

"I don't know, really. I just knows that's where I gotta be right now."

"Are you having trouble staying with your auntie Evelyn?"

"How's that, Mr. Daniels?"

"Are you having a hard time getting along with your aunt and uncle while you stay with them at their house?"

"Oh, no, sir! They's been mighty good to me since I came back from that prison. Pretty much gave me anything a man could need. They gave me food, a roof over my head. They even kept up with where and when I needed to be places, and took me there whenever I did. Can't ask for much more than that."

"Then why, Bo? Why do you feel so strongly that you need to leave?"

"I just have things back at that prison that need tending to, Mr. Daniels."

"What kind of things?"

"Can't say as I know. Just things I reckon."

Bo's attention was suddenly drawn to an empty chair across the room. Not thinking much of it, I reached into my bag to pull out my recorder.

"Mr. Daniels, who is Skipper McGee?"

I froze with the recorder still in my hand. "What did you just say?"

"Marcus says to tell you he spoke to Skipper McGee," Bo said. "He wants you to know that Skipper says 'hey.'"

My head grew incredibly light and the room began to spin. The tape recorder dropped from my hand and crashed onto the floor. Voices swirled as I struggled to get control.

"Mr. Daniels, are you alright, sir?" I heard from across the room.

As I picked my head from my hands and looked in the direction of the voice, it was Marcus Brown. He was sitting on the edge of the chair Bo had been staring at.

"Marcus?"

"Yes, sir, Mr. Daniels," he said. "Are you gonna be okay?"

"Is this another dream?"

"Oh, no, sir," he said with a slight laugh. "This here ain't no dream."

"Mr. Daniels!" Bo shouted excitedly. "You can see Marcus a-sitting there?"

I dropped my head back into my hands and rubbed my eyes hard.

"He can see me, sure enough, Bo," Marcus said. "It might take him a minute or two to get used to the idea, though."

The three of us sat there quietly for awhile, maybe even a long while. I didn't dare lift my head again, and neither Bo nor Marcus said a word while I struggled with what was happening. Skipper McGee was one of my friends from my childhood – one of my *imaginary* friends! In fact, it was Skipper that my father had chased away with the threat of violence, just before all of my unseen playmates left for good.

"Mr. Daniels, Skipper says to tell you it's okay now," Marcus finally said. "He says that now that your daddy's passed on, they've talked. Your daddy understands."

Tears filled my eyes at the idea that my old friend Skipper, the one soul always there for me as a kid, had somehow connected with the one that had never come to know me at all. The tears grew to an uncontrolled blubbering, and I felt two large arms wrap gently around my shoulders.

"There's no need to feel sad, Mr. Daniels," Bo said. "What you're learning of is a powerful good thing."

At that moment, I knew I had gone completely crazy. I lost control like never before. It felt as though I were watching myself from another part of the room. With my head buried deep in my hands and tears cascading like a thick river rolling over a waterfall, thoughts of my distant father pushed the river along. Images of him flashed across my mind. Snapshots of all the moments in our lives together, when instead of talking, he yelled and I cowered. It was as though each scene were being played out as evidence of our tragic relationship, and in the end this strange documentary would not be stopped until each and every incident was out on the table. The major breakdown I had fought against for so many years had finally come.

Someone should have walked in on us. That's what I remember thinking when the images finally quit and the room stopped spinning long enough for me to post a thought of my own. Bo's big arms were still around me, and I felt a slight rocking motion from within his big frame. He was holding me like a child, gently waiting out the storm. We must have been like that for a good while, because the heat from his big arms was causing me to sweat where they rested.

"You sure enough cleaned out a whole peck of them bad thoughts there, Mr. Daniels," Bo said as I lifted my head cautiously.

"Is Marcus still here," I asked without looking around myself.

"No, sir, Marcus is gone."

Relieved, I lifted my head again and tried to regain some semblance of composure. That's when a second shock blew any chance at a return to sanity. "I'm sorry, son." A blurry apparition floating in the middle of the room said softly. "For all of that."

As an image of my father reached out with both arms in my direction, a quiet, white light drifted from his hands and covered me like a blanket.

"Dad!" I yelled, struggling to push myself out from under Bo's big arms.

Slowly, the image faded; but the serene stillness that had washed over me with that gentle light remained. In one miraculous moment, demons that had been chasing me for my entire adult life went away in an instant. To that point in my life, I'd taken a cornucopia of medications to help ease anxiety, been dissected during hundreds of individual therapy sessions, and poured out more emotions during group sessions than most folks ever feel in their entire lifetimes. And while all of these did make me feel better about the burdens I carried, it was always to the symptoms they were designed to address. But in that moment, I felt cured; released from the extra baggage I secretly carried around. Somehow, I got the sense that the same might be true for my dad.

"That were a mighty powerful moment, Mr. Daniels," I heard Bo say after a few minutes of total calm.

"You saw him too, Bo?"

"I did, Mr. Daniels. Looks like your daddy's found a bit of peace for himself now," he said, sounding more like a wise old sage than a man with autism and a child's outlook.

There wasn't much else said between us. Bo smiled his trademark smile, and I smiled back. As I gathered up my things, Bo just stood there as if waiting for me to leave. He stuck his hand out when he thought I was ready.

"Congratulations, Mr. Daniels," he said with pride as I shook his hand.

I nodded but didn't say a word. It felt as if I didn't need to; like, somehow, a deeper connection between us had been established that no longer required it.

"You know, Mr. Daniels," Bo said after I'd made my way over to the door to leave. "Some folks aren't gonna think much of the story you could tell of what happened here."

I turned in his direction and chuckled. "By that do you mean they're going to think I'm crazy?"

Bo laughed with me. "Not everyone, Mr. Daniels. But, yes, sir, I reckon some folks will think you're a bit touched."

"Bo, there are some people that will tell you I lost my mind a long time ago,' I said before pausing. "And I'd say that after today they might just be right."

Bo smiled so big I felt it radiate all the way across the room and onto my own face. "And what do you think, Mr. Daniels? You thinking you've lost your mind, then?"

I paused again, sure of the answer but taking my time to enjoy that same certainty.

"I don't know for sure, Bo," I said. "But for the first time in my life I think I can honestly say I don't care."

I walked out onto the grand steps of the courthouse building, and as I looked out over the tiny town of Chases Corner, words spilled from my mouth, as if under their own power.

"Lord – 'Here am I'."

Chapter 33

What is sanity, anyway? Are we sane if everything about our lives conforms to the accepted norm, or can be rationalized or reasoned back into place when it strays?   If true, back in the Chases Corner County Courthouse with Marcus Brown and my dad was the day that Mark Daniels officially crossed the line over to insane. There was no way to rationalize what happened in that room: no safe explanation.

Of course, Dr. Keller could have helped with the repudiation process. A few more marathon sessions back in his office, and a subsequent increase in the dosage of my meds would certainly have been enough to get me back on track. He'd proven he was up to the task many times before, and though this was – in no small way – a very different kind of episode, I knew Dr. Keller could have coaxed me back onto the reservation. But as I wandered out of the courthouse that day, dazed, spent and literally numb, I knew I was never going to see Dr. Keller's face again. Never again going to listen to his soothing, calming, rationalizing nonsense.

After the ride from the courthouse over to Molly's for lunch that day, I think I realized that the balance of my life would forever include whispers and side conversations about the tragedy of Mark Daniels' decent into erratic, insane behavior. My reasons for not rationalizing – and ultimately rejecting – the incident at the courthouse were very simple: to do so meant I would have had to put aside a reconciliation that I was not prepared to let go of. I *wanted* to believe – and in believing, I had found peace. It is a powerful thing, this belief stuff. I hadn't known that before.

When I got to Molly's after my meeting with Bo at the courthouse, I was still in a bit of a fog. And here's another one of those details that is hard to explain: I was focused on nothing but having lunch! By that, I mean I had no other agenda. I simply wanted to eat. There were no pressing issues I felt I needed to be mulling over during my meal, no guilt for having interrupted my work schedule. I just wanted to enjoy lunch. Having lived with me for every day of my life, that was huge. It was the first meal I could ever recall that wasn't salted with anxiety.

As I walked up the steps to Molly's, my cell phone rang with Bart's number flashing, a call I promptly ignored. Inside, I noticed that the restaurant was packed with people, most of whom I had never seen before.

"Well, if it isn't our good friend, Mr. Daniels," the hostess said with an unusually elevated level of welcome, even for her.

'Hello, my dear," I said. "Is there going to be a wait for a table?"

The hostess started to giggle. "Does it look to you like we're more crowded than usual, Mr. Daniels?"

"I would say so. Quite a bit more."

She giggled again.

"Just never you mind about that then, Mr. Daniels," she said rubbing my upper arm. "We'll just have to slide you into the VIP room away from all those other folks milling about."

"No, really, I don't need to have—"

"Maggie!" the hostess shouted as she started off toward the French doors of the VIP room. "The restaurant is a might bit too crowded today for Mr. Daniel's liking."

"Is that right?" Maggie said as she came around the corner from the kitchen. She was beaming from ear-to-ear.

"It's sure enough the truth," the hostess added. "He said so himself."

The two of them were nodding and smiling like old women with an adult secret they were keeping from a youngster.

"Now, let's be clear here," I said a little more sternly. "I did not ask to be put in the VIP room."

'Well, sir, if there's a VIP in this restaurant today, I'd sure enough say it would have to be you," Maggie said. "Why don't you go on in and I'll fetch you a glass of tea."

The hostess held open one of the French doors and handed me a menu before walking off with yet another giggle.

After settling into one of the places at the VIP table, I was beginning to come down from the cloud I had floated on from the courthouse. A knock came at the door.

"Maggie, you don't have to knock" I shouted. "Just bring me that delicious tea."

When the door opened, it wasn't Maggie that stepped through, but rather the old woman I had seen in the kitchen. "Mr. Daniels?" she asked tentatively.

"Yes!" I said, spurring the woman to an immediate and very pronounced smile. "You're the world famous Molly, right?"

I reached out my hand, but Molly bowed slightly rather than accept it. "We are all very pleased to have you back, sir," she said with impeccable Southern charm.

"It's good to be back," I said. "Molly, I have to tell you, you're one heck of a good cook!"

"Thank you, Mr. Daniels. But I must admit that there are others who do most of the work associated with the food preparation here."

"I'm sure there are, but are all the recipes your own?"

"That they are, sir. That they are."

"Well, if you ever want to make a bundle of money for yourself, I have a few publisher friends back in New York that I'm sure would offer a pretty penny to put them in a book."

"I thank you kindly for your generous offer, Mr. Daniels, but I'm afraid that the meals from the recipes I have accumulated will forever be restricted to our humble establishment here in Chases Corner."

"I guess there's no sense giving away the secret formula then."

"Something like that," she said before bowing again. "Enjoy your meal, sir. I will leave you with a recommendation of our special today."

"Is it as good as the chicken?" I asked.

"Yes, I believe it will bring as much satisfaction to your taste buds as our fried chicken."

As Molly made a graceful exit, I marveled over the majesty about her. She reminded me more of the Charleston upper-class – that of Trevor Galax circles – than of a proprietor of an eating establishment in a bumpkin town like Chases Corner. She'd swept in and out of the room as if on a cloud, the refinement of her movement giving way to the probability that Molly was a transplant.

Maggie made it back without knocking.

"Here you go, Mr. Daniels," she said, setting two glasses of tea in front of me. "I brought you an extra since I can't see through the doors to this room to know when you get to the bottom of your glass."

"Well timed, Maggie. I thank you for that."

"Shall I tell you about the special for today?"

"No, need," I said waving her off. "Molly recommended it herself, so whatever it is, just bring it along."

"Molly recommended today's special to you?"

"Yes, she popped in to say hello. She said I would enjoy it as much as the fried chicken."

'Did she?" Maggie asked, leaking yet another series of short giggles. "A bowl of Charleston stew it is then ... and I think you may even enjoy it *more* than the fried chicken."

Within seconds of Maggie leaving to place my order, the cell phone rang again. This time it was Carl, and no doubt that when Bart had been unable to get me earlier, he would have tattled on me to the boss. Once again I didn't answer - I had no desire to talk to sane people. Especially not the two that I knew would try to talk me out of my insanity.

After a few minutes, Maggie was back with my food. It was the most delicious bowl of anything I've ever had placed in front of me. In the middle of lapping up the last remnants of tender pieces of beef and crisply cooked vegetables swirling in a spicy brown sauce, another call came in from Bart. This time I shut the phone off completely. I sat there for quite a while after finishing, enjoying the afterglow of the meal. I considered asking for a second bowl, but by the time Maggie came back to collect my plates I had another idea.

"Maggie, do you have anyone else scheduled for the VIP room this afternoon," I asked.

"Do you mean, is there anyone else coming along to eat in here?"

"Yes. I know you're busy, but I was wondering if I could just hang out here and try to get some work done rather than heading all the way back to my hotel."

Maggie laughed out loud. "Well, sir, I reckon we'll find a place out front to squeeze in any new customers that might happen along," she said. "I'll check with the girls, but I'm sure it would be okay."

"Great. Could you add a cup of coffee to the bill then?"

"I'll do it. Anything else? Maybe a piece of Molly's custard pie?"

"I'm tempted, but I think I'll let the stew settle."

"Whatever you like," she said, deftly manipulating the door with hands loaded with dishes. "You let me know if you change your mind about that pie."

When she brought my cup of coffee, I very nearly gave in to the pie idea; but I had to work to do. I didn't know what that was exactly, but with a renewed vigor I pulled out my notebook and began to try and make sense of what was happening. After a purposeful series of shapes and lines, circled words and numbered lists, the question began to work itself out.

After some time, Maggie peeked her head in. "You still okay in here, Mr. Daniels?"

"More than okay, Maggie." I replied, putting down my pen and noticing for the first time that my fingers were cramping.

"This might be your last chance for pie, Mr. Daniels," she said. "The girls are getting ready to start setting up for supper."

"Supper? How long have I been in here?"

"Oh, you don't have to worry about that, you're fine right where you are."

"Thanks, but what time is it."

"It's just a little before four o'clock, Mr. Daniels." Maggie said. "Why? Is there someplace—"

Before Maggie could finish an out-of-breath Billy Thorton squirted past her and into the room.

"Oh, thank goodness, Mr. Daniels. I been looking for you for over an hour."

"I've been right here, Billy."

"I know that now, Mr. Daniels," Billy said. "But who would of know'd to look in the VIP room. I been by here three times looking out there in the dining room."

"Okay, settle down. You've found me, so what did you need?"

"Mr. Deaver sent me over with a message for you."

"Mr. Deaver?"

"He's the security guard over at the courthouse," Maggie added, hanging around for the excitement.

"Yes, sir, that's who he is all right," Billy confirmed, his breathing slowly returning to normal. "And he said for me to tell you that the judge has decided to go ahead and send Bo back to the prison."

"Decided? Was there a formal hearing? Was Mr. Galax present?"

"Them's a whole bunch of questions all at once, but here goes," Billy said, holding up three fingers. "Yes, the judge decided. No, there wasn't no hearing. And Mr. Galax was on a conference call when the judge was talking to old Bo." Billy looked proud as he pushed the final finger down. "Any other questions, Mr. Daniels?"

"No, but thanks for finally tracking me down," I replied, reaching into my wallet.

"I suppose Bo just ain't used to living outside that prison," Maggie said. "I reckon it's gonna be hard for him, if they ever do let him out of there."

"If you need anything else, just give me a holler, Mr. Daniels," Billy said. "I'll be around."

"I will, Billy. Thanks again."

Billy seemed to be giving me a thorough scan as he slowly made his way back out of the VIP room. "You're looking mighty relaxed, Mr. Daniels," he said. "How'd you get rid of them wrinkles on your forehead?"

Maggie giggled and I smiled. "Get out of here, Billy," I said, and with that he bolted back out the way he came. "You better bring my check along, Maggie."

"Sure thing, Mr. Daniels. You want me to wrap up a piece of Molly's pie to go?"

"How about you wrap up two pieces?"

"Two pieces? You'll ruin your appetite if you eat you two so close to dinner, Mr. Daniels."

"No worries. I'm not planning on eating both of them by myself."

"Well, then, sharing a piece of Molly's custard pie is a sure enough way to make a friend for life," she said as she left the room.

After she'd gone, my attention returned to the notes crammed onto a single page in my notebook. In the center was one sentence, circled for emphasis, from which all other shapes and words radiated.

CLEAR BO BUCKMINSTER OF THE MURDER OF MARCUS BROWN.

Those were the first words I'd written that day, and as I sat there waiting for Maggie to return with my pie, I circled them again, over and over. The significance they would have on the rest of my life was not lost on me as I sat there in the VIP room of Molly's World Famous Restaurant. They meant I had become an advocate rather than a reporter; the consequence of which could very well be the end of my career with *The New York Times*, or any other independent news outlet for that matter.

Yet there in the VIP room of Molly's World Famous restaurant, I began to feel with absolute surety what I was supposed to do.

Chapter 34

From the parking lot at Molly's I powered up the cell phone. Three more incoming calls from Bart's number were recorded. Skipping straight to the contacts screen, I found the number I wanted and made the call.

"This is Trevor Galax. How may I help you?"

"Trevor, it's Mark Daniels."

"Mr. Daniels, you are very much a hunted man. Your colleagues have been somewhat frantic in their attempts to reach you."

"I'm aware of that, Trevor, but I need to talk with you about Bo."

"You really should be here just now. Things are truly starting to break on the story your friends are working on."

"I'm sure they are, but obviously things are breaking here as well."

"If by that you mean Mr. Buckminster's return to prison, I assure you it was not entirely unexpected."

"Did you do anything to stop it?"

"And what is it you would have had me do, Mr. Daniels?"

"Find him another place to stay, for starters."

"Another place to stay? And with whom would you suggest?"

For just an instant, I wanted to snap at him. It passed. "Trevor, I'm beginning to worry that you may not be representing the best interests of your client."

"Mr. Daniels, there is much we should discuss, but none that I feel comfortable speaking with you about over the telephone."

"I didn't hear a denial just then."

"Nor do I feel the need to provide one. Can I tell your friends that you will be returning to Charleston?"

"You can tell them I have things to take care of here first. Should I tell your client you will be coming this way to do your job representing him?"

"Really, you and I must sit down and talk face-to-face."

"I might have expected that response. I don't understand what's going on yet, but believe me, I'm going to get to the bottom of it."

"May I say you sounded more like a detective just then, rather than someone reporting on a story."

"You can look at it from whatever angle you want. Just know that I'm not going to let Bo Buckminster be railroaded back to prison permanently."

"Bo is very lucky to have you on his side, Mr. Daniels. Once again, I wish you would decide to come here to Charleston so that we might—"

I hung up the phone and pulled out of Molly's parking lot. I knew where I needed to go and didn't want to hear about any other plan. When I got to my destination, Father Hanaway was standing in front of the church talking with what looked like a construction contractor. The old priest was pointing up to a peak on the top of the church roof, waving both hands at times in dramatic fashion. As I pulled into the driveway of his house next door, the contractor noticed me but waited for Father Hanaway to finish before nodding in my direction as I got out of the car.

"Hello, Mr. Daniels," Father Hanaway shouted with a big wave. "I'll be along in just one minute."

I waved back and watched as the old priest made a few more wild gestures, then put one hand behind his ear while he listened to the contractor's response. After shaking the man's hand, he began a lively jog over to me.

"Mr. Daniels, it is indeed a pleasant surprise to see you,' he said, out of breath from the short jaunt.

"Pleased to see you as well, Father," I said, reaching back into the car. "I was hoping that you might have some time to talk."

"Of course. For you, I have all the time you need."

He reached out to shake my hand, but I stuck a piece of Molly's pie in his hand instead. "I come bearing gifts,' I said.

"Oh. My, if that is a piece of Ms. Molly's custard pie you may truly count me as your most loyal servant."

"It is indeed. Can we sit on the porch and talk while we get after it."

"I believe there's nothing else for us to do in this situation except to eat that pie," he said with a coy grin. "I may even be able to rustle us up a cup of coffee to go with it. I've recently acquired a second coffee cup to use for guests such as yourself, and I'm anxious to try it out."

Father Hanaway headed for the screen door to his house, but spun around quickly in the middle of the steps to say something. "Oh, by the way did I mention we're getting a bell?"

"You didn't. Who's getting a bell?"

"The church!" he said emphatically. "With the help of Reverend Johnston, we were able to secure a sponsor to put a bell tower on the top of the church building."

"Is that right?" I said as the old priest started up the steps again.

"Yes, that's what I was doing just now. The gentleman I was with is from the company that will be installing it, and I was just giving him my ideas for how it might look."

"That's terrific."

After making his way inside, Father Hanaway hustled straight to the kitchen and began working on getting the coffee ready. "I failed to ask how you've been, Mr. Daniels," he said over the sounds of pots clanging. "How are you then?"

"I'm doing well, Father."

"Yes, I noticed straight away that you looked much more relaxed today than the last time we were together."

As he finished his last sentence, Father Hanaway came around the corner holding two plastic forks.

"I've only an old fashioned percolator to brew coffee with, so I'm afraid it will be some time."

"That's no problem." I said.

"If you'd like, we could go ahead and start in on that pie." He held the plastic forks up higher. "By the time we're done, we may have some coffee to wash it down with."

"That sounds good."

The old man brushed past me to lead the way back out onto the porch, and I noticed that without the flush from his little jog from the church, his face was somewhat pale. As we sat in the porch chairs, Father Hanaway seemed to take a longer time to settle in.

"I wouldn't worry too much about not having the coffee while you eat this custard pie," he said delicately unwrapping the saran wrap. "Molly's pies are always so moist, it's like eating and drinking at the same time."

When Father Hanaway chewed his first bite of the soft custard his whole face relaxed, and a few satisfied murmurs escaped. But as he swallowed, his face became strained; followed quickly by a slight gag response.

I'd been about ready to take my first bite, but paused. "What's the matter, Father," I asked. "Is there something wrong with the pie?"

The old priest waved me off without lifting his head. After a minute or two he seemed to regain his composure and took in a deep breath. "I'm very sorry," he said, as out of breath as he'd been after jogging over to meet me. "It's not the pie."

I looked at the piece of pie sitting on the end of my plastic fork.

"Go ahead and eat it!" he said. "It may be the best pie you will ever taste."

I did as he suggested, and he was right about the pie. "So if there's nothing wrong with the pie," I said after swallowing the first bite. "What's wrong with you, Father."

"I'm not well, I'm afraid."

"Not well? Do you have some kind of bug?"

"No, nothing of the sort," he said blandly. "I'm afraid I'm dying, Mr. Daniels."

There was a heavy moment between us. I set my pie down on the porch, sensing he wasn't just being dramatic.

"You know, it's not something I'm sad about either," he said, appearing to regain some measure of strength. "It's just such a disappointment that I'll probably never be able to enjoy that heavenly pie again."

I stayed quiet to give the old priest the floor. After a while he simply popped to his feet as if nothing had happened. "Well, I guess I should go in and check on that coffee," he said, before disappearing into the house.

When he finally made his way back to the porch, Father Hanaway was holding two cups of coffee, walking delicately so as not to allow any of it to lap over the sides of the cup.

"I'm sorry about the writing on your coffee cup, Mark," he said with a chuckle.

After turning the cup to see what was written on it, I too laughed a little. It read "Property of The South Carolina Dept. of Correction."

"A priest has boosted a coffee cup straight from the man," I said. "What's the world coming to?"

We both laughed heartily at the image, and the tension of the old priest's confession melted away.

"You really should eat that piece of pie," he said pointing to my pie on the floor.

"It's okay, Father," I said. "I had a really big lunch, anyway."

"So, how are you feeling?" he asked out of the blue.

"Well, as I said earlier I'm feeling fine."

"No, I mean about what you've just learned?"

"Are you asking me about how I feel concerning your health?"

"Yes, exactly. I have cancer in its very latest stages, and I'm absolutely going to die soon," he said softly, gazing intensely into my eyes as if looking for something specific. "How does that news make you feel, Mr. Daniels?"

"Do you want me to be honest?"

"Of course I do."

"I'm happy for you."

The old priest smiled from ear to ear, and fell back in his chair seemingly satisfied. "Then it's true," he said.

"What's true?"

"You've seen Marcus Brown."

I didn't answer, but it didn't seem that I needed to. "Why would you say something like that?' I asked.

"Why would I say it ... or how would I know about it?"

"Okay, how would you know?"

"I would tell you that only in *knowing* there is an afterlife could anyone possibly feel joy for someone about to die."

"So you saw that in me just now?"

"No, of course not," he said with a laugh. "Unfortunately I don't have any such gift."

I laughed with him. "Then how?"

"I talked to Bo this afternoon," he said, laughing hard enough to make it difficult to get the last word out. "He told me you saw Marcus there at the courthouse."

In the few jovial moments together that followed, any walls between the old priest and I came down completely. The first time we met, he'd given me a case of the willies, touching so close to home about things I didn't wish to speak of. By then I saw him as someone I could speak more openly to than even the good Dr. Keller.

"And you believe Bo's account of things. No doubts; you just believe him?"

"I believe everything Bo tells me. He's incapable of lying."

"That must take a lot of trust."

"It's not trust, Mark. It's *faith*."

"I thought faith was something you put in God."

"Ah, but God can come to us in all manner of forms or shapes," he said. "For me, I simply can't speak with Bosephus Buckminster without seeing the hand of God at work. He is as blessed as any person I have ever known."

"And what about you, Father?"

"What about me?"

"You get kicked out of the church you've dedicated your life to; you spend a good part of your best years being ridiculed for the work you do; and you wind up here in this hick town, practically living in squalor."

"Let's not forget about this terminal disease thing," he added.

"Right."

"So, you'd like to know if I feel blessed."

"Well, yes, that's exactly what I'd like to know."

The old priest thought on the idea for a minute, either struggling to find the right words or trying to decide his answer.

"Yes, well, I would say that I have been abundantly blessed, Mr. Daniels," he said with a certainty in his voice.

"In what way?"

"In all ways. You see, the trials and tribulations you have listed – and believe me, there have been many more – have all served me well. Each with a singular purpose for which I am eternally grateful."

"And that is?"

"Well, to strengthen my faith, of course. While I may have had doubts, and at times perhaps even been angry with God for the predicaments I have found myself in, each and every time I have come out on the other side with even more faith than before."

"So your faith is your blessing?"

"It is, Mr. Daniels. And as for my work, God has provided yet another great blessing for me, one that will see to it that all my years of study and analysis will continue after I am gone."

"And what would that be?"

"You, Mr. Daniels."

"Me?"

"That's right, my friend, you are what may turn out to be my final blessing."

"Father, I appreciate that you're willing to share your work with me, and there's no doubt I am completely re-examining my own life's work right about now."

"But?"

"But I don't have any idea what my future holds. Except to say I think I am probably going to have to look for a new job when all this is over."

"And what will you do then?"

"I don't know," I said. "The only thing I know for certain is that right this minute, I'm determined to do whatever it takes to help Bo be acquitted of a murder."

"And if that doesn't happen?"

"Do you mean if Bo isn't acquitted?"

"Yes. What will you do if that's not part of God's plan for Bo?'

I stopped before answering, as the circled and re-circled image of the words from my notebook found their way into my thoughts. "I'd find it difficult to believe that any God – yours, mine, or anyone's – would send an innocent man like Bo back to a place like that and call it a plan."

"And what would that do to your faith?"

"Father, I'm here, and there are definitely some weird things going on in my life right now..."

"Wonderful things!"

"Maybe so. Who knows at this point. But I still wouldn't say I have any *faith* at all. At least, not the kind you're talking about. I'm more afraid I might be losing my mind."

Father Hanaway's smile remained through the entire exchange, small breaks in it appearing every now and then when a grimace would shoot across his expression. Either the pain he was feeling had kept him from taking on the challenge of my previous statement, or he simply chose to leave it alone. After a few minutes he seemed to gather strength and resumed our conversation with a burst of energy.

"Enough of the talk about faith and such," he said, surprisingly. "What do you say we turn the topic of our discussion to the discourse of science?"

"Amen to that, Father."

"A very proper ending to that part of our discussion," he said. "Will you excuse me while I go inside to retrieve some papers?"

"Absolutely, Father."

I took the opportunity to retrieve my notebook; but digging in the bottom of my bag for my tape recorder, I felt a couple of pieces of plastic from my tape recorder. It seemed that when I'd dropped it back at the courthouse, I'd damaged it beyond repair.

"It looks like you may be in the market for a new tape recorder, Mr. Daniels," Father Hanaway said as he stepped back out on the porch while I fiddled with the broken recorder in vain.

"Yeah, and I'm afraid it's not going to be that easy to replace," I said. "It was one of those oldies-but-goodies."

As I slipped the recorder back into my bag, my hand brushed against another item. I pulled it out of the bag. It was the small, digital recorder I had given to Bo.

"That looks just like a little device Bo showed me the last time we were together,'" the priest said. "He was quite proud of it, I must say."

"Yes, I believe it's one I gave him," I said. "Our deal was that he would hold on to it unless he had to go back to prison. I guess he returned it somehow when I wasn't paying attention."

"Can you use it now?"

"No, not really. It only holds about five minutes of conversation."

"That's too bad. I have so much I want to share with you."

"Not to worry, Father,' I said sliding the digital recorder into the outside pocket of my bag. "I have all the technology I need to keep up with you right here in this notebook."

"I'll try not to rush through things," he said. "I can at times ramble."

"Ramble away. I've gotten along fine with just my trusty partner here for many years."

"Where would you like to start then?" he asked.

"I suppose since I just had the shock of my life, how about we start with me."

"Certainly."

"Why am I seeing dead people?"

The old priest shuffled the papers on his lap and brought one of them to the top of the pile.

"Mark, do you remember me talking about the Fragile-X gene, the one that is now being used to help diagnose autism and its carriers."

"I do. I actually did a bit of research on the topic since we met last."

"Good, then we have a foundation from which to resume our discussions. Stop me anytime if I lose you."

"I will."

"For starters, you may recall that there are roughly five or six different levels of the mutated gene. Variations that have to do with the number of repeats of certain protein levels contained within."

"That I recall. I also seem to recall that when it reaches a certain number of repeats, the likelihood of producing a child with the full blown symptoms of autism increases."

"That's correct. And since the nineteen-eighties there has been a relatively simple test that can be performed to pinpoint this mutated X gene and the number of repeats it has."

"What does that have to do with me seeing Marcus,' I asked.

"I'm getting there," he said. "Have some faith."

"Right, faith,' I said laughing.

"You of course recall that when you were here last, you cut your hand on the screen door?"

"Yes. What about it?"

"Let's just say, I took the liberty of using some of the blood you left behind that day to ... well, you could say ..."

"You did one of those DNA tests?"

The old priest paused as if caught in the middle of a burglary. "I'm very sorry, but yes I did. I've set up a small lab on top of my bathtub."

"How accurate would you say a DNA test performed in the bathtub of an old mill house is?"

"You'd be surprised," he said. "I've had my own results crossed checked with large out-of-state facilities many times."

"And what did you learn from your test results of my blood test, Father?"

"It is apparent from the test that you are indeed a carrier of the mutated Fragile-X gene," he said, sounding like a doctor delivering bad news. "And it would appear your version is very high in number of repeats and very low in protein."

"So, you're saying I'm going to have children that with autism?"

"Not necessarily," he said quickly jumping to an easier tone. "What it means is that it's possible. As we discussed the last time you were here, there are other factors."

"Such as my choice in a wife,"

"Yes, and simple chance."

"And it's the *fully* mutated version of the Fragile-X gene that would produce offspring with autism."

"It would," he said softly. "But either way, you *will* pass the mutated variety of the Fragile-X gene on to your children. There is a very high likelihood that you will have a child living on the autism spectrum."

"The autism spectrum?"

"Yes. That's how people within the autism community refer to the many different varieties and forms the disorder takes. From my experience it is a very appropriate description."

I took a couple minutes to take it all in, as Father Hanaway allowed me to ponder the news uninterrupted. I scribbled in my notebook, and inside one of the shapes I inserted the name Karen.

"Father, let's say I forgive you for the invasion of my privacy," I finally said, sitting back in my porch chair. "How do your test results help to answer the question of why I'm seeing dead people?"

"I believe there is another side-effect of the mutated Fragile-X gene that science has not yet documented."

"And what would that be?"

"Those with certain levels of protein restriction – certain degrees of mutation, if you will – also have the ability to, well - as you say, see dead people."

"What?"

"Okay, I understand your reluctance to believe that statement," the old priest said, obviously ready for my incredulity. "So let's not use the words 'dead people'."

"What words would you use then?"

"Just one," he said. "Angels."

"A lack of proteins is what causes people to see angels," I said with a cynical tone. "That's what all your years of research have come to?"

"Well, in a word, yes," the old priest admitted. "That is to say, a lack of proteins inside the Fragile-X gene seems to. But there seems to be another important factor."

"And what would that be?"

Father Hanaway paused and reached out to put his hand on my knee. "The trick seems to be in accepting that such a thing is possible."

In spite of the crazy morning, and despite the butt-kicking all my previous beliefs and boundaries had taken just hours before, there still seemed something of a stretch in what Father Hanaway was saying. It did shed some light on the whole 'accepting the gift' thing.

"And what happens when protein production shuts off completely and a child is born within the autism spectrum you speak of?"

The old priest smiled broadly. "That child has much more than the gift of seeing angels," he said. "They are the most blessed of all God's children, for they themselves have the chance to *become* one of his heavenly messengers."

"To become one?"

"That's right, Mark. There is one fundamental criteria that all angels have."

"That they're mentally retarded?"

"Oh, no, there are plenty of angels without any manner of mental incapacity whatsoever."

"Okay, then you've confused me enough to be lost here," I said, standing to walk to the edge of the porch facing the church. "What is the one fundamental criteria you're talking about?"

The church property was busy with workers getting it ready for the new bell, and while the old priest continued to delay his answer, I used the pause to watch them at work. In between hammer blows, I heard a thump on the floor of the porch.

"Father Hanaway!" I shouted as the old man finished a drop to his knees by falling in a clump, face-first against the floorboards.

The old priest lay there without moving, but as I made my way back across the porch, there was a slight but noticeable twitching of his hands, as if he were fighting something.

"Innocence," he whispered weakly as I bent down to help him.

It was his last word on Earth. As his eyes closed, the corners of his mouth pulled into a Mona-Lisa-like smile, and I felt his final breath blow against the sensitive skin along the inside of my forearm.

Chapter 35

Within an hour of his passing, every resident or guest inside the town limits of Chases Corner had made their way to the church property to pay their respects to Father Hanaway. Everything in the town came to a halt, and even the staff at Molly's restaurant closed-up shop and made their way to the church grounds. One by one they passed through the rusty screen door. The squeak it made each time became the signal that another could go in. Sitting exhausted in one of the porch chairs, I counted each squeak for a while, but gave up somewhere near one hundred. As I sat there, I felt a hand rest against the back of my shoulder.

"Mr. Daniels, I understand you were here at the very end," a familiar voice said.

I lifted my head to confirm the arrival of Reverend Lee.

"I was, Reverend," I said groggily. "I didn't even know he was that sick until today."

"Yes, well, Father Hanaway was determined to press on as if he knew nothing of his illness."

"What was wrong with him?"

"Cancer," he said plainly. "Though in recent months, all manner of maladies had overtaken his body."

"He just keeled over and that was it," I said after a moment of silence. "Just dropped dead in the middle of a sentence."

"Mark, I know it may appear that way to you, but believe me when I tell you, I don't know how he was able to make it this far. Except that there was one thing he absolutely wanted to take care of before he passed."

"And what was that one thing?"

There was a pause as the reverend adjusted his suit jacket and took in a deep breath. "Why, that would be you, Mr. Daniels."

"Me?"

"Yes ... or at least, he wanted for you to be ready."

"Ready for what?"

"To inherit all of this, of course," he said, sweeping his hand toward the house.

"He wanted me to have the house?" I said with a snicker.

"Oh, no, I will be taking over the house," he said. "It belongs to the church."

"Wait a minute," I said sitting full upright in the chair. "Are you telling me that you're moving in here?"

"It is where the pastor from the Church of All People lives," he said. "That part of Michael Hanaway's work has been left for me."

"Look, I've been freaked out enough today already," I said. "Are you saying that you'll be moving from the big city and the great big old stage you've built for yourself, to take over a Podunk church in the middle of cow-country?"

"It doesn't sound as attractive when you say it like that, but yes."

"Why?"

The reverend unbuttoned his suit jacket and took a seat in the same chair Father Hanaway had fallen from earlier that day. He looked back in the direction of a dozen or so men from the church, frantically working on the bell tower.

"You know, they've decided to honor the old man by getting that bell into place right away," he said. "We'll be ringing it for the first time at a midnight service in his honor tonight."

"Why are you doing it, Lee?" I asked again.

"When they ring that bell," he said, appearing to ignore my question, "it will serve a purpose that none of us even imagined when we talked about getting it. We all thought about how great it would be to ring the bell to announce services on special occasions or holidays. I don't think it even crossed anyone's mind that its first purpose would be as a memorial."

"You're staying because of the new bell?"

"No, of course not. But I would say that little bell and I have both found a higher purpose."

"God's purpose for Reverend Lee Johnston?"

"Yes. *His* purpose for *me*," he said. "Isn't that a kick in the pants!"

Sitting there, I noticed that this Reverend Lee Johnston looked nothing like my Reverend Lee Johnston. It was as though he had made a complete transformation.

"So, are you prepared to make do with this?" I asked, nodding in the direction of the house.

The reverend laughed out loud. "I suppose I am," he said still chuckling. "That is, once you get all of those mounds and mounds of papers out of the house. It might be made fairly cozy, I would think."

"Once *I* get it all out?" I asked. "And why would that be *my* responsibility?"

"Father Hanaway insisted on it," he said. "He told me a number of times that one day you would understand what to do with it all. Perhaps that is *your* purpose?"

"While I admit that I find Father Hanaway's work interesting, I've got just one thing on my mind right now."

"And what would that be?"

"I'm going to make sure that Bo Buckminster doesn't get railroaded back to prison."

"Hmm ..." the reverend hummed. "That would seem to put your purpose somewhat at odds with my own."

"How? I thought you came here to help get him off?"

"I did. Or at least I thought I did. Now I only know that someone will need to step in for Father Hanaway to cover his weekly visits with Bo."

"You won't have to carry that burden for long. He's innocent."

"Yes, I believe that as well," he said. "But nonetheless, I'll take over that chore for as long as is necessary. God's will be done."

The Sun had long since set and the thick darkness of a cloudy night had settled in. The reverend and I sat quietly as Chases Corner slowly ran out of visitors to parade through the cluttered and cramped mill house. I couldn't help but think of the irony surrounding me and my new best friend, and of how absolutely unexplainable this bizarre new connection would be for Carl Odette. That dogs had stopped chasing cats was manageable. That they were eating from the same bowl was beyond any words I would be able to find as an explanation for Carl.

"What time is it, Reverend?"

"It's a little after eight," he replied, struggling to get the right angle on his watch in the darkness.

"Well," I said forcing myself up and out of the chair. "I've got to get a shower. I'm starting to smell myself over here."

"I was going to say something," the reverend said. "But I was afraid that I was the one casting the odor."

"No, it's me. And if I'm going to do it, I better get going before I fall out right here on this porch."

"Will you be back for the ringing of the bell?"

I thought over his question for a moment. Midnight seemed a long way off, considering my ridiculously early start to the day.

"I suppose," I said. "If I can keep myself from passing out on the bed back at the hotel, that is."

The reverend nodded politely, and as we parted I responded in kind.

Chapter 36

Back in my room, the message light was flashing with what seemed like extra vigor. The front desk guy had mentioned that I had received a number of calls during my absence – the last of which had been placed just twenty minutes prior. I knew who they were from, but as hard as I might have tried the motivation to listen to them wouldn't come. I'm sure it was simply a matter of not wanting anyone to try and talk sense into me.

There was a moment just before getting into the shower that I almost gave in to the urge to put a good night's sleep under my belt before returning to Chases Corner. I was as tired as I'd ever been in my entire life. Physically, mentally and spiritually there was simply nothing left in the tank. But the notion that there was still something left in the day, something I couldn't afford to miss, pushed me off the bed and into the bathroom to turn on the shower. With zombie-like motions, somehow I made it through an abbreviated hygiene ritual.

Despite the shortcuts I had taken getting ready, it was still almost ten thirty when I got down to the lobby. I had planned to bring my bag, but after grabbing the strap I decided I was way too tired to lug it around. I didn't think I'd need it anyway, and having another free hand to grab a coffee and a couple cookies seemed prudent.

"Darn it!" I yelled, at the sight of an empty countertop.

"Hello, Mr. Daniels," the front desk guy shouted from his perch. "Is there something wrong?"

"No, I was just hoping there might be something to snack on over here."

"I'm afraid we put the snacks away after ten o'clock."

"That's a bummer," I said. "I'm heading back over to the church, and I wasn't able to get dinner this evening."

"Oh, you're going over for the midnight service for Father Hanaway?"

"Well, yes, and I was hoping…"

Before I could get the whole sentence out the front desk attendant quickly passed around the partition behind the front desk and emerged from a door in the hallway. "Listen, if you're going back over there why don't you just take what we have in stock with you," he said, fiddling with a set of keys until finding one to unlock a cabinet under the counter.

"I could, I suppose."

He set about the job of filling up the two large trays that sat on the counter during the day. After digging through another cabinet, he pulled out a jumbo box of Saran wrap and covered them both over.

"You shouldn't worry too much about being hungry, Mr. Daniels," he said, stacking one tray on top of the other and handing them to me.

"Listen, I was just looking for a couple of cookies."

"Oh, no," he said, laughing at my response. "I was hoping you'd be so kind as to take these cookies over to the church."

"Okay, I get it."

"The reason I said you shouldn't worry over being hungry is you'll likely have your choice of a whole table-full of casseroles and the like."

"I'll take these with me then," I said. "And I'll make sure they know where they came from."

"Thank you kindly," he replied. "And will you have your cell phone with you, Mr. Daniels?"

"What's that?"

"The folks that were trying so hard to reach you earlier kept asking me if I knew if you had your cell phone with you. Should I tell them you do?"

"You can tell them I got the message, and I'll call them when I get around to it."

"I'll do it, Mr. Daniels. Have a good evening."

I didn't have my cell phone with me, but it wasn't a conscious act. It was in my bag, and after deciding not to take it with me I hadn't even given it another thought. However, driving the dark and winding roads back to Chases Corner made me think that might not have been such a smart idea.

When I pulled up in front of the church, there was still thirty minutes before the midnight bell ringing. The new bell was being hoisted into the hastily constructed bell tower on top of the church, and a round of applause broke out as two men straddling the eaves of the church quickly ratcheted a few bolts to hold the bell in place. It swayed slightly when the ropes used to hoist it were let loose, and one of the two men quickly reached in to the clapper to keep it from ringing prematurely.

"Careful, young man," I heard the Reverend Lee shout. "We haven't time to tend to broken limbs."

The group milling about laughed at the new pastor's quip, followed by round of applause as the man pulled his hands away from the bell and it steadied it on its new perch. One of the parishioners tapped the reverend on the arm to get his attention, then pointed in my direction. He started toward me immediately.

"Mark, I'm so glad you were able to make it back," he said as he walked up to the rental car. "You looked so exhausted when you left, no one could have blamed you for sleeping through it."

"I wouldn't have missed it for the world," I said. "It looks like your bell is ready."

"Indeed. Your timing could not be any more perfect."

"Perfect may be pushing it a bit," I said, as I reached into the back seat to retrieve the cookies. "These are compliments of the Marriott Courtyard hotel."

"Wonderful," the reverend said accepting the plates. "Though I dare say we have our fair-share of food in the sanctuary. Are you hungry, Mr. Daniels?"

"Starving, actually."

"Well then, let's you and I make our way over with these fine treats, and we'll see about getting you a plate of real food to take care of that condition."

It may have had something to do with not wanting to eat inside a building where I assumed the good Father Hanaway's corpse was resting, but I didn't feel comfortable heading for the church.

"You know, I think I'll use the time before the service to rummage through Father Hanaway's eclectic archives."

"I suppose there's no time like the present to get started on that chore," he said, seeming to sense my reluctance. "Why don't you do that, and I'll send one of the ladies over with a plate for you."

"Thanks, Reverend, that would be good."

"Consider it done," he said, turning with the cookies and quick-stepping back toward the church.

I hadn't really wanted to go back into the old priest's messy abode, but felt compelled to do so. Inside, the house was brightly lit, with extra lamps and rows of rows of candles having been brought over from the church. The light gave detail to what were previously mound-like shapes along the walls, and revealed smaller stacks invisible on my past visits. It also exposed more of the dust, cobwebs and other signs of neglect. Not knowing where to begin, I grabbed a chair from the kitchenette, put it next to the first pile, and dug in. There didn't seem to be any method or purpose to what went into each pile. The first pile was a hodge-podge of old magazine articles – reprints from medical journals or handouts from seminars or lectures Father Hanaway had attended. By the time I started on the second pile, a very rudimentary filing system began to reveal itself. While the first pile had been mainly medical information of one kind or another, the second contained a whole myriad of documents concerning angels and cherubs and the like. Some were very official looking treatises put out by the Vatican, others as simple as a few pages torn from a children's book; but all had the same theme. I was encouraged by even this small level of organization, and my interest was renewed.

It was while in a mode of increasing curiosity that I came across a document that snapped my investigator reflexes to attention. About halfway down the pile of material on angels, a paper that appeared to have been typed on an old-timey typewriter was hanging separate from the rest. The title grabbed my attention: "The Fragile X Gene as a Marker for Angels to Come."

The first paragraph of the faded blue-black words typed below the title, were a continuation of my final conversation with Father Hanaway from just hours earlier. Once again, the hair raised on the back of my neck as I read through the opening paragraph:

The purest of all innocence is the foremost quality an angel must possess. Only those incapable of the tainted or corrupted thoughts our mortal minds can concoct will have the chance to one day wear the wings of our heavenly Father's glorious messengers. When this is recognized, one can come to understand that those for whom we now reserve pity may instead be deserving of veneration and praise. They are the fortunate ones; we are no more than their servants. Along with the increase in recorded Fragile-X mutations, God is simply creating a corresponding increase in the pool from which he can draw and recruit for his heavenly army of Angels.

I was lingering on that first paragraph when I heard the sound of a bell ringing outside from the direction of the church. I knew that it meant I was missing his midnight tribute, but it felt for just a moment as if the old priest were there with me in the shabby little shack, perhaps looking over my shoulder and guiding me through the mess he'd accumulated.

"Father Hanaway?" I asked out loud. "Are you here?"

With the last clang of the new bell, a small breeze fluttered through the screen door and caused a few loose papers from some of the piles to sail around the room. As they settled back in, a yellowing, hand-written note came gently to rest at my feet. It appeared to be a thank-you message the old priest had probably forgotten to send. It was signed simply: *Your Friend, Father Michael Hanaway.*

Chapter 37

As the room began to fill with natural light, I knew my interest in Father Hanaway's papers had grown to the level of obsession that night. Sunlight was pushing its way back into the room, drowning out the artificial light brought over by the parishioners. Its victory meant that I had gone yet another night without enough sleep, the thought of which reminded me of just how physically exhausted I had become. On a mental level, I was still wide-eyed, as if coming off a full night's cramming for a college exam. By the time the first Carolina gamecock began his morning calls, while I had not yet come to an understanding of Father Michael Hanaway work, I had at least come to know his motives.

If at that point I no longer thought the old priest was crazy, within Father Hanaway's work and research there was plenty to make that case. It was no mystery why the man had been ostracized by the church. For nearly his entire adult life, he had been chasing the unseen – determined to find an answer for the unknown. His ideas and theories stretched the imagination to breaking point, making them difficult believe in. He must have recognized that only a very few would ever be prepared to affirm his propositions, but he pushed on. I suppose he had faith that he would one day find someone to believe with him. On the morning after his passing, the first in many years without the old priest and his strong faith and conviction to drive his work, there remained at least one casual believer in the world to greet the morning. I stood up with difficulty, and had begun to brush away a layer of dust from my clothes when I heard a polite knock on the screen door.

"Mr. Daniels? Are you up and stirring in here?"

"I am," I said, as the Reverend Lee let himself in.

After a few minutes of studying the newly opened spaces left by my filtering through Father Hanaway's piles, Reverend Lee stepped directly toward the kitchen. "Mr. Daniels, I hope you didn't take my request to go through Father Hanaway's papers to be urgent," he said, stopping at the entrance to the kitchen. "By the way, if you'd like, I could try to get that old percolator of his to make us both a cup of coffee?"

"I think I just got carried away last night. And yes, I could definitely use a cup of coffee."

"And did you make any progress?" he said from the kitchen, already looking for the parts to the percolator.

"Well, I've at least identified the stuff I think is worth keeping," I replied. "I brought along some boxes from the hotel and should be able to get most of the important papers cleared out of here before I leave this morning. Anything left can be taken away."

"That is good news," he said, sticking his head back around from the kitchen. "But I was talking more about making progress with understanding the good Father's work."

"Oh, that," I said, while the reverend waited on my answer. "I can't say I understand his work just yet, but I have at least come to understand what he was trying to get at."

The reverend smiled. "If he were here with us now, I do believe the old man would consider that a major victory," he said, before slipping back into the kitchen to finish making the coffee.

I used the opportunity to run out to the car and retrieve the boxes I'd brought along with me the night before, and I felt my cramping legs wobble slightly as I made my way down the stairs. I was just about to fall into a nasty tumble, when I felt something push hard against the front of my shoulders. It was forceful enough to prevent my fall and caused me to pause before carrying on to consider what had happened.

"Thank you, Father," I said with a laugh. "You can go now. I've got it from here."

A gust of wind gently swayed the new bell on top of the church, producing a couple of small clanking sounds just shy of a ring. When it stopped, a black bird landed on the edge of the roughly hewn tower before darting off toward the sunrise and disappearing as a small dot against the morning sun.

"The coffee's on," Reverend Lee shouted from just inside the screen door. "Do you need help with something?"

"I just have a few empty boxes I still need to bring in."

"It will be my pleasure to help you fill them," he shouted "With the work you did last night, it would appear I might even be able to make enough room to have a place to sleep tonight."

As the reverend and I got after the job of filling the dozen or so boxes I'd brought with me not a word was said between us. There was a level of comfort that seemed to communicate all that needed saying. Lee Johnston and I had always been at opposite ends of things, jousting and fencing as two adversaries whenever we met. Neither of us ever trusted the words the other used, and were we always listening for language intended for leverage or to manipulate. It's hard to hear what someone is saying when you're on the lookout for what was not being said. I think the two of us liked that game, thrived on it even. But in the dead air between us now, working on a task together that neither one of us could have predicted would be ours, there came a commonality that seemed to say we were not so different after all. No longer having anything to gain from the other's mistake, I think we found we could become friends.

"What will you do now?" the reverend asked as he handed me the last of the boxes to stuff into the trunk of my rental car.

"Right this minute or for the rest of my life?"

"Let's start with right this minute."

"I plan to go back to the hotel and collapse. I'm way behind on my beauty sleep."

The reverend laughed. "And when you have once again regained your stunning appearance ... what then?"

"I don't know, Lee. I'll try to get up with Trevor Galax to see what he has up his sleeve for Bo's hearing."

"That's scheduled for this Friday, isn't it?"

"Yes, the day after tomorrow," I said. "I don't know how much I can do, but I know I have to try."

The reverend nodded his head a few times, as if holding back from telling me it was pointless.

"And after that, Mark? Do you think there's a story in Father Hanaway's work?"

I slammed the trunk and slipped past the reverend, giving myself time to think of an answer for him. "Probably," I said, getting into the driver's side. "There's definitely something in those boxes, but ..."

"But what?"

"I just don't know if I'm the guy to dig it out."

I closed the car door and rolled down the window. Lee Johnston stuck his head through. "Then I shall leave that between you and our Maker to work out, Mark," he said without argument.

His handshake was brief, and as I backed out of the driveway the reverend didn't wait for me to finish before walking sharply in the direction of the church.

All the way back to the hotel, I fought sleep. I did everything I could – rolling all the windows down and cranking the radio to keep from running off the country roads. I was singing along with an old Beatles song when I pulled into the Marriott parking lot. Hank was out in front, picking up trash with a pointed stick, and must have heard me coming. By the way he was standing, he appeared to be waiting for whatever was making the noise to come along. Embarrassed, I quickly turned off the radio as I pulled into the parking lot.

"Mr. Daniels, could I have a word with you?" he shouted from the other side of the parking. He approached quickly as I got out the car.

"Sorry about the radio, Hank," I said, meeting him halfway.

"Oh, that's no trouble. Soon as I saw it was you, I figured you must have been trying to keep from nodding-off."

We shook hands.

"There is something I need to give you a heads-up on, though," he said. "And I sure do hope I did the right thing."

"What's that?"

"They's two fellas up there in your room, Mr. Daniels. One of them is the man that called you so early with the emergency the other morning. The other one says he's your boss."

"My boss? A tall, good-looking man?"

"That'd be him, I reckon."

"Did he tell you his name?"

"Which one?"

"The tall one."

"I believe he said his name was ode ... oder ..."

"Carl Odette?"

"That's it! He sure enough said Odette."

"What in God's name is he doing here?"

"I hope I didn't do wrong by letting them into your room there, Mr. Daniels. It's just that the one fella kept saying they were worried about you, and when the tall one said he was your boss, why I ..."

"Don't worry, Hank. I'm fine with you letting them in. I just wasn't expecting that little twist. At least not yet."

"I could always run them off if you like?"

"That won't be necessary. I think I know what they're here for."

Hank was quiet for a second. "It ain't a bad thing, is it, Mr. Daniels?" he asked as I walked toward the hotel entrance.

I stopped to consider my answer for both of us. "You know, sometimes change is a good thing," I said turning around. "But I've had so much of it lately, I'm starting to feel like I'm living someone else's life."

Hank smiled. "This place has a way of doing that to folks, Mr. D. You wouldn't be the first."

Tired and effectively numb, I made my way through the lobby to the elevator. On the way up to my floor, I got a look at myself in the reflection of the mirrored doors, and what I saw fit precisely with how I felt. I looked like a man about to be unemployed, and I couldn't help but wonder if being an ex-reporter with *The New York Times* would be as much of a consolation to me as having an ex-fiancée had been a week or so earlier.

Outside the door to my room, I heard voices, and while poised to slide the key card into the slot, I nearly turned back around. The problem with that was that I really didn't have anywhere to go; at least not one with a bed I could crawl into. The voices stopped with the sound of my key card. Inside, Bart was sitting on the edge of the bed while Carl had made himself comfortable on the small couch.

"Well now, to what do I owe the honor of such a distinguished delegation?" I said, taking the offensive.

"At least he's alive," Bart said looking over at Carl.

Carl didn't answer or even look Bart's way. He was studying my face like a granite statue.

"Hello, Carl," I said. "If you'd let me know you were coming, I could have cleaned up a little for you."

"We tried to call you. Many times," Bart said.

"Yeah, well I've been having some trouble with my cell phone."

"And the hotel phone?" Carl said, cool but calm. "Are you having trouble with that as well?"

"Carl, you of all people should understand just how difficult these new systems are," I said sarcastically. "So many buttons to push."

Carl continued to stare with unblinking eyes. Bart on the other hand was bouncing his head back and forth between us, looking for the next volley as if watching a tennis match. I sat down at the small desk in my room and noticed my computer was on. Behind Bart, the contents of my bag were scattered across the bed.

"Did you find what you were looking for?" I asked.

Bart looked nervously at Carl for the reply.

"Give him the copy, Bart," Carl said.

Bart leaned over to the coffee table in front of Carl and grabbed a small stack of papers, then walked them over to me. "That's a story that's running tomorrow morning. It's the first of three parts. The second will run Friday, and the third a large spread in the Sunday edition."

There was a picture clipped to the front of the papers. It featured Senator Hunter standing and speaking at a table-top lectern with a very ominous looking symbol attached to it. Two men sitting to his right wore garb that could only be associated with a Klan-like organization, while a third, sitting to his left, sported a baseball cap with the confederate flag emblazoned across it. I read through the story behind the picture, and details of a long-secret racist brotherhood were slowly put forth in a methodical fashion. It was well laid out with very little supposition.

"I take it you got someone to roll over," I said after getting through the first installment.

"Yes. We have inside information," Carl said, standing and walking toward the sliding glass door that led out to the balcony. "We thought you should have a read-through."

Carl drew back the curtain and let a rush of morning light into the room.

"I'm sure Bart's done a great job with—"

"Since your name is on the byline," Carl said cutting me off. "We just figured you should know what you're getting credit for."

I hadn't noticed it at first, but there on page one was indeed both Bart's name and my own. "I didn't ask you to do that," I said. "This is not my story."

"Don't be an asshole," Bart said in a high pitched voice. "Of course it's your story."

"It's not the one I came down here to do, Bart. You're the one that stumbled across—"

"Stories don't always lead where we expect them to," Carl snapped. "That angle may not be the one you started out with, but it's the one we we're going to run with!"

"Listen, I didn't ask you to add my name to the byline. Have you even considered that there might be more than one story?"

"More than one story?" Carl asked, moving pointedly back toward the coffee table. "You say there's more than one story?"

"Yes. I just happen to be working—"

"And which one would that be, Mark?" he said, snatching another group of papers off the table. "Would that be the story about a crazy old priest that thinks we'll all be retarded in a couple of generations or so?"

"That's not what he's saying in that paper."

"Or, would it have something to do with what's coming out of your notes here?" he said, grabbing my notebook from the table. "Like maybe the one where you say you must *prove* Bo Buckminster is innocent?"

"My notes might not make sense to you, but I know exactly—"

"You know what, exactly, Mark? Do you need me to deliver that letter to Karen for you, by the way?"

"What did you do, go through my entire hard drive?"

"Just your most recent documents."

Carl tossed the items back down on the coffee table. "Mark, I'm just going to say it," he said as he calmly settled back into his seat on the couch. "You're obviously having trouble coping, and we need to get you back to New York for some help."

The room went silent. The way Carl had sat himself back down on the couch, I supposed both he and Bart had been expecting me to blow up. That I didn't, surprised all of us.

"Carl, there's no question you have to run the story about Senator Hunter," I said. "It may even get you guys a look by the Pulitzer committee."

"So, let's run with it, buddy," Bart said nervously.

"I can't go with you on this one. I've got to finish what I started here."

Bart shook his head and looked back in Carl's direction, as if to say the path was clear for Carl to take things to the next level.

"Mark, I believe you've had a very serious breakdown," he said. "I have no choice but to take the appropriate actions necessary to protect the paper."

"Breakdown? What makes you so convinced I've had a breakdown? Just because I'm standing up for a story I'm doing, doesn't mean I'm—"

"You convinced us yourself!" Carl said.

"I did?"

"Yes. We have it on tape."

My eyes darted back toward the bed, scanning the material strewn from my bag. I found what I was looking for.

"You listened to a tape from a broken tape recorder?" I asked. "That thing isn't even working. Nice try though."

Carl reached into his pocket and pulled out a pen-sized digital recorder – the one I'd recently given to Bo. When he clicked the play button with his thumb, for a moment my heart jumped up into my throat. There was just one voice on the tape: my own. Me talking to Marcus Brown, with no response. Me hollering out for my father and my imaginary friend. Me crying like a baby. At the end of the tape, Bo Buckminster could be heard comforting me as I sobbed, before the tape abruptly cut off. It was beyond embarrassing.

"Man, no one is passing judgment," Bart said breaking the deafening silence that followed. "You've beat this sort of thing before."

"This isn't like before," I said, holding on to what little defiance I still had left.

"It's not up for discussion," Carl said. "We all have to look at this for what it is."

"I swear, it's not what you think," I said.

Carl looked down and watched himself rub his hands together. I knew the conversation was over and braced myself for the proverbial hammer dropping. "Mark, I'm going to need your credentials." he said, turning his attention away from his hand wringing.

"Maybe that's a little too drastic," Bart said.

"Bart, we talked about this. If you can't be neutral, you can wait for me in the lobby."

For just an instant, I thought about giving in. On the face of it, I couldn't blame Carl for the stance he was taking and there really wasn't a middle ground for us to meet on. I was either going to have to rollover to the idea that I had once again lost my mind, or I was going to have to convince Carl that this –and any other episode he and I had gone through together – was not a matter of me flirting with crazy. In short, I would need to get Carl to accept my new *gift*; even as I struggled to completely accept it myself.

"Bart, can you reach behind you and pass my credentials to your boss," I finally said as my response.

Bart reached around and found my press passes on the bed. "Come on, man, think about what you're doing here!" he said, holding on to the credentials while he waited for my response.

"This is the best thing for everybody," I said.

"Oh, bullshit," Bart snapped as he threw the passes over to Carl. "You're just a stubborn son-of-a-bitch; and believe me, you're going to regret this for a very long time."

I already regretted it. Not that I'd been fired by one of the most prestigious news outlets in the world, but that the two of them, Carl and Bart, would be leaving there extremely disappointed in me. They were the last two people that I hadn't completely let down long before, and the sense that I would now be alone in the world was not lost on me.

"Mark, I sincerely hope you change your mind and seek help for yourself," Carl said as he stood up and reached for his bag and buttoned his suit jacket. "I'm not going to leave you without a cell phone or laptop, but you'll need to turn them in to IT when you get back to New York."

I nodded my head.

"Naturally, you'll no longer have access any to company resources. Including email, I'm afraid."

Bart stood up and threw a pillow from the bed against the head board, then stomped past me to the door without so much as a glance. Carl walked over to me and stuck his hand out, which I shook with little effort. As the two left and made their way down the hallway, I heard Bart curse at Carl, loud enough for me to hear through the door.

"Well, Mark, if you *are* going crazy," I said out loud to myself. "There's no one left to keep you from finishing the job properly."

At last there was nothing standing in the way of me and a coma. After using two large swipes of the arm to clear the items from my bag off the bed, I collapsed onto it. I was able to muster enough strength to kick my shoes off, but physically that was all I could manage. My mind raced for a few minutes, trying to force me to replay the conversation with Carl and Bart, but my body would have nothing of it. As I began to black out, one word kept popping into my head: *freedom.*

Chapter 38

In total darkness my eyes fluttered, trying to work out the difference between being opened or closed without a speck of light. I rolled my head just enough to catch a small burst of bright red in the background, a color that slowly formed into the shape of numbers on the alarm clock radio.

"Damn," I said, sticky lips and gooey mouth making it difficult to form even that one word.

After slowly throwing my legs off the bed and wiping my mouth against my sleeve, I got after the job of removing the crust from my eyes. It was a few minutes after three a.m. on Thursday morning; and that was if I'd only slept through just one cycle. I wasn't really sure, and after lighting up the lamp next to my bed I checked the date on my watch to make sure.

"Okay, Mark," I said to myself. "You're alone, unemployed, and very likely half-way to becoming a full-fledged, delusional psychotic. Now let's make this a great day!"

When a man hits a low spot in his life, he can feel it all the way to the core. I had had my share of low spots, and so I was fully aware of the consequences they could bring in terms of mood and attitude. That morning in Chases Corner there were no consequences – at least, none that I could feel. I wasn't feeling sad or bummed-out about getting canned, and I wasn't even feeling sorry for myself for the predicament I found myself in. I actually felt lighter than a feather that morning, as if not having a job, friends, or a significant other had removed all responsibility.

Having a thing taken away, something you've worked hard for most of your adult life to hold onto, it is at first a shock. In my case, that initial period was blunted by extreme fatigue, and by the time I woke up after some eighteen-hours sleep, it had played itself out. I don't suppose I would have ever have admitted that maybe, deep down, I didn't really want to be a reporter. But once I no longer was, it seemed as plain as the nose on my face.

One sign of a return to normalcy that morning was that I felt an urgent need to get myself and my surroundings in order again. With my things strewn all over the hotel room, my first task was to get everything together and put it back into place. With a trunk-load of boxes yet to be introduced, bringing them into a mess simply would not do.

After getting things tidied-up and put back in order, I took some time to apply tight hospital corners to each layer of bedding. I knew I was going to have to use the bed as a staging area for sorting documents brought from Father Hanaway's house, and I wanted to have a steady base for my own piles. Finally, after wiping down all flat surfaces with a damp washcloth and stuffing all trash into a single plastic bag outside my door, the room was ready.

For the first time in a couple of days, I took the time to go through my entire personal grooming routine from start to finish. Nails and aberrant hairs were clipped, teeth flossed and whitened, a double-shave was followed by a cooling moisturizer gently massaged into the face and neck. Inside and out, I was a new man again.

It had taken well over an hour and a half to get me and the room in tip-top shape, which meant at four thirty it was still probably too early for fresh coffee. But I was anxious to unpack the trunk of the rental car and headed down the stairs to the lobby. There I found the night watchman and the bounding aroma of fresh coffee.

"Hank, don't you ever go home?" I asked.

"Sure I do," Hank said, still pulling on the spout for the first cup of Java. "Well, now, don't you just look good enough to meet the president," he said as he turned in my direction. "You look a whole bit better than you did coming in here yesterday morning."

"Yeah, I clean up pretty well. Can I get a cup of that Java you have there."

"I suppose for a big-time celebrity such as yourself, you could have just about whatever you have a hankering for."

"Celebrity, huh," I said with a touch of sarcasm. "Tough to pass as a celebrity when you're unemployed."

As I moved over to the coffee pot Hank was looking at me with a strange eyes. "Mr. Daniels, are you saying you was let go by *The New York Times*?"

"Yes. That's what my boss was here for yesterday morning. You let him in to do it."

"He fired you as a reporter?" Hank asked again, as if needing to confirm.

"He did indeed."

When I took my first sip of coffee, I noticed that Hank was still having trouble putting the pieces together.

"Don't worry about it. I was ready to move on to something else, anyway."

"So you break a case as big as that, and they fire you?" Hank was scratching his head and I realized I might be the one missing something.

"What are you talking about when you say a case as big as that?"

"What you been doing the past twenty-four hours, Mr. Daniels? Sleeping?"

"Well, as a matter of fact ... yes."

"Oh, my. You haven't been watching no TV then?"

"You know, Hank, I've always found that pretty tough to do with my eyes closed."

"Well, sir, I reckon you probably oughta go ahead and take a look now that you're up and about. Pretty big stuff brewing down there in Charleston."

Hank was smiling like the proverbial Cheshire cat, and I was playing along when it hit me what he was talking about.

"It's Thursday morning. The story has run in *The Times!*" I said.

"Well, I can't say as I know it's in your paper just yet. But the cable news channel's been talking about it since last night."

"Right. They would have leaked it to pump up circulation."

"You sure did upset old Senator Hunter's world there, Mr. D. I always did figure him as a bit of a scoundrel, anyway."

"Do you get copies of *The New York Times* here, Hank?"

"No, sir."

"Damn!"

"Now, don't go getting your rooster feathers ruffled. I called the fella that fills the newspaper machines here every morning and asked him if he could get his hands on a copy before he came out."

"And can he get one?"

"He said he could. I figured you be wanting one."

"Boy, Hank, I sure do appreciate that. I've really been out of it."

"Don't mention it, Mr. D." he said proudly. "You sure you're fired? You and that Mr. Kennedy been mentioned all over the cable news shows. Can't see how they could let you go now."

"I'm afraid so. I didn't have much to do with that story. I don't really know why they put my name on it."

"It sure is a good thing. We got us a bad enough reputation here in the South, still hanging on from all that segregation nonsense. Them boys got no place running things."

"It's a pretty big scoop, I'll say that."

Until I heard Hank talking about the impact Bart's story was going to have, I don't think I'd really considered it. As wrapped up as I was in Bo and the wild events at the courthouse in Chases Corner, I suppose I was out of mental bandwidth.

Hank moved over to the television in the lobby area and turned the volume up. "If you wait a few minutes, they been running the story every half hour or so on this channel."

"Thanks, Hank. I might just wait for the paper."

"Suit yourself, Mr. D. What you got planned for the day, then."

"I don't know. I've got a load of boxes I need to get out of my car; but after that I'm kind of open."

"The reason I asked, is to see if you was planning on sticking around."

"I'm staying at least through Bo's hearing tomorrow, I suppose. Why do you ask?"

"Well, sir, this is rather delicate, but the folks at the front desk will need you to stop by to see them if you're planning on staying."

"What about?"

"Seems your company called and stopped any further charges on the card you gave when you checked in."

"Really?"

"Yes, sir. I'm truly sorry about it."

"Nonsense. You didn't have anything to do with that. I'll just give them one of my personal credit cards."

"That'll sure be enough take care of things." Hank pointed over at the television.

"In a breaking story we're following here at CNN, in a feature running in this morning's edition of The New York Times, *South Carolina Republican Senatorial Candidate, Wilson Hunter, is facing a bombshell revelation about his activities with a white supremacists group."*

As the anchor person spoke, Trip Singletary's photo flashed across the screen, followed by a film montage of Senator Hunter on the campaign trail.

"In a scandal that has already swept up a number of local and state politicians in South Carolina, the word from insiders is that as the story unfolds

over the next few days, candidates and politicians form surrounding states such as North Carolina and Georgia may also be implicated in what is being called the Hate and Racism Scandal, or Hategate."

"Here it comes, Mr. D," Hank said, looking over to get my attention.

"Two reporters and a freelance photographer working for The New York Times *have filed the story, one the paper says will run today and tomorrow before culminating in a large spread set for the Sunday edition."*

"Wait for it...," he added.

Just as he said it, the byline photographs of Bart, Trip, and me appeared on the screen.

"The reporters, Bart Kennedy and Mark Daniels, and the photographer, Trip Singletary, apparently risked their own lives getting to the bottom of the story, and at one point were forced to negotiate the release of Mr. Singletary, who was being held captive by associates of Senator Hunter."

"You're famous, Mr. Daniels," Hank said.

"Now I understand your celebrity comment."

"Yes, sir, I'd say you're a celebrity this morning – round these parts or any other for that matter."

"Not something I was really wanting at this point."

"Not that you need anything to cause people to recognize you around here. Most folks know who you are by now, anyway, Mr. D."

"You're right about that."

"Thing is, you weren't planning on heading down Charleston way in the next day or two, were you?"

"It's a possibility, I suppose. Why?"

"Well, sir, don't take this the wrong way about Southerners, 'cause it don't have nothing to do with how people think in Chases Corner."

"What are you talking about?"

"You have to keep close to mind that while they don't speak for the rest of us, they's some folks along the way to Charleston that might think Senator Hunter – and all he's done – ain't such a bad thing."

"You're saying there's a few bigots left in this state."

"Not just bigots – *mean* bigots," Hank said, switching to a very serious tone. "Mr. D., there's just some folks you don't want knowing what you look like when they's mad at you. CNN ain't done you no favors by putting your picture up there for every nut to get a gander at."

I had come downstairs in a fabulous mood; one that in spite of the wacky twists and turns I'd been through, had me looking ahead to the future. Now my future was still going to be dominated by the past. "This is crazy," I said. "Let me get on over to the front desk and give them my credit card."

"You want some help unloading, Mr. D."

"What's that?"

"You said you had some boxes to unload from the car."

"Oh, yeah. That would be great, Hank."

"How many you got?"

"A dozen or so, I would guess."

"I'll run and get a luggage cart to stack them on while you get things straight with the folks at the front desk."

"Great, I'll meet you at my car."

Hank stopped to turn the volume back down on the lobby television while I lingered a while, sipping coffee and reading the news ticker running underneath the CNN anchor. Over and over ran the same words: "Three Reporters from *The New York Times* Break 'Hategate' Racism Scandal in the Deep-South."

While curious at first, the more I watched the more agitated I became. That morning I had been surprised to wake up actually feeling good about the end of my career, but by sticking my name on their story Bart and Carl had made sure that I wasn't going to be out after all – just off the payroll and covering my own expenses. As I walked toward the front desk to square accounts, for the first time in many years the cost of my hotel room became an issue. There was an extra strain as I reached for my wallet, knowing my personal card was coming out.

"Good morning, Mr. Daniels," the front desk attendant sang. "Did Hank speak to you about—"

"Yes, he told me what happened."

"I'm very sorry about this. I was going to call up last night, but Hank said he'd take care of it if I let you sleep."

"No reason to be sorry. You didn't do anything."

"I'll just need a new credit card to keep on account. You're paid up through this morning."

"How much does the room cost, anyway?" I asked.

"The corporate rate for that room is ninety-nine dollars a night."

"Is there a discount for Triple A?" I asked, handing him my shiny Visa card.

"There is, but I think you have the best available rate. Do you have a Triple A card?"

"No. Just trying to establish a point for negotiations."

The front desk guy smiled nervously, unsure how serious I was being. "Do you want me to see if I can find you a cheaper room?"

"No, that won't be necessary," I said with a laugh to let him off the hook. "I just haven't paid for a hotel room in so long, I don't really know what a fair price is."

"Well, you have an excellent rate, Mr. Daniels," he said as he swiped my card.

He had to swipe it a second time, and we both began to worry about the card still being valid.

"There you go," he said, confirming it went through. "Do you know how long you'll be staying?"

I had to think it over for a second or two. "Not really," I said. "Do you need to know now?"

"No. That's just one of those things I'm supposed to ask," he said as he handed me a slip of paper and a new key. "I'll trade you out this key for your old one and you'll be all set."

After thanking him and heading for the exit, the front desk attendant tossed out one more comment. "Oh, and congratulations on your story, Mr. Daniels!"

"Thanks, but I really didn't have much to do with it," I said, starting off again.

"What exactly do you think is gonna happen to old Senator Hunter?"

"I'm not sure," I said, slowing, but not turning around this time. "I'll let you know after I read what's in the paper this morning."

Hank was waiting for me at the rental car with a gold-plated luggage cart.

"A little fancy for moving boxes," I quipped.

"Only the best for our celebrity guests!"

"I can tell this is going to be a long day," I said "Do you think everybody I see today is going to have a comment about the story in *The Times*."

"Can't see is how they'd miss something like that, Mr. D. You better get your best smile ready for folks."

"Great."

After we got all the boxes stacked, Hank took the back of the cart while I pulled it through the lobby.

"Just bringing in a few things to make my room feel more like home," I said to the confused front-desk guy. "There should be a man coming later with new drapes to hang. Would you mind keeping an eye out for him?"

"Mr. Daniels, we can't really let you—"

"Take it easy, Tristan" Hank said as he wheeled his end passed the front desk. "He's just funnin' with ya."

At the room, Hank helped me unload the boxes in three neat stacks just inside the door.

"What are you going to do with all these boxes of papers, Mr. Daniels," Hank asked, standing in the doorway.

"Well, that's a tough question. I'm not really sure what I'm supposed to do with them."

"Come again?"

"About all I can tell you is that I'm about to become an expert on the life's work of Father Michael Hanaway."

"On his ministering work?"

"No, on some research he was doing."

Hank paused. "I heard tell he was doing some of that," he said scratching his head. "Can't say as I know much about it, though."

"I'll try to get a summary together for you from all this," I said, waving my hand in the direction of the boxes.

"Nah, that won't be necessary, Mr. D." Hank said laughing. "I'll call up when the newspaper fella comes by with the paper."

"Thanks, Hank."

Alone in the room with the boxes, it felt a little like being alone with Father Hanaway's ashes.

"I sure wish you would have put all this on discs, Father," I said out loud, sitting on the edge of the bed.

During the first filtering of the old priests' papers the night of his memorial, my interest had been sparked enough to work through the night. While his ideas about autism and its connection to angels was a real hook for me, it was more like the way a good Michael Crichton novel might drag one in. Plausible science fiction rather than believable fact. Rested and reinvigorated, I was having difficulty finding the same level of motivation to begin the second round of sorting. I grabbed the first box off the top of the closest pile and set in on the bed.

I'd just taken the top off when the phone rang.

"They's here, Mr. Daniels," Hank said when I picked up. "The newspaper fella just dropped-off your copy of *The New York Times*."

"I'll be right down."

By the time I made it back to the lobby, Hank already had the newspaper open on a coffee table, with a few of the hotel staff scrunching in next to him to get a look.

"Here you go, Mr. D," Hank said flipping me another rolled-up copy. "You famous reporters get one of your very own."

With the paper unrolled, the headline jumped off the page: "SC Senate Candidate Linked to the Klan." The subtitle beneath promised more to come: "Investigation Turns Up Group with a Goal to Re-Make Southern Politics and Return to Policies of Segregation."

From the first paragraph to the last, the story was filled with so many details that it was obvious Bart, Carl and Trip had more than just an insider. The sheer volume of information, in such a short period of time, meant they had to have flipped someone at the very top. In a writing style that matched Bart to the letter, the initial installment opened with teasers for what was to come, followed by a very concise history of the organization as an introduction. Tracing itself to the original founder of the Klu Klux Klan, none other than the Civil War hero Nathan Bedford Forrest himself, the group claimed to be a continuation of that organization. The details of the group's history, after keeping its very existence secret for nearly a hundred and fifty years, seemed to prove that someone with knowledge of *everything* was rolling over to the max. With less than seventy-two hours between the time I had left Bart in Charleston and my reading the story in the paper, and considering Carl would never had gone to print without verification, there could even have been more than one.

When I'd finished, I realized the story I'd just read through was substantially expanded from the draft I'd read the morning before, and I knew my former colleagues had stayed hard at work while I'd slept.

"Those are big doings, Mr. Daniels," Hank said as I folded up my copy.

He and the cabal of hotel employees hanging with him appeared to have been waiting for me to finish. As I stood up, one of the group began to clap, inciting a round of applause from all.

"Really, I didn't write that story," I said.

"You must've had some hand in the thing, Mr. D., or they wouldn't have put your name right there on the front page with the other fellas," Hank said.

"Well, I mean I was there last Monday night in Charleston as things were starting to break, but I don't deserve—"

"The good Lord does love a humble man, Mr. D." Hank said "But he don't mind a fella taking a little credit now and again, either."

"Okay, Hank. Thank you very much,' I said.

"Mr. Daniels?" one of the employees asked.

"Yes?"

"How far is this whole thing going to go? Do you think it will reach into the governor's office?"

"You know, we're both just going to have to read about it tomorrow in the next installment."

"Come on now, folks, we probably ought to be getting back to work," Hank said. "I'm sure Mr. D. can't just give it all away. Who'd buy newspapers?"

"Thanks, Hank," I said as the others finally drifted off.

"No trouble. I still don't know if I believe you about getting fired and all, but I get that you don't want to be answering a thousand questions."

"I appreciate that."

"Were you planning to head into Chases Corner today, Mr. D?"

"Well, I was thinking about going over to Molly's for some biscuits and gravy."

"Get ready for ten thousand, then?"

"Ten thousand what?"

"Questions. These folks around this hotel are paid to be polite. I'm not so sure them over at Molly's is going to be so cooperative with the 'no questions' rule"

"Oh, crap, I didn't even think of that. You think word is out in town?"

"Mr. D., Chases Corner might be a little off the beaten path, but they do get cable TV and all."

"What are my options?"

"Well, sir, Stella will be putting the free continental breakfast out in a few minutes or so. How about I just have her run you up a plate with a little bit of everything when she's done."

"That would work," I said. "I was just going to come back here anyway to get after all those boxes of papers."

"I'll see that she does it, then. I'll have her fetch you up a pot of coffee too."

"You're a good man, Hank," I said, awkwardly reaching out to shake his hand, still a bit uncomfortable with all the kindness.

"That's no trouble," he said. "I'll be heading home in just a few minutes, so you'll be on your own for lunch."

"I think I can manage."

"But don't make any plans for dinner," he said as he shuffled away. "I'll take care of that fer ya."

"No, really you don't have to—"

"You'd be doing me a favor, Mr. D. The wife puts that little extra into the job when she knows she's cooking' for someone other than just her and me."

With that, Hank pushed open the door from the lobby marked maintenance, and I hustled to my room to get started on the only job left to me: digging through thousands of papers collected by a dead priest.

Chapter 39

So engrossed was I in Father Hanaway's material that when a knock came at my door, I hadn't noticed I was reading in what was slowly becoming the dark of night. It was Hank at the door, and he was holding a tray of plates covered in aluminum foil.

"Evening, Mr. Daniels."

"Hi, Hank. Come on in," I said, motioning for him to enter.

"Were you sleeping, Mr. D?" he asked as he set the tray on the coffee table.

"No, I've been reading through these papers the entire day."

"You really ought not to be reading in the dark, you know," he said, flicking on a light. "It strains the eyes."

"Thanks, I hadn't noticed the sun was going down."

"Must be some powerful good reading. About the only thing could make me read like that is a good Louis L'Amour novel."

"Really. You're a big reader?"

"Not much anymore, since old Louis's dead, but I read everything he ever wrote at least once. Some two or three times."

"I can't say as I've ever had the pleasure. He wrote Western novels, didn't he?"

"Yes, sir. They's all pretty much the same. Different names and such, but if you've read one you've read them all."

I laughed. "Why read them all, then?"

"I don't know, some writers just hook you, I suppose."

"I feel the same way about Gustave Flaubert."

"Who's that?"

"Gustave Flaubert."

"Flaubert, huh?"

"Yes, he's a French writer."

"Is he dead too?"

"Yes, he's been gone a while."

"I won't bother looking him up, then," he said. "I think I'll keep trying to find a live one. Are you hungry, Mr. D?"

"Now that you mention it, I'm starving."

"You didn't read straight through lunch time, did you?"

"Unfortunately, that's exactly what I did."

"Well, then," he said, pulling off the aluminum foil covering the first plate and wadding it up tight. "Let me introduce you to some of the finest low-country cooking you're ever going to eat."

On the plate were a few very pink shrimp, smothered in a sauce with vegetables and small bits of something that looked like red peppers. Next to it, the shrimp and vegetables pressed against a slim border that separated them from a clump of yellowish colored grits.

"Now they's people that will tell you shrimp and grits is a New Orleans dish, but the fact is the best you'll ever eat comes from Charleston," he said as he picked up the plate and put it into the small microwave in my room. "And the best cook that's ever come from that fair city just happens to be my bride."

As we waited out the thirty seconds he'd programmed in, a tangy, spicy smell began seeping out of the microwave. He removed the plate, and the full aroma arrived well before he set it in front of me.

"Now, I'm afraid if we put these biscuits in the microwave, we'll ruin them for sure," he said as he unwrapped another plate. "But the Mrs. buttered them up proper while they was still hot, so you won't miss out on much."

Hank stood over the table, waiting for me to sit down. After motioning for me to eat, he lingered to catch my reaction to the first bite.

"Oh, Hank, that's fabulous," I said, taking a bite of the shrimp and vegetables.

"Now I know they's separate on the plate and all, but the best way to enjoy those is to catch a little of the grits on your fork, then scoop up a shrimp or two."

I did as he suggested. "Your right, the texture of the grits is just the right mix."

Hank watched the next couple of bites with a proud smile across his face. "Well, I suppose I should let you eat your meal in private instead of hovering over you like this," he said, picking up the last plate and sliding the tray off the table. "That last plate is a slice of pecan pie, so I sure hope you have a sweet tooth."

With a mouthful of shrimp and grits, I nodded, holding up one finger and mumbling. "Hank, don't go," I said after swallowing, trying hard to clear my mouth. "If you've got the time, I'd love some company."

"What's that?"

I took a drink of water and started over. "Do you have a minute to stay and chat?"

Hank looked surprised at my request. "I suppose I could keep you company a while," he said. "Anything in particular you'd like to talk about?"

"Not really. I've just been cooped up here all day."

"I understand that," Hank said as he pulled out the other chair at the small table and sat down.

"Hank, tell me about Chases Corner?" I asked, figuring an open ended question asked of Hank would give me time to finish my dinner.

"What would you like to know, Mr. D.?"

Having just taken a large mouthful, I had to make him wait. "You know," I said, wiping my mouth with a paper napkin his wife had included. "What was this place like as you grew up? What kind of changes have you seen, that sort of thing."

Hank waited just long enough for me to get another mouthful. "I didn't grow up here," he said. He seemed to be determined to put aside the perception he was a talker at the one time I wanted him to talk.

"Where did you grow up, then?" I mumbled.

"Charleston."

Down to just one word answers, I had to let things stay quiet between us while to finished the food. Hank sat patiently until I'd soaked up the last of the sauce with a wipe of the remaining biscuit.

"Sorry, Hank," I said still chewing the last bite. "I didn't mean to be impolite."

"No trouble, Mr. Daniels, that's the way most folks get after my wife's cooking."

"And you said she's from Charleston, too?"

"Born and bred."

"What brought you two to Chases Corner?"

Hank was quiet. He seemed to be thinking of an answer, or perhaps whether or not he should give it. "Our youngest son was born late in life. We had a total of five: two girls and three boys."

"You moved here to give your youngest a better place to grow up?"

"No, sir. Tyson passed a couple weeks after his seventh birthday," Hank said, emotion building slightly in his voice. "We moved here shortly after. That was about twenty years ago, give or take."

Patterns are something reporters are trained to look for, and though my life had been shaken to a jumble, I was still a reporter. An older couple have a child late in life; the child dies; the couple moves to Chases Corner. With old Mr. Brown as a template, I knew there were more connections, but I considered carefully whether or not then was the time to try to tie them all together.

"Hank, can I ask you a delicate question? A question about your youngest son?"

"What would you like to know?"

"Was he ... well, slower than other kids?"

"You mean did he have autism?"

"I suppose that's exactly what I mean," I said, a bit surprised. "No offense, you understand?"

"None taken. Tyson was challenged with autism, sure enough. Though I can't say we knew as much back in those days."

"What do you mean, you didn't know as much?"

"We knew he wasn't like the other children when he was alive. We loved him just as much, but when a child is handicapped like that, you know something is wrong. We just didn't have a name fer it, I reckon."

Hank was being very open with his answers, but after my experience with Mr. Brown at Molly's restaurant, I didn't want to step on a raw nerve. "So, you found out Tyson had autism *after* he had passed away?"

"Yes, sir. He'd been gone a couple of years before we was able to put that together."

"How?"

"What do you mean by 'how', Mr. Daniels."

"How were you able to find out something like that after your son had died?"

"Before I answer that one, I think I'd better ask a couple questions of you first."

"Okay, fire away."

The hesitation I saw in Hank was the same I'd seen in Atticus Brown's eyes. "Are you one of them that has the *gift*?"

It was my turn to hesitate. Not because I didn't know the answer by then, but rather I had not yet said it out loud. "Yes, I think I might have the gift."

Hank's expression remained stoic. 'That's what they're saying.," he said. "But have you accepted it?"

A warmth began to flow from the tips of my toes to the top of my head, and I could feel a calm, knowing smile stretch across my face. "Yes, Hank, I believe I have accepted it."

Hank nearly burst into tears, barely holding back a torrent of emotion that caused him to choke up to the point of nearly gagging. As I waited for him to gather himself, a sensation like none other I'd ever experience settled in. I felt free.

"Mr. Daniels, are you able to …" Hank said softly.

"I could try. But you have to understand, this is all very new to me."

We waited like that for some time, both looking for something to happen, but neither one of us really knew what that might be. Eventually, the look of anticipation on Hank's face slowly began to be replaced by one of polite disappointment.

"Mr. Daniels, it sure enough was good of you to try." Hank finally said, catching a small tear that leaked from his eye. "They say it ain't just something that can—"

"Hank?"

"Yes, Mr. D?"

"Tyson's here. He say's you shouldn't cry."

Chapter 40

The rest of that evening and the morning that followed were the first of my time in Chases Corner with a normal sleeping pattern. I was in bed by ten and up by five thirty, and not a dream or disturbance to interrupt a minute's worth of solid snoozing. I woke ready for the day – a day that began with the makings of something big. The hearing for Bo Buckminster's request for a new trial was set for ten that morning. The judge's options were limited: he could either throw out the old conviction or let the original verdict stand. If, as everyone seemed to think, the verdict were set-aside, it would then be up to the county prosecutor to decide whether retry Bo on the original charges. Something that with sixteen-years and the death of a key witness, did not seem likely. But if it did come to a new trial, I was ready. I would be Bo's chief advocate, unhindered by the ethics of my former employment. All my years of experience at *The Times*, all the years of learning to scratch and dig my way to the truth, would be available for Bo. I was ready for a fight.

The day also forecast an opportunity of utilizing a whole new skill set apparently at my disposal: that of talking to the dead. Acting as the intermediary between Hank and his dead son, Tyson, should have been the single most bizarre role of my lifetime. I would have thought it enough to put me completely over the edge and send me back into the arms of Dr. Keller and his soothing medications. Instead, it was the most fulfilling and satisfying event I'd ever been a part of. Helping a good man patch a small hole left in his heart left me on a high no drug could ever match. In fact, the power of it all had been so strong that after Hank left, I took the symbolic steps of tossing my medication in the toilet. I was hooked, and anxious to meet up with another old man as he sat for breakfast at Molly's restaurant.

At precisely six forty-five, I went downstairs, anxious and excited at the idea of sharing a cup of Java with Hank. When I got to the lobby, he was nowhere in sight.

"Is Hank milling about someplace?" I asked the front desk guy.

"No sir, Mr. Daniels. He didn't come in last night."

"I don't understand? He brought me dinner."

"Yes, but he wasn't supposed to be on until eleven o'clock. After he got back home, he called back and said he was feeling a little under the weather."

"Oh, I'm sorry to hear that."

I was disappointed, but certainly could understand. Hank had become very emotional over his encounter with his son the evening before; and when he'd left, he looked exhausted. He seemed so relieved and happy, I hadn't even thought about the toll the whole affair might take on him; let alone how much more would have to be drawn from the well when he returned home to share the news with his wife.

"Is there something I can get for you, Mr. Daniels?" the front desk guy asked when I lingered. "The coffee's ready. I made it myself."

"Thank you, but I'm all set for now," I said. "I was thinking I might head in to town and get some biscuits and gravy with my coffee."

"Can't blame you for that, Mr. D." he said. "You planning on going over to the courthouse later this morning?"

"I wouldn't miss it for the world. Why do you ask?"

"I just didn't know if you were still working Bo's story," he said, reaching under the counter as he said it. "The newspaper fella left-off another copy of *The New York Times* for you," he said, tossing the latest edition on the counter. "Got your name all over it again.

As I picked up the paper the headline punched me in the nose:

THE KLAN IN THE WHITE HOUSE? Secret Klan Group Planning to Run Their Man for President: More Southern Senators Implicated in Scandal!

It was set in the boldest type used by *The Times* for any story short of a declaration of war, and as with the day before, my name was attached to the byline.

"I really haven't had anything to do with this story," I mumbled, as I quickly scanned through the text under the headline.

"I sure can appreciate the modesty, Mr. Daniels, but with your name up there at the top, you better get ready for some serious attention. This thing looks like it could be the biggest story about government in these parts since General Lee surrendered."

As scanning gave way to serious reading, the front desk guy's bold pronouncement started to feel like a major understatement. Detailed on the front-end of the story was an accounting of a plan by the Klan-like group, a scheme to eventually put up three candidates for party nominations for president of the United States: two democrats and one republican. Senator Hunter was one of the democrats, while a Georgia congressman and a sitting republican senator from Tennessee filled out the trio. With decades of ultra-secret planning and behind-the-scenes machinations, the story claimed the group had succeeded in getting the two members into national office, with Senator Hunter slated to be the third. Once in place, all three would eventually run for their respective parties nominations for the presidency, with the ultimate goal of getting one of them into the oval office.

With the power of the highest office in the land available to them, the real agenda could then be enacted: appointing like-minded judges to the federal bench and eventually to the Supreme Court. While standing in doorways had failed to prevent the march of civil-rights legislation, after the sixties the group had apparently taken a longer-term view.

The tale was so bizarre it read more like a novel than a *Times* feature. Bart was at the top of his game for this one, spinning the yarn like a master. I was just about to turn the inside flap when I was coaxed along by the front desk attendant.

"Um ... Mr. Daniels, you can feel free to take that with you," he said.

"I'm sorry," I said, noticing for the first time that a couple had come into the lobby and was standing behind me. "Please, go ahead. I'm just reading here."

"No, we weren't waiting for that," the man said. "I just told the wife I wanted to shake your hand. It took a whole lot of courage to do what you did, but we're sure glad you did it."

"Thank you, but I really didn't have anything to—"

The man reached and grabbed my hand. "We're not activists or anything, but it would have been sad to see so much progress just thrown away like that."

He shook my hand like I'd just saved his child from a burning building. The woman leaned in and gave me a giddy peck on the cheek.

"Well, we don't want to take up any of your valuable time," the man said, finally letting go of my hand. "We just wanted to make sure you knew there are people out there that support you and what you've done."

They'd already said they would leave me alone, and setting the record straight seemed like it would only prolong things. "Thanks," I said.

"No, thank *you!*" the man said, holding up a hand for a high-five.

After I'd slapped the man's hand, the two headed toward the parking lot, stopping just outside the sliding doors and waving back at me one more time before going to their car.

"You're a rock star, Mr. Daniels," the front desk attendant said. "Better get used to that."

I suddenly felt the need to get out of the lobby before any other guests came through. Folding up the paper, I stuck it under my arm, and after waiting a few seconds to watch the young couple pull out of the parking lot, I headed for the relative obscurity of my rental car.

Driving to Chases Corner I spent a good deal of car time thinking about the 'rock star' comment from the front desk guy, and about how Bart was on the verge of living out his glory days. No one was better suited for the role – at least, no one that I knew personally. And yet from his writing, he had to have been successfully fighting the urge to celebrate with a good drunk. His words were crisp, clean and sharp, and though he probably would argue otherwise, I knew there was no way he could have been so masterful without being stone-cold sober.

When I arrived at Molly's, there were people standing all the way up the steps waiting to get in. I suppose I was holding onto the futile hope that news of the second installment hadn't yet reached the crowd inside, but as Hank had pointed out, Chases Corner was wired to cable TV. Which meant I was either going to have to stutter and stammer my way into Molly's, or – as I had with the couple back at the hotel – just quietly acknowledge any praise and move on.

I heard Billy Thornton's back tire skidding through the gravel of the parking lot after I'd pulled in behind the restaurant.

"Congratulations, Mr. Daniels," he said right away. "Shouldn't you be back there in New York City at some press conference or something?"

"No, I've got work to do here, Billy."

"I saw your partner, Mr. Kennedy, this morning on the television."

"Did you? Which channel?"

"All of them!"

"All of them?"

"Well, near about. My pop was watching CNN and he was on there. Then a few minutes later he was on that morning show answering the same questions."

"I'm not surprised, Billy. That's a big scoop he's uncovered."

"Why ain't you on no TV show, then, Mr. Daniels?"

"I really didn't have much to do with it. Bart Kennedy's the one that wrote the piece that's been in the paper the last two days."

"Why's your name on it, then?"

"It's a good question, son. One I don't really have an answer for."

Billy pedaled along with me as I walked to the entrance of the restaurant, a confused look across his face as if he were trying to figure something out.

"There he is!" a man at the top of the stairs said when he noticed us. His comment was followed by a round of applause from those on the stairs, with folks stepping aside as the man at the top opened the door for me.

"Thanks very much," I said waving them off. "That's really not necessary."

"Mr. Daniels!" Billy shouted, looking over at me from his bike with huge eyes. "You accepted your gift!"

"What's that, Billy?"

"Ah, that there *is* a big story!" Billy said, an excited smile breaking out. "I reckon I know why you ain't up there in New York. Ain't no better place for a man to be on a day like this than right gosh-darn here."

Billy balanced the bike between his legs and started applauding with the group. As I slowly walked up the steps, the hand-clapping and occasional hoots spread inside and throughout the crowded restaurant. As I reached the top of the stairs and looked in, every single guest at each and every table was standing.

"Good morning, Mr. Daniels," the big hostess said as she leaned in close. "You're among friends," she added softly.

A thought popped into my head as she spoke, and I spun back around in the doorway. "Hey, Billy!" I shouted, catching him just as he was about to ride off. "Are you going to be around later?"

"I can be," he said, foot still at the ready on the pedal. "You need me to do something fer ya?"

"No, I just want to talk to you about something."

"Alright, then. I'll stop back this way after you finish up with breakfast."

Billy immediately sped off on his bike, and I was ushered into the restaurant. With everyone on their feet and still applauding, for just a second I truly did feel like a rock star.

"Thank you very much, but please, don't let your biscuits get cold on my account."

The crowd let out a collective chuckle, and when they all sat back down it was once again obvious that there were no seats available. The hostess sensed my concern.

"Don't you worry, Mr. Daniels," she said, going grabbing a menu. "We got you all set up in the VIP room again."

As we started across the restaurant, heads nodded in acknowledgement at each table we passed.

"I reckon there may be a few folks that might want to stop by and stick their head in on ya," the hostess said, stopping at the door to the VIP room. "I'm not sure how good we can be at the job, but would you like us to try and keep you some privacy?"

"Oh, that won't be necessary," I said, not wanting to offend anyone after such a warm reception. "I'm sure I'll be fine."

"I hope you enjoy your breakfast, Mr. Daniels.," the hostess said, stopping at the French doors as I took a seat. "Your waitress will be along shortly."

"Is Maggie working today?" I asked.

"She is. She'll be taking your order."

I was glad Maggie was going to be my waitress, even though after thinking about it she'd been the only one that had ever waited on me anyway. It didn't take long for her to turn up.

"Good morning, Mr. Daniels," she sang as she popped into the VIP room with an extra level of perkiness. "How's it feel to be the biggest VIP in town this morning?"

"Thanks, Maggie, but I really didn't have much to do with it."

"How's that?"

"The story in *The Times*. I didn't write any of it."

"Oh, yes, your newspaper story. I heard about it, but haven't read any just yet."

"Did you catch any of the coverage on CNN?"

"I don't get cable."

Maggie's smile seemed to stretch a little further across her face, and in the still moment that followed a silly giggle slipped out that she immediately tried to suppress.

"Okay, Maggie, what gives?"

"What do you mean Mr. Daniels?" she said, followed by another giggle.

She appeared to be enjoying the moment so much I had to chuckle a bit myself. "Come on, now," I said as she nearly broke into a full blown laugh. "I always seem to be missing something when I come here. Why don't you have a seat and fill me in on the big secret once and for all."

Maggie swallowed back most of the giddiness and seemed to be pondering my invitation. "I probably shouldn't, Mr. Daniels."

"Look, I know you're packed out there and all, but you gotta take a minute to put me out of my misery. I always feel so stupid about not getting it."

Maggie started to giggle again as soon as I mentioned the restaurant was busy.

"Alright, that's it," I said, standing and pulling out the chair next to where she was standing. "Take a seat right here and start talking."

Maggie looked back in the direction of the French doors, getting more serious the longer I held the chair out for her. "I'm not sure how much I can even tell you, Mr. Daniels."

"Is it because you *can't* or you *won't*?"

"No, sir. It's more like I don't know all that much."

Maggie's expression changed to the point of looking a little afraid, and she continued to glance back and forth at the doors. I was just about to let the pressure off when she suddenly caved.

"Fine then," she said, dropping into the chair. "I don't suppose there's nothing I can tell you that you couldn't figure out for yourself on a day like this."

"Now that's the spirit," I said, pushing in her chair and resuming my own.

"What specifically would you be wanting be know?" Maggie asked.

"I prefer to start with a more general question."

"And what would that be, Mr. Daniels?"

"What is this place, Maggie?"

"What do you mean? It's a restaurant."

"No it's not," I said, staring her down as best I could. "We both know it's more than just a greasy spoon."

"I reckon I'm in the dark a bit about whatever a greasy spoon is, but people gather here to eat a meal and enjoy each other's company. Doesn't that make it a restaurant?"

"It would – if there weren't so many other odd things going on here while all that is taking place."

Maggie looked back again in the direction of the French doors.

"Who is it you're afraid of?"

"I'm not afraid at all, Mr. Daniels. This ain't a place for fearing."

"Then why do you keep looking back at the doors like you don't want to get caught?"

"More like I'm looking for some help."

"What kind of help? There's nothing to worry about when it comes to…"

"Mr. Daniels, they say you've accepted your gift," Maggie snapped, interrupting me in mid-sentence.

"I might have," I said after a slight pause. "Why?"

"You really ought to be talking to Molly about this stuff. I'm really not the one to give you the answers you're looking for."

I couldn't tell if Maggie was evading me or if she legitimately didn't think she was the best person for the job. "Then, would you mind stepping out and asking Molly to come in here for a minute?"

"I can't do that, Mr. Daniels."

"Again, you can't or you won't?"

Molly started to giggle again. "Listen, Mr. Daniels," she said through a chuckle. "If you want Molly to come in here and speak with you, why don't you just try thinking on it for a minute."

"Do what?"

"Close your eyes a second or two and concentrate on getting old Molly to stop by the VIP room."

"I don't understand what you're asking. If you won't go get—"

"Just try it, Mr. Daniels! What could it hurt?"

Maggie seemed determined for me to try and use some sort of ESP powers to conjure up the owner, but was serious enough for me to abide by her request. I closed my eyes for a few seconds and pictured Molly coming through the French doors. A knock came shortly after.

"Come in."

As the door swung open I lost a breath or two.

"Is that her then?" Maggie asked.

I looked over at Maggie with a queer eye. "You don't see her?"

"That's what I been trying to tell you, Mr. Daniels. Can't nobody see her, 'cept those with the gift."

"Good morning, Mr. Daniels," Molly said. "How can I help you this morning?"

Maggie stood and pushed in her chair. "Well, if she's here now you won't be needing me hanging around. Do you want me to put in a breakfast order for ya, or would you rather wait a bit?"

Stunned I didn't answer.

"I'll just check back with you in a while," Maggie said, resuming her giggles after passing back out into the restaurant.

Molly smiled as Maggie left, then sat down where she'd been sitting.

"Who are you?" I asked right away.

"My name is Molly. I run this place."

"Let me say it a different way. *What* are you?"

Her smile broadened. "How about we just say I feed those with important work to do for the Lord."

For the first time I noticed an ever so slight echo of light outlining Molly's person. "Are you dead?"

"I can't serve *everyone* that comes in here, that's one way to put it."

"Are you an angel?"

Molly borrowed Maggie's giggle for a second. "No, Mr. Daniels, I'm no angel. You might see a few in here on any given day, though."

I don't know how, but at that point – despite her evasive responses – I was beginning to put things together. It was as though the answers were coming into my head on their own. "So, you run a restaurant for angels?"

"I run a restaurant for those with important work to do for the Lord."

"I didn't think dead people ate meals."

"Well, Mr. Daniels, sometimes when people stop for a meal, the food isn't necessarily the point."

"I will say this, Molly. Your chicken might just be enough to raise the dead."

Molly laughed lightly, and I was suddenly very comfortable with her. Like I had been with my imaginary, childhood friends.

"I thank you for the compliment. Is there anything else you'd like from me, Mr. Daniels?" she asked politely. "I do have customers to tend to."

"Just one more thing," I said as she stood. "Is it the restaurant that's so special, or is it the whole town?"

Molly smiled her compassionate smile one last time. "Let's just say, one couldn't be without the other."

I studied her answer a moment; not wanting to let go of a peaceful warmth that had begun to fill my veins like some astral transfusion. "Thanks. I think I get it," I said. "I appreciate your time, Molly."

"Enjoy your breakfast, Mr. Daniels," Molly said, standing as she spoke. "There is one other place you might look for an answer to your question, Mr. Daniels."

"About this place?"

Molly nodded. "I believe you will find some measure of peace within the words of Hebrews 13:2."

Molly bowed her head politely, and as she stepped out of the VIP room I felt enlightened. The answers kept coming even after she left, as if Molly were an attendant at the gate of knowledge rather than the oracle behind it. She had simply swung open the gate to let me browse for myself. Wandering around inside, I was either making up answers out of thin air, or finally unlocking an encyclopedia that had long ago been shut away.

A knock on the French doors took me away from the lesson.

"Come in, Maggie."

The doors opened slightly.

"Hey there, Mr. Daniels. It's me." Marcus Brown stuck his head through the opening.

"Marcus?" I said, somewhat surprised. "Don't you normally just pop into a room?" I noticed the same, ever-so-slight outline of light around him as well.

"Not around here, Mr. Daniels. It don't work that-a-way here at Molly's place."

"Well, come on in," I said. "Do you have something scary or world-shattering you need to disclose to me this morning."

"No, sir. Not exactly."

"What do you mean by 'not exactly'? You've dropped a couple of bombs on me lately."

"Yes, sir. I understand how you could be feeling a bit squeamish about me popping in on you and all. I was just hoping you might be so good as to consider doing me a favor?"

"Me ... do *you* a favor?"

"Yes, sir. That's what I was hoping."

Though I knew I wasn't dreaming, part of me was still waiting for the floor to open up or the ceiling to come crashing down. "I'm happy to do whatever I can," I said. "Come on in and have a seat."

Marcus shuffled the few feet from the French doors to the chair across from me, keeping his head bowed as if needing to avoid eye contact. "Mr. Daniels, you can say no if you want to" he said, speaking into his lap.

"I'm sure I'll be fine with whatever it is. Just go ahead and ask."

Despite my assurances Marcus hesitated a while longer. "Mr. Daniels," he started, lifting his head. "You know my daddy comes in here for breakfast every day, right?"

"I do. We talked together one day when I was here."

"Yes, sir. Well, what I was hoping was … you know, if you felt good about it and all … was that when he comes …"

"Oh, Marcus, you mean you never?"

"No, sir."

"You can't speak with him yourself?"

"No, sir."

"And there's nobody out there that will do it for you?"

"No one can, Mr. Daniels. You're the only one – least ways, the only one since I been coming here."

I had to pause to let the latest piece of the puzzle to settle in. Marcus waited without as much as a twitch. "Yes, of course. That's my gift, isn't it?"

"It's sure enough a part of it, I suppose."

The sliver of light outlining Marcus seemed to flicker slightly while he waited on me to soak it all in.

"I'll ask Maggie to bring your father here to me when he comes in. Would that be good for you?"

"Yes, sir. That would be just fine."

There was some sort of emotion on Marcus face, but it wasn't a feeling I could read. It's hard to explain, except to say there was a touch of satisfaction to it – maybe a tinge of sadness, strangely mixed with a little joy. It was mesmerizing to look at, and as he left the VIP room I wondered if something of the same expression might now be stretched across my own face.

Maggie stuck her head in shortly after Marcus left. "You ready for your breakfast yet, Mr. Daniels?"

"I am, Maggie. And I need you to do me a small favor."

"What ya need, Mr. Daniels?"

"What time is it?"

"It's about a quarter past eight. Is that the favor you was asking about?"

"No, no. I was hoping that when Atticus Brown comes in this morning, you'd ask if he could join me for a few minutes."

"I reckon that would be easy enough. He's asked about you a time or two since you two chatted the other morning."

"Great! I'll take some biscuits and gravy in the meantime. And how about another cup of..."

Maggie had already stepped into the room with the coffee pot in hand. She poured me a fresh cup.

"That's quite a gift you have there," I said as she poured.

"Oh, no, Mr. Daniels," she said quickly. "I ain't got nothing of the sort. There's really just a few—"

"I meant being able to read your customer's minds."

Maggie smiled. "I get what you mean, there. I suppose that would be a pretty good thing for a waitress to have."

Just as Maggie closed the French doors behind her, I heard her voice just outside. "You can't go in there, Billy. Mr. Daniels needs his peace this morning."

"Maggie, he told me to come on by after he ate his breakfast."

"Well I ain't even put his order in yet. Now you git!"

I jumped up to head for the doors, but before I could get there one of them flew open.

"Hey there, Mr. Daniels," Billy said, half in and half out, a result of Maggie's firm grip on the back of his shirt collar.

"What'd I tell you boy," Maggie said with a yank of the collar that stretched it to the point of threads starting to tear.

"It's okay, Maggie," I said, just in time to keep my waitress from ripping the shirt off the boy's back. "I need to speak to Billy."

"You sure Mr. Daniels?" she said, loosening the tension but not her grip. "Your biscuits and gravy will be right up."

"Yeah, just bring the breakfast in when it's ready," I said. "There is one other thing you can do for me, though."

"What's that, Mr. Daniels?"

"I need to look something up. Do you happen to have a bible around here somewhere."

Billy was trying to adjust his shirt back into shape, but a big bubble had grown where Maggie's grip had been.

"What ya need to look up, Mr. Daniels," Billy snapped, starring back at Maggie.

"Now you hush-up, boy," Maggie said wagging her finger. "You ain't off the hook for pushing past me like that."

"I want to find out what it says in Hebrews 13:2, Billy," I said.

"She don't need to be rustling up no bible for you over that one, Mr. Daniels. That's one they make us study first thing, over at that school I go to."

"He probably could tell it to you, Mr. Daniels," Maggie said. "That is if he hasn't been slacking off on his lessons and such."

Billy just shrugged and rolled his eyes. He didn't speak until Maggie had gone.

"She's always acting like I'm gonna steal the silverware or something'" he finally said.

"She's just doing her job. I think I might have asked her to give me some privacy."

"Ah, it ain't that at all. She's just ornery."

Billy looked up at the ceiling and squinted his eyes, as if he were trying to remember something. "First off, I gotta tell you Mr. Daniels – they's different ways to say that one."

"What do you mean by different ways to say it?"

"Well, though they all mean the same thing, I think it kinda depends on what particular bible you're-a-looking at to give you the exact words used for it."

"That's true with a lot of quotes, Billy. How about you just give me the version that's in your bible?"

"Yes, sir. It says; *'Be not forgetful of strangers, for thereby some have entertained angels unawares'.*"

"That's pretty good, Billy. I'm impressed."

"I could try to spout off one of the other version if you like?"

"That's okay, Billy. Why don't you just have a seat."

Billy dropped in the chair, still trying to shrug his shoulders to get the bump to settle in his shirt. "So, what is it ya need me to do, Mr. Daniels."

"Nothing. I just wanted to talk with you a bit."

"Talk? About what, Mr. Daniels?"

"For starters, I'd like to know what you meant when you said I'd accepted my gift."

"What part you having trouble with?"

"Well, why did you say it?"

Billy looked at me oddly. "Mr. Daniels, did you see all them people on the steps waiting to get in?"

"Of course I did."

"There you go then."

"There I go then, what?"

Billy rolled his eyes the same way he had at Maggie. "Mr. Daniels, if you seen 'em, that's about all a fella needs to figure things out."

"In order for you to know I saw people out on the steps, you'd have to have seen them too, wouldn't you?"

Billy fumbled with a fork on the table. "What's your point there, Mr. Daniels."

"That must mean you have this gift everyone is talking about also."

"Oh, no sir. Half the folks around here can see 'em. That ain't *your* gift."

"It's not the gift?"

"No, sir, that's not it."

I waited a moment to see if Billy would volunteer the obvious, but he did not. "Help me out here, Billy. What exactly is it then?"

"Well sir, we ain't supposed to talk about it, that much I can tell you."

"Why not?"

"Don't know, really. I reckon because it ain't nobody's business. Least ways, nobody but the person that's got it."

"Then how would I know for sure if I have it."

Billy peeked back at the French doors, as if checking to see if the coast was clear. "Mr. Daniels, have you spoken with anybody here at the restaurant today? Anybody other than the folks that work here or maybe Mr. Galax?"

I hadn't seen Galax out front when I came in, so I assumed he must have arrived after I'd made it to the VIP room. "I didn't even know Bo's attorney was here. But yes, I spoke with Molly this morning."

Billy smiled. "There's your evidence,' he said. "That's how you know what degree you is."

"What degree I am? You mean there are different levels – like a yellow belt or a black belt."

Billy shot me a queer glance. "Oh, you mean like that karate stuff?"

"Yes. They have different degrees or skill levels."

"I get what you're trying to say, there, Mr. Daniels. I reckon it's just like that karate stuff then."

"And so, different levels can do different things with their gift. Is that how it works, Billy?"

"Yes, sir," Billy said with a proud voice. "There is one other mighty important part to it, though."

"What's that, Billy."

"What you're supposed to be a-doing with it. They say at my school, a gift ain't no good, unless you put it to good use."

"And how do you figure that part out?"

"Well, sir, here's about all I can say about that." Billy glanced back at the door and leaned in closer. "Whatever gift you have, you're supposed to use it to help along someone with the next level up from you."

"Help them along?"

"Right. So if you look on it, I've been a helping you, cause whether you know'd it or not you was the next level up from me. Of course, it probably weren't right I been taking your money and all – "

"Let's just call that a bonus, Billy." I said to cut him off. "So who do I help?"

Billy paused a minute, and turned his eyes back to the ceiling.

"Billy, you need to run along now and let Mr. Daniels eat his breakfast," Maggie huffed, as she came in to lay out the morning feast.

"Yes, ma'am," Billy said with a shrug, before standing up and sliding in his chair.

"Are you off to school?" I asked him.

"No, sir. I'll be hanging around at the courthouse with my pop for the hearing."

"Your dad has a booth again?"

"Yes, sir. Could get mighty busy today."

Maggie had finished laying out my breakfast, but was hanging around, probably to make sure Billy left.

"What school do you go to?," I asked as I poured the gravy over my biscuits.

"The Arden school."

"Okay, Billy, you need to scoot," Maggie said abruptly.

"Maybe I'll see you at the courthouse, Billy," I said before taking my first bite.

Maggie started toward Billy.

"Now don't you go putting another hump in my shirt," he said to her as he backed up toward the doors. "Sure thing, Mr. Daniels. Enjoy them biscuits."

Billy's last sentence was spoken outside the VIP room as Maggie hustled him the rest of the way out and closed the door behind them.

Alone with my breakfast, I took the time to focus on the biscuits and gravy. After finishing, I did what I could to get re-focused on the main event for the day, and tried to get my head around a plan for what I was going to do for Bo's hearing. I even thought about stepping out to look for Trevor Galax to have a word with him, but I still felt a little uncomfortable about being around him. After jotting a few notes in my book, another knock came.

"Mr. Daniels," Maggie said sticking her head in once again. "Mr. Brown just turned up."

"Perfect timing," I said, closing my notebook. "Please ask him to come by."

Maggie slipped back out into the restaurant and made it back with Atticus Brown just as I was pushing the plates to the side.

"Mr. Daniels, don't fuss with those,' she said, leaving Mr. Brown at the door to hop over and grab the dirty dishes from me. "I'll get them."

Atticus Brown stood in the doorway looking somewhat confused, maybe even a little afraid.

"Good morning, Mr. Brown," I said, pushing myself away from the table and getting to my feet. "Won't you please come in and join me?"

Marcus' daddy hesitated, only moving from the doorway enough to make room for Maggie to pass with the dishes. Maggie deftly closed the French doors behind her with her foot, leaving Mr. Brown just inside them.

"Is there something wrong?" he said after a few seconds of looking terribly uncomfortable.

"No, nothing like that Mr. Brown. I was hoping we could talk a little more. Won't you please sit down?"

Mr. Brown slowly shuffled to the chair, never taking his wide-open eyes off me as he did.

"Why are you all shut up in here?" he asked after taking his seat.

"There's just so many people out in the..."

I stopped in mid-sentence after noticing Mr. Brown's eyebrows raise up.

"You is one of them after all, isn't you?" he asked

When I nodded, Mr. Brown exhaled noticeably and his head drooped toward the table.

"Mr. Brown, would you like to talk with Marcus?"

The old man started to sob slightly. I gave him a few minutes to gather himself.

"Yes, Mr. Daniels," he said, raising his head slowly. "After all these years, I'd sure enough like that very much."

I wasn't really sure what the next step was. We waited together quietly for a while, but nothing happened right away. Finally, I remembered that earlier Marcus had knocked on the door and come into the room just like everyone else, and I gave up on trying to conjure him up out of thin air.

"Mr. Brown, will you excuse me for a minute?"

Atticus Brown looked perplexed, but slowly nodded his head. As I opened the French doors to the restaurant and scanned through the crowd, I spotted Marcus sitting at a table all by himself, looking hard in my direction. I waved for him to come over and stepped back in with Mr. Brown. I left one of the doors open for him, and as soon as I'd taken my seat again, Marcus arrived. He was smiling broadly.

"Mr. Brown, your son is with us now. What would you like to say to him?"

Chapter 41

As Hank had the evening before, old Mr. Brown looked physically exhausted following the short conversation with his son. Afterward, he thanked me and simply walked back out into the restaurant. I followed him, waving for Maggie to come over so she could help him to a table. Curiously, instead of walking with him to a seat in the restaurant, Maggie took him straight to the door and helped him down the stairs out front.

I'd packed up my things and was standing at the register when she came back in.

"Is Mr. Brown not eating this morning?" I asked.

"I reckon not," Maggie said. "He said he was powerful tired and thought he ought to be getting home."

"I hope he's alright."

"He looked mighty peaceful, Mr. Daniels," Maggie said. She looked at me like a proud parent. "It's a good thing you did in here."

I had to wait at the register, but when the hostess made it back to her post, she would have nothing of my paying. "Mr. Daniels, this ain't no day to be expecting to pay for nothing," she said. "People in this town are mighty excited for you."

"Thanks. But again, I didn't have much to do with *The Times* story."

"Yes, sir," the hostess said with a grin. "You did say that, didn't you?"

Stepping off the stairs on my way to the parking lot, I could see Mr. Brown shuffling down the sidewalk; but from the distance I couldn't tell whether he was happy or sad. I was worried that he'd skipped his breakfast, but was even more concerned about the toll connecting with Marcus might have had on him. After glancing at my watch and noticing it was nearing nine thirty, I had to put it out of my mind in favor of hustling over to the courthouse to be on time for Bo's hearing.

While I'd been steadfast in my denials over involvement with the series running in the paper, I was hoping my new celebrity status would hold a good seat for me at the courthouse. As I parked my car, I saw that the large crowd winding its way out the doors to the courthouse and down the stairs was going to prevent me from getting a good seat either way.

That's when I heard a very loud whistle and noticed a hand waving above the crowd just near the doors.

"Mr. Daniels, up here!" I heard over the murmurs of the crowd. "You're gonna have to hurry!"

I could tell from the second shout it was Billy, though how I was going to make it to where he was standing was a large obstacle. I tapped a person in the last row of folks waiting to get in, and that person quickly tapped the person in front, they in-turn the one in front of them, and so on all the way up the stairs and to the door. Within moments, a clear pathway was made for me – straight to where Billy was standing. As I started up through the middle of the crowd, everyone began applauding, and I knew there was a seat waiting for me in the courtroom after all.

"There ya go, Mr. Daniels," Billy said as I reached him near the entrance. "Why, the president himself wouldn't get an easier time of it."

"Thanks, Billy!"

"Ain't nothing I did, Mr. Daniels. You're just a popular fella is all."

I smiled – partly at the sarcastic way Billy delivered his last comment and partly because it felt pretty good to be popular.

"Mr. Daniels," came a voice from the doorway to get my attention. "You better get on in here so I can pass you through."

It was my security-guard friend; he'd taken a break from the line inside to get my attention. As I walked his way, he held the door to the courtroom lobby open for me. "We wouldn't want things to get started inside without our famous, big-city reporter up front for the proceedings."

"Thanks very much," I said. "I guess I'm running a little late."

"I reckon I can understand that," he said, nudging me a little as I turned in the doorway to speak to him. "You remember how to get to the courtroom?"

"Is it the same one as last time?"

"Exact same one."

I hesitated a minute, lifting my arms for a pat down.

"We won't worry about that today, Mr. Daniels," the guard said. "I think we'll just have to trust you don't mean any harm."

When I was slow to get started, the guard put his hand on my shoulder and guided me the first few paces toward the double doors beyond the screening tables. After reaching the doors, I looked over my shoulder and saw the guard and everyone in the lobby watching me like I was a child heading into school for the first day of kindergarten.

Down the hall there were a dozen or so more people waiting to get into the courtroom. The bailiff standing at the door motioned to me over the heads of those waiting. "Good morning, Mr. Daniels," he said excitedly. "We gotta get you seated; court's about to be called into session."

As I walked into the courtroom, I saw that nearly every head was already turned in my direction. The bailiff walked me down to the same seat I'd occupied during the preliminary.

I sat down, and a man seated directly behind me said, "Atta boy, Mr. Daniels," and patted me on the shoulder.

"Congratulations, sir," I heard another small voice say from a seat next to him, followed by a lighter pat on my shoulder.

The prosecution's table was fully manned, though in front of me the defendant's side was empty. After a few minutes, Attorney Galax stepped into the courtroom from the side-door Bo Buckminster had come through the first time. The look on his face was oddly distant, and when he made way to his seat he didn't seem to notice I was sitting directly behind him.

"Trevor?" I whispered to the back of his head after he'd sat down.

"Mark, I'm sorry I didn't even notice you," he said spinning around.

"You'd be the first one this morning that didn't," I said, reaching out my hand.

"Yes ... yes, congratulations are in order, I suppose."

"You of all people would know that they are not."

"Nonsense," he said, still slightly distracted. "You certainly played a large role in breaking that story."

"I didn't write any of it, and you know it."

Galax paused, staring at something and nothing at the same time, obviously considering something other than my comments.

"Is there something wrong, Trevor?"

The question seemed to snap him out of a small trance. "Oh, no, I'm sorry," he said. "I'm simply caught up pondering over what we might hear from Judge Jefferson."

"You sound as if you already know what's coming."

"I have my suspicions, of course; but I assure you, I would not attempt to predict a man like Judge Jefferson." Galax gathered some level of composure. "He is most unpredictable."

"What are your suspicions?"

Just as I finished my question, the bailiff walked to the front of the judge's bench. "Please rise. Court is now in session, the Honorable Preston K. Jefferson presiding."

"It looks as if you will have your answer straight from the proverbial horse's mouth, Mr. Daniels."

After all in the courtroom had come to their feet, Judge Jefferson made his way from the side-door to his bench at an unusually rapid pace for an old man. He dropped a large file in front of him and took his seat. "Be seated," he said. "Is the defense ready?"

"We are, Your Honor."

"Will the defendant be joining us, Mr. Galax?"

"He will not, Your Honor. Mr. Buckminster has decided to waive his right to be present at these proceedings. I have filed the necessary document with the court recorder."

"Very well. Is the prosecution ready?"

"We are, Judge Jefferson."

I was stunned by the first move on the chessboard. In my mind, I suppose I had been picturing a scene where everyone in the courtroom cheered and gathered around Bo after the judge's decision was announced, and then paraded him out the front door to a life of freedom. Him not even being in the courtroom not only blew that image, it was certainly not a good sign.

"Gentlemen, I'm not going to drag this out. Each of you will receive a full copy of my decision, and you may read it and dissect it at your leisure."

"Your Honor, may I make a motion at this time," Galax said, standing bravely with his interruption.

"You may not, Mr. Galax," Judge Jefferson snorted. "Take you seat."

Galax slowly slunk back into his chair.

"In the matter of a request for re-trial of the conviction of one Bosephus Buckminster on the charge of murder in the first degree, the court finds insufficient evidence to grant such a request."

There was a collective groan in the courtroom.

"You may make you motion now, Mr. Galax," Judge Jefferson added.

"That will not be necessary, Your Honor."

"Does the prosecution have anything they wish to add?"

"Nothing at this time."

"Then let us all brace ourselves for the backlash that is sure to follow. This court is adjourned."

After a pound with his gavel, the judge picked up his file and scooted back out the side-door of the courtroom as quickly as he had come in.

"What the hell just happened, Trevor?" I asked as the murmurs in the courtroom raised to a near raucous.

"Our beloved lady justice has just taken a very large crap upon our system, I'm afraid."

As those in the courtroom rose to their feet and began to break up into small buzzing cabals, Galax slumped a little lower in his chair and began flipping his pen in one hand.

"I take it you knew this was coming," I said, still in disbelief.

"I had hoped to make a motion to postpone things for another week or two; but yes, I had a peek at the judge's decision before I came in."

"A postponement? Jesus, Trevor, you didn't so much as utter a single objection!"

"What is it that you think I should have objected to, Mr. Daniels?"

"The decision! How about you object to the decision?"

"That is what is called an appeal, and I'm afraid without new evidence that avenue is no longer available to Bo."

"You just rolled over!"

"You may think as you wish," he said, finally turning in his chair to face me. "But this is not the outcome I had hoped for. Though, frankly, I saw it coming."

"So what happened then? More undulations?"

"Some very large ones, I'm afraid. Something more akin to a valley, perhaps."

Galax turned back around as if we were through. He probably hoped I would leave, but in the pause that followed I found a new resolve. "This isn't going to stand, Trevor," I said calmly.

"And may I ask why you think it will not?"

"If Bo needs new evidence to keep his fight going, by God I intend to find it!"

Galax pushed himself up from his chair, gathering the few papers in front of him and sliding them into his briefcase. "Mr. Daniels, how would you like to get direct evidence of exactly what happened that afternoon sixteen-years ago? To find out precisely what went on that day, and know once and for all who killed Marcus Brown?"

"I'll find that out one way or another."

"I am offering you an easy way," he said with a blank look that suggested he might not be playing games.

"And what would that be?"

Galax pushed in his chair and looked to see if the way out was cleared of people. "Come to my office today at four p.m.," he said plainly.

"Today? I'm not going to drive all the way down there on a—"

"It must be today. If you wish to find out exactly what the circumstances were on the day Marcus Brown died, I assure you there will be no other time."

He stared at me with a pair of penetrating eyes I hadn't anticipated.

"Fine. I'll see you at your office."

"I will look forward to it." He was halfway to the exit when I decided a final shot across the bow was warranted.

"There *is* one other way Bo might be allowed to stand for another appeal."

"And what would that be?" he asked, turning just his head.

"Lackluster representation."

Galax allowed a slight nod before heading to the exit.

Chapter 42

By the time I made it back to the hotel from the courthouse that morning, I'd talked myself into an even more vigorous crusade to free Bo Buckminster, no matter what it took. The initial shock of the morning's events required driving a few miles of country road before it passed, but seeing Galax walk out of the courtroom had crystallized things for me. I realized that all my questionable decisions the past week had led me straight to that moment in the courthouse. From choosing not to work the "Hate" story with Bart, to calling Carl on his ultimatum and subsequently getting fired from the only real job I'd ever known; I felt as if these otherwise unexplainable actions might actually have had a purpose. Meeting Bo hadn't just been therapeutic - I was *supposed* to be there. At a time when even his own attorney had thrown him under the bus, it seemed to me that I was destined to take over the fight for Bo. The fighting spirit in me was fully aroused by the time I made my way into the lobby at the Marriott.

"Welcome back, Mr. Daniels," the front desk guy said to get my attention as I walked past the counter. "Things didn't go so well for Bo this morning, huh."

"Not well at all, I'm afraid," I said, backing up slightly to compensate for not noticing him initially. "But it's not over – not by a long shot."

"Will you be doing a story about him for your newspaper?"

"I'll be writing about it for somebody," I said. "I'm just not sure who yet."

"Well, I reckon if anybody can get people's attention right about now, I'd say you got some mighty fine credentials."

"Thanks," I said.

I considered his words as I rode the elevator to the next floor, and another large piece of the puzzle fell into place. When Carl had come down with his challenge to get in line or get out, I'd allowed myself to be fired in order to keep working a story I knew I'd have no place to publish. Something that was at best counter-productive and at worst pretty stupid. But, as was the case so many other times during my career, my former boss had saved my bacon – even as our time together came to a close. By leaving my name on Bart and Trip's story, Carl had ensured I would have enough clout behind my name to find a home for my next story, whatever that might turn out to be.

He'd seemed angry with me that day, but somewhere deep down I figured he must have been still looking out for me. It was the only thing that made sense. Having to explain why I wasn't around for press conferences and such after the "Hate" story broke could only have made his life more difficult, and the truth was we both knew I didn't deserve the byline. Bart might have asked him to do it; that would fit with Bart's character, too. But Carl would have had to approve it. Why he did only made sense in the context of Carl being Carl – looking out for one of his own. My world was still very much upside-down, but motive and opportunity were suddenly very clear for a move forward with a killer story.

Though I knew I'd have to leave the hotel within an hour to get to Galax' office in Charleston by four, back in my room I fired up the computer. I surfed the Internet, thinking about how great it would have been to have the Librarian to fall back on for help. As I muddled through a number of legal websites all by myself, I felt a twinge of pride to be doing my own homework. The deeper I got into each site I visited, the more notes I scratched in my notebook. In an hour's time, I was able to fill four entire pages, which was something of a record for me. When the time came to leave for Charleston, I was ready to get to the truth. That's what Trevor Galax had promised, and I fully intended to give him the opportunity to keep his word. But if he didn't, I was also ready for battle.

"Going out again, Mr. Daniels?" the front desk guy asked as I got off the elevator.

"I'm taking a short trip to Charleston, but I'll be back this evening."

"We'll hold your room for you."

"Thanks," I said, stopping to broach another topic. "How's Hank feeling?"

"Oh, I haven't really spoken with him personally," he said. "But if you bump into him on your way to Charleston, you could ask him yourself."

"What's that?"

"He's gone, Mr. Daniels. He quit his job this morning."

"Quit? What's he going to Charleston for?"

"Moving there, I reckon. Least that's what they say."

"Really?"

"Sure enough. He packed his stuff into a trailer this morning. The manager says he's heading down there to be with family."

"To be with family?"

"Yes, sir. Seems his wife's kin is from there. She must have got a sudden hankering to be back with them."

As I stood there taking in the latest twist, the front desk guy seemed to be waiting for something.

"Did he leave any kind of word, or..."

"Just this, Mr. Daniels," he said, pulling an envelope out from under the counter with my name scratched on it. "One of the fellas that helped pack him up brought it by while you were upstairs."

The front desk guy looked as though he were waiting for me to open it in front of him, but I opted against that and waited until I was sitting behind the wheel of the rental car in the parking lot. I pinned the envelope against the wheel with a thumb on each corner, trying to predict what might be inside. Finally, I opened it.

Mr. Daniels,

Thank you kindly for sharing your gift. After our son passed away, we heard talk of folks in Chases Corner that might be able to help us find the answers we was looking for. He left us so sudden like. We had no idea we'd be waiting on a fella from New York to come through, but I sure do hope you found some of those answers for you own self. It's time for me to take my bride home to claim back what little life we have left together.

I'll pray for you to find the peace you deserve.

Hank.

Atticus Brown had walked straight from the restaurant earlier that morning after our talk with Marcus, and I'd gotten the sense it was the last time I was going to see him as well. After reading Hank's note, I couldn't help but wonder how many others living in Chases Corner were there just for the smallest of chances they too might connect with a lost loved one. Not to mention how easy it might be for me to deplete the population if I hung around long enough. It dawned on me that there were probably just two types of people in town – those who were born there, and those who came looking for something.

Upon my arrival in Charleston, the fire inside me stirred with each local landmark I passed along the route to Galax's office, stoking the coals of determination. There wasn't anger or anxiety diluting that condition, something that was as big a surprise to me as it would have been to Dr. Keller. It was instead a simple conviction that I could not be stopped.

"There seems to be a continuous thread of inevitability in the way Bo approaches his condition," Father Hanaway had written in one of his early notes from the prison. "He seems genuinely to believe that he is in the service of good."

I never was much of a believer in the good-versus-evil thing. So many of the *good guys* I'd been exposed to over my many years as a reporter, were so terribly flawed they made it difficult to make such a clear distinction. From my experiences, whether you were on the side of good or evil usually depended primarily on perspective. Bo was the exception to that rule. In his simple view of the world, there was no compromise – no concept of the ends justifying the means. Which meant that as a staunch defender of Bo, I too must have been squarely on the side of good. By the time I pulled into the parking lot for Galax's offices in downtown Charleston, the one challenge that remained was in determining who the *evil* players were that I was up against.

From the very first moment I met him, something nagged at me about Trevor Galax. In his role as the cunning Southern barrister, he could not help coming across as a bit smarmy at times. But even forgiving him that trait as a by-product of his occupation, there remained an element of untrustworthiness that lingered behind his eyes. From every conversation there seemed to be something left out – held back for reasons unknown. He never actually lied to me, or at least I never caught him. He did, however, have a penchant for not saying things that probably should have been said.

The door at the entrance to the offices of Johnson, Galax, and Kicklighter was locked, and the lights in the lobby ominously dimmed. I could see a brighter stream of light coming from a hallway to the left of the reception desk, and from the flicker of shadows I knew there were people stirring inside. After a minimal knock, a menacing fellow with slicked-back hair and a barrel chest that pushed against his black suit coat came out from the light. He unlocked the door and opened it a third of the way.

"Please come in, Mr. Daniels," he said.

He locked the door behind me and punched a number into a keypad next to it, then spun around without looking back. "Please follow me, sir," he said as he walked away.

When I hesitated, he simply paused without turning around.

"I'm here to meet with Mr. Galax," I said, as if to confirm we were both on the same page.

"Yes, sir," he said, this time shooting me a slight glance over his left shoulder. "If you will follow me, Mr. Galax will join you shortly."

The big man waited until he heard my shoes against the marble floor in the lobby before resuming his march toward the lighted hallway. We walked to a door that looked heavier than the others and was equipped with a even more serious looking keypad above the door knob. After punching in a series of numbers, the man opened the door, stepped into the room to look around, then turned back to face me.

"You can wait in here, Mr. Daniels," he said. "Mr. Galax will be along shortly, but I'm afraid I'm going to have to hold on to your bag."

"Can I at least take my notebook out?"

"You can take it out. I'm not sure if Mr. Galax will allow you to use it, but be my guest."

I pulled out my notebook and handed the bag to the man.

"Would you mind flipping through those pages for me?" he said, staring at the notebook.

When I gave him an odd look, he shrugged his shoulders but continued to wait.

"Thank you, sir," he said after I'd proven it was a notebook. "If you'll leave it there on the table, Mr. Galax will let you know if you can use it for notes or not."

The room was overflowing with white light, intensified by barren walls. With the exception of the black, polished conference table and eight uncomfortable looking chairs, there wasn't a single other item in the room.

"How often does this room get swept?" I asked the man, who smiled slightly in reply.

"As often as is needed," he said, and then he stepped out of the room. When the door closed behind him, it made a slight clang, a sign the core was made of metal.

I'd conducted interviews from inside secure meeting rooms before, though usually from within the Pentagon or some other government agency wrapped in a blanket of security. That day was a first for an attorney's office, however, and it only added to my growing suspicions concerning what side Trevor Galax was on. Attorney-client privilege is one thing, but a bug-swept room with a metal liner was not something one would expect a simple country lawyer would be in need of. I suddenly felt a bit naive for coming, and a little stupid for knowing there wasn't anyone else in the world that even knew I was there.

The sound of someone punching in a code at a second door located on the long end of the conference room, startled me enough to cause me to stand up quickly.

"Mr. Daniels, I thank you for taking me up on my offer of hospitality," Trevor Galax said as he walked into the room.

"I didn't come here for your hospitality, Galax."

"Galax huh?" he replied, as he took a seat and a set a thin manila folder on the conference table. "You know, the use of just a last name to address someone can come across as rather combative, Mr. Daniels."

Trevor Galax's comment reminded me that I was trying to be the opposite of what was expected. "My apologies, *Mister* Galax." I said plainly. "But under the circumstances, perhaps we could get right down to business."

"Indeed. We all have reasons to be brief." He turned his attention to my notebook. "I'm afraid I am going to have to ask you to delay the taking of notes until after our session has ended."

"I expected as much. Let's just get started."

Galax opened the thin file he'd placed on the table and slid it across to me. As I sat back down, he stood up.

"While you look that over, I shall retrieve our interviewee," he said, and with that went back out the same way he had entered.

Inside the folder was a one-page, handwritten statement that from its condition was likely an original. The top of the page was marked with the date of Marcus Brown's death, and the words themselves were reported as those of Corey Aycock.

After practice was over, me, Marcus and Bo was cutting through the woods in back of the ball field on our way home. We'd been doing batting practice and Marcus was the last one to hit. He was hittin' some cannon shots at the end there, dropping his last four swings clean over centerfield fence. Bo was sort of patting him on the back as we walked, saying over and over that he was the next Babe Ruth or something. That's when Trey Hunter came running up behind us to catch up. He had to stay back after practice, and since it were him that was pitching when Marcus was hitting them shots, the coach was giving it to him pretty good.

When Trey heard what Bo was saying, he called him a couple words like dummy and retard and told him to shut up. Bo said he was just praising Marcus for how good he hit the ball, and that's when Trey raised his bat up and told Bo that if he didn't shut his mouth he was going to hit him a lick with the bat. Marcus stepped between them and told Trey he was sorry for hitting so many of his pitches over the fence, and that it wasn't Bo's fault. I ain't never seen no one ever get as mad in the face as Trey was right then. Then he screamed and hit Marcus a hard one on the side of the head with the bat. Marcus bent over front-ways and fell on his knees, and Trey hit him again on the back of the head. I guess he was dead after that.

Beneath the statement in was what appeared to be the signature of Corey Aycock. I sat there a minute, less surprised than stunned. I'd figured something of the sort for the real story, or I had at least come close enough in one of the many possible scenarios that had ran though my head, the idea that Trey Hunter was the murderer wasn't totally unfamiliar. But for Bo, the document itself was exculpatory – and it had been handed to me by his own attorney.

When Galax returned, a scraggly-haired man with a greasy-billed John-Deere baseball cap was with him. The man had multiple days worth of stubble, wore clothes of various sizes, and possessed a smell that quietly slipped into the room ahead of him. The two took seats directly across from me, Galax sliding his chair to one side, as if trying to put some space between he and the man's odor.

"Mr. Daniels, please allow me to introduce you to Mr. Corey Aycock," he said.

Corey Aycock lifted from his seat enough to reach a hand across the table; it felt as leathery as an old baseball glove, left in the rain and dried in the sun.

"Mr. Aycock," I said, after we'd sat back down. "It seems you have certainly unlocked the lid to the proverbial Pandora's box lately."

"Ain't no Mr. Aycock around here," he replied.

I paused. "Corey, then. And you can call me Mark."

"Mr. Daniels," Galax interrupted, "I believe he's referring to the fact that as of today, Corey Aycock will no longer exist. Mr. Aycock will be starting a new life once he has left us."

I studied the rough-looking man across from me. A new life of any kind seemed warranted.

"Is he entering the witness protection program?"

"You might say that," Galax answered. "Though not in an official capacity, you understand."

I paused again, trying to decide if there was any benefit to further explanation. "How can you be a part of the witness protection program in an unofficial capacity?"

"Let us just say that Mr. Aycock has provided a valuable service to our country, and he will now be allowed to continue a life unmolested."

"You mean he's being tucked away someplace to keep him quiet."

The cold, blank expression on Galax's face was a sufficient answer.

"That would be considered witness tampering, Mr. Galax," I added. "A very serious offense."

"Witness tampering? For what trial? This whole affair with Senator Hunter will require no witnesses. The senator and all of his cohorts have confessed. Justice will be quite swift in that case."

"Don't talk to me about justice, you hypocrite!" I barked at Galax. "You know damn well what case I'm talking about."

"If you are alluding to our mutual friend, Bosephus Buckminster, there will be no additional adjudication in that matter. You know that as well as I."

"I know nothing of the sort. You may think it's over for Bo, but I'm not going to let—"

"Mr. Daniels! I do not mean to be rude. You and I may argue all you would like on the matter of Bo later on, but Mr. Aycock has very little time with us this afternoon. If you have questions of him, you must ask them quickly or they may never be asked."

I could hear slight murmurs of conversation outside the door Galax and Corey Aycock had entered through, suggesting that Galax's sense of urgency was valid. Then again, there was really only one question that needed to be asked anyway.

"Who killed Marcus Brown?" I said, getting straight to it.

"Trey Hunter," Aycock replied.

"Why?"

"He was mad, I reckon. Trey could be like that. He had a powerful-bad temper."

"What would make him so agitated he'd take the life of someone like Marcus."

"He didn't need no reason. I don't think he was expecting to kill Marcus when he done what he did. He just lost it over things that happened during that baseball practice. One minute we was walking, and the next old Marcus was dead on the ground."

Corey Aycock looked down at his hand, then up to the ceiling; all the while avoiding a zone that would cause him to make eye contact with me.

"Is that what you want people to believe?" I asked.

"I don't much care what you believe. You asked and I told you. Am I done now, Mr. Galax?"

Galax slowly looked in my direction. "Mr. Daniels, I'm afraid time has—"

"Then he's going to have to be late," I snapped. "You dragged me all the way down here, and I intend to get a few more answers to my questions."

"Such as?"

"Why didn't you come forward during Bo's trial?" I said, turning back to Corey Aycock.

After a pause, Aycock finally took me on eye-to-eye. "It weren't that easy, " he said. "I was still just a kid."

"You were old enough to tell the truth."

"I told the truth! That ain't what came out, but back in them days the truth didn't mean squat around here."

The sudden flash of fire in his eyes as he spoke told me that Corey Aycock was probably as much a victim of the cover-up as anyone. From the look of him, and what I knew of his life after that fateful day, the road had been hard for him.

"I understand it wasn't your fault, Corey," I said with far less intensity. "Just tell me, who was behind pinning Marcus' murder on Bo ... and why?"

"Senator Hunter was a powerful man, Mr. Daniels. Him and his family could do just about whatever they pleased when it came to the law. Trey Hunter was part of that family."

"So to keep his son out of trouble, the senator hung the murder charge on the only one of you that wouldn't be able to defend himself."

"The senator, the sheriff, probably the judge too for all I know. They told me that if I didn't keep my mouth shut about what happened, they was going to pin it on me." The fire in his eyes was doused by tears that welled up behind them. "Now I ask *you*, Mr. Daniels: what was I supposed to do?"

Despite the determination to see justice for Bo, it did seem that Corey Aycock had been made to suffer something of an injustice himself. His life had been thrown away that day, as much as Bo's had – though Corey Aycock's prison was one that allowed him to remain on the outside most of the time.

"Mr. Daniels," Galax said. "You and I can speak further on this, but I must insist that we allow Mr. Aycock to begin his journey."

I thought about objecting further, but with a slight nod of the head I acknowledged Galax stern request. With that, Galax guided a now emotional Corey Aycock back toward the far exit, helping him along as if he were a man of advance years.

"Corey," I said as Galax opened the door for him. "If they brought you back to testify, would you tell the truth in court?"

"I am afraid," said Galax, "you simply must adjust your plans to account for the fact that Corey will not be coming back."

"Hold on there," Corey said, interrupting Galax. "Mr. Daniels, you know I been there in that prison with Bo for a while."

"That's what I understand."

"Well, sir, if it makes you feel any better, he ain't all that bad-off up there. He's got friends – folks that look after him and all."

"Maybe so. But he doesn't deserve to be there, and you know that."

"True enough. I'm just saying, he's doing some folks some real good just by him being there, is all."

Aycock looked at me as if he wanted my approval. When I wouldn't give it to him, his chin dropped slightly and he shuffled through the exit. Galax followed him, closing the door behind them.

After a few minutes, Galax returned alone. "Now that you've heard it from the horse's mouth, so to speak, what will you do?"

"I'm a writer, Mr. Galax. What other weapons do I have beside the pen?"

"Yes, well a writer needs a place to publish what he has written."

"Don't you worry too much over that. Haven't you heard ... I'm probably going to share in a Pulitzer Prize nomination."

Galax was unimpressed and unflinching. He certainly hadn't been obliged to set up the meeting with Corey Aycock, and there was no way he would have, if he had thought it would somehow jeopardize whatever it was he was he had planned.

"I'm sure you will do your best, Mark," he said, in an almost condescending tone. "I think in the end, you will follow your heart."

We both sat there a moment, in a room that was perfect for the thick silence between us. I was sure he was expecting more questions and seemed more than ready to oblige. I just couldn't decide on the tact to take. "Why did you bring me here?" I finally asked.

"I thought it might bring you some level of peace."

"You thought I might find solace in knowing for certain that Bo is getting screwed over? That he really is in that prison for nothing?"

"Not at all. I was hoping you would come to understand that Bo's situation is part of a much larger plan. One in which great benefit has been realized in its conclusion."

"Bo's in prison, but the senator is, too – so everything is just swell. Is that what you mean?"

"A great good has been done for our community and if you were to—"

"Oh, just get off that line of BS will you, Trevor! I don't see the connection at all. Why in the world would it be necessary for Bo to stay locked up if the senator is singing like a bird and everyone involved with your little scandal is being brought down like apples in autumn?"

"It was a pre-condition to the senator's cooperation."

"What? What the hell does that mean? The senator is knee-deep in the biggest pond of crap he's ever going to wade through. Why would he care one way or another if Bo's conviction is overturned?"

"That would be an obvious answer, if you were looking for it in an unbiased fashion."

"Humor me, then."

"To protect his family."

"His *dead* son. The senator is worried they might dig up his dead son and throw him into prison in place of Bo?"

"Of course not. Let us just say that Southern families tend to be larger than most folks know."

Galax was leading me down a path again, something that considering where we had arrived was a waste of time. The cat-and-mouse game seemed to be the only way Galax could pass along information, tossing out tiny bits of it only after the previous one had been picked up.

"Trevor, as with just about every other conversation I've ever had with you, I've quickly grown tired of the riddles and tiny morsels of information you toss around like bread crumbs," I said. "If there's something else you wanted me to take away from this little visit, you might want to go ahead and spit it out."

Always the chess player, Galax calmly studied the board before his next move. "Mark, have you ever seen Senator Hunter up close?"

"We've never met, if that's what you mean."

"Then perhaps in pictures or TV clips you may have seen ... have you ever looked at him with a more inquiring eye."

"What should I be looking for?"

"The senator is not a small man. In fact, large men run in his family."

"Please, Trevor, I don't think I could handle—"

"Perhaps you will humor *me* this time, Mark. Have you ever wondered why Bo's father left his mother? Skipping town without a trace as he did, and not a peep from him thereafter."

"I heard he didn't get along well with Senator Hunter, if that's what you're saying."

"Have you wondered why? You know, the senator was mighty generous to Bo and his momma."

"Look, I was serious about all the hint-dropping and ..." I stopped myself in mid-sentence when the pieces finally fell into place. "Wait a minute. Are you saying what I think your saying?"

"It could be. To what do you refer?"

"Senator Hunter is Bo's father?"

Galax lifted his hands and shrugged his shoulder slightly.

"Bo is the senator's son?" I asked again.

"Whichever way you say it, there are those that believe it to be so."

"Did you at least bring any of this stuff up in Bo's original trial?"

"I did not represent Bo in his original trial. I played a different role then."

"And that role was?"

"I represented the Hunter family during those proceedings."

"The Hunter family? You mean you helped bury the information."

"It was not necessary for me to do such a thing. Most of the information was buried by the system"

"But this was a murder trial?"

"Yes, but Senator Hunter was not the one on trial. The judge would never have allowed any inquiry of that sort."

"And that was Judge Jefferson, I assume."

"That is correct."

"Wow" I said, allowing a few seconds for the quiet room to do its job. "So the fix really was in this morning. Everybody that matters knows Bo didn't do the thing, but still he's dragged back to prison."

"Bo was not dragged anywhere. Let us both recall that he chose to go back to that place, even before this morning's events at the courthouse."

"Come on, counselor! You're talking about a man with the mental capacity of a small child. You do understand the role that could play in his decision-making process, right?"

"If, by that, you are inquiring as to whether or not I understand the limitations of Bo Buckminster's mental capacity, I understand it completely. You might even say I have deeply personal understanding of it."

"How so?"

"My wife and I have had two children born to us with the afflictions of autism. Two otherwise lovely daughters ... but suffering with the effects of autism none the less."

"Really?" I was stuck for a response to such a dramatic bit of information. "How old are they now?"

"Our oldest shall celebrate her fourteenth year later this month," he replied, then he stiffened and looked over the top of my head. "Our youngest was lost to us just over three years ago, I'm afraid." He seemed to be fighting an unusual torrent of emotions, his face becoming even more rigid. Just as it looked like he was ready to let loose with what was probably many years of pent up sadness, a very translucent and hazy apparition began to slowly manifest itself into the chair next to him, directly to his left.

"Was she a blond child ... say, seven or eight years old when she passed away."

Galax was instantly startled and returned his eyes directly to mine. "Yes. She was seven."

"And did she have two very deep dimples on each of her cheeks when she smiled."

A solitary tear dropped from the left eye of Galax's otherwise stoic face, followed by a second from the right eye. They merged at the end of his chin.

"She's here with us now," I said, quiet and calm, trying to help the Southern gentleman maintain the decorum his culture demanded of men like him. "She's leaning over like she wants to lay her head on your shoulder."

Galax maintained a rigid, upright position in his chair, almost as if by moving he was afraid he might chase away the vision of the little girl he could not see. "That's what she used to do when I came home at the end of the day," Galax finally said, his lips barely moving. "She would sit like that with me for hours."

As Galax spoke, the girl lifted her head. She held a very wide, happy smile, then pointed to it before pointing once again, this time to Galax' face. "She wants you to smile, Trevor."

Galax face muscles began to twitch slightly, as he forced the corners of his mouth upward. "Mark, can she speak to you, then?"

The little girl bowed her head slightly and moved it side-to-side to suggest she could not.

"But you understand what I'm saying, don't you," I said to her.

The huge grin returned to the girl's face as she nodded her head in acknowledgement.

"Can she?" Galax asked quickly.

"Yes," I said without taking my eye off the proud, boastful expression now written across the girl's face. "I believe she may understand all this better than you and I ever could."

Galax dropped his head into his hands, and it fell to within inches of the table. There was not even the slightest attempt to hold back the tears that began to flow. His little daughter did her best to get him to feel her touch, at various intervals trying to rub his arm and back, even attempting an outright full-body hug.

After many minutes Galax at last raised his head and wiped the moisture from his face and now very red eyes. He straightened his tie as if readying himself for a meeting with a client.

"You know, my Chelsea had a very deep and comprehensive form of autism," he said, with just a slight quiver to his voice. "She was unable to communicate directly with others."

"That was her name? Chelsea?"

"Yes, she was named for her blessed grandmother," he said, looking to his left slightly with his eyes, as if hoping to catch a glimpse of his daughter. "Is she still here?"

"Yes, she's still with us."

"Will she understand if you tell her how much I love her?"

With that the little girl used her finger to draw the outline of a heart on her chest, and then held both hands to it.

"You just did, Trevor, and she says that she loves you very much as well."

A sort of high pitched yelp escaped from Galax' mouth, and his face and neck shuddered slightly, as if he'd just bitten into a sour apple.

Chelsea began to wave her hands to get my attention, then pointed to herself and towards the door.

"I think Chelsea has to leave now, Trevor."

Once again the little girl began to wave her hands to get my attention. Using one finger, she pointed to her mouth, then using the same finger traced the outline of the slight, golden glow that surrounded her.

"She wants you to know that she's become an angel."

Galax eyelids first dropped, then squeezed tightly together. "You are and forever will be my dearest angel, Chelsea."

The girl waved her hand excitedly, as a little girl might do from the stage after her first successful dance recital, then blew a kiss first in her father's direction, then one to me. With the last kiss blown, she slowly faded away, still waving her hand rapidly goodbye.

I allowed a few minutes of nothing.

"Are you okay, Trevor?" I finally asked.

"Has my Chelsea gone?"

"She has. She blew you a kiss before she left us."

As the two of us sat there, through many more minutes of complete and utter silence, I realized that I finally understood Trevor Galax. I had searched mightily for his motivations, and had found he was probably less a part of the story of the injustice done to Bosephus Buckminster, and more a part of my own, bizarre, developing tale. His motivation was simple: he wanted to speak one last time – and for the first time ever it turned out – to the beautiful little daughter that had obviously held so much of his heart.

I waited until I could sense a return to a more normal rhythm to his breathing before starting a new conversation, this time under an entirely different perception of the man himself. "Trevor, you just traded with me, didn't you?"

"Traded?" he said, looking in my direction for the first time since his daughter's farewell. "How do you mean?"

"I couldn't understand why in the world you would be giving me this information about Aycock, the senator, and the like. But you swapped it – all for the smallest of chances that somehow I might be able to connect with your daughter."

"Perhaps. It has been the focus of my life for a very long time."

"But how did you know that I could? I mean, I didn't even know. Hell, I'm still not sure if this isn't all just a part of my going stark-raving mad."

"Yes, well I didn't know. Until a few days ago I had placed all of my hope in Molly's restaurant and Bo."

"Molly's restaurant?"

"I have been going to Molly's for many years. As I said, I have an older daughter with autism; though in no way near to the extent her younger sister had to."

"And let me guess, she goes to the Arden school there in Chases Corner?"

"She does."

I didn't need to know any more from Trevor Galax, and from his appearance it seemed the events of the day had sapped him of the considerable emotional strength he usually displayed.

"Trevor, what will you do now?"

"Me? Oh, I don't know. If you are successful with your story, it is certain that I shall be swept up in the added scandal that is sure to follow. If not, I think an early retirement might still be in order."

"*If* I'm successful. I think you've given me enough here to write a pretty powerful story. With everything that's already been written about Senator Hunter in *The Times*, this should dove-tail quite nicely."

"You may be right about that," Galax said, as he slowly stood and pushed in the chair he'd been sitting in. "I just can't help thinking about one of the comments that Bo continues to make about his time in prison."

"And what would that be?"

"That if God wanted everyone to know he did not kill Marcus, it would not be such a difficult thing for him to do."

"I think it won't be such a hard thing for the *New York Times* to accomplish, either."

"Yes, and that in itself would be a bit ironic, don't you think?"

"How so?"

"In the scenario you describe, you would be doing God's work for Him directly, would you not?"

"Well, He and I would have the same goal at least."

Galax made his way to the door he'd entered with Corey Aycock originally. "It would indeed," he said, after pausing to turn back in my direction. "If that truly is God's plan for Bosephus Buckminster."

As I stood up and grabbed my unopened notebook from the table, I felt a sudden chill. "Thank you again, Trevor," I said. "It was a pleasure doing business with you here today."

"It is my thanks to *you* that is paramount this day, Mr. Daniels," he replied, opening the door halfway and turning away from me. "You can have no idea just how much peace you have brought to my life today. A peace that has been lacking for so very long."

He stood frozen for a moment, as if soaking in his own words.

"There is a man just outside the door you came in. He will see you out."

With that, Trevor Galax walked into an uncertain future – a future he had willingly traded for the chance to exercise gnawing questions from his past.

My future was much more certain. I was about to write the story of my life, a story that would tie in nicely with the one I was already an undeserving candidate to win the Pulitzer Prize for. As I made my way out of Galax' offices, I even considered that within a few days, there was a pretty good chance I would have my old job back.

Chapter 43

Back at the Marriott that evening, as I fast walked through the lobby the clock behind the front desk said it was half past eight, but it felt more like the crack of dawn. To finally know exactly what needed to be done was pouring adrenaline into my system.

"Welcome back, Mr. Daniels," I heard from behind the counter. "Everything go okay in Charleston?"

"Fine," I said, never breaking stride on the way to the elevator.

"Are you in for the night? Would you like a wake-up call?"

"Just coffee," I replied as the elevator doors swung open the instant I pushed the button. "Is it possible to get someone to make a fresh pot?"

"Sure thing, Mr. Daniels. I'll be happy to—"

The elevator doors closed on the front desk guy's response, and as I made my way to my room it felt as though I was on the way to some kind of redemption. During all the craziness of the previous two weeks I had lost a relationship with terrific woman, flushed the career I'd toiled at my entire adult life straight down the toilet, and perhaps even let go of the few remaining strands of sanity that allowed me to function in normal society. And yet, I knew that the one thing I still had mastery over was going to help me get it all back. I could write - and no one had ever questioned that. I was determined to prove it yet again, and in doing so show once and for all that Bosephus Buckminster did not kill Marcus Brown. Maybe not in a court of law, but at the very least in the court of public opinion. The challenge ahead of me had less to do with writing a good story, as it did with making sure it was a story that could get into *The New York Times*. I knew there needed to a be a very serious filter applied to my writing, but since my sole purpose at the time was to get Bo out of prison, I had absolutely zero need for people to believe I could talk to angels, and felt not a single qualm about writing the truth, some of the truth, and nothing but the truth that was believable.

As I'd been unable to take notes while visiting with Corey Aycock and Trevor Galax, the one thing I wanted to take care of right away was updating my notebook Not being able to capture my thoughts during a meeting was a situation I usually dealt with by simply transferring everything from my head immediately after a session ended. But for the three hours that followed my meeting at Galax offices I'd needed both hands for the job of driving back to the Marriot. That drive-time left me with a slew of mental notes just floating around waiting impatiently to be set free, and after I'd prepared things at the desk in my room to be ready to capture them, as if from a script there was a knock on the door.

"Here ya go, Mr. Daniels."

It was the front desk guy, and in each hand he held a Styrofoam cup of coffee.

"Fresh from the coffee maker," he said, as if proud to be playing a part in something big.

"Thanks, but you didn't have to deliver them to me."

"No trouble, Mr. Daniels. I reckon you've got some mighty important things you're wanting to get after. If there's anything you need, just call down to the front desk."

"Thanks," I replied, as he handed me both cups. Unable to offer a handshake, I nodded my head before kicking the door closed with my foot.

"I'm on for the rest of the night!" he shouted from the other side of the door as if he'd never moved, indicating that I'd probably just kicked the door shut in his face.

After a few gulps of Java I began with a usual review of the previous couple of days worth of notes. Having caught myself up, I flipped to the first unused page in my notebook, and grabbed my pen to start the job of scribbling in the latest items. I was quickly frustrated by a pen that wouldn't work, and after flicking, licking and rapping it a few times on the table, I got up to grab another one from my bag.

When I made my way back to the desk with a fresh pen, my eyes were quickly pulled to the still open notebook – and blood immediately started to pump across my stomach. On a page that I was certain was completely blank before I'd stepped away, there were two fresh lines scratched across the middle of the page. The words were written in a handwriting that matched mine exactly, but they were as new to me as any I had ever read.

> *There will be some that will appear to you as angels, but they do not do My work. Understand that sometimes I must put my angels in places where they can do the most good.*

"Oh, come on now!" A voice shouted from behind me. When I turned in my chair to have a look, a young man was sitting on the couch and staring up at the ceiling, shaking a fist. "Do you have to take the fun out of everything."

"Who are you?"

"Well, I suppose from you're little tip there, you can probably figure out I'm not one of His little do-gooders."

"You're not an angel?"

The young man let out a raucous laugh, and it seemed to echo with an eerie bass undertone. "Damn, you really are a reporter."

As he stood up from the couch I recognized the younger features of Senator Hunter. "Are you Trey?"

"That clinches it then! You're a goddamned reporter, alright."

When he'd finished, the outer edges of his eyes grew blood red, and with a swipe of his left hand through the air my notebook went flying from the desk and slapped against the wall.

"Well, Mr. Yankee reporter, the good news is that I'm here to help you with your little job getting old Bo out of that prison."

As he took a step towards me, every muscle in my body froze in its last position. "What do you want?" I mumbled.

"What do I want? I want to help you."

"Help me? How would ..."

Trey Hunter held his hand up to his lips, and as he did my mouth went numb. "Shush now," he said. "I had hoped to come here and convince you I was one of them pussy retards you got popping in and out on you, but it looks like the Big Guy's tipped you off and screwed that up for me."

With another swipe of his hand my bag was lifted and hovered over the bed, before turning over and shaking all the contents out on the mattress. When the bag was empty, it darted across the room and slammed through the window with a loud crash.

"You're eyes look mighty big, there Mr. Daniels. What's the matter – did you think your special little gift was going to limit the visits to just the good guys?"

Trey reached out with his left arm, and with a shout that sounded as if it came straight from the bowels of hell, my laptop lifted off the bed and into his outstretched hand. When he opened it with the other hand, the screen came to life in an instant, and as he scrunched his eyes tight it looked as though he was scrolling through every single document from my hard drive in a matter of few seconds. When he'd finished, he sucked in a breath of air, powerful enough to pull the bedspread part of the way off the bed, and with the exhale the laptop flew across the room and embedded itself in the wall with a thud.

"So look here, Mr. Daniels, you and me are a team. We need to get that big, stupid bastard out of that prison for good. You know – we're like partners working together to do what's right and all."

Frozen in fear I felt the blood beginning to pump even harder across my stomach. The coffee in the cup I was holding sloshed over the top edge of the Styrofoam, and my arms began to shake, hard enough to cause the pen in my other hand to launch from my fingers like a projectile. The room was spinning and faster and I squinted hard to fight a total blackout.

"So what do you say, Mr. Daniels? Care to make a deal with the devil?"

Still involuntarily muted, I couldn't answer.

"Sorry about that," he said, wiping his hand through the air in my direction. "Shall we work together on getting old Bo out of that prison?"

"I won't need your help with that" I said. "I've got enough material to…"

With another swipe I was silenced again.

"That's not the answer I wanted to hear!" he shouted with a piercing anger in each word. "You don't know what I can do!"

Trey gritted his teeth so hard, the grashing they made sounded like marble stones being crushed under the weight of a steam roller. The reddish hue that outlined his frame grew brighter, and it appeared he would burst into flames at any moment.

"That will be enough of trying to scare Mr. Daniels," a third voice said from across the room.

"Well if it isn't my simple-minded hemorrhoid himself," Trey said, turning in the direction of the voice. "Tell me something – how many times do I have to kill a son-of-a-bitch like you before you finally stay dead?"

"A good man dies once and lives forever," Marcus Brown said calmly.

"Oh, yes 'a good man dies once and lives forever'..." Trey said, mocking Marcus. "Well, it ain't just the good ones that can pull off that trick, grits-for-brains. I'm doing quite nicely, thank you very much."

"You'll never find peace from where you are, Trey."

"Who says I'm looking for peace?" Trey snapped. "I got a job to do, and your buddy up there in that prison is getting in my way!"

"Bo also has a job to do, Trey."

"Well, he needs to go do it someplace else! That prison's where *my* people are!"

"They's all God's people, Trey. As long as they's still breathing, all God's people have a chance to feel His love."

"Is that how you got to that cheese-eating father of mine. You promised him some of your precious *love* from that god of yours?"

"Your father did the right thing, Trey. He's done God's work."

Small flames shot from Trey Hunter's eyes. "The right thing? You mean to tell me that helping to keep an innocent man in prison for something he didn't do is the right thing these days?"

"God's plan ain't always so simple to figure out, Trey. He works in mysterious ways."

"Plan? There's no plan to all this! My illustrious father is only doing what he's always done. Showing preference for that illegitimate imbecile over me!"

"A father will always try to protect his child, Trey. It don't make no never-mind how he got to be his son. He's kin sure enough."

"And what was I?" Trey screamed. "I was the one that had his last name! The one he introduced as his *only* son!"

"I' know your daddy wishes with all his heart you'd turn away from the darkness you've run to. That's love enough right there."

"Don't try and feed me that crap, black boy. I got work to get back to here. You can't stop our Mr. Daniels from doing what he feels needs to be done."

"No, I reckon I can't, Trey. But you can't make him do something he don't agree to neither."

"Well, there you go then. Mr. Daniels has already decided he's going to get that goofy sasquatch the hell out of my prison."

"Maybe so, Trey. But you and I is just going to have to let things happen as they was meant to."

"Is that right," Trey said, turning his attention back to me. "Mr. Daniels, if you could have anything in the world your heart desires – what would that be?"

I was still muted and couldn't answer.

"How about that pretty little blond firebrand that walked out on you? Would you like to get her back?"

Trey Hunter's eyes grew bigger and redder as he waited for my answer, before he realized once again I could not respond.

"Oh, shit," he said exasperated, wiping his hand in the air with quick strokes. "Okay, let's try this again. What can your new buddy Trey get for you, in exchange for helping me make sure our good friend Bo get's out of that prison?"

The room was spinning so fast, that even though Trey Hunter had made it possible to speak, dizziness was causing me to feel a blackout coming on. I could feel my eyes begin to roll back into my head, and my neck and shoulders became incapable of keeping my head from dropping to my chest.

"Oh, no you don't," Trey snapped, pulling my head all the way back with a swipe from his left hand, and levitating my medication bottles from the bed with his right. "Take some of this crap and get yourself right," he said, making the bottles turn over in mid-air and causing dozens of pills to fly straight across the room and into my open mouth.

"You can't do that, Trey Hunter!" I heard Marcus say.

"I just did it, retard. He's either going to help me or you can have him for good."

Nearly unconscious, I heard a few loud bangs against the hotel room door. "Mr. Daniels, are you alright in there? What's happening?"

"Damn it!" Trey Hunter shouted.

"It's time to go Trey," Marcus said.

"Mr. Daniels, if you're in there please come to the door and let us in!"

As Trey Hunter stood upright and took a few steps back away from me, all items not bolted down were caught up in a tornado-like swirl in the middle of my room. As he and Marcus Brown faded away, the items floating in mid-air fell abruptly back to Earth, and as I passed out I heard the crash of the hotel room door being broken down.

Chapter 44

A lot can happen in a year. Even if during most of it, nothing really happens at all. Days, weeks, and even months can go by with nothing but the same old routine to suck up the clock. One day rolling ambiguously into the next; bereft of even a single watershed moment to distinguish one from the other. Then one day you look back, and you see something you can take from it.

That pretty much describes the year that passed after my last day in Chases Corner, South Carolina. I spent the first three months of it at a quiet, non-descript facility in Westchester County, an hour or so outside New York City. Not much happened during my stay there, with the exception of getting to know Dr. Keller even better than I had known him before. He came to see me regularly – twice a week – even adjusting his days should a conflict arise over holidays, vacations, or emergencies. He was my only visitor during my entire stay, an isolation I maintained voluntarily. When soul-searching, or head-shrinking, or whatever it was I was supposed to be doing at that place, I really didn't want to be mingling with those closest to me. Even if they would have come, I didn't want them to be a part of the mess. When you are released from the nut-house, people can overlook the reasons for your stay there. They can move on from it after you return to the person they knew before. That is if they are spared the details of how you made it back. Like taking a tour of the sausage factory, it's the details of the process that can cause people to change the way they feel about something; or in my case someone.

Until yesterday that was just a theory. Yesterday, I finally mustered the courage to reach back to someone that cared about me.

"Mr. Daniels, your lunch appointment has arrived," the maitre de at La Masion restaurant said in a French accent, one that seemed to have become much thicker than what I remembered.

When I'd arrived earlier, Claude was excited to see me. He called me by name, though at first I couldn't for the life of me remember his, and had to sneak a peek at his name tag. He offered belated congratulations for my part of the Pulitzer Prize.

"I was surprised to hear you had left the newspaper," he said, after hugging me briskly. "Mr. Odette and Mr. Kennedy still come in quite often, but they say only that you have found some bigger fish to fry."

"Something like that, Claude" I replied, unsure of how to respond, but grateful that Bart and Carl had kept my cover. "It looks like you've been promoted while I was away."

"Yes, this is true. I have now, as they say, great powers at my disposal, no?"

"Enormous power. You are officially a mover and a shaker in this town."

Claude grinned and put his hand on my shoulder. "I like this idea of yours."

As we walked back toward the front of the restaurant, I felt moisture building on my palms, a dampness I couldn't seem to wipe off against the man-made fibers of my new suit coat. I'd almost decided to drop off and visit the men's room when a familiar voice called my name.

"Mark? Is that you?"

A sudden flight response nearly took hold of my next actions, but after an awkward few seconds I was able to suppress it.

"Hello, Carl," I said nervously, offering him my wet hand. "It's good to see you."

"Good to see me?" he said. He ignored my offer of a handshake, and pulled me to him in a strong, back slapping hug. "You have no idea how much I've missed you, my old friend!"

Just three words – *my old friend.* Not what many would consider the most powerful three words in the English language, but at that moment there could have been none more precious.

"Bart sends his regards. He was so excited when I told him I was meeting with you today, it was all I could do to keep him from jumping on a plane to be here."

"Really? And how did you manage that?"

"I didn't tell him until an hour ago. He's in California and wouldn't make it back in time."

"Very nice. You always did have a way of staying one step ahead."

"Your table is ready," the Maitre de said with a smile. "Follow me, please."

As I followed behind Carl, he had to stop intermittently to speak to acquaintances offering greetings. None came my way, which hurt a little.

"Mark, you look so different," Carl said as soon as we got to our table.

"I was just thinking the same thing ... or that maybe I've become invisible."

"You mean to these people," he said, glancing around the room. "They aren't real people, Mark. Real people don't lunch at fancy French restaurants in New York City."

I laughed a little and knew just what he meant. "What does that make us, then? I seem to recall we ate here quite a few times over the years."

"Yes, but you were always the one that chose this place. The only reason I suggested it this time was because I knew you liked it."

"Well, then that might be yet another one of the changes in me these days."

We waited out a moment of silence that was not unwelcome.

"Seriously, Mark ... you look great."

"Thanks! I feel pretty great right about now. Though I have to admit the past year has been a little lonely at times"

"I wish you would have let us come see you."

"A nuthouse is just not the best place in the world to receive guests."

"I understand, but I tried to track you down after you were released. We certainly could have met somewhere ..."

"I had to go through some stuff, Carl. It wasn't easy, but I made it through."

Carl smiled and nodded his head. "Indeed you did! You know, Bart hasn't been the only one inquiring about you. Susan has stayed pretty close with Karen since she moved."

"You didn't break your promise, did you?"

"No. Neither Susan or Karen have any idea we've talked."

"Sorry, I'm just a bit guarded from past experiences."

"I understand. But keep in mind, it's probably just a matter of time before Bart spills the beans to Karen. That bomb could go off on both of us at any time, so you might want to ..."

"I'll be taking care of that one myself, very soon."

Carl smiled even broader. "I hope so. She's a good woman, and she worries."

I smiled and nodded again uncomfortably, a sign Carl correctly read as a plea to move on. "So, let's talk about your book!"

"It's just a manuscript right now, but did you have time to read it?"

"It's good, Mark. It's really very good."

"Any qualms about forwarding it on to your friend at Random House?"

"It's already done. As well as to another at Penguin."

The maitre de stopped back to drop off water. "Gentlemen, on such an occasion as this, I have decided to handle your order personally."

"Thank you, Claude, we're honored," Carl said a bit surprised.

"Well, it is only right that such movers and shakers are served by one of their very own. Wouldn't you agree, Mr. Daniels?"

"I would agree, Claude," I said with a laugh, as Carl looked on somewhat puzzled.

"Mr. Odette, will you be having the usual?"

"If the usual is an Asian salad – then, yes, I'll have the usual."

"And Mr. Daniels, it has been some time but I believe I can still remember your favorite."

"Okay, surprise me then."

Claude looked at me with a wrinkled brow. "Mr. Daniels, if it is a surprise then I'm afraid I will have missed the mark."

"That's fair enough. Don't surprise me, then."

Claude put his hand on my shoulder again and smiled, and it felt for a second like I never left New York.

"You know," Carl said, soaking in the exchange with the maitre de, "If it's that easy for you to fit back into this place, it might be just as easy to do it across the street."

"Thanks, Carl, that's really tempting," I replied delicately. "But *The New York Times* isn't a restaurant. I think my days as a reporter are pretty much over."

"Having read your manuscript, I might agree. Just know the door is always open."

"Considering how we left things last time around, that means a lot to me."

The rift between us seemed to have been easily repaired, and at that moment I couldn't help but feel a little silly. Maybe the time away was the main reason it was so effortless – time does heal most wounds. I just couldn't help feeling a little stupid inside, as the separation from Carl had been totally of my own doing.

"Okay, let's try this one more time," Carl said, cutting a little of the emotion hanging in the air. "Getting back to your book, I think you're going to need a literary agent."

"I thought I'd wait until there is some definite interest before I—"

"I'll give you some names before you leave today, but both publishing houses I sent your manuscript to want to meet with you. One of them called me back the very same day."

"No kidding!"

"As a budding novelist you're a hot commodity."

"Yeah, a little strange, huh?"

"I don't know, you've always been a pretty talented writer."

"I meant the *budding novelist* part. The same story I pitched to you as non-fiction might just turn out to be a best seller in the fiction section."

"Don't worry, you're far enough out there with some of the angles that the mainstream isn't going to confuse it with reality."

"Do you think some might?"

"Maybe. There are some people that *want* to believe, even if something is presented to them as fiction. Just look at all the readers that still think Dan Brown *really* uncovered the secret of the Holy Grail."

"What about you, Carl?"

"What about me?"

"What do you think about the whole fiction versus non-fiction classification for the book."

Carl paused, looking for words. "I think it's a good book,' he said, straightening himself and leaning closer to the table. "If there are those that will take from your story a belief that angels really do exist ...well, I fail to see a downside in that."

Carl looked at me as if he were daring me to ask another question. I think he knew ahead of time the answers I would be looking for when we met.

"Carl, why were you so insistent that *I* be the one to cover the Buckminster hearing."

Carl pushed away slightly from the table. "You were the right man for the job."

"Why me, and not someone else?"

"I needed a good reporter."

I was trying hard not to play investigator on my friend, but I sensed that was exactly what Carl was trying to get me to do. "Carl, I'm sure you know this by now, but over the past year I've learned that Dr. Keller is incredibly good at coaxing people to get things off their chest."

"That's certainly his reputation."

"Yes it is, and he's told me many times that a thing left unsaid between two people never goes away. That no matter how long it's ignored, it will always be there."

Carl's eyes fell off of me and onto his suddenly wringing hands.

"He also says that it eventually starts to act like a pothole in the road that's never repaired," I added. "Every time you drive around it, the hole just keeps getting deeper and bigger. Until one day the road just can't be travelled anymore."

Carl still wasn't allowing himself to look in my direction. "So, you're thinking I'm a pothole now?

"Not you, specifically," I said. "But whatever it is that's lurking behind your eyes right now might certainly be."

Carl drew in a deep breath and picked up eye contact with me.

"Now there's the ace reporter I've come to know," he said. "It seems the good Dr. Keller has taught you a few life-lessons to bolster your interviewer skills."

"I've spent enough time with him," I said. "You also know that, as a reporter, I can suspect and even project, but I can't move forward -"

"...without confirmation. Stop giving the professor lessons, Mark."

We both laughed, which lightened the mood. I could tell Carl was girding himself for something.

Carl shifted in his seat. "Susan is from Brooklyn. Did you know that?"

"I don't think I did."

"She was also raised a good Catholic girl."

It took me a minute to realize that he had handed me a clue and was waiting for me to acknowledge it. "Let me guess – you're prepping me for the *ultimate* Susan Odette backchannel connection," I said. "She knew Father Hanaway?"

"She did. They were very close when she was young," he said. "He helped her a great deal. I think she helped him with his work as well."

A dead silence fell on our table.

"Carl, is that why you put me on the Buckminster story? Susan asked you to?"

Carl went back to watching his hands. "I'm ashamed to admit it, but yes – Susan had a hand in it."

"She wanted you to assign the story to me as a favor to her?"

"Not exactly. Father Hanaway reached out to her and asked if she could use her influence to get me to send you down there."

"I've always known there was something," I said after letting the latest bomb-shell settle. "I just couldn't put my finger on it."

"Mark, I've spent my entire life trying to avoid doing things I would regret later. I swear to you I didn't agree easily."

"I understand, Carl. I know what kind of man you are."

"Knowing your background as I did, I should have just dug in my heels with Susan and said no."

"Why didn't you?"

"You mean, why didn't I say no?"

Carl paused for a moment, as if there were still one more cat to let out of the bag, and he was trying to figure out how to do it delicately.

"Aside from Susan being the love of my life, and her practically begging me to do it," he said, lifting his head and looking over the top of mine. "Let's just say that I am familiar with the information you've included in your novel about the Fragile-X gene."

"Familiar? Do you mean personally?"

"I do."

"Wow!"

"There is a history of autism in Susan's Family."

Carl and I allowed his admission to get comfortable with us at the table.

"So, is that why you two have never had children? You don't want to be responsible for bringing a child with autism into the world?"

Carl hesitated. "No. Two of Susan's siblings were born with autism, and I can tell you there's great love in her family."

Carl had thrown me another twist, and he gave me the time to process it.

"Then I guess there's one big question left," I said.

"And what's that?"

"Are both of her siblings with autism still alive?"

Carl breathed out heavy, as if the deep breath in he'd taken in earlier was only now being let out. "Her youngest brother was ten-years-old when he died."

Carl had laid in the final piece to the puzzle. There was enough of it already put together for me to have seen the bigger picture without it, but with Carl's final addition came a sense that the job was at last complete. There was just one more question to ask, but that question would need to be saved for Susan Odette directly.

"You have no idea how ashamed I am for being so unprofessional," Carl said, appearing to need to lift the silence between us. "If I could go back to the day I gave you that story, I would definitely take a different – "

"Let it go, Carl," I said, cutting of his lamentations. "I've come to the realization that everything happens for a reason. If you'd told me this stuff six months ago - I probably would have punched you in the nose. But from where I sit today, I think I've come through it all much better off than I was before."

Carl stared at me with big, disbelieving eyes, before shaking his head and letting his face muscles relax. "You have no idea what a relief it is to hear you say that."

"You have no idea what a relief it is to *say* it," I replied. "Ultimately, it was the writing the book that brought me to a point of reconciling all the negative stuff."

"Yes, and when your book comes out, you'll probably have a small fortune to help ease that reconciliation along even further."

Just then the maitre de came around from behind me with two very large salads in his hands.

"Mr. Daniels, have you written a book?" he asked, placing a salad in front of each of us. "I will be the first to buy it, you can count on this."

"Don't you want to know what it's about first?"

"I do not care. You have always been one of my favorite writers," he said, flipping his hand in the air and rolling a finger. "Can I get you gentlemen anything else?"

"I think we're good, Claude," Carl said as he unrolled his silverware and spread his napkin across his lap.

During the time it took for us eat the big salads served at Le Maison, Carl and I took a break from clearing the air. Carl tore into his greens like a man on a mission, while I just picked at mine. Stirring around the thoughts in my head as much as the bits of lettuce and sharply cut pieces of chicken.

"Sorry about that," Carl said after finishing. "This diet Susan has me on keeps me so hungry, it's as if I turn into an animal when you put food in front of me."

"Do you feel better now?"

"It didn't even scratch the surface."

Carl's eyes moved to the still abundant salad on my plate.

"Would you like some of mine?" I said, pushing my plate in his direction.

"Thanks, but if Susan were to find out, I'd be relegated to fish-bone soup when I get home." He was blaming it on Susan, but I knew his diet restrictions were more likely a part of the discipline he lived his life under.

"Carl, before we leave here today there are a few other things that have to be said."

"Okay." Carl said, then he wiped his mouth one last time and tossed his napkin on top of his plate. "Fire away!"

"First, you need to know how extremely grateful I am that you never turned in my termination paperwork."

"I know that, Mark. You don't have to—"

"No! I absolutely have to! If you hadn't held off, I don't know how I would have lived the past twelve months, let alone pay for almost three months of in-patient care from Dr. Keller."

"Listen, sometimes things are said in the heat of argument that—"

"Don't go there either, Carl," I said, determined not to let him talk. "We both know I deserved to be fired. I put myself in that situation."

He stared at me with a look I could not read. I'd expected him to continue his attempt at humility, but he just sat like that for a moment. "Mark don't go around for the rest of your life heaping praise on me for the way I handled things in Chases Corner?" he said, as he stood up and brushed off a few bits of lunch from his tie, apparently readying himself to leave.

"Don't be humble, Carl. You saved my butt, plain and simple."

Carl paused and looked down at his shoes. "I sent you there – remember?"

"Of course I remember, but you couldn't have seen the way things were going to play out for me."

Carl stood there for what seemed like several minutes, staring blankly. "I don't know about all that, Mark. I think in my head at least, I knew that story had the potential to push you over the edge."

"But in your heart?"

"In my heart? Well, they do say love is blind. No matter how crazy it may seem now, for Susan's sake, I think I wanted to believe that nutty old priest really had stumbled on to something. I guess more than anything else in the world, I want for Susan to find her own kind of peace."

"I think we all find peace in our own time, Carl."

"You'd be one to know that, my friend." Carl stuck out his hand to prepare for a goodbye. "Mark, I'm so happy for you!"

"Thanks," I said, pushing away his hand and stepping from the table for a man-hug. "And thank you for the help with my book."

"I would say it was the least I could do," Carl said. "Oh, and by the way, the tab is being picked up on *The Times* account."

"Tell the folks in accounting I appreciate the meal."

We'd finished hugging, but Carl hesitated before stepping away. "Hey, could I ask one small favor of you?"

"Of course, Carl. That's what friends do."

"I know you didn't want me to say anything to Susan just yet, but would you mind if I let her read your manuscript, rather than waiting for it to hit the bookstores."

"If you can hold off until tomorrow to give it to her. I've still got something to take care of later this afternoon."

"Oh, certainly. I didn't mean right this minute. I just want to get ahead of the curve when it comes to her getting all excited over the story-line. You and I know it's a novel – but I'm afraid she's going to be one of those people that just wants to believe it's real."

"Do what you have to do, Carl. As long as you can hold off for twenty-four hours, I'm fine with it."

"Thanks. That will help."

Carl walked away slowly, as if finding it hard to break with the moment.

"Carl, one other thing before you leave," I said, which caused him stop and turn back in my direction. "After Susan reads the manuscript, would you mind if I to get together with her?"

"Are you looking for some feedback?"

"Feedback would be good," I said. "But I was thinking I might be able to lend a hand."

"Lend a hand? How so?"

"Let's just say, I may be able to help her find a little of that peace you've wanted so much for her to have."

Chapter 45

That afternoon, I drove along a tight, winding road that intersects the north-facing lane of the Taconic Parkway, ready to face one final gremlin on the road to redemption. Thinking on how easy things had gone with Carl over lunch, I was at least hopeful. There was also a degree of foreboding whenever I thought about my next meeting, because I was worried it could very well end as a loud confrontation.

When I pulled up to the main entrance to Catskills Institute for the Challenged Child, an old man with a clipboard waved for me to stop.

"Greetings," he said cheerfully. "Are you here to visit a resident?"

" I'm not actually. I'm here to see one of the staff."

"That's different. Who are you here to see?"

"Karen McDonough."

"Oh ... Ms. McDonough," he said. His voice jumped along each syllable. "She's a fine lady. Is she expecting you?"

"I'm an old friend. I just happened to be passing through the area."

"You just happened to be passing through *this* area? We don't get a whole lot of that."

"I just live on the other side of Fishkill."

"That's not too far away at all. So, how come a good-looking fella like you hasn't stopped in to visit with her before? She's single, you know."

"Is she?"

"Yes, sir. She was engaged a while back, but it didn't work out. You know I can't understand why that knucklehead she was supposed to marry would ever let loose of such a catch."

The security guard had moved uncomfortably close, looking in through the driver's side window.

"Well, you know … I was once … I mean, a long time ago I was engaged …"

"I'm just playing with you, Mr. Daniels," the guard said, slapping the driver's side door before walking back to the guard house. He returned quickly. "Stick this on you dashboard," he said, handing me a guest card. "Then take a right into the parking lot and park in any of the spaces marked visitor."

He got a kick out of his little ribbing, while I was somewhat stuck on what had just happened.

"How did you know who I was?" I asked, putting the card where it could be viewed through my front window.

"I saw your picture on TV a few times last year."

"Really?"

"Ms. McDonough still brags on you a good bit."

He was giving me such a snickering smile, I couldn't help but throw one back.

"I'll give Connie at the reception desk a heads-up and see if she can track her down for you. Last I saw Ms. McDonough, she was out on the grounds."

"Thanks! You've been very kind."

The old man suddenly got serious and walked back over to my window. "You're welcome," he said, becoming almost grim. "But don't be expecting the same courtesy on your way out if you do anything to upset our little Ms. M."

"I'll absolutely remember that. And don't worry, I'm not such a knucklehead anymore."

The guard smiled again and waved me on. It didn't take long to park the car, as every one of the visitor spaces was open. As I made my way across the lot, a portly, middle-aged woman came bounding down the stairs faster than her size should have allowed her.

"Hi, Mark," she said, a bit out of breath. "I'm Connie Hampton."

"Hi, Connie; Mark Daniels" I said, reaching out my hand, only to have it grabbed and patted by both of hers.

"Yes, indeed. Mr. Mark Daniels!" she said with a slight giggle at the end. "I just know Karen will be so pleased to see you." As she stood there, still holding the bottom of my hand with her left and rubbing the top with her right, a few more giggles escaped. "Right! Then let me just run and see if I can find her." She turned quickly and started off in couple of different directions before choosing one. "You can just wait right here, and … well, I'll just bring here right back here."

"Okay, then. I'll be right here."

As I looked around the grounds, I could understand why everyone had taken to the outside. It was a beautiful mid-afternoon that can only be enjoyed in the Catskills mountains in the spring. The first signs of life were popping everywhere, and the whole scene seemed to be getting greener as I watched.

After about ten-minutes, I started to get a little worried that Mrs. Hampton might have hustled her way into a heart attack. I looked around and I noticed two young girls playing next to a big mountain rock. One of them was sitting on the big rock, holding a doll and chatting away, while the other was twirling effortlessly in what looked like a choreographed homage to the sunny day. During one of her twirls, the girl noticed me, and then quickly scampered to crouch down behind the big rock, out of view. Curious, I walked over to investigate.

"Good morning!" I said to the girl sitting on the rock, who up close looked to be about eleven or twelve. "What's your name?"

The little girl paused slightly, but then continued playing with the doll, yakking away as if I weren't there. I peeked around the big rock to turn my attention to the hidden dancer. "Hi there! I saw you dancing. I hope I didn't startle you."

The little girl shook her head.

"My name's Mark. What's your name?"

As she stood, I noticed she was wearing a very old fashioned dress. "Willa," she said. "My name is Willa."

"That's a pretty name. Is it short for something?"

"Wilhelmina."

"I like either one."

"Hey!" the girl sitting on the rock shouted. "Hey, you!"

"Do you mean, me?" I asked.

"Yeah, I mean you. You can see her?"

"See who ... Willa?"

"Yes, Willa! What are you retarded?"

"No. And yes, I can see Willa. She's a wonderful dancer."

Willa blushed, but immediately resumed twirling and leaping around the big rock.

"Tell me this," the girl on the rock said, letting her doll drop. "How come you can see Willa?"

"It's a hard question. Are you the only one that sees Willa here?"

"There was a couple of the kids that were here before. But no grown-ups."

"That's too bad. It is such a joy to watch her dance."

"But you're a grown-up!"

"I am a grown-up. For a long time now."

"Have you always been able to see … well, girls like Willa."

"I think I did when I was your age, but then for a very long time I was just like the rest of the grown-ups."

"But now you see them again?"

"Yes."

There was suddenly a tense hesitation behind the little girl's eyes, as if she were trying to decide to jump over a chasm.

"Do you see the mean ones?" she whispered.

I wanted to put my hand on her shoulder for comfort, but as I stepped toward her she shifted higher up the big rock.

"Yes," I said in a soothing tone. "I see them too."

"You need to be careful," she said, relaxing a bit. "They can break things and get you in trouble."

"I've had that happen to me," I said with a chuckle. "I got in a whole bunch of trouble, too."

"When Willa's around, the mean ones can't show up."

"Is that right? Willa keeps watch over you, does she?"

"Not all the time. She can't always be here, cause she looks after others, too. But she gets here fast as she can when one of them mean ones turns up. She don't always get here in time for me to stay out of trouble, though."

"It sounds like Willa is a good friend to have."

"Do you have a friend like Willa?"

"I do."

"What's her name?"

"It's not a her. His name is Marcus."

The slightest hint of a smile appeared across the little girl's face, and her shoulders seemed to relax a bit.

"Are there other grown-ups like you?"

"I don't know. I think so, but I'm still learning about all this myself."

The little girl on the rock sat silent for a moment. "Okay. You can be in our club. My name is Talia."

"It's nice to meet you, Talia. Who else is in this club I'm joining?'

"Just me and Willa right now."

"I'm pleased to be a part of your club. Shall we shake on it?"

The little girl hesitated. "Sure," she said sticking out her hand.

As I was shaking Talia's hand, I heard a voice shouting my name back from the direction of the entrance to the main building. I turned to see Connie Hampton with a familiar figure standing next to her.

"I've got to go meet with someone now, Talia; but maybe we can speak again soon."

"That would be nice," she said simply.

I looked around for Willa.

"She's gone," Talia said. "She doesn't like Mrs. Hampton."

Talia picked up her doll and regained her perch on the big rock. As I got closer to Mrs. Hampton and Karen, I noticed they were both looking wide-eyed in my direction; Karen sporting a slightly open mouth. When I was a few steps away, I saw them look at each other again. Mrs. Hampton whispered something to Karen and then, just as I approached, she called out, "Well, I'll leave you two to talk."

As she hustled back up the long steps to the entrance, Mrs. Hampton looked back in our direction, shaking her head and nearly stumbling on one of the stairs.

"Hello, Karen."

"I could barely recognize you from a distance, Mark."

"You're still as lovely as ever."

"Thank you," she said, still wearing a wide-eyed look.

"What was that all about?" I asked.

"Do you mean between Mrs. Hampton and I?"

"Well, yeah. Was I not supposed to interact with any of the—"

"Oh, no, that's fine," Karen interrupted. "Believe me, it's more than alright."

"Okay … then what gives?"

"It's just that, in the year that I've been here that's the first time I've seen Talia interact directly with anyone," Karen said. "Mrs. Hampton has been here longer, and she was as surprised as I was."

"She's a very nice young lady. I'm in her club now."

Karen seemed to remember that a hug might be in order, and she stepped awkwardly toward me. "But enough about that for now," she said after a faraway squeeze. " Mark Daniels, I'm mad at you!"

"Mad at me?"

"You shouldn't just drop-off the end of the Earth like you did. There are people that worry about you."

"People?"

"Yes, people. I think Carl was talking about hiring a private detective at one point."

"Did he?" I said smiling. "Well, I missed Carl."

"You should. He's a good friend and he deserved better." Karen was showing a little discomfort, but for some reason I was having fun with it.

"I missed you, too, Karen."

"Oh, I'm sure," she said, blushing. Karen was avoiding the very direct eye contact I was trying to initiate. "Does Carl even know you're back yet?" she asked, pushing the hair off the back of her neck and letting it fall.

"Yes, we met earlier for lunch in the city," I said. "I called him last week for a favor."

Karen look puzzled. "Last week? I spoke to Susan just last night, and she never so much as ..."

"Ah, that would be my fault."

"Your fault?"

"Yes, I made Carl swear he wouldn't tell Susan anything about our meeting. At least until ..."

"Until what?"

"Until I could get here to see you in person"

She blushed an even deeper red. "That's very sweet," she said, turning her head completely away from me. "But it wasn't necessary. You don't owe me anything."

"Oh, yes I do," I said, turning her back around by the shoulders to face me again. "I owe you a lot!"

"Such as?" Her voice cracked slightly.

"For starters, how about an apology."

Karen couldn't speak, and I knew from her twitching lip it could only be one of two things that was building inside her.

"I know I've sabotaged a lot of good things in my life," I said, moving on. "But wrecking what we had together was the worst of all of them."

Karen looked down, and somehow I knew the tough little bird I had come to know wasn't going to pick her head back up chirping. "Thank you," she said after a few seconds. "That means something to me."

As I let go of her shoulders, it felt as though I were letting go of a rope attached to a very large anchor – one that I'd been dragging around for a while.

"So ... that wasn't as hard as I thought it was going to be," I said somewhat flippantly. "I think I could have another go at it if you need me to."

Karen's answer was a punch in the arm with the same balled-up little fist I'd last seen at Il Vagabond's. "Would you like to come inside? We could talk some more in my office?"

"I'd love to, especially the talking part. But I've got a dinner meeting in the city that Carl set up for me."

"At the paper?"

"Oh, no. It's with a publisher."

"A publisher? Like in a book publisher?"

"Actually, yes. Two of them to be exact: Random House and Penguin-Putnam."

"Really? Is it a behind-the-scenes peek at how a Pulitzer Prize winner got the story?"

"No, actually it's a novel."

"I didn't see that one coming."

"Yeah, I don't think I saw it either. But I think it's pretty good."

The two of us stood there, sharing a few of the best moments we'd ever spent together, not saying a word, but with so much going on between us.

"So, you drove all the way out here from your apartment in the city, just to turn around and head back."

"Actually, I've been living in Fishkill for the past few months."

"Fishkill?"

"Yes, it's a nice little town."

I could tell Karen was fighting an instinct to give me the what-for over being so close and not visiting, but she fought it off well. "What are you going to do now?"

"After the meeting, I have a plane to catch for South Carolina."

"Still working on follow-up to your big story?"

"No, just visiting a friend."

A fairly serious look crawled across Karen's face. "Is it a *lady* friend?"

"No, no ... nothing like that. It's just a very good friend. One that may need my help from time to time with some work he's doing."

"And after that?"

"You know, I'm not sure. I had a long cell phone conversation with my new agent on the way up here, and he seems to think I may be coming into some money rather quickly."

"That's always a good thing."

"Yeah, my funds were pretty much drying up, but it looks like I'm not going to have to do anything drastic like get a job."

"That's even better. Are you going to move back to your wonderful city?"

"No, I think I'm going to stay around here for awhile. I was hoping I might even be able to come by and see you every now and again."

"That would be nice."

We grabbed hands and I kissed Karen on the cheek. "Besides, now that I'm in Talia's club, I'll probably need to be here for meetings and such."

"Yes, you probably should attend," she said, pulling away and taking a more serious posture. "Seriously, Mark, being able to connect with her earlier was more amazing than you know."

"We just hit it off."

"Very few people can do what you did with her."

"Oh, I don't know. When someone is living on the spectrum, I think it's just best to try to go where they are instead of asking them to come to you."

"Spectrum? Are you talking about the autism spectrum?"

"Yes, of course. Why do you ask?"

"I guess I just...you know...wondered where you learned about it."

"I was a reporter. You do remember that, don't you?"

Karen smiled. "I do remember," she said, nodding her head lightly. "Anyway, that's quite a gift you have."

"Yeah. I'm beginning to recognize that there are a number of gifts in my life that I've overlooked for a very long time."

I slowly began to walk away backwards, knowing I needed to get on the road but not wanting to take my eyes off Karen.

"You know what they say," she said

"What's that?"

"You should never look a gift horse in the mouth."

I laughed as I looked at her over the roof of my car from the driver's side. "I've never really understood that expression," I said. "But I *have* learned that when you look at it from the other end, you can get kicked pretty hard."

As I pulled away, in the rearview mirror I saw Karen bring her hand to her mouth as if she were holding back her emotions, and from the big rock out on the grounds came a happy wave.

It was springtime, and it was like God was starting over.